Chasing Petals

THE ROSE DUET, BOOK 1

KRYSTAL KAE

DARK ORCHID PRESS

Cover Design: Martin Endeavors, LLC
Editor: Rebecca Joy Editing

Paperback ISBN: 979-8-9895730-4-2

Before You Read

This book contains mature themes, including a history of violence, bullying, and child abuse (of a main character), both verbal and physical. The romance includes dark sexual themes such as dubious consent and somnophilia, as well as stalking. (But don't worry—our MMC is actually a cinnamon roll who would rather die than hurt her.)

Cheating (in the past, not a main character) and a contentious divorce and fight for child custody. Discussion of weight, body image, and unhealthy eating habits. Discussion of infertility and reproductive health (main characters) and brief mention of miscarriage (side character, in the past). Depictions of death and murder, including murder of family members.

1

And Then There Was One

Clara

The dishes are looking at me dirty again. In fact, the whole house seems to have exploded within the past four days.

Between my job and shuffling the kids around, the whole place is in disarray. I groan at the realization that it might just take me all weekend to fix it up again. But for what, exactly? It's not like I'll be entertaining any company.

There are pieces of clothing scattered about, because apparently, there aren't enough hampers in the house. Reusable water bottles cover multiple surfaces, to-go containers fill the trash to the brim, and the whole house needs a good dust, sweep, and vacuum.

There just isn't enough time during the week when the kids are around. And when they're not here, I'm still bustling about, trying to make it to games and practices. I've never missed a single one, and I'm not about to start now.

We get home from extracurriculars, eat a quick meal, and then dive into homework, just to get ready for bed after that. I'm worried that my kids are doing too much, that they aren't enjoying what little time they have as a thirteen-year-old and a nine-year-old. But they assure me, time and time again, that they're happy and they love everything they're involved in even though we barely get to spend time together.

I'm trying, I really am. But it still doesn't feel like enough.

Julie, my oldest, notices me staring at the overfilled trash can and waves a hand in my direction. I blink, snapping myself out of my thoughts as I meet her gaze. Her pale brown hair is swept up into a ponytail with flyaways here and there from her cheerleading practice. My daughter has been blessed with some kind of beauty gene that must have skipped over me. With all of the social media influencers she follows and videos she watches, she's halfway to becoming a model of some sort. I allow her to wear makeup as long as it's minimal. It was a compromise between the two of us.

"Want me to take that out?"

It's funny how something as small as my daughter taking the heaping trash out without being asked lifts my spirits.

"That would be great, Julie. Thank you."

She sets her overnight bag at the bottom of the stairs and makes her way into the kitchen to do just that. I don't waste time going to change out of my work clothes. Instead, I skirt around the island of fake marble countertop and plant myself at the sink.

"Mom! I can't find any underwear!" my youngest yells down the stairwell. I roll my eyes. Obviously, he hasn't put away the laundry at the foot of his bed. I do all the hard work of gathering, washing, drying, and folding. The least he can do is put his crap away.

But no, that would be too helpful.

"Never mind!" he calls down a few moments later, before I can reply. I let out a sigh as Julie makes her way back inside, a scowl on her face.

"What's wrong?" I ask, already filling the sink with hot, soapy water. Luckily, the kids know to at least rinse their dishes before leaving them to die in the sink. It helps the tiniest bit. The dishwasher has been making a strange sound, and I'm afraid to use it for fear of flooding the kitchen or something.

"Do we have to go?" Julie groans. My heart sinks, although I try not to let it read on my face.

If I had a choice in the matter, she would get to stay if that's what she wants. Their dad is due to pick them up in about ten minutes, and with the house such a wreck, I contemplate foregoing any chores for the moment and waiting outside. I don't need him coming in here and seeing the destruction. I don't need to give him any more ammunition to argue that the kids need to spend more time with him.

Our divorce was final about three months ago. And even though he was the cheating bastard in our relationship, we were granted joint custody. Our children bounce between homes on a week-to-week basis, but this weekend, Joe was adamant about taking them on a surprise trip to an amusement park three hours away.

Before this year, it was an annual thing. We would make our way there, spend a couple days riding thrill rides and munching on all the eats and treats the park had to offer, just to come home and crash.

This was the first summer we didn't go together as a family, and now since we're into September, the park is in its last few weeks of operation before it closes for the winter. I may not be a fan of most of the rides, but it's the memories we created, the laughs we had, and the smiles on our kids' faces that kept me going back every year.

Only now, I have been replaced by a fake, blonde bimbo who doesn't seem old enough to even drink. And don't get me started on how she's closer to Julie's age than mine and my ex-husband's.

"Mom," Julie begins again when I fail to answer. My trips down memory lane are getting in the way of responding.

"Sorry, yes." I clear my throat, stifling the hurt that's trying to surface. "Your dad was very adamant to have you this weekend, but I'll let you in on a little secret…"

I pause my dish scrubbing so I can listen to hear if Emmett is near, but when all is quiet, I continue.

"Your dad and I came to an agreement. If he gets you this weekend, then I get to choose when I take you two to the Mall of America."

Her jaw drops open, revealing her perfectly straight teeth thanks to her braces. She had a painful crossbite that had to be corrected by traditional braces. To this day, she reminds me of how stupid she looked, but deep down I know just how appreciative she is that she had it done. Now it's just a memory, as long as she keeps wearing her retainer at night.

"You're joking." She gapes at me, and I can see the excitement building in her eyes.

I nod. "I promise, I'm not. I know how bad you've been wanting to go, and that Emmett wants to go to the theme park there. I was even hoping you could each take a friend with you, and I think I can save up enough to get adjoining rooms so you and Mags can have a bit more privacy."

At the mention of her best friend since diapers, Julie makes a bee-line across the kitchen and wraps me in a huge hug while she squeals. I try to keep my wet hands up and away from her, but I fail, returning her embrace full force.

"What'd I miss?" Emmett is already halfway down the carpeted steps and eyeing us with suspicion. Julie and I separate, and my hands dive back into the water.

"Mom's going to ground you if you don't pick up your clothes. The house is a pigsty." Julie rolls her eyes as she collects a few more items of trash and places them in the now empty bin.

I grin, reflecting on how Julie sounds just like me. Quoting me, even. She might not have got her beauty from me, but she did get my brown eyes and has some of my mannerisms. Her athleticism, though—I have no idea where she got that from, because it certainly wasn't from her dad or me.

A flash of yellow zooms by out the front window and I still. Anger is beginning to fill my veins, and I rinse my hands quickly and dry them off.

"Emmett, please pick up your clothes and put them in the laundry room. I'll be right back."

I shoot out the kitchen door just as I hear a groan from my youngest. I'll never understand why it's so hard to pick up after yourself.

The air outside is warm, but luckily, the humidity is dying down a bit so it doesn't choke you. Little Miss Bimbo is already getting out of her car, breasts pushed up and peeking out of her tank top, gold jewelry around both wrists and her neck, as I make my way through the garage. The one that Joe always swore he would finish, but never did. There's no insulation, heating or cooling.

"Where's Joe?" I ask as soon as I'm within earshot, not wanting the kids to hear me from inside as I almost stomp through the building that houses my van and miscellaneous yard materials and totes.

"He had to work late. I'm here to get the kids." God, her nasal voice will haunt me in my dreams tonight. It's almost like she's pushing to make it worse.

The hell you are.

"That's *not* what Joe and I agreed to." I draw my phone out of my back pocket and begin to dial him up. My hands are threatening to shake with my nerves.

"He's not going to answer," she adds, mumbling, as she shifts her stance in her rubber flip-flops. I hope her legs catch on the leather of her car with how short her shorts are. I wouldn't even let Julie out of the house in something so small.

When the ringing in my ear comes to an abrupt halt and is sent to voicemail, I'm already fuming. "Joe, if you want the kids this weekend then *you* need to pick them up."

I end the call and stow the phone back in my pocket. "Sorry you wasted your time coming out here."

I start to turn, but her nails-on-a-chalkboard voice halts me in my tracks.

"You don't have to be such a bitch."

I'm not normally one to throw punches, but she would make an excellent punching bag for me to try and test it out.

"What the hell did you just say?"

Her slim body goes rigid for a moment at the confrontation before she crosses her arms. If she thinks her sunglasses are hiding the narrowing of her eyes, she's mistaken.

"I *said*—" She emphasizes the "d" to the point that I want to cringe. *Say it again, I fucking dare you.*

"Ladies..." A deep voice of a man tears my heated stare away from the woman just feet away. "You have an audience."

To say I'm taken aback by the stranger who appeared out of thin air on the street is a mild understatement. His golden hair on top of his head wraps around into the slightly darker hair along his jaw. His upper half is barely concealed by a tank, ripped out at the sides, showing off nothing but muscle. His calves, too, are thick with a lean curve to them. I don't recognize him, that much I know.

Our small town has the same people, the same children, running about again and again. Some take to the streets on schedule every day, walking in rain, sunshine, or snow. This man, however, I have never seen before. And with that giant-ass wolf tattoo on his arm, I would know.

It's hard to drag my attention away from him, but I force myself to blink away to see where the man is referring to. Sure enough, my kids are poking their heads out of the garage door, one stacked on top of the other like some old cartoon.

"Well, hi." Chassidy begins to twirl the ends of her hair, now that there's a man present. Sadly, this isn't the first time I've witnessed her act with men.

Hello? You screwed around with my husband and broke up our already failing marriage. Can you at least act like you're in a committed relationship?

I hate the fact that this woman will be spending time with *my* children this weekend.

Offering a small crack of a forced smile to the devastatingly handsome stranger, I lower my voice as I step in closer to the suntanned twig before me. "Either Joe picks them up, or forget about this weekend."

I bite my tongue as I swivel around and into the garage, promptly closing the door as I make my way in. When I turn, I find the man gone and a fuming child of a woman screeching her tires as she leaves.

The house is starting to take shape again thanks to the extra time with the kids at home. The dishes are done, sweeping and vacuuming are now complete, and Julie even took it upon herself to light a candle warmer so the house now smells of fresh cookies. It makes me want to eat some raw cookie dough. Perhaps a run to the store is in order tonight. With the extra time, I guess I could drown my sorrows a bit.

I pack the kids some snacks for their road trip tomorrow, and as much as I want to tell them where they're going, I refrain. I don't think I would be able to act happy about their first amusement park visit without me. But, I try to assure them that they'll have fun with their dad. I purposefully omit any mention of Chassidy, not knowing how much they overheard outside. If they were witness to any of it, the both of them are smart enough to not say anything. Since they've been helping me clean the house without much of a fuss, I assume they heard enough.

It's almost an hour after they were supposed to be picked up when Julie gets a text from her dad, stating that he has arrived. I had purposefully put my phone back on silent after leaving Joe a voicemail with the ultimatum. I don't want to argue, I just want him to hold up his end of our agreement. I'm not going to badmouth the kids' father, as much as I want to. So I just stated that there had been a misunderstanding and he should come when he could to pick them up.

Catching Emmett trying to stash his handheld game in his bag, I stroll over to him and hold out my hand. The look of defeat in his eyes when he realizes that he's been caught almost makes me cave, but I can't.

"Come on," he whines. His glasses slip down his nose and he pushes them up with a rough finger. "Julie has her phone, what do I have?"

"Homework," I state, very matter-of-fact. "I know you have some missing assignments in math and reading, and more than likely, they're stashed in your school bag. Take it with you."

Emmett groans, rather exaggerated. "But, Mom!"

"Don't start with me. You know the deal. Keep your grades at a C or higher and you get your electronic privileges back."

"We should get going, Emmett." Julie already has her hand on the doorknob, a wary look in her eyes.

"Come on, I'll walk you guys out."

"Dad lets me play whenever I want," Emmett mutters, but the jab is only surface level. I was always the disciplinarian during my relationship with Joe, and I knew it would make me the bad guy at times, but it was something I stood firm on. I'm not going to get hung up on it, and I don't want the divorce to sway the way I'm raising my children. Sure, I had thought it would be a joint effort, but Joe is definitely trying to take on being the "fun" parent. It is seriously annoying and has pissed me off more times than I can count.

I could be fun too. But now, only having one income, we can't just drop everything and go on a sporadic road trip. I have to be careful with my money since there's no child support. We split costs for school and clothes, and feed them when they're in our respective care. Fun and spur-of-the-moment activities are another story.

I have been toying with the idea of picking up a second job for when the kids are away, but the idea of starting over from scratch at a new place of employment with unknown people…it's a daunting task I can barely bring myself to try. I might as well wear a sign on my head indicating that I'm having money problems.

Opting not to open the garage, the kids and I take the breezeway between the house and garage to make our way around to the driveway. I can hear the sound of Joe's diesel engine the moment we step outside. When he filed for divorce, he practically ran to the nearest car dealership and bought the stupid gas-guzzling red truck. We'd had our vehicles paid off for nearly two years, and then he went off and bought a sixty-thousand-dollar truck as soon as he was "free" to do as he wanted.

Funny, considering I thought we had been in agreement on all of our financial decisions over the years. But hey, I guess I'm not sixty grand in debt on a vehicle—he is.

Joe's glossy, light hair comes into view as he hops out of the truck. Chassidy is in the passenger seat with her arms crossed. I'm sure she's trying to give me the death stare behind her glasses. I'm only waiting for her to stick her tongue out like the child she is.

"Bye, Mom." Julie turns and gives me a tight squeeze before skirting around her dad on her way toward the truck. I try to place an arm around Emmett, but he shrugs me off as he follows after his sister. I try not to let it get to me, even though deep down, that action stings. He looks so much like his father; if he were to gel his hair like his dad, he would be the spitting image of Joe in his youth. Though Emmett's hair isn't quite as light as his father's, it's nowhere near the darkness of mine.

"Really, Clara?" Joe is perturbed, and I knew he would be. Especially since I chose to ignore any calls or texts after my voicemail. "A bit childish today, aren't we?"

"You should ask Chassidy. She called me a bitch in front of our children." I try to keep my face void of any frustration, knowing that I'm on full display to everyone who is now sealed inside the truck.

"Well, sometimes you—"

"Don't you dare, Joe," I cut him off, fully aware of where he was going with that. The audacity of this man! And to think, I was married to him for almost thirteen years. We got married before we could even legally drink.

His face reddens, and he opens his mouth to speak but then closes it once more. His blue eyes that I used to admire hold nothing but hatred now. The man I once knew, once loved, is gone.

"You said that *you* would be here to pick them up. And with the way she squealed her tires when she left, I still stand by the decision of not letting the kids leave with her. You try to pull that shit again—"

"And you'll what? Hm?" His voice rises and his brows take a drastic dip. "I know you can't afford any more lawyer fees."

Ouch. Hard to believe there was a time when I would have done anything for him. I was *that* enamored.

Deciding to not let this go any further, I choose to take the high road—even if I want to get in a full-out screamfest over how he wronged *me* to begin with. *He* was the one to throw our family into a tailspin with his little piece of ass in the truck. *He* was the one who sank his dick into somebody else and then decided to end our marriage when I wasn't enough for him anymore.

"Look, Joe. I'm not comfortable with her picking them up or dropping them off. End of story."

I give a brief little smile and wave of my fingers to the kids, and without another glance at my ex-husband and the steam being emitted from his carefully styled head of hair, I leave them and round the corner of the garage. I don't stop until I'm in the breezeway, where I sink down against the side of the garage until I'm a heap on the concrete.

Tears burn my eyes as I turn my gaze up to the clear blue sky above. I don't want to be alone. I don't want my kids taken away from me on *my* weekend, but I was the one to agree to it even though I hadn't wanted to. I hate being alone in a house that is usually filled with sounds of music, electronics, or voices. I know Julie and Emmett are becoming more independent, and spending more time to themselves than with me, but still—just having them present is all I want. My kids are my freaking life.

I don't want to share them and their time with the man who broke my heart and shattered our vows. Our marriage might have been crumbling, but I fully believed that we could work through it. I chose to believe that we could conquer anything, until I found out that he cheated.

Once he had done that, there was no going back.

2

The One

Seth

The only downside to moving so much is not taking my furniture with me. I only bring along what fits in a small U-Haul that I can attach to the back of my truck. That usually consists of my clothes, computer shit, and my gaming devices. There are a few odds and ends as well, but nothing that I can't carry with my own two hands.

I usually opt for bigger cities than Alton. They make it easier to blend in while still having some sort of forest area nearby. If I can have the trees right outside my back door, then that's even better.

Pembrook, which is just about twenty miles away from Alton, would have been more ideal, but when I saw this place up for rent, I snatched it. The small, two-bedroom home is set back far enough from the main road, and with a dense tree area behind, it's almost too perfect. The small town of Alton is literally across a highway bridge, lying just on the other side. As long as I can get internet out here, and I was assured that I could, I'm all in.

That's the beauty of working remotely. I could literally work from anywhere in the United States. As long as I take care of my work and get shit done, nobody cares where I am. Hell, I can even make my own hours, to an extent. Meetings that should be nothing more than an email are my biggest complaint and time killer. But in the end, the freedom that comes with my job is why I have stayed with the company for so long.

Even though the house is in fairly good condition upon my arrival, I still clean it from top to bottom before my furniture delivery, which is to come between the hours of two and four. I crank up the central air and get to work, stripping down to nothing more than my shorts and letting my music play on full blast from a portable speaker. Given how far back I am from the road, I don't think I could blare the music loud enough to be heard from there. I'm already growing grateful for the privacy I haven't had in so long.

Except for the fact that apparently nobody delivers food out to the middle of nowhere. Guess I hadn't anticipated that when moving here. Goodbye, DoorDash and Uber Eats. You will be sorely missed.

Running to the nearest gas station in Alton, I survey the little town as I drive by. Several wave, some stare, and it is made very clear quite quickly that I am a curiosity of sorts. I grab a sandwich, a few drinks and bags of chips before fueling up my tank and heading back to my new humble abode.

I hope that after a while, the eyes on me might lessen, but I guess only time will tell. Alton is a quaint little town with a population just tipping over eight hundred. There are more people around at this time of day than I might have expected, but I remain as pleasant as I can be with any gestures.

Usually, I stay in a location for six months to two years. Sometimes it depends on the terms of my lease. Other times, I'm just bored and want to move on to something new and fresh. I've been living this way for over a decade now, ever since I left the only home I had ever known and didn't look back.

Some would call this life lonely, but it's how I prefer it. I don't have anyone to answer to. No one depends on me, and there are no responsibilities outside of paying my own bills and doing my own work. Other than that, things couldn't be simpler. And that's how I like it. Can't disappoint anyone with the life I currently have.

The furniture arrives almost at the end of their window. I had been growing wary, worried that I might find myself sleeping in my truck tonight without a bed. But luckily, that won't be the case.

The two guys that were sent to deliver it are...an interesting choice. Both scrawny men with hardly any meat on their bones. I end up helping them move things into the house just so they don't damage anything, or themselves, for that matter. My security deposit was just as much as my monthly rent, and I don't want to mess up my chance of getting that back someday.

A bed and dresser for the bedroom. A small couch and entertainment center for the living room. The little two-person table for the dining room looks like some sort of joke. It's laughable just how tiny it is in the room, but I don't exactly plan on having any guests to warrant anything bigger. I guess I should have paid more attention to the measurements online.

I tip both guys a few twenties and send them on their way, thankful to get them out of my hair.

After my bed is made, I toy with the idea of starting to put my office together in the second bedroom. Although I usually get excited about doing something so menial, today that isn't the case.

After the long drive here and being cooped up in my truck and then this house, I'm ready to get some energy out. I'm not exactly dressed for going into Pembrook and checking things out, but the urge to run tells me that I need to get outside. Stretching my legs will do me some good and give me some time to explore what little my eyes have seen so far in Alton.

Strapping my phone to my arm and plugging a bud into my ear, I take off. My blood begins to pump as each foot kicks off, the gravel of my driveway skidding away behind me. I offer a small raise of my hand in a polite wave to a vehicle going by, only to be snubbed.

Whatever. Nice to meet you, too.

A couple of school buses pass beneath me as I make my way over the two-lane bridge. The lack of noise coming from them tells me that if they're not empty, they're nearing it.

On my side of the bridge, it's mostly woods. This side, leading into the little hub of Alton, has cornfields on my left and more trees on my right.

Traffic begins to pick up from the end of the workday, and as soon as I see a sidewalk, I leap over to it and keep going. There are several people out walking their dogs, kids at play on bicycles and scooters, and the occasional golf cart or ATV.

I grin as a neon green side-by-side turns a corner and heads in my direction. Now that thing is a beauty. I wouldn't mind getting behind the wheel of one of them myself. I've never really been one for outdoor toys such as that. I've been a computer guy most of my life, so I can't explain the newfound fascination I have with it. Perhaps I'm merely smitten by my favorite color, it's hard to say.

House after house, there is life of some sort, be it a dog roaming around or the occasional person mowing their lawn. The little town is busy. But even so, it's still quiet compared to the larger cities I've lived in.

I catch eye after eye searching me as I pass, and more often than not, they offer friendly hellos either by a tip of a hat or a wave of their hands. It is a bit strange how obvious it is that I'm the new guy around. I don't think there will be any blending in around here.

One older man, who if I had to guess is in his eighties, is sitting at the edge of his worn down shed of a garage, just still as a statue in his overalls. He eyes me the entire time I pass, which even at my speed, feels like an eternity. I wouldn't be surprised if the old man has a shotgun stored nearby for trespassers.

I round the next corner and the wind shifts. A sweet aroma fills my nostrils and has me skidding to a stop. Closing my eyes, I inhale as deeply as my chest will allow as I try to catch my breath, pulling out my earbud as if that will help my sense of smell.

Vanilla.

A warm, sweet mix of vanilla, as if it's straight from a bottle. It is mouthwatering, filling my head and rendering me completely useless. I inhale again, concentrating on it, hanging on to every molecule that the air gives me, and when I find the strength, I take off in its direction. It carries me as if I'm weightless, when really, I'm probably stomping the pavement with each foot like a madman on a mission.

It is intoxicating. The smell is so potent that I long to chase after it until I can wrap my hands around it like it's a tangible thing.

"Sorry you wasted your time coming out here."

A woman's voice rolls over my skin, creating a trail of goosebumps as if I've just been touched by her. I might be starting to perspire, but it feels like I just experienced a blessing from some divine creature, begging to be worshiped.

Standing a short distance from an open garage is the one responsible. It's a large, two-story house with gray vinyl siding. The house and garage match, trimmed in a stark white with various bushes and rock landscaping around them. That's about all I take in before I return my attention to the women in view.

A brunette beauty has a scowl on her face, indicating that whoever she's talking to is on her shit list. It reads all across her round face. The light breeze whips at her shoulder-length, dark-chocolate-colored hair, and I want to sink to my knees as the vanilla hits me again like a brick wall. How can she be so deliciously potent from so far away?

The woman is a bit shorter than me, with a curvy figure that begs to be touched and caressed. Her dark eyes pop against her fair skin even from this distance. She looks fierce, and I would hate to be on the opposite end of whatever she's doling out.

There's movement behind her. Two petite frames are moving about the garage as if they're sneaking around the inside perimeter, and my feet are moving once more the moment I hear an irritating voice call the curvy one a bitch.

"What the hell did you just say?" She grows louder, totally oblivious to the young ones who are now peering out as if they're afraid to get caught. They aren't very good at hiding, if you ask me.

"I *said*—" I cringe at the younger woman's tone as I come to a halt at the end of the driveway.

"Ladies..." I try to remain calm as both of them turn their attention on me. I lock eyes on the one who smells of vanilla, trying to reel my thoughts back in and stay focused. My feet become weighted to the ground, and I struggle for a moment to continue. "You have an audience."

The lusciously beautiful one makes my mouth water as her eyes roam over me quickly. I'm sure she thought it was fast enough that I wouldn't notice, but she was wrong. She turns to find the kids, and judging by the way her posture stiffens at their arrival, I have just saved her from doing something she might regret.

"Well, hi." The one next to the awful yellow car tries to drag my attention away, but I only ignore her. She needs to fix her damn voice before she opens her mouth again. She reminds me of those porn videos, calling for Daddy to fill her up.

I don't make a habit of watching shit like that, but once they refer to each other as Mommy and Daddy, I cut out. I'll never understand the need to bring up a mother or father during sex or anything related to it. It's an instant turnoff for me. Along with that damned voice.

"Either Joe picks them up, or forget about this weekend." The curvy one leaves us before anyone else can get in another word.

The girl by the yellow car is fuming, balling her fists as the garage door begins to whir, coming to life as it closes. I want to run after the curvy one, but not with the audience. There are children present, and obviously someone who wasn't welcome.

I turn and head back the way I came, but it's difficult. Like I'm trudging through sludge as I attempt to leave while my body is telling me not to. But I'm eager to get back and fire up my laptop. I have to find out who the hell this Joe is, but more importantly, find out the name of my mate.

I didn't think there was a mate in the cards for me. My family prides themselves on carrying on their lines and their pack mentality bullshit. If you can't reproduce, you're as good as dead. I guess in a sick way, by their standards, I am.

Rewind to age twenty. I'm on the verge of getting married, at the doctor's office getting tested for everything known to mankind at my fiancée's request, when I find out there isn't any kind of chance of creating a child of my own. Apparently, that was a deal-breaker for her and she dumped me. My family couldn't understand how I could possibly be sterile, and you would swear I brought dishonor to the whole fucking pack instead of just my immediate family.

My ex had wanted children. Loads of them, in fact. And when she found out I couldn't give them to her, she moved on quicker than a shot fired from a gun. Three years together, and our relationship was ripped away. I was devastated.

There was nothing I could do to persuade her to stay. Anything that came out of my mouth wasn't good enough, as if our time together and leading up to our wedding meant absolutely nothing. How could she possibly be so shallow to give up our relationship over the first obstacle that came our way?

When I realized that perhaps she had never truly loved me, I left with nothing more than what I could fit in my suitcase and backpack. And I haven't returned to the place I used to call home since.

It's better this way. Can't let anyone down when you have no one around.

But a mate? How could I have one? I can't fathom why I would even be granted one, since I can't procreate. Is this some kind of sick joke?

I've heard how powerful it is, finding your connection. That it's almost like time stands still as your body tries to register and then scream at you that the person you belong with is present. The phrase "I would move heaven and earth" takes on a whole new meaning when you come face-to-face with the one who completes you.

I'm huffing and puffing as I storm into my new home and retrieve my laptop. The stroke of keys as I type in my password illuminates my screen and I sink back onto the couch, oblivious to the sweat coating me.

Once I locate the property records, I find out just who lives there. The house with the woman and children.

Clara Rose Serring. I let her name roll from my lips, and before I can groan out how beautiful it sounds, I note the name beside hers from the previous year and my mood sours.

Joseph Franklin Serring.

Thanks to social media, I'm able to quickly put puzzle pieces together to form a quick summary of Clara's life.

Clara Rose. *My* Clara Rose.

She is fucking beautiful. Her body began to grow more curves after each child. Her chest is fuller, hips a little wider, but nothing short of stunning. If I ever have the chance to see her naked, I will die a happy man. And if I ever get my hands on her, damn. I might just have a heart attack. Just imagining my fingers sinking into her skin has my dick hardening in my shorts.

There is one social media outlet that she seems to post on more often, but then I note the date of the last post. It was well over a year ago. What has transpired since then to take her away from her usual posting schedule? There was usually about one post a month, and it was either about hobbies, trips, or her children. Julie and Emmett.

They are the ones I witnessed sneaking around the garage in the hopes they wouldn't get caught.

Sorry, kids, but your mom was obviously upset.

The deeper I dig, the more my heart begins to ache for her. I notice how she became more and more absent from pictures. She must have been the one taking them instead of being in them, and when she did get in front of the camera, there was a sadness to her facial features. Smiles never fully reached her eyes when she was pictured next to her now ex-husband.

From what I gather, they were high school sweethearts. They moved into the house in Alton shortly after they married and Julie came into their lives. Post after post, picture after picture, I'm drowning in the life of Clara and my yearning for her only worsens.

I know without a shadow of a doubt that her ex must have done something wrong, and that suspicion is solidified when I locate the divorce filing.

And don't get me started on the whiny little tot of a woman who was next to the yellow car. It's quite clear that she is Joe's new woman, if you could even call her that.

Chassidy. She looks and sounds like a stripper or some sort of adult entertainer. She posts daily, sometimes more than that. That absurd duck face is prominent in a lot of her photos. Makeup is plastered on her face one minute, she's posing in a bikini the next. Is she even a legal adult yet? The videos of her taking shots at bars—with Joe in the background, might I add—make me wonder if she just lured men to pay for her drinks so no one would ask to see an ID.

My stomach churns, thinking about Clara trying to compare herself to her. It's something women do, whether they really want to do it or not. And the fact that Joe is being paraded around makes me think of him as nothing more than a sugar daddy of some sort. He traded in Clara and the mother of his children...for this chick?

But I guess that's good news for me. I don't know how much he's in the picture now with Clara, but judging by these photos, he shouldn't be a problem.

I want her. The need to talk to her, touch and feel her, has my body vibrating.

There is one picture I keep going back to. Clara is staring out a window in what looks to be a living room of some sort. A small tyke is asleep on her chest, Emmett, and a younger Julie is curled up beside her. Joe, or perhaps someone else entirely, must have taken the picture, and my whole world now resides in this one frame.

It would be a bit stalkerish of me, but I want to blow it up, print it, and frame it.

I would be whatever she needs, whatever her children need, as long as I could be a part of her life.

Looks like I'll be staying in Alton a lot longer than my one-year lease.

3

Screw Yard Work

Clara

The house is too quiet.

I'm in a mood the moment I wake up and realize that nobody is home. There are no creaks of the floorboards upstairs in the kids' rooms. Zero stirrings as they start their day, eager to be the first ones downstairs and racing to get to the biggest television in the house. No arguing over which show or influencer is more stupid. No curses muttered only for them to freeze in the hopes that I didn't hear them speak it in the first place.

I sigh heavily as I get up from the bed, rubbing my face as if I could ease away the pain of their absence.

Last night I stayed up too late, losing myself in one of my favorite television shows while spooning refrigerated cookie dough into my mouth until I made myself sick. Stupid, I know. But for whatever reason, I wanted my body to feel just as upset as my head.

I probably need a therapist. It's something I've been contemplating ever since Joe filed for a divorce. I had been blindsided, not even offered the slightest courtesy of a heads-up. I think that's why I bury myself in work and the kids' after-school activities. If I keep my brain busy, then

I don't have to wallow in my own self-pity. When the kids are gone and I'm alone, I have less than ideal ways of coping, if you could even call it that.

My argument that I just don't have the time to go for an hour-long appointment every couple of weeks to talk to somebody is growing more and more weak. I could use my lunch break at work, for starters. Two, I could try to go in before work, knowing that the one office on Farley opens an hour before my day job starts. Three...

Why the hell am I focused on this today, and first thing in the morning? It's Saturday.

Because I'm sad, lonely, and depressed. God, how pathetic am I?

I scrub my face at my bathroom sink, ridding myself of the oils built up on my face overnight, and I poorly rearrange my little bun at the back of my head. Retrieving my light robe, I leave my end of the house and stroll out to the living room, plucking away at my phone to find some music to fill the silence.

Emptying the dish drainer gives my iced coffee enough time to do its thing before I add creamer, some splashes of milk, and syrup until I get the color of beige I need before I even attempt a taste test. When I'm done doctoring up my coffee, I decide to go out on the back porch for a little while.

My phone is playing as I step outside, quickly embraced by the early morning warmth. I have little doubt I'll be sweating later. Especially since I know the yard needs mowing. Now that the teenager next door has begun school again, I'll have to take up that task on my own. He's a godsend during the summer months, and he only charges me ten dollars per mow as long as I keep my gas tank filled. I always try to pay him double, hoping to keep him coming back, and so far, it has worked.

He's a few years older than Julie and started up a little lawn-mowing business of his own last summer. It has been to my advantage, considering how much I loathe mowing. Come to think of it, the last time I did mow we had a self-propelled machine. It's been a while since I've had to worry about the yard at all.

Closing the door, I turn to take my place in my rocker when I notice the pinkish-red bloom of a rose in my seat. Its petals are large and open, rendering me motionless for a moment as I study it. The coloring is a stark contrast to the dark blue chair that it's nestled on.

I look around, eyeing my backyard. There are no rose bushes around here, certainly not on my property. The tree line out back doesn't show any for as far as my eyes can see, either. Our landscaping is simple, and easy to care for, since neither Joe or I have a green thumb. The neighbor closest to me has some daffodils that pop up in the spring, but that's about it for anything on my end of the street.

But this flower, the way it sits, looks like it was strategically placed here. There is no way in hell the wind simply carried it and delivered it on my chair.

There's only a camera by the front door in case of guests or packages delivered. Since I can't get here quickly from my work on a normal day, it has definitely proved useful. Working in the next town over a guaranteed five days a week, it's nice being able to check on things when I'm not so close by.

So where did this gorgeous rose come from?

You stupid, fucking machine.

The mower has stopped once again as I tried to reverse, sputtering before the engine goes silent.

I just filled the stupid tank with gas, so what gives?

Drawing out my phone, I pause my music and search for videos for the stupid thing I'm sitting on. I've barely done two passes on the side of my yard and can't keep the damn engine running.

The first man to light up my screen has such a thick Southern accent, I can barely understand him. Going back, I select another video, and this one has a long-winded intro that soon has me rolling my eyes. It reminds me of some of those recipe sites that have to tell you every little detail about their life before actually diving into the recipe.

Stupidly annoying and not at all helpful.

In the third video I select, the man is seated, holding the camera at my point of view, instructing me on how to start the engine. I begin repeating after him, trying to commit his instructions to memory.

Thank God this side of my yard is on a dead end. Saves me a bit of embarrassment since I'm just a bit further away from prying eyes.

Brake. Choke it. Turn the key. Push the—

Why are there so many fucking steps? Just let me mow my damn yard!

A hand shoots into view and knocks on the front end of the mower, my heart rate spiking at the sudden and unknown presence. I jolt, sending my phone to the ground as I clutch at my chest from the interruption.

"Jesus!" I exclaim, eyes wide as I take in the person who snuck up on me. My heart doesn't calm down when I note that it's the same tattooed man who appeared out of nowhere yesterday at the end of my driveway.

His mouth is moving as he points to his ear. I blink at him for a moment, confused, when it suddenly registers that I can't hear him because the damn lawn mowing guy is still instructing me in my ears.

"Sorry, sorry." I pull my buds out, breaking our eye contact. I can't help but notice how golden his are, now that we're so close. They are freaking beautiful.

His lighthearted chuckle is music to my ears now that the man in the buds is no longer filling them. If velvet had a sound, it would be this man's voice.

"I'm the one who should be sorry. I didn't mean to scare you. I *did* try to get your attention before, though."

I nod my head slowly as he picks up my phone and hands it back to me. The man is dressed almost the same as yesterday. Running shoes, shorts, and a loose tank that's ripped out along the sides. I don't know what I've done to deserve a glance at this fine specimen of a man before me, but I can't deny that he is hot. The way his muscles move as he places his hands on his hips shouldn't be this satisfying to watch.

Geez, am I eye-fucking him? I totally am, and I can feel heat rush into my cheeks.

"Can I help you with something?" My lips roll inward, nervous at the sudden encounter.

"Actually, I was trying to ask you that same question. Is everything alright?"

What are the chances he might do me the favor of taking off that scrap of fabric he's using as a shirt so I can get an unobstructed view of what's beneath?

Oh, dear God, Clara. No!

"Well," I begin, wondering if I should attempt to play the single mother who doesn't know what she's doing. Or, I could be stubborn and assure him that I can figure it out. I somehow settle in the middle. "I normally pay the kid next door to mow, but since school has started back up, I'm afraid I'm on my own now."

He studies my mower for a moment, allowing time for my gaze to freely roam over him before his mouth starts to move. The darker coloring of his facial hair piques my interest. It's a stunning combination to the prominent coloring on top of his head.

"And what seems to be the problem?"

How stupid am I that I need a freaking YouTube video to figure this out?

The man seems genuinely concerned, however. Not a note of mockery to his tone or body language whatsoever. Perhaps this new guy is just being...friendly. Which is usually considered a normal and neighborly thing around our small little town, but...he's *new*. It could just be Midwest Nice at its finest, and if I'm lucky, I might just get to benefit from it.

"I um...well...it shuts off every time I try to reverse it. I thought I was doing all of the right steps, but maybe I'm getting them out of order? Honestly, I don't know where I messed up." My free hand slaps the top of my legging-clad thigh, aggravated that my little knowledge of mowing has already garnered unnecessary attention.

"Mind if I give it a go?" He tips his head in the direction of the mower and I ponder it for a moment. I could say, "Thanks, but no thanks," but at the same time, I just want to get the damn yard done before the real heat of the day begins. I can already feel my oversized shirt clinging to my back. If my arms didn't jiggle so much, I would undoubtedly be wearing a tank top. Only mine wouldn't be ripped out at the sides like his. The more covered I am, the better.

"Sure," I mutter as I remove myself from the mower, and rather ungracefully, might I add. The man slides onto the seat with ease, the large bicep closest to me showing off his phone that's strapped to it. It's almost double the size of my phone.

I watch as he makes quick work of turning it on, pushing, turning, and pulling mechanisms until it roars to life. When I try to thank him, my voice is drowned out by the sound of the blade lowering, and I jump back. When he takes off, I stand there for a moment, dumbfounded.

I didn't ask him to mow my yard, but in hindsight, maybe I should have clarified. I take a few long strides to catch up to him, hollering that I can take over, but he merely points to his ears, pretending that he can't hear me when I know damn well he can.

The teasing grin that forms on his bearded face is evidence enough. I stand there, stunned, as he begins whipping the machine around the yard. When he comes back toward me again, he just offers a small salute with two of his fingers.

He shows no signs of stopping.

I'm not sure if I should be concerned that this man is taking it upon himself to save a damsel in distress, or just grateful that I'm escaping yet another mow. I decide to go with the latter for now, and disappear to go fetch him a water bottle. The sweat glistening off of his muscles before he even sat down on the mower makes it evident that he has already been outside for some time, but it hasn't completely soaked through his powder blue tank yet. Given the time it normally takes to mow the yard and maneuver that mower, I have little doubt it will be drenched in no time.

I, on the other hand, am already hot and bothered that this man is taking this little weight off my shoulders without me even asking. I want to gawk at him from my kitchen, but I know with the daylight pouring in I don't really have a place to hide.

Placing the cold water bottle on my neck, I let my eyes wander over him while his back is turned. My mind is obviously interested in his good looks, trying to pick off his clothes in an attempt to visualize just how striking he would look underneath it all. I shouldn't be ogling him like this, but yet here I stand, completely smitten by this man who has once again shown up unannounced and out of thin air.

Then there's that tattoo of his...

When the mower turns, I try looking at his hands for any kind of ring, but nothing catches a glimmer from the sun.

He could have left it at home.

Granted, he could have. He has more muscle and athleticism in his whole body than I probably have in my index finger. He's totally out of my league, and if he isn't taken, I'm sure he has women falling for him left and right.

Hell, even Chassidy flipped a switch and tried to flirt with him yesterday. There's no way he isn't spoken for already.

But damn, I'm going to enjoy every glance I can take without coming off looking like the desperate woman that I am. Not having sex in almost two years might make anyone a little crazy about the first man to show any kind of interest.

Even if that interest is for my mower, in the first place.

I have to admit, the now-memorized sight of him will be on my mind when I grab my vibrator later. Hell, I might even use it in the shower after being outside. Why wait until tonight?

Deciding I have wasted enough time inside, I leave the air-conditioned kitchen and make my way back out to the deck. When he looks up, I try to draw his attention to the water I grabbed from the fridge. When he nods, I make the trek out to the yard and unscrew the cap for him.

He comes to a brief pause on the mower, lifting the blade and granting us a slight reprieve from the overbearing noise. Enough for me to try and speak again.

"You really don't have to do this," I state, trying to offer him a way out. He grins, handing the bottle back to me now that it's halfway gone.

"I've got nothing better to do." He flashes a smile that I'm sure could wet the undergarments of anyone—man or woman—and continues on.

I find that very hard to believe. He seriously has nothing better to do than mow some stranger's yard? Yeah, right.

Returning to the deck, I sit in my chair. The single rose found in my seat, that now sits in a small vase in the kitchen, flashes through my memory as I wait. I try scrolling through multiple apps on my phone, but I can't concentrate on anything besides the hunk in my backyard.

God, Joe would have a fucking field day with this. Good thing he's probably already at the amusement park by now and out of my hair for the weekend.

I play with the idea of taking a picture of the man when his back is turned. Sweat is beginning to form along his spine as he maneuvers through the yard with an ease that I certainly don't have. Deciding it can't hurt, I take a quick picture with his face turned away so he doesn't know.

I feel like a creep, but a part of me still can't believe that this is actually happening. Perhaps I fell off of the mower and hit my head on the landscaping blocks. This is all a dream and I'll come to with a concussion of some sort. That seems more logical at this point.

I delete the picture out of guilt.

He disappears to do the front yard and I slink back into my chair. I can finally breathe now that I'm not on display for him. It only took him about twenty minutes to do my backyard. Joe always paid someone to take care of it—the landscaping, mowing, weedeating, everything. Before I met him, I had only operated a push mower, and while that thing made your body work harder, at least I could start and use the damn thing without much fuss.

But without Joe's income, I've had to cut back on things. I can't afford the yard workers, name-brand grocery items, and luxury meats. Hell, I even had to switch insurance companies because my old one kept upping my rates. I know the fact that our insurance agent was best friends with Joe had something to do with it, but regardless, severing another connection with my ex helped lift my spirits a little bit. And saving an extra seventy-five dollars a month helped, too.

When the mower turns off, I leap off the top stair of the deck and go off in search of him. I'm surprised to find that he has parked it in its usual spot in the garage, and the man stands quickly as he takes an earbud out of his left ear.

"I hope you'll tell me the name of the man that mowed my yard."

I'm met with that charming grin as I hand him his water again.

"Only if you'll tell me yours." He beams as he takes a large gulp of water. His beard comes down about an inch from his jawline, offering me the bob of his Adam's apple as he swallows.

"Clara," I say. I want to stick out my hand to shake his, but I still have no idea if this man is a killer in disguise or what. Perhaps I watch too many crime shows if my mind instantly goes to that dark of a place.

"Very nice to meet you, Clara." He then sticks out his hand and mine is shooting out to meet his. I mean, it would be rude if I didn't return the gesture. "I'm Seth."

Seth, I repeat in my head. His large hand wraps around mine gently, and as much as I want to leave it there, I let it slip out before it lingers too long.

"Thank you for mowing my yard, Seth. Although, you really didn't have to—"

"It's fine, really." He takes another swig before those golden eyes turn back to me. "I just moved in and I've been stalling on getting things squared away."

"And you would rather mow?" I snort a rather unflattering laugh and click my mouth shut soon after.

"Believe it or not, yes. I was out for a run, trying to explore the town a bit, but...there really isn't much town. I think I've roamed its entirety twice by now."

This time when I laugh, it comes out a bit more gracefully. "Did you not know where you were moving to?"

"Yeah, it's small." Seth rubs at the back of his neck. "A lot smaller than I'm used to."

"What brings you here?" I inquire further, longing to hear his deep voice continue. I don't think I've ever carried on a conversation with an attractive man for this long before, and honestly, it's helping take my mind off of my lonely weekend. It's a nice change of pace.

"Nothing in particular."

I raise a brow, suddenly getting serial killer vibes. Seth couldn't be more vague in that answer, and it is a bit concerning.

"I'm a programmer and work remotely," he states when he observes my shift in attitude. "I pretty much move when I want to, wherever I please. I usually stick to bigger cities, and I decided to change things up this time. Little did I know that you can't get anything delivered in a small town like this. Not even a pizza."

The rigidness of my body softens, knowing his plight all too well. I grew up in Pembrook, where I currently work, and having various restaurants deliver at whatever time of day you want is definitely a luxury service that's a hard thing to lose after moving out here.

"There's pizza at the gas station, but unfortunately, no, they don't deliver. Their hours suck, by the way."

"Noted, thank you." Seth lifts his shirt to dab at the sweat on his head, so I'm given a quick glimpse of what lies beneath the cotton and damn, it does not disappoint. Tight and toned ridges of muscle are on display, and what little I can see of his happy trail is enough to send my mind straight into the gutter.

My mouth snaps shut again as I blink away, trying to focus on anything else in my garage to get my mind off of his body.

Grill. Gas tank. Rake. Hose. Leaves that have made their way into the garage and died.

"I was thinking about going into Pembrook tonight. Checking things out. I saw a Chinese restaurant that I might try."

Food, okay. I've got this. *Relax, Clara.*

"Which one?"

"The Wall, I think?" He finishes off his water before tossing the bottle into the nearby recycling bin with perfect precision.

"If I were you, I would steer clear of that one. Health inspector has been there a lot lately. I wouldn't chance it."

"Oh?" His attention and curiosity is heavy, and I'm unable to meet his gaze this time around.

"Yeah, um..." *Focus.* I need to just freaking focus on food, not his body like he's a piece of meat at the perfect temperature for consuming. I know I'd never even stand a chance with him. He's probably taken, and if he's not, I know my kids come first. What guy isn't going to be scared off by the schedule and minds of a thirteen-year-old and a nine-year-old?

"If you're wanting good Chinese, I would head the opposite direction and go to The Gold Dragon in Benson. Their crab rangoons are literally to die for."

There's that heart-stopping smile again. I seriously might swoon if he doesn't stop that right now.

"I appreciate you steering me away from making a bad decision."

I nod my head as he begins to move past me at a slow pace. It seems unnatural for his height. He's about a whole head taller than me.

"Wait, let me get you some money." I'm aware that I still have a twenty-dollar bill in my purse, as I was holding out hope that the boy next door might take pity on me and mow my yard one last time.

"That won't be necessary." Seth tries to brush me off as he keeps walking down my drive, and I have half a mind to chase after him. It would be easy, considering how slow his strides are. More like half strides.

"Please," I beg. "It's the least I can do."

He pauses his retreat and then swivels and begins to backtrack. I steal a quick glance at his wolf tattoo before looking up at him. "Actually, there is something."

My eyes widen, suddenly unsure of what he could possibly have in mind.

"You wouldn't by chance be free tonight to join me, would you?"

I'm stunned into a moment of silence, my brain short-circuiting at the words that just left that mouth of his. My eyes dart between his lips and eyes before I cross my arms uncomfortably.

"Obviously, I'm new around here. You're the first friendly face I've met. Would you care to join me for dinner?"

There's no fucking way he just did that.

"Don't you have a wife or something you'd rather take?" There's no way he's asking *me* to join him. The mere thought is absurd. Maybe I'm jumping to conclusions, though. Perhaps he's just friend-zoning me.

"Free as a bird." He waves his empty and ringless hand between us.

"Or lone wolf." I shrug, referring to the open-mouthed wolf tattoo. The detailed work on it is amazing, I have to admit. There isn't a drop of color in it, but the shading and attention to detail is fascinating.

At the sound of his laugh, my nerves retreat ever so slightly.

"I guess you could say that, yes."

I argue with myself over the possibility of joining this man for dinner, and the chances of him killing me later. On the bright side, if he tries to murder me, our town is quiet enough that I'm pretty sure they would bring out their guns, knives, and hunting gear with a single scream. And while I normally try to remain cautious in all of my decisions, the thought of being cooped up in my empty house tonight is enough to sway me in a new direction.

I think for a moment, willing to risk everything on this crazy whim for some reason I can't comprehend. "I'll see you there at six thirty."

4

It's a Date

Seth

I can't fault Clara for being wary of the new stranger in town. I only hope that I didn't come on too strong in asking her to go out with me.

After returning from her house, I hop into an insanely cold shower to cool my body down. The mere touch of her hand had me wanting to pull her in close and take her mouth. Run my hands down her body until she caved to my touch. If I thought she would let me, I would have carried her inside and fucked her right then and there.

The mere thought of doing that makes my erection grow incredibly hard. *Painfully* hard. I want to rub one off, but I refrain from touching the damn thing that's causing me so much grief at present.

It's her. She's the one.

The moment I got a whiff of that sweet scent of hers, my knees wanted to buckle. She was mumbling to herself, hunched over and trying to see her phone screen. The green and yellow mower beneath her, silent. It was almost too perfect, like the stars had aligned and given me the exact moment to place myself in her life. Little does she know, I'm not going anywhere. There is nowhere she can hide from me now. I would chase her to the ends of the earth.

Clara opted to drive herself, and while I didn't love that idea first off, it's probably for the best. If I was going to be shut into a vehicle with her, her smell would drive me mad with desire. We probably wouldn't even be able to leave the little town of Alton before I hurl myself at her. I only hope that being in a crowded restaurant with a table between us will be enough to calm my ass down. But even then, a table would be too much distance.

I know I have to tread lightly. I already know her better than she's aware of, and she is just coming out of a marriage that resulted in two children. I can't give Clara a reason to push me away. No, I want her to want me just as much as I want her. She has no idea how her mere presence calls to me like a damn siren's song.

I should have asked for her phone number, but I didn't want to come on too strong. That and, if she had my number, there might be a greater chance of her trying to back out and decide against dinner. Though I don't peg her for the type of woman to stand me up. Deep down, I know I intrigue her.

She was eyeing me from inside her house, eyes flicking away each time I tried to make contact with her. The blush that crept up into her cheeks was amusing, to say the least. I thoroughly enjoyed bringing that out in her.

The drive to Benson is quicker than my phone predicted. I shave off four minutes, peeling down the highway in my truck. I smirk as I stick my tongue out at my device, proving my arrival time wrong and beating the clock. I use the extra fifteen minutes to do a deep dive into the restaurant, looking at its food and layout, putting way too much effort into trying to pick out the perfect spot where my Rose and I can sit. I'll slip the attending host a few bills to ensure that I get the spot I want, if it's available.

My Rose.

Her beauty makes the flower I left her pale in comparison. I only wish I could have been there to see her retrieve it. I hope it brought joy to her morning before she began her attempt at yard work.

I have to give her credit, though. Even though I swooped in to take that chore off of her hands, she had been adamant to figure it out herself.

Sorry, Clara. Today isn't going to be that day, and it won't be for a while. Not now that I'm around.

A silver van pulls in and my back straightens. Recognizing the license plate, I exit my truck. As much as I want to meet her at her vehicle and get the door for her, I refrain.

Don't come on too strong.

Pretending I haven't seen her, I begin to cross the parking lot, making my way toward the front door of The Gold Dragon. The red sign has the name of the restaurant in gold letters, with Chinese written beneath its English. Smells waft out of the building with each opening of the front door, and my stomach growls. I only grazed on some chips today after exploring and mowing. I seriously need to make a grocery store run and stock up on some things. I can't just live off of gas station food, but I guess there are worse things I could do.

"Seth!" The sound of my name coming from her lips sends a shiver through me, only to be replaced by a warmth when vanilla floods through my nostrils.

Fucking divine.

"I guess we're both early, Clara. I'm glad you could make it." She quickens her steps to join me as I pivot to wait for her. Her brown hair is down and straightened, bangs covering a part of her forehead and resting a bit below her right eye. The length, just barely grazing her shoulders. Her jean capris and sandals show that she's comfortable, but her top is hands down dressier than what I witnessed her in this morning. The purple material hugs her breasts but gathers beneath it. Loose fabric hangs down from there, covering up any pockets she might have in her bottoms. Her hand is gripping her purse tightly, and when I draw my eyes back up, I note her necklace. It's an interesting piece she chose to wear. I will definitely be bringing that up later, but for right now, I need to get something in my stomach.

Clara awkwardly shrugs, a shy smile sweeping across her face after she rolls her lips. "Shall we?"

"You lead the way." I open the door and let her do so. I would follow this woman wherever she goes. All plans of picking a place to sit leave me as she approaches a hostess and tells her the number of our party.

Clara is almost too polite in every interaction with the staff. I know that before long, I'll lose count of how many times she says the words "please" and "thank you." It makes me wonder about her upbringing. Either someone instilled manners in her, or she had some sort of unpleasant experience herself to warrant this kind of behavior. Regardless, it's refreshing. Manners are lost on so many, anymore.

Before I know it, we're seated at a booth that is far from the ideal spot I had initially hoped for. We both slide in, and I must be grinning like an idiot as she thanks the hostess once more before bringing her attention back toward me.

"What?" Her lashes blink a few times before I shake my head away from my train of thought.

I choose to just state the obvious. I don't think it could hurt my case any. "You're very polite."

She rolls her lips again, a slight gleam coming from whatever she put on them, but the color is subtle. Apparently, she thought enough to dress up a bit and apply makeup for me. Perhaps this is more of a date for her too.

"Sorry?" She forms it as a long and strung out question.

Her confusion is cute. "It's nice. Some people just ignore the pleasantries. You treat them like...you know, people."

"What a weird thing to say." She ponders that for a moment. "Thank you? I guess?"

"It's a compliment, I swear." I flash her a smile, and though it takes a moment, I can see her shoulders relax a bit. "What's good here?"

I begin skimming through the menu even though I already narrowed it down to two while in my truck.

I was glad to see that The Gold Dragon isn't your typical Chinese buffet sort of restaurant. I'm not crazy about those, or really, buffets in general. I would rather have my food prepared for *me* to eat, and me only. Not dozens or hundreds of people coming through and touching the same damn handle for the fried rice.

"Well, I tend to gravitate toward the General Tso's or sesame chicken. I used to love the Szechuan, but since having kids, heartburn really kicks me in the ass whenever I eat something spicy." Her face falters for a moment, a sadness touching her eyes, I assume at the mention of her kids. Those earthy brown eyes have probably seen more heartache than I care to admit.

"They could have come. I wouldn't have minded." That's a bold-faced lie, I have to admit internally. Especially since tonight I want her all to myself for our first meal together. But I would have gotten over it.

"They're with their dad this weekend." She takes a sip of her drink and I detect a small hesitancy in her hand. It's clear that this is shaky territory, and I know that last night has something to do with that sore spot.

I shouldn't, but I press on to test the waters, knowing that I need to be ready to pull back in a split second. "I don't mean to pry"—but I am—"is that what last night was about with that blonde pip-squeak?"

Her eyes shoot to mine, gluing me to the padded seat of the booth. "I'm sorry. I shouldn't have said anything."

The wheels are turning inside her head, and I would give just about anything to hear what she's thinking regarding me, the blonde, or both.

"I guess if I don't tell you, our town will. News travels fast, and unfortunately for me, my failed marriage is the most exciting gossip it's seen for a while."

She leans back, appearing to clasp her hands on her lap. Our waiter appears and takes our orders quickly. I barely acknowledge his presence except to tell him what I want and utter my thanks, but I hardly take in the sight of the young man scribbling in a notepad. When he finally leaves, I'm the first to break the silence at our table. The restaurant has been busy since we arrived, and as much as I would have liked to be tucked away in a corner somewhere, the noise around us drowns out most of the conversations within earshot.

"Clara, you don't have to tell me anything you're not comfortable with. I don't give a rat's ass about gossip. If it's not coming from your lips, then I won't believe it."

She's careful there. A brief flash of something reads across her face before she masks it. Appreciation, perhaps? I can't be sure.

"I..." She's rendered silent for a moment as she contemplates something. So I wait patiently. Eagerly awaiting whichever direction she decides to take it, so I can see just how comfortable or uncomfortable I make her.

"My ex-husband cheated on me with that pip-squeak. Blindsided me when he filed for divorce, and he hasn't tried to hide his infatuation with her." She's unable to look me in the eyes as her face sours. "Chassidy is her name."

Yep. Stripper name. How could I forget? But Clara doesn't know just how deep into her history I've dived. I want to know everything about her and her life, even the bits she may not want to disclose herself. Though, one way or another, I am going to know *everything* about her.

"We hate her. Got it." I reach for my drink, noticing how she perks up at that.

"We?" she repeats after me.

I'm quick to reply. "Yes, we. She called you a bitch in front of your children. Instant dislike. I'm on your side."

"But..." Her loss of words is cute as she searches our table as if there's something imaginary there. "Well..."

Her words fail her again, and I want to reel her back in from whatever well she's just taken a nosedive in.

"Thank you." Her mood levels out, and when she's finally able to look at me again, her mouth opens once more. "And thank you for yesterday. I didn't realize my kids had snuck up on me."

They won't get away with that on my watch. I have superb hearing, for starters. I shouldn't have been able to hear the stripper call Clara a bitch from that distance, but I did.

"Do you have kids?" she asks, suddenly falling shy again. I want to bring her out of that, to carry on a conversation like two grown adults. She's nervous, judging by her bouncing knee beneath the table that she may not be aware that I know about. It suddenly occurs to me that this might be her first outing with another man since her long relationship with Joe. A real douchebag—the epitome of one, if you ask me.

"I do not. Free as a bird, remember?" I lift up the corner of my cheek, hoping she'll take the bait on that one.

"Or a lone wolf." Her voice is barely audible, and she's smiling to herself. It's enough to bring her out of her slump.

I decide to let her in on my life a little bit to put her more at ease. She just opened up about her ex, and I feel as if I need to divulge a bit more information. For every piece of her she gives me, I'll give something back in return. If only she knew just how much I really want to give her.

Everything. Fucking everything, every little piece of me.

"Tell me about your tattoo." She points to my arm as her knee stops bouncing. I push up the gray sleeve of my shirt, showing it off in all its glory even though she had been eyeballing it earlier. The wolf's mouth is wide open with a ferocious look on its face. The perfect way to lock the anger of my past away, a reminder of what it took to push and drive me from the only home I had ever known.

"A bit of backstory," I start. I haven't shared this with anyone. Haven't talked about it to a single person since I left. Clara is going to find out sooner or later, so I decide to go ahead and get it out of the way. "I was engaged once. The love of my life, or so I thought."

Shifting in my seat, I let my elbows rest on the table as I deliver a blow that I know she won't be expecting. She deserves to know it all, no matter how much it pains me to think there's a chance it could happen again. "She dumped me when she found out I can't have children. Called the wedding off and shut me out. I left my hometown shortly after, and haven't been back since."

Clara's emotions flare. When the shock wears off, her brows move inward as she scoots forward in her seat. Her breasts come to rest on the edge of the block of wood between us.

"You...she...what a bitch!" She flinches when she realizes just how loud that last sentence flew from her mouth. There are a few turned heads in my periphery, but I keep my focus solely on her. "What about adoption? Fostering? There are so many children out there who could use a home. A family."

"She wouldn't even entertain the idea. I was practically as good as dead to her since I couldn't produce offspring of our own."

"Wow." Her eyes begin searching the table again, as if the rectangle might give her more to say, but she only grows more agitated when she repeats herself. "Just...wow."

I spare her the details—that I looked up my ex a few years ago, just for shits and grins. Turns out, she got knocked up shortly after I left. She had been adamant about waiting to get married to have kids. Once I was out of the picture, she was pregnant before she married the guy.

"How long were the two of you together?"

"A few years. Had I known that was a deal-breaker, I wouldn't have wasted another day on her." I shrug. I'm a bit surprised at myself for how easily I'm talking about a secret I locked away long ago.

"Understandably." Clara shakes her head, brown hair swaying at her shoulders. "I am so sorry. That's awful."

"It was. But I moved on. It took some time, but I did it." I pat my arm where the wolf is now hiding again. "I got this tattoo to remember the pain, and why I left. It was almost a cathartic experience. Like I could finally leave it in the past."

Her nod is slower now, as if she can understand that. My troubled past is a lot further behind me than hers, but I figure that to a point, she might be able to relate. And if not now, perhaps someday in the future.

"Well, the tattoo is stunning. A bit scary, but beautiful at the same time." She then scrambles over her next set of words. "S-sorry. I didn't mean beautiful. It's...handsome? No."

As much as it amuses me, watching her fumble to find something more masculine to call my tattoo, I put her out of her misery. "Clara, it's fine. You can call it beautiful. Art is subjective. I take no offense."

Clara's genuine smile is enough to make my heart soar. She could have called the wolf on my arm "cute as a button" and I would probably still be in a pile of mush.

In a crowded restaurant, her vanilla scent is minimal. The smells in the air are enough to keep her mouthwatering fragrance at bay, and I can concentrate on this. On the conversation between us.

Knowing how flustered she grew when she mentioned my tattoo being beautiful, I think to turn that compliment onto her. My head tips to the side, and I observe her neck as she peers out at the people around us, taking everyone in. I don't want it to be too much if I state the obvious. That she is the most beautiful woman here tonight. Stunning, even.

"You look nice tonight, by the way," I offer her as I break my stare when her head turns back in my direction.

"Now that I'm not in my bum day mowing clothes?" Her hands return to her lap and her knee begins bouncing again. I want to stretch my leg out under the table and still the motion in her.

"Bum day mowing clothes," I repeat, amused. I figure she should have been in something a bit more breathable than the leggings and that baggy shirt. She would have been awfully hot had she got the mower working on her own and did the whole yard.

She also deflects my compliment.

"You don't clean up so bad yourself." I can sense her growing wary again. I know that she likes my tattoo, but I want to know what she thinks of me. Does she envision taking my clothes off? Mentally undressing me until I'm stark naked before her?

I have done so about ten times since we arrived, starting in the parking lot.

"Thank you," I acknowledge as our waiter reappears, bringing an appetizer into view. The peaks that appear over the plate indicate crab rangoons. Clara said they're the best, and I wanted to put that to the test. Was I so absent when the waiter was last here to not realize she even ordered them in the first place?

She utters her thanks, and when she catches me grinning at her, the color rises to her cheeks again.

Will she have that same reaction when I fill her between her hips? I wish I could know how soon I'll get to find out. My erection is pressing into my jeans, making me uncomfortable.

"Is this a date?" Her brown eyes never leave mine as she rolls her lips inward again, her leg stopping its movements as she does. It makes me wonder if that's why she's so nervous. Am I really the cause of it?

"It's whatever you want it to be, Clara." I try to be smooth in my delivery, but her lowering brows tell me I might have had the opposite effect. "If we're merely friends, then so be it. But I would be lying if I said I didn't hope that this was a date. But I will leave that up to you."

Her gaze falls again, her vulnerability shining through at my statement. This dinner can be whatever she wants, whatever she *needs* it to be.

"We just met." Her voice lowers again.

"Officially this morning. Yes, we did."

"But you don't know me."

"Perhaps I want to get to know you."

"Why?" She looks at her Diet Coke, almost shrinking in her seat.

Because your scent calls to my soul like a drug meant for me only.

Yeah, that doesn't sound like a psychopath talking. Knowing how she was cheated on by her husband, I know why she's suspicious. Appearing out of nowhere and inserting myself into her life, I have to be ringing a few alarms in that pretty little head of hers.

"Honestly, you're the first interesting person to talk to me here besides the movers and the cashier at the gas station in Alton. I'm pretty sure a guy who sits in his garage wants to shoot me every time I run by, and everyone else seems either intrigued or scared of me, judging by the looks I get."

"You're forgetting Chassidy." She eyes me, disbelief evident.

"Not my type." I brush off the audacity she has to bring her up again. I thought we were in agreement that we dislike her, end of discussion. Don't let that woman take any more from you than what she already has, Clara.

Chassidy can have Joe, but that's it. Keep him far away from my Rose. Realistically, I know that he's still in the picture since the kids are with him today, but still. He's done enough damage.

"What is it?" That damn leg of hers is beginning to taunt me worse than her ex who I have never met.

Her brows lower again.

"Your leg." It stills the moment she realizes I've caught her.

"I..." Her pale skin is deepening more with her embarrassment. "A date is too much pressure. It's been a long time since I've been on one."

I want to ask if she's been on any dates at all since she and her ex parted ways. I want to keep digging in my attempt to get to know her, but I hold back. If she hasn't been on any dates since then, and since she married her high school sweetheart—which I'm not supposed to know—then it has been well over fifteen years. No wonder she can't stop bouncing her leg. She hasn't been out on a date with a stranger in her entire adulthood.

Glad I could be her first. And last.

"Then it's not a date. Just two people getting to know each other over good food. At least, I hope it's good. I have yet to try these things, so we'll see." I gesture to the plate between us, offering her to go first. "After you."

Timidly, she leaves the back of her seat, her hand coming into view as she picks up a yellow wonton and pries it apart. Her hands no longer show any indication of having a ring there. If she ever had an indent from one, it isn't there anymore.

"Okay." She forces a smile, and I try to soothe her with an easy one of my own.

It's more forced than I would have liked, but I eventually agree, snagging a rangoon for myself. "Okay."

5

Just Friends

Clara

It's hard to remember a time when I've smiled so much.

Our dinner started off a little weird, and while I still don't know what Seth is expecting to get out of this little outing, I choose to try and enjoy myself. After all, it beats sulking around the house while my kids are off enjoying themselves. So I guess I'm grateful for the company, and the food before me that I've begun to pick at. I don't want to fill myself so full that I feel miserable, like last night.

The conversation has morphed into exactly what one might expect when two strangers get together. Seth fills me in on his computer background and how he used to get in trouble at school for working around their firewalls and letting kids gain access to whatever the hell they wanted. Turns out, he was even turning a profit for doing so. Quite the little devil and entrepreneurial spirit, if you ask me. I'm trying to imagine a younger version of the man before me. Prior to his facial hair, that is. I have little doubt that he was attractive even then, and probably an athlete of some sort. When he states he was into football and basketball, however, I know there's no chance in hell he would have had any interest in me if we had met back then.

I *still* find it hard to believe that he has any in me at all. Interest. I try not to dwell on the fact that he might have considered this a date at first. And while I did insist on driving myself, I still can't fathom why he's being so nice to me. Except that maybe he wants to get laid.

But even so, with his good looks, he could have literally picked anyone else but me. Lord knows when I was intent on mowing I had dressed for comfort, not to attract the opposite sex. No one in their right mind would have found my clothes to be any kind of turn-on.

Seth practically licks his plate clean, and considering his tongue never touches it, it amazes me just how shiny it is now that the food has disappeared from it. I offer him some of my sesame chicken if he's still hungry, and he helps himself to a taste but then he requests a box for me from the waiter. He all but devoured his Szechuan chicken and fried rice, and somehow didn't gulp down his drink from the spice of it. Either the spice level has gone down, or he has a crazy high heat tolerance.

"I have to ask..." Seth wipes off his mouth with his cloth napkin before he continues. I wonder if his beard would tickle if our lips ever meet. Not that I think they will, but I can't deny that I'm curious to find out. "Is there any kind of meaning to your necklace? The moons on it...any significance?"

"Actually, yes." I've tried to keep the talk of my kids and ex to a minimum unless asked, but since he brought this up, I figure it doesn't hurt anything. He already knows I'm a mother with two children and he hasn't gone running yet.

"They're the moons from when each of my kids were born. Julie is the top one, Emmett is the bottom."

"Waning crescent and gibbous," he states, throwing me off-kilter a bit. Joe had thought it was stupid when I bought it. He couldn't have cared less about their moons, astrological signs, nothing. He considered it useless knowledge. I would never claim myself to be an expert on those subjects, but that doesn't mean I can't enjoy looking into or studying them occasionally.

"That's right. You know your moon phases." I'm pretty sure the smile on my face is just stuck on me now, permanently. I'm growing more comfortable around Seth. The ease that our conversation has fallen into certainly helps.

"I do." He smirks to himself. He has to know how hot he is, right? There's no way he doesn't. "It's really neat, though, your necklace. Can't say I've seen something like that before."

Before I saw it advertised online, me neither.

It's difficult to remember a time when Joe and I had enjoyed a night out like this. If we ever managed a dinner together without the kids, he was usually on his phone. It's refreshing that mine hasn't come out of my purse, and Seth's has remained face down on the table the entire time. I'm pretty sure it vibrated a couple of times, but he never bothered to even look at it.

My heart skips at the thought of how date-like tonight has turned out to be, even if we agreed that it isn't that. I'm grateful that we aren't in Pembrook, considering that's where most friends, coworkers, and acquaintances live, and there's less of a chance of running into anybody I know here in Benson.

It feels sneaky, even if we're just chatting. I haven't had many male acquaintances or friends over my lifetime. I know I'm not anything to be desired first off, and I just feel awkward around them. I'm not thin, pretty, or funny. I'm not good at sports and I'm uncoordinated to boot. I was smaller when I met Joe in high school and fell head over heels fast. Then, two kids later, my body filled out even more, boobs began to sag, and I stopped chasing after a body that I knew I would never have again.

Fucking Chassidy is everything I'm not and have never been. Of course Joe sought out someone else. I can't even place when he stopped being affectionate toward me, when he started withdrawing.

My mood plummets, and I begin to scan around the restaurant that is now emptying. It's hard to say how long we've been here at this point. My food is probably dying in its container and I have downed another drink since we finished eating. I've completely lost track of time.

Excusing myself to the bathroom, I find a clock hanging on the wall on my way and see that it's almost nine. I hurry, unsure of how to end our little dinner. Seth has certainly taken my mind off of my worries and troubles tonight. It was nice focusing on him and learning about a lifestyle so different from my own. A little part of me is envious of his ability to just pick up and go. Move to new places on a whim while still having a job intact.

I am a receptionist at a local dentist's office in Pembrook, and I've almost been there eight years now. I'm stuck, so to speak. I have worked my way up in my salary, but it always paled in comparison to Joe's work at the event center. He's the director, and the amount of money he makes is ridiculous.

When I return to the table, I can't sit down, but I don't know how to wrap up the night.

"I take it you're ready to go?" Seth sets his phone down as soon as I approach.

"If that's alright. I think this place closes soon."

Seth takes a turn looking around us, and when he sees just how few people are left, he nods. "Sure thing."

I lean into my seat to snatch the handle of my purse as he stands. He takes my leftovers and lets me lead the way out. He was adamant about paying for dinner, especially since he was the one to invite me in the first place. I tried to split it, and when that failed, I offered to do the tip, but he wasn't allowing me to do that either.

The humidity has dropped dramatically within the few hours we've been inside. There's a faint glow in the distance from the disappearance of the sun, and the parking lot is practically empty as he walks with me to my van.

My nerves are gathering again, thinking about this hunk of a man I have been blessed to have dinner with. There were several women in the restaurant, both young and old, who kept stealing looks at him, and I recognized the longing looks and hushed whispers. I only hope it isn't too obvious to him that I'm attracted as well.

We come to a stop at my hood and I thank him for the meal. He offers me my box, and just when I'm about to open my door, he clears his throat. "Could I get your phone number?"

I pause, heart thumping a bit too loud.

"You know, in case I need a good food recommendation?"

My spirits sink slightly. I don't know why I was getting up my hopes of anything else. I set my purse and container down in my seat and return my attention to him. My response is short, trying to hide my disappointment. "Of course."

Seth hands me his phone with a new contact already pulled up. I quickly type in my name and number and hand it back to him. It feels more like a mini tablet than a phone.

What do you say to somebody who you aren't on a date with? I had fun tonight? Nope, too predictable. Thanks for the free meal? No, makes me sound like I was in it for that alone. Thank you for letting me stare at you all night, tearing your clothes off in my mind while I try to choke down a piece of sesame chicken? Wow. How pathetic am I?

"Talk to you soon then. Drive safe." He flashes a perfect grin and takes a few steps backward before I can offer a reply to tell him to do the same. He then turns to give me his back, retreating toward a truck about six parking spaces away.

I think I might be breaking open that bottle of Moscato tonight that's hidden in the back of my fridge. And my favorite vibrator.

I talk with myself practically the entire way home in incoherent ramblings.

There is no way Seth is interested in me in any kind of romantic way, and I'm coming up with all of the different reasons as to why he wouldn't be, convincing myself that there's some bombshell he would rather be with.

He is living the life of a bachelor. He can do whatever, whenever he wants. There's no way that Seth would want to be bogged down with a single and tired mom of two who is still trying to figure out this new life she's trying to lead. Attempting to piece things together and pretend that I have my shit together when in reality, I sometimes don't know what the fuck I'm doing.

But he asked for your number.

He said, "Talk to you soon."

How soon is he thinking? Will I catch him walking or running by my house? Two days in a row—and at different times, might I add—he has placed himself in the little corner of Alton where I reside.

He said he lives on the opposite side of the highway, which for me is no easy trek, but considering he has been in my neck of the woods each day, that distance must be nothing to him by foot.

We couldn't be more opposite. He is fit and handsome beyond words. I don't normally take to guys with facial hair either, but the way he wears it is almost sinful. I, on the other hand, love sweets a bit too much and sometimes don't know when to cut myself off from food. My emotions and food are tied to one another.

Oh my God. If he ever invited me for a run I would probably pass out before I reached the end of my street.

There's no way we could ever work. And hopefully, he knows that with this body of mine he shouldn't even try to ask me to work out with him.

Go for a walk? Sure. Run? Put up my headstone now.

Julie could probably keep up with him, though. I hate the thought of her running around town by herself, even though I have no reason to believe it isn't safe. But I know deep down, with her good looks, all it would take is just one sick freak to snatch her up. If Seth was running by her side, nobody would mess with her, and it would put this mother's worried head at ease.

Why am I even entertaining the thought that that could be a possibility after just one dinner with Seth? I grumble, frustrated with where my thoughts are taking me.

Pulling into my garage, I cut the engine and hop out. The light is on in the breezeway between the house and my van's home, and I turn my key to let myself inside.

When I'm greeted with the silence of an empty home, my mood takes another dark turn.

Tomorrow. They'll come home tomorrow.

I kick my shoes off and set my purse on the counter, leftovers in the fridge. Nothing but the under-cabinet lighting illuminates the kitchen, but it's nice to see that it is still clean. Minus the one dish in the sink from my lunch. I'm traipsing through the living room when my phone goes off, alerting me to a motion detected on the front door camera. It's probably a deer, stray cat or something, but I check it anyway.

The doorbell sounds before I can get the video to load and I freeze in place, wondering who would be coming to the house so late at night.

When I see Seth standing on the front porch, a confusing bunch of reactions catapults through me. I can't make much out, except that he's looking at his phone.

Is he coming to kill me, or did I forget something at the restaurant? Even so, he has my phone number now, so why wouldn't he call?

At a snail's pace, I move through the house. I don't turn on any lights and I stay away from the windows as I make my way to the front door, and then a text message sounds on my phone. I wince, nervous that he might have heard its chime through the door, telling him that I'm close by. I silence it, making sure that it can't make any more noise. That's when I see the text in my drop-down bar.

> **Did you make it home ok?**

I could ignore it. I could watch the video feed until he leaves. So why am I being a stupid idiot, unlocking the door to a man I just met?

I hesitate, meeting his golden eyes that are still bright beneath the porch light that illuminates his hair. "Everything alright?"

"I didn't like how we left things." His brows are furrowed, and he's tense. So stiff that I can't tell if he's breathing or not.

"Talk to you soon. Drive safe?" I repeat the words he had parted with. "You could have texted instead of showing up unannounced." Then I add, "Again."

"I'm sorry, I..." His words trail off and while my mind is heading toward all of the missing persons and criminal shows I watch, nothing about his attitude or body language makes me want to shut the door in his face.

"What is it?" I ask, letting the door open a bit more.

He's the first to break eye contact, his gaze dropping as if he's struggling with something internally. He inhales deeply, slow and exaggerated. His pecs grow shadows as the lines of them catch the streams of both light and dark around us.

"Clara," he breathes on an exhale, and his gravelly voice has me bracing myself against the doorframe.

"Are you alright, Seth?"

The question is barely out of my mouth as his hand shoots out, wrapping around the back of my neck and drawing me to him. A small yelp is swallowed up as his lips meet mine, my widened eyes trying to register what's happening.

I'm rendered into a temporary state of shock. His mouth moves against mine, coaxing my lips to return his fervor. His tongue darts out to taste, and a low groan goes through his chest as he pulls me in closer.

Eyes fluttering closed, I surrender to it. His beard pokes at my face, but I let my hands wrap around his neck, keeping him close. The neediness in his grasping touch is enough to make my legs shake.

He walks me backward, shutting the door behind him as he pins me against the nearest wall. My hip bumps into the small table that houses a few decorative pieces, the wood hitting the wall as its contents threaten to knock themselves over.

Seth is snacking on me as if I'm his only chance to live. Stealing my breath until I become lightheaded. I struggle to tear my mouth away from his and when I do, he keeps going until he reaches the corner of my neck.

"What..." I'm failing to catch air. "What are you doing?"

It has been so long since my body experienced anything like this. Hell, maybe it never has, to this extent. The spot between my legs is throbbing, and all I can think about is sex. I don't want him to stop, but at the same time, this is too damn good to be true.

Yanking his head back, he leaves wet remnants of his lips on my neck. "Telling you goodnight."

"F-funny way of showing it." My chest doesn't have the room to expand fully, not with his on top of mine, nearly crushing me like his lips did my mouth.

"Where's your bedroom?" His heated gaze is going to burn a hole through me.

"My...bedroom?" I shoot him a look, confused as hell.

"Your. Bedroom," he growls, sending my body into a frenzy. Surely, he doesn't want to—

"Clara—" He takes my chin in a rough hold, forcing me still and locking in on my gaze.

"D-down the hall. On the right." My head won't budge as I try to nod in that direction.

Releasing my chin, Seth bends and scoops me off of my feet. I yelp again, trying to swat at him as he pivots and turns down the darkened hall. He might as well be made of stone.

"Put me down! You're going to hurt yourself!"

A low rumble of a laugh surges through his chest as I cling to him while at the same time I try to figure out how I can be put down without bashing my head into the wall behind me.

Seth picked me up as if I'm light as a feather, but the bulging muscles in his arms tell me a different story. He's going to throw out his damn back or something.

God, this is so humiliating.

I didn't close the blinds before leaving for dinner tonight. Light pools in from the nearby streetlight, casting horizontal lines almost across my room. My unmade bed is a tangled mess of both comforter and sheet as Seth sets me down.

I take in a mangled breath, thoughts going a million miles a minute.

It's not dark enough in here.

He's crazy mad.

I don't have any condoms.

He might claim that he's unable to have kids, and my tubes have been tied, but that doesn't protect me from any STIs he might have. Or is it STDs again? Does it fucking matter at this point?

Seth's pupils are dilated when I settle on them. He tears his shirt up over his head, revealing chest hair that matches the coloring of the hair on his face. His tattoo looks sinister now, its menacing mouth trying to devour me.

Sitting here, I'm dumbfounded by the man undressing before me. He takes hold of the bottom of my shirt and begins to lift. I try to push it back down, but fighting against him is useless as he hauls it off and over, tossing it to the ground.

I'm shirtless before him, panting as if I'm ready to have a panic attack at the man who's removing his pants before me. My arms cross over my middle section, uncomfortable with my stomach and the way it creases near my belly button. I'm riddled with stretch marks, too. Something that has lessened, but their scars still remain.

There's too much light in here. He can see too much, and this is all happening too fast.

Joe is the only man I have ever been intimate with. The only one to have seen me naked. Over time, I covered up more and more, and over the last few years of our relationship, his interest in me, and sex, diminished drastically. I think Joe stopped wanting me before I even realized we had any problems.

Seth is undoing my pants and peeling them down the curves of my hips. While I want to protest, I can't deny what he's making me feel right now. For whatever godforsaken reason, he wants me. I don't understand why he does, but I want him too. I would be a fool to try and say otherwise. The way my body comes alive for him as if fire is shooting through my veins and straight south is almost too much to process.

His beard grazes my leg as he stands again, dragging it across my flesh and creating a trail of goosebumps in its wake. I shiver against it, trying to enjoy it even though my head is telling me all the reasons I'm not good enough for him.

When he tries to reach for the clasps of my bra behind me, I stop him.

"Please, don't." My pleading makes him stop and his back straighten. I don't have perky breasts, and my nipples don't exactly point in the direction he might expect anymore. Over the years, my chest began to droop, and after breastfeeding two kids, I know they're not anything special enough for intimate times such as this.

"Lie down," he instructs. The tone of his voice carries over my body and lets me know that it's an order, not a request.

I swallow hard, nervous that he might back out at any given moment. Am I crazy for wanting this? For wanting him? Why in the hell does he even want me in the first place? Perhaps he's merely a chubby chaser trying to get his fix.

Carefully, I turn and crawl further onto the bed, pushing the wadded-up blankets out of the way so I can lie down without the bulkiness of them at my back. I then turn to sit, seeing he has rid himself of all his clothing as I slowly lean back.

Every curve of muscle has my throat going dry at the sight. The lines of his abs are so defined that he almost looks photoshopped. The creases deepen with the dim lighting and slants from the blinds. His erection, though. Damn, it's big. Does he have to go up a pant size just to get that thing to fit in his jeans?

"Take off your underwear." His chin dips down as his eyes roam over my body. It's almost too much, watching him watch me with his bright eyes.

On shaky limbs, I lift my rear enough to slip them off, and he bends to take them from me, skimming my legs with his fingers as he passes.

My body, my channel in particular, is throbbing so hard I think something might break down there. Not sure if it's possible, but I might be the first to make it happen. It wants to be filled so bad that it hurts.

Seth parts my legs, kissing the inside of my knee as he inches onto the bed. His beard is a newfound layer of pleasure that I have never experienced before. It tickles a bit, but it isn't enough to make me want to push him away.

Maybe I was in a car accident on the way home. Perhaps I'm suffering life-threatening injuries and I'm on my deathbed dreaming up impossible scenarios that I would never actually experience in my waking life.

It isn't until his fingers enter me that I'm brought back down to reality. They swirl into my heat, coating themselves in my arousal, and I struggle to keep my eyes open, gazing at the ceiling.

His thumb arrives at my clit, creating circling motions that have my legs falling apart and to the sides, opening wider for him. I inhale sharply, reveling in the feeling of being touched *there*, and by someone else.

Lips meet the bare spot between my breasts as he works me with his fingers. The sounds that the both of us are creating down there are a bit embarrassing.

When his fingers disappear, I'm left panting and bereft. But that doesn't last long as his erection seeks to replace them, and my mouth drops as he begins to enter.

"Look at me, Clara."

My eyes are screwed tight as I try to adjust to the head of his cock. My forearms are crossed over my stomach as if I could hide away from him, until he seizes my wrists and pins them by my shoulders. In that quick movement, his cock plunges the rest of the way inside and a scream leaves my lips, forcing my eyes fully open to catch Seth hovering above me.

"Fu—" I can't even form words. My head goes blank as I stare into the eyes of the man who is adamant on claiming me.

"I know you can take me." He grits his teeth as he retreats for a brief moment before he rolls his hips forward again. A garbled shriek leaves my lips as he fills me and I try to move my hands but it's pointless. I'm not going anywhere.

Eyes watering, I peer up at him, both pain and pleasure radiating as he repeats the motion a bit slower.

"You're the one, Clara."

My puzzlement with his statement is brief as he captures my mouth. His chest hair is soft, brushing against my skin as he begins to search for a rhythm between us, and with each drive I moan into him. I couldn't stop the sounds from slipping out even if I wanted to.

I swear my eyes are going to roll into the back of my head as my necklace falls to the base of my throat, then off to the side.

Grabbing my left knee, he pulls it up and out before rocking into me again, and I swear there's no human way possible that he could plunge his dick any deeper. My jaw drops as I take him inside, further than anything has ever reached before. That, I am certain of.

Seth is invading my body, my mind, and my soul. I'm also willing to bet his cock is trying to rearrange any organs inside of me that it comes in contact with.

Once both my wrists are free, Seth steadies himself at my sides. My hands fly up to his arms, gripping him tight to the point that my fingertips are trying to take on the beast that's tattooed on him.

Our combined moans fill my ears with each rock from him. He buries his head in my neck again as one arm snakes between us and begins circling my clit once more. My legs tighten on him and my body begins to build to that precipice that wants nothing more than to rip me apart.

His name is on the tip of my tongue, but each raspy plea falls flat. I rise higher and higher until his thumb, in combination with his thrusts, propels me over the top.

My back arches into his chest as my body begins to spasm. Cries of total and complete ecstasy rack my body as I shake with each wave of my orgasm. Seth quickens his movements, and just when I think I can't take anymore, he spills.

The sound of him finding his release is the sexiest response I have ever heard. His movements become jagged and disjointed, and his arm beside me struggles to keep him above me.

I reach out and cup the side of his face, still reeling from the aftermath of what I have just experienced. My thumb brushes across his hair, back and forth as if it could bring me back down to earth.

This time, I bring his lips to mine.

6

What Just Happened?

Clara

Is that what sex is supposed to feel like? One husband and two kids later, I can certainly say without a shadow of a doubt that I have never experienced lovemaking like that before. Hell, I even came before Seth did. I don't think that's ever happened to me. No, I *know* that's never happened to me before.

I lie in bed, a cloudy and dreary day outside my windows as I reflect on last night, my brain constantly turning.

Joe has the dick of a string bean compared to Seth, and it had been the only one to ever enter me. It impregnated me two times, so I guess it works in that aspect, but damn.

Chassidy can have him. Fuck it. It's not like I'm holding out any hope to have him back anyway. That door closed long ago.

I stretch as I turn over, but I find my bed empty. My face falls, saddened at the mere possibility that what we did was nothing more than a one-time thing. That would make for an incredibly awkward encounter should I see him around Alton. Which given the size of the town, is very possible.

Sitting up, I adjust my breasts and my bra. One boob is trying to free itself, and my band is apparently trying to do a one-eighty. I'm a bit sore beneath it from wearing an underwire bra all night, but since Seth had insisted on staying I bit my tongue and kept it on. But now, I'm the only one in bed.

Did he really slip out and leave me? I didn't think I was one-night stand material, but I guess I don't know his standards.

Is it really so bad if that's all I am, though? I'm not sure how to even begin the whole dating game in the first place. Sure, I've toyed with the idea of putting myself out there, but things have changed so much over the years since Joe and I got together.

It amazes me to even say it, but Seth has set the bar incredibly high for anyone to follow after him.

My face is growing hotter by the second as I reflect on last night. Taking me by surprise at my door. Carrying me down the hall. The whole ordeal breathed a whole new life into the word *fucking*.

I begin to fan my face. I'm at war with myself, thinking about how wonderful it was and yet feeling disturbed at how I let him come in and take me like that. But deep down I knew once I opened that door there was no way I could have stopped him.

I hadn't wanted to stop him, either. I think I wanted it just as much as he did.

The bedroom door swings open and I jump out of my skin as Seth appears with a coffee cup in hand.

"I—" I'm trying to peel my soul off the ceiling at his sudden and quiet appearance. "I thought you might have left."

I swallow hard, trying to avert my eyes from the sight that he is, now that the room is brighter than last night. The way his boxers fit low on his waist is teasing me to pull them down the rest of the way. He doesn't disappoint, no matter the lighting. I think I would still be drooling with the lights turned off.

A playful smirk crosses his face. "Did you really think I would just up and leave after last night?"

I blink at him, still stunned that he didn't. "We don't really know each other."

"And that's something I'm hoping to fix." He sits on the edge of the bed, taking a sip of his coffee.

Just make yourself at home, I think.

"Why?" It's all I can manage to ask when everything else fails.

Seth's face falters, his smirk wiping away slowly. Honestly, I have no idea which way this will go. It feels like my life is a wreck, and every day there's something making me think that I'm not good enough. And that didn't stop with the arrival of Seth, either.

Not only that, but maybe I'm not a good enough mother, housekeeper, or employee. That's just to name a few. It's a constant battle.

"Clara I...I can't explain it, but I *feel* something when I'm with you."

Yeah, an orgasm will do that to you.

"When I first saw you on Friday night, you were obviously pissed off, but there was something about how you handled it once you found out your kids were watching. You cared more about them and what they witnessed than what you really wanted to do, which was probably to claw her eyes out."

My head tips side to side, thinking. There isn't really anything wrong with that statement. There was a time I wanted to ring her neck until she turned blue. I guess I have made some progress since then. Being able to stand in front of her and not get the police called on me should count for something.

"Yesterday, even though the mower was trying to get the best of you, you pressed on. I have little doubt that you would have figured it out on your own, but I wanted to help."

"I would have got it done," I agree, although I don't want to think about how long it would have taken me to be victorious. "Eventually."

Seth smiles again. If only he knew how much I want to melt at the sight of it.

"But last night wasn't supposed to be a date." I hug the sheet around me closer, blushing as I recall how the night ended. I don't regret it. At least, not yet anyway.

"I lied." He takes a sip of his drink before looking at me again. "For me, it was a date. And just for the record, I thoroughly enjoyed all of it. All of you."

I can't tell if he's just flattering me or if what he's saying is true. I don't know him well enough to even try to decipher it.

"Be honest." I drop my gaze to my hands in my lap, afraid to look at him as I stir up the courage for my next question. "Are you just wanting a fuck buddy or something? Because if you do, I don't think I can be that for you. You're eventually going to leave, anyway."

The quiet that falls over the room is uncomfortable. I never thought I would be fuck buddy material, but his silence makes me think maybe that's all I am to him. I deserve to be happy someday. With someone who *makes* me happy. I'm not going to settle for anything less if I'm ever offered that opportunity.

Seth moves, setting his cup on the coaster on the nightstand, and scoots across the bed. His hand lifts to my chin and pushes it up, forcing me to look at him. I'm reluctant to do so, eyes roaming up his upper half before finally meeting that heart-stopping gaze of his.

"Don't ever refer to yourself as that." His deep tone is stern, almost scolding, until his eyes soften. "And I know what my past looks like, but you'll be first to know that I plan on staying for a while."

"Longer than your one-year lease?" I push, eager to see how he answers that.

"Much, much longer." His thumb skates across my bottom lip, pulling it away from my teeth that are attempting to bite at it. He's fixated on that small action, and the hunger that fills his eyes has my heart flip-flopping around my chest like a fish out of water.

"I wouldn't dream of leaving, Clara."

For whatever goddamn reason, when my name rolls off of his tongue, I believe him.

Seth tries to get me to take a shower with him, but I won't budge in my refusal. He certainly puts forth some effort into making me do so, but I'm scared to let him see my body without the cover of night. Granted, I know my bedroom was lit up more than I would have liked last night, but it was still better than the light filtering in through the windows now.

The promise of shower sex is tempting, especially when he sees just how big the walk-in shower is, but I scurry away from him like a cat from a bath. It also sounds like an accident waiting to happen. And while he might be strong enough on his own and willing to do it, it doesn't mean that I wouldn't fall and crack the textured glass doors with my head or something.

I'm in the kitchen when he strolls out of my bedroom, freshly showered but wearing his pants from yesterday. They're unbuttoned at the front, showing the V that leads down to the most rigid part of his body. At least, it felt that way last night as he was screwing me.

My iced coffee isn't even enough to calm me down from the heated thoughts soaring through my mind as he approaches, clearing his throat.

"I wasn't sure how you take your coffee. Otherwise I would have made you some this morning."

"That's fine. It's a measured art that I get wrong half the time anyway." I set my glass down but keep my hand around it, willing the cold to work its way through me. I probably need an ice bath.

The more I move around, the more I am reminded of last night. I guess not having sex in so long has made me a bit weak in the downstairs department. Not only is my vagina aching from Seth, but the insides of my thighs are sore from him spreading them apart. The mere thought of him between them again has my head spinning, and I grip the counter with my free hand to steady myself.

"Is it alright if I have another cup?"

Unable to find my voice, I just nod. He brushes past me, his arm grazing my shoulder as he passes. My brows pinch as I take in the sight of Seth's back, and the air in my throat gets stuck. One, two, three...I can't keep track of the number of scars that had been hidden until now. Some as if they had just barely clipped him, others long and drawn out. Something deep down inside of me stirs, pained by what might have caused those raised marks on that devastatingly beautiful body of his. The whole lot of them are healed now, but it doesn't make seeing them any easier to swallow.

Clearing my throat of the lump that's forming, I divert my gaze and try to focus on anything other than the sight that has me aching for this new man in the most uncomforting way. It's probably none of my business to inquire about them, as we barely knew each other. That's even putting it mildly.

Seth makes quick work with the coffee grounds and water. Flipping my machine to hot brew instead of cold, he turns and leans against the counter, crossing one leg over another.

I have to sober up from my obsession with him and his body, no matter how sexy, alluring, and troublesome it might be. One glance at his hips and the markings on him are almost forgotten. After one lay, it's all I can think about, and I'm starting to think the throb at the apex of my thighs is more from the desire to repeat it all again instead of recovering from last night.

Prying myself away from my lusty thoughts and flashbacks from last night, I can't help but blurt the first thing that comes to mind. "You were honest with me yesterday, about not having any children of your own?"

His brows pinch as his expression morphs from a playful one to another that is more serious. "I was, yes."

I bob my head slightly, suddenly afraid of the news I'm about to deliver. I don't know why it worries me so much. Maybe it's because he made me aware that there are people in the world—like his ex-fi-ancée—who would dump you the moment things don't go according to plan.

"You should know that I can't, that I won't have any more children of my own." I swallow, fully turning to face him. "I had a C-section when Emmett was born and had my tubes tied."

There had been a time when I wanted five to six kids, but the paralyzing sickness from both kids and the havoc that Emmett caused on my spine caused me to rethink it. I cried for so many nights after I came to the conclusion of doing the tubal ligation. But in the end I knew it was the best decision for me and my body, even if it pained me to do so. Joe had been furious at first, and made the hurtful comment that if I could just keep my weight under control, maybe my pregnancy with a second child wouldn't have been so bad. I had put on a lot of weight with my second pregnancy, and while most of it came off after delivering, it didn't make what he said hurt any less.

Tears begin to form, burning my eyes as I beat myself up over it all over again. I don't know why I was so blind to not see all the red flags throughout the one and only relationship I've ever really had. I can only assume that it was because I loved him and only ever wanted to make him happy. But I failed in that, too.

"Hey." Seth steps forward, wrapping me in a hug that is almost suffocating. I snap a hand over my mouth as a hiccup leaves me. If my body isn't going to send Seth packing, then perhaps my spontaneous outburst and negative feelings toward myself will.

He backs away, taking me by the shoulders and lowering his head until mine tips up.

"I came to terms with the fact that I may never be a father." His thumbs start to rub at the thin fabric of my robe under his touch. "But you, you have already been blessed with two beautiful children."

His head looks at the furthest wall across the kitchen and in the dining room. Julie and Emmett's school photos hang in there for all to see. Little does Seth know, there used to be a family photo that sat in the center, slightly above them.

I smashed that motherfucker to pieces in the backyard the first night they stayed with their dad in his new house. Joe had paid a lot of money to have it framed, and I took way too much joy in destroying it, just like he had destroyed me and my life.

"They are," I agree. Their photos are from last year, since we haven't received the new ones yet. Coincidentally, picture day was just last week at their schools. The way they can change so much in a single year never ceases to amaze yet sadden me at the same time. Emmett has already moved on to another set of glasses even.

"But I can't have you meet them. Not yet." I sniffle, still trying to keep the tears at bay. He's too new and I'm unsure. I already have enough problems with Chassidy, I don't think I could handle the possibility of Joe finding out and going off about it. That, and I don't want to introduce anyone to Seth until I'm one-hundred-percent sure that this isn't just some sort of fling. Because I still have my doubts that this is even real. I'm not sure if that will upset him or not.

When our heads turn to one another once more, there's something in his eyes that tells me he isn't that type of guy. I can't explain the gut feeling I have that he will protect me and honor my wishes, no matter what I ask of him. Is it strange to be trusting him this early on?

"I understand that. But I hope that means you won't ask me to stay away, because right now, I don't think I can. At least, not for long, anyway."

This man is too good to be true. I mean, come on—what's the catch?

"I guess you could start by mowing my lawn," I tease, trying to lighten the conversation that has grown heavy.

"I'll mow your lawn every damn day if you ask me to." He purses his lips, as if his statement has a double meaning.

I roll my eyes as I shake my head. "Hell no. Gas is too expensive."

7

My Purpose

Seth

Clara takes one sip of my coffee and practically spits it out within a nanosecond. The most disgusted look I've ever witnessed on her full face has a belly laugh forming within me as I take my cup back from her.

"What the hell is that?" She fans her mouth and sticks her tongue out, as if air will somehow help her plight. I guess she was just lucky enough to spew her hate of it into the sink.

"Why are you asking me? It's *your* coffee grounds."

"You drink your coffee black?" She takes a long draw of her iced coffee and swishes it around her mouth. I can tell by its color that we clearly have different tastes. "Are you a psychopath?"

I would be one, for you.

"Well, what are you drinking?" I snatch her drink from her and even though it's almost gone, I take a little sip. I'm taken aback by the sweet overload that overtakes my mouth and makes my taste buds scream. "That doesn't even taste like coffee!"

She giggles, the first time I've heard that sweet sound this morning. "Exactly!"

I shake my head, completely stunned at how anyone could drink something so sugary. I have the fleeting thought that perhaps that's why she smells so sweet and heavenly. Regardless, it doesn't make me love her any less.

I'll learn how to make her damn coffee and I'll serve it to her in bed. That day will come, mark my words.

"You're a bit odd, you know that?" She downs the rest of her drink and dumps the ice in the silver sink, rinsing the cup out before she places it in there.

Her mood has improved as the morning went on. She hasn't showered yet, but the smell of me on her is absolutely exhilarating. If I thought I could get away with another round like last night, I would. But I don't want to push my luck. Because of my actions so far, I've already driven her further and faster than I initially anticipated.

Hell, I can't even remember the last time I screwed around without a condom. But last night? I slipped into her without a single worry, and faster than Pavlov's dogs salivating at the sound of a bell. The desire to consume her was too great to possibly ignore.

I had followed Clara home last night like some obsessed stalker, keeping a distance in my truck and parking at the end of her dead-end road instead of in her driveway. It was like I was moving on autopilot as I approached her front door. I didn't even have a plan as I rang her doorbell. Then I panicked at my inability to think straight, and followed up with a text. Had she not answered the door, I would have felt really fucking stupid.

I shake my head, trying to blink my way back into the conversation at hand. "It's probably from being cooped up and buried in computers all the time. I should get out more."

And into your bed, preferably.

"I'm a bit weird on my own, but..." The wheels are turning inside that messy head of hair. Her bedhead is a good look on her, and knowing it was my hands that mussed it up has my cock straining against my jeans. "What did you mean last night?"

"Sorry?" I look her dead in the eyes, hoping that she might be intimidated by me and drop it. I didn't mean to talk to her like that. I know *exactly* the statement she's referring to. The comment I made about her being "the one."

The more I'm getting to know her, the more things are falling into place. We're both coming from crappy relationships that left damages to our well-being. I can never have children, and she has two of her own and is done. For whatever reason, I was drawn to Alton and to her. It couldn't be more perfect. My *Rose* couldn't be more perfect.

My only regret is not having been the one to help raise her children and spare her the pain and heartache of a lying and cheating ex-husband. She didn't deserve that. Clara strikes me as someone who would never waver in her faithfulness in a relationship.

"Never mind, forget I said anything." She drops it just as quickly as she brought it up.

I have the rising suspicion that this won't be the end of my unfiltered statements, but for now, I'm safe. Her posture straightens a bit, her silk robe parting slightly as she pushes her shoulders back. The swell of her breasts becomes more pronounced and it takes every ounce of strength to tear my gaze away.

"I hate to ask you to leave, but my kids are coming home today. I'd like to get some things done around here before they do." While Clara is trying to be polite, it still sends a pang of sadness through me.

"Anything I can help you with? I can be pretty handy."

My dad runs his own hardware store, there's an uncle who's a plumber, and I began yard work at an early age. My family home has about twenty acres, give or take. There was always something to do, things to be worked on. I think that's why I like computers so much. Working in garages and with our land had me wanting to go as far as I could away from it all. I can remember the countless times my parents hollered at me to do something useful. There were so many instances they would flip the breaker to my room, turning off my electronics and forcing me outside.

"Thank you, but I think I can handle what's left." She offers a shy smile as she crosses her arms, closing the gap at her front. I want to pout.

Her modesty is something that will take time to work on. It's clear that she isn't comfortable showing off certain parts of herself, but there isn't an inch of her that I don't want to worship. My hands can't fit enough of her, and I'm going to make sure she knows she is worth every kiss, lick, touch, and desperate grasp of mine.

"Let me just grab my things then." I down the rest of my coffee in two gulps and follow after her example, rinsing the mug before leaving it in the sink. I take off toward her bedroom and quickly make the bed, inhaling the scent of the two of us combined.

I can't remember the last time I slept with a woman all night. Anytime I entertained the company of one, I slipped out before I could fall asleep. I was always up-front about my intentions with them, too. I had needs, and sometimes working it out on myself just didn't suffice. Most didn't give it much thought, just grateful to get me in the sack in the first place. Some didn't even shy away from telling me just that, but I did what I had to do to get by.

Until now.

Sensing Clara's approach, I raise my shirt over my head to put it on and grab my shoes and socks from the floor just as she turns the corner.

"When can I see you again?" I blurt, and she comes to an abrupt halt.

She tucks some hair behind her ear, stalling in her response. I have to know when it would be alright to contact her. I've already pushed myself this far.

"I promise I won't stop by unannounced." Even though last night, I failed. "Especially if there's a chance your children are around. But I do want to see you again."

Her throat moves as she swallows, her frame slowly leaning back and away from the doorway. "How soon are you wanting to see me again?"

If I had any say in the matter, I would never leave. I want our lives together to begin now. My days should start and nights should end with her. I'm well aware that her kids will come into play at some point, and while I don't know much about them except what little Clara has posted on social media from time to time, I will do my absolute best to get to know and befriend them. I know I'll never be able to replace their actual dad, but fuck if I won't be the best damn stepdad that they could ever have. I'll figure it out.

"Not to sound too eager, but as soon as you want. You've got my number."

She's biting back a smile as she takes a full step back, and I take that as my cue to leave. I'm not going to prod anymore, even though I want to.

When I emerge from the hall and reach the front door, I slip on my socks and tie my shoes. When I meet her gaze, she's rolling her lips again. The top one is slightly smaller than the bottom. Someday, they'll be wrapped around me.

That mere thought has me surging forward, pinning her against the wall again and taking her mouth. The sweet taste of her so-called coffee lingers, and I wonder if she can taste the bitter bite of mine. She whimpers, surprised by my sudden attack just like last night.

Her hands are fisting my shirt as I grind my hips into her, and I let one hand squeeze her breast. The thickness of her bra is too much. I want to feel her, *every* inch of her. That is now a goal.

Before I let myself travel down the same road as last night, I fight my own body to pull away. It's like attempting to pull a screw out of a wall with your bare hand. Clara's face is flushed, eyes fluttering as if she's trying to get her thoughts in her mind right.

This time, I tuck her hair behind her ear for her. Her brown color shows small slivers of gray near the root that you have to focus to look for. I kiss her on the forehead, taking in a deep breath as if I can carry her scent with me, and leave without another word.

Closing the door behind me, I give a half-ass grunt. My dick is hard, and my jeans are too much. The friction as I descend the porch steps and cross her lawn provides an agony that has me wanting to pivot and return to her, to screw her until I find relief.

But I can't. As much as it pains me, I have to leave the ball in her court now. I don't want to scare her away or be too overbearing.

You're the one, Clara.

Why did I even fucking say that? Of course she would hang onto that. She has no knowledge of my world or the sacred connection that comes from finding your mate. I can't tell her that my body comes alive for her. That I'm intoxicated by her scent and that I would literally lay down my life for her.

No. She would think that I don't really have legitimate feelings for her. That it's just my DNA or whatever, telling me that I do. While pairings with humans are rare, it still happens. In reality, it's far less frequent than "once in a blue moon."

Humans have trouble wrapping their heads around it, and while I want Clara to be different, I'm not going to concern myself now with the possibility of her rejecting me because of it. She's going to fall in love with me, and at her own pace.

"Is that your truck?" A man calling out from my right garners my attention. He's dressed in khaki shorts and a polo, a large water jug in his hand. It's obvious by his critical squint of a stare that he's skeptical of the unknown man walking toward his truck that just so happens to be parked out front of his house on the street.

"Yes, sir." I plaster a fake smile on my face. "Afraid I had some trouble getting to a friend's house last night. I'm going to try and start it again before I call for a tow."

"Need any help?"

Small town nice, still going strong.

"Not sure yet. Hold that thought." Unlocking my vehicle, I pop into my seat and give the key a turn. When the engine roars to life, I shut the door and offer a small wave of my hand as I drive off.

I stop at the gas station and top off my tank. When I notice someone coming out with a pizza box, I decide to take a peak and see what offerings they have for the morning.

Settling on a few pieces of sausage breakfast pizza and a couple of cake donuts, I return to my truck. I'm tearing into one slice and munching on the crust of it by the time I return to my new home.

There's a small hope in my chest at the possibility of ending my lease early to go live with Clara and her kids. Sure, I like my newfound place and its seclusion, but it's too far away from her. Hell, I could be living next door and I would still think that. I don't know what kind of timetable we'll have about this mate business, and I'm not sure how patient I can be.

Guess there's a first time for everything. Literally.

A blue sedan is parked in front of my place, stirring up a slew of questions. I don't think my new landlord would be paying me a visit. I pull up behind it, noting that it has an out-of-state license plate. The grip on my steering wheel tightens, on edge with the familiarity of somewhere I vowed to never go again.

As soon as I open my truck door, I'm hit with a whiff of something that is setting off alarm bells.

Familiar. Woodsy. But not forgotten.

I have an unexpected visitor, and the mere thought of who I suspect it to be has me bolting from my truck and leaving my food behind. There are no other cars around, nothing else alerting me to the un-invited guest other than his smell. When my front door is already unlocked, I let out an irritated huff and brace myself for someone who I haven't seen in over a decade.

"Cousin! 'Sup?" Carter, the cousin closest to my age of them all, is strolling out of the kitchen with one of my chip bags, shoes already off as he plops down onto my sofa. His hair is receding a bit and it's hard to believe that so much time has passed. Were it not for the scar along his jawline, I might need to do a double take. His scruffy facial hair is a bit out of place too, like it's having trouble deciding which direction and how thick it wants to grow.

The sound of him crunching on my chips is as irritating and per-plexing as his arrival.

"Carter," I start, closing the door behind me. "What are you doing here?"

"Well, good to see you too." Another crunch, and he begins to talk while chewing. Guess he hasn't changed that much, after all. "Is that any way to treat your favorite cousin?"

Yeah, my favorite. That's why you have that scar. While there were times we got along growing up, there were others when we literally fought with teeth and claws.

"What do you want, Carter?" I reform my question. I've worked really hard to keep my whereabouts hidden. With each move, a new address and local phone number even. Although, I haven't been here long enough to get a new one yet; it's still on my to-do list. My employer is the only one I bother to keep up-to-date on these things, and I wait until the last possible minute to renew my driver's license if necessary. I know my methods aren't foolproof, but I have tried.

"Did you just get here? Everything is so bare." He studies my new home that I have only slept one night in so far.

"Carter," I growl, growing more impatient. I had cut ties with *everyone* from my old life. Family, so-called friends, everyone.

"Okay, okay." He sets the bag of chips on the couch beside him and begins licking his fingers. I cringe as he takes his time taking off the seasoning that stains them. "We need you to come home."

I stand there, unblinking, as I try to register what he just said. Then a booming laugh erupts from me at the mere thought of it. The audacity!

"I'm not joking, Seth. It's time to stop fooling around and come back home."

"You're an idiot if you ever thought that I would." I take a step forward, growing heated. "I've moved on. I want nothing to do with the family that practically disowned me."

"That's a bit of an exaggeration, don't you think?" He scrubs at his beard, the scratching pressing on my nerves. "Time has passed, people change."

"Bullshit," I spit, and his eyes snap to mine. I could beat the shit out of him now, just as I did when I gave him that scar. In either form, I know I could take him. And if he doesn't stop pestering me with this nonsense, there's a good chance this will have to be taken outside.

And that beer belly on him, that's an indicator of just how little he's taking care of himself. My gaze barely skims over his hand, noting a ring that looks like silicone instead of metal. Probably married with children of his own already.

"How did you even find me?" My nostrils flare, trying to figure out his why. Maybe he has known about my whereabouts for a while now, but I can't move from my spot until I find out why the hell he's here, until I know how he pinned me down in the first place.

"Tanner's in law enforcement now. He got a hit when your new landlord did a background check." Carter speaks nonchalantly.

Fuck. You can't tell me that's even legal. It's not like I'm a missing person. I at least had the decency to leave a note when I left, telling them all to go to hell. And Tanner, of all people? I have trouble believing he has enough strength and endurance to make it through any of the tests he would have to pass to become a police officer. Maybe he's doing something clerical instead.

"After all this time, why now? I thought I made it very clear that I wanted nothing to do with any of you."

"Yeah, yeah." He waves me off as if I left on good terms. It infuriates me that he can just gloss over the countless blowups about how big of a letdown I was. The only offspring of Mike and Alice, unable to produce a child. Who knew it would be the end of the only life I had ever known?

Over the years, I have seen advancements—some surgeries or hormone therapy that might give me the chance to create a family of my own making, but the damn risks associated with them were too high to sway me into trying them. That, and I hadn't met anyone I was willing to go through that for. And as my thirties kept ticking by, I began to write it off altogether.

With Clara, I won't have to worry about that. A new life and future are just in front of me, dangling with hope of ending my sad and lonely days. I can finally plant roots here, away from my past and the scars it left on me.

If only I can get my damn cousin to leave and go home.

"Your dad is sick, Seth." Carter leans forward on the couch, letting his elbows rest on the knees of his roughly worn jeans. "They're giving him about six months."

This news about the man who raised me might have been a gut punch to some, but not to me. My last memory of my old man is one that I could never forget. His face, full of disappointment and an anger that made me realize I was dead to him. My mom, quiet and reserved in the background as he yelled and cursed at me. As if I could merely flip a switch and decide to impregnate my ex-fiancée but was simply deciding not to. As if I had a choice in the matter.

One thing is for sure, however. It was the last damn time he ever inflicted any type of abuse on me. The fear instilled in his eyes, as the tables finally turned and I fought back, is nothing more than a proud memory now.

I remain stiff, barely letting my mouth part to speak. "My condolences, then."

"Dammit, Seth!" He stands, my bag of chips falling from his lap and sending crumbs scattering about on the wooden floors. "They want you to come back home. They want you to take over their estate and marry—"

"Fuck that, and fuck you!" I shoot back. My bones are vibrating with anger, trying to alert me that if I don't calm down, shit is about to go south. While I might have the space to change in here, I don't want to risk any damage when I have only been here for three days. I'm not taking any chances on trashing the place.

Storming through the living room and tiny kitchen, I make my way out the back door. I swivel to find him in my doorway, staring at me, puzzled at my outburst.

"You need to leave, Carter. And don't come back. I'm not going back there, and not even the death of a parent can get me to return."

"Come on, Seth." He takes a step out onto the cement steps, apparently oblivious to the rage funneling and taking root inside of me.

Not even the rose bushes that are prominent along the backside of my house sway me from losing my shit. Thinking of her and that small token is still not enough to calm me down. Even if their blooms are starting to become more sparse. I'll find flowers elsewhere for my Rose, even in the dead of an Iowa winter.

The mere remembrance of being inside of her, the connection I have already formed with her, solidifies my need to stay. Nothing, and no one, will take me away from Clara.

Packing up and leaving was never an option in the first place. Now, with her at the center of my world, not even dear old dad on his deathbed can persuade me otherwise.

"Go home, Carter!" My voice turns primal as it leaves my body.

"Do we really have to do this?" he grumbles as he takes off his shirt and begins to shed his pants.

It appears we do.

Bones begin to crack. Teeth elongate, and my body bends this way and that, trying to accommodate my changing size. Everything burns as the shift overtakes me, human Seth taking a back seat since he was getting nowhere.

A guttural exhale leaves my lungs, fighting for air through the agony. Even after all these years, changes brought on by myself or the full moon never get any less painful.

My clothes expand until they have nothing left to give and begin to shred as they fall from me. I'm huffing, letting my anger take hold and ground me. There isn't a damn thing that's going to convince me to leave. Not my cousin or my fucking father who I wrote off so long ago.

So, I'll have to send a message.

8

Chew Me Up and Spit Me Out

Clara

Something's wrong.

I can tell by the way Julie's head is hanging low as she gets out of Joe's truck, and I'm already crossing my arms and biting my tongue.

She has a phone of her own and didn't text me at all over the short weekend. Since this was supposed to be my weekend and I had let Joe take them, I insisted that he bring them back so I can have dinner with them before bringing them to him for the week. It was almost too easy to get my ex to agree, and now I'm wary about why he didn't put up a fuss about it.

"Well, okay then," Joe remarks as Julie skirts around him, denying him the hug he was after. Emmett, on the other hand, is nothing but glee as he gives some electronic device back to his dad. My eyes narrow, and I send up a silent but stern prayer to whoever might be listening about how that better not be a phone.

We agreed. No phones until they turn ten, and even then they don't leave the house unless they have some sort of after-school activity where they might need one. Emmett is usually in some sort of close proximity to Julie anyway since their schools are connected, so I don't see the need to change our rule.

"What's wrong, Julie?" I ask as she approaches, not knowing which way this is going to go. She's my straight A student, but lousy at lying. "Did you not enjoy the park?"

She freezes, confusion flickering across her face, and then turns back to her father as if she's looking for something.

"We had a change of plans." Joe shuts both doors on his side of the truck, closing Chassidy inside. She's scrolling through something on her phone. I note how the phone is too close to her face, giving me the suspicion that she's trying to use it as a shield as she watches us behind dark sunglasses.

Was she the reason they could only go out of town this weekend? Was it her schedule that took my kids away from me on *my* weekend?

I thought they were going to have mild sunburns after returning from Wacky Wonders, the only amusement park we ever made the trek to every year, no matter what. One of my yearly complaints was its lack of shade amongst all of the rides and eateries.

"Please don't be mad," Julie mutters, shrinking in size as she clutches the strap of her bag on her shoulder with both hands.

"Mad at what?"

"We went a little further north than we anticipated." Joe's words are lighting a fire and I can feel the blaze igniting. He's lucky I'm not a fire starter, or his body would be next. Let's add the truck in there too.

"We went to the Mall of America!" Emmett exclaims, and it's all I can do not to go off. "Thanks again, Dad!"

He hugs his father, then brushes past us and Julie decides to follow after him. Her shoulders are caved in, acting as if she's the one in trouble. She couldn't be further from the truth.

I look over my shoulder, my face reddening as I watch them disappear from view. "What the fuck, Joe?" I finally snap. "That wasn't the fucking plan!"

"Now calm down—"

"I will not fucking calm down! You crossed into another damn state without running it by me. What happened to the park? You were taking them to the park!"

"I'm their father, and like I said, there was a change of plans."

Chassidy has her sights on me now, too. Her beady little eyes are watching me from over her pink phone. She isn't trying to hide anything anymore, with the tilt of her head.

My voice is cracking under the pressure of the damn hatred and frustration coming out of my mouth. "That doesn't give you the right to—"

"To what, Clara? To spoil my kids?" His name-brand shirt seems to tighten at his neck as he yells back at me. "You're just jealous because you don't have my money to do things like this anymore. Back the fuck off!"

Jealous! Of him? The hell I am!

"Joint custody, Joe." I step forward, pointing to the ground between us with each word. "Joint. Fucking. Custody."

"You know I could take the kids if I wanted to. Don't push me." He has threatened that several times before today, and this isn't the first time we've sparred with our words. While I want to believe that he would rather have more alone time with his little plaything than take on our kids full time, I wouldn't put it past him to try and take them from me, just out of spite.

"I'll be expecting them at eight tonight. Don't be a minute late," he sneers as he returns to his truck that's still roaring from the engine. Even with how loud it is, it wasn't enough to drown out our exchange of words, and I wouldn't put it past Chassidy to roll down her window just to make sure she could hang on every word.

The smug look on her face makes me want to vomit.

It isn't until he steps on the gas, soaring down the road and blazing past a stop sign, that I realize a few neighbors have emerged from their houses, some peeking from behind blinds and curtains, all playing witness to the scene.

I want to rage. I want to scream and beat something until my hands are bloodied and my voice goes silent from the force of it. I don't know how to handle this...this anger. I'm feeling so helpless and out of control, unable to financially and mentally fight for what I want most—my kids.

Julie and Emmett might be home, but our dinner at the table is mostly silent. So quiet that I'm pretty sure the sound of everyone chewing is raising my blood pressure. Though, not as high as it was when Joe was here.

I waited out in the garage for a while after he left, stewing and shaking from all of the emotions that were trying to get the best of me.

I am hurt. Beyond repair, possibly, at the damage Joe is doing to me. Feeling backed into a corner with nowhere to turn, and no rescue in sight. It sickens me, and my already failing appetite is beginning to take a turn for the worse.

Excusing myself to the bathroom, I dash out and make my way to mine just in time to rid my body of the food I just consumed. My eyes water and my throat burns as I expel it all, dry heaving in the aftermath.

When I finally quiet and my stomach is empty, I flush it down, shut the lid, and collapse on the floor. The cold tile is a welcome feel on the backs of my arms, the temperature a cool compress to the back of my head, too.

Is this my rock bottom? Please, please tell me that things can go up from here because I don't know how to survive if things get any worse.

"Mom?"

Julie's hesitant, singsong voice interrupts my wallowing in self-pity, and instead of rushing to my feet to meet her, I just lie there. She's probably worried about what she might walk into. I'm sure my vomiting wasn't very quiet either.

"Are you okay?" She draws a little closer, and I keep my gaze straight ahead at the ceiling, noting how the vent up there needs to be taken down and cleaned.

"I'll be out in a few." I swallow, my throat sore from the torture it just went through.

I can hear her footsteps as she slowly creeps into the bathroom, and before long, her head comes into view. Even in my periphery, I can tell that she's still cowering. As if I'm mad at her, when really, she is innocent in all of this. Joe has made it perfectly clear that I have zero control over what he does. He knew how much I wanted to take the kids there. I have talked about doing it for years, even. I've always wanted to go, and when our children were finally potty trained, I was even more ready to make the trip and do it. Together.

Why drive all the way up there when we have so many shops nearby?
It's a waste of time when you can spend money here or online.
Why would you want to walk around a crowded mall like that?
We have a bigger amusement park closer than that.

Time and time again, Joe shut me down. Yet I give him a goddamn inch and he goes for hundreds of miles and across state lines at the first opportunity I give him.

Fucking prick.

I guess the only good thing to come from our marriage is our kids. I will never regret our relationship for that exact fact, even if it angers me to reflect on the past and relive moments that would be better off forgotten.

Julie and Emmett are still worth it.

My eldest takes a seat on the floor beside me, her braided hair falling forward and over her shoulder. She's wearing one of her favorite cheerleading shirts, a deep navy blue one that's a bit faded from all the wear, but nothing could make her any less beautiful than she is.

"I'll be fine," I mutter, although my voice betrays me with its infusion of sadness. The mere sound of it has a lump forming in my throat. Tears are beginning to pool in my eyes, and even though I keep them wide in the hopes of them drying, my plan fails. They leak from the outside corners and run down my face and into my hairline.

"I'm sorry, Mom," she sniffles before her voice cracks. "I think Dad might have overheard me talking to Mags when we stopped for gas. I was just so excited that I wanted to tell somebody."

No, no, no.

I sit up, and too quickly. I blink rapidly to restore some sort of equilibrium before I can focus on her.

"You have absolutely nothing to be sorry for." *The bastard.* "None of this is your fault, you hear me? None of it. This is between me and your father."

She slaps her hands on her bare thighs. "You keep saying that, but nothing seems to be getting any better."

I can feel the color drain from my face at that remark. Well, any color that might be left that is. I have been trying, time and time again, to keep the kids out of this. I keep the trash talk about Chassidy inside my head or get it out over a bottle of wine while on the phone with my mom when the kids are away. I try not to make snide comments or fight with their dad when they're around. I keep pretending that this is just the new normal and that we're still adapting to it but dammit, I'm freaking coming up short there as well.

My kids shouldn't be thrown into the middle of this. They shouldn't be used to get a rise out of me. Is that his goal in all of this? Try to show me off as an unfit mother if I lose my temper so he can nab them out from beneath me and gain full custody? Hell will have to freeze over first.

As much as I don't want to think of myself as a violent person, something about Joe and Chassidy, whether together or apart, brings about the worst in me.

"I'm *trying*, Julie. It may not seem like much, but I am." I force the words out, hoping I don't break.

"I know you are, Mom." She sniffles as she looks away, then down into her lap. "I don't want to live with Dad. I want to stay here with you, but..."

This is the first time she's come right out and said it. Staying here. I find it easy to believe, though. Every time she's picked up or dropped off by her father, that bubbly and outgoing personality of hers shuts down. She's almost a different person when she's around him. At least, from what I can see.

"What is it, hon?" I try to press lightly, afraid that she might back off and retreat.

"This is my home." Tears are springing to her eyes and falling fast. My heart sinks even further. I'm pretty sure it's in the basement now.

"I don't like being split up between the two of you, and I don't understand why Dad treats you the way that he does. He didn't used to."

"I know, honey, I know," I try to soothe, placing a hand on her knee. "He's not treating you badly though, is he?"

Better not be. Throw me under the bus all you want, but you'd better not fuck with our kids. I don't take him for someone who would, but then, I never thought he would be capable of cheating on me in the first place. Guess I was a fool from the start.

"No." She shakes her head. "But he's almost *too* nice. He wants to buy us everything. Take us everywhere. It's getting to be overbearing. He's trying too hard."

Yeah, he's trying to buy you off.

God, it makes me sick that he would stoop so low to try and wrangle the kids away from me with gifts and trips. No wonder Emmett was in such a good mood when he got home. I had taken away electronics, and that was probably the first thing Joe bought for him. Julie, on the other hand, is growing into her own. She is sensing the bullshit.

"Believe me when I say that there is nothing I would like more than having you and your brother here all the time. I know I may not be the perfect mom, but you two mean *everything* to me." I pause for a moment, letting that sink in, but then Julie starts shaking her head.

"I don't want to go to his house this week. I want to stay here. I like my room and my things. I like having my third grade teacher down the next block. I like being able to ride the bus with my friends."

Damn, can my heart break any more?

"Have you..." I swallow, considering what I'm trying to ask her and the response I might get. "Tried asking your dad if you could stay here?"

She snorts, shaking her head vehemently. "He just laughed at me. Told me that I wasn't old enough to know what I want."

"You're going to be fourteen soon. I think you've got a great head on your shoulders to have an idea of what you want." I scoot my bum across the floor so I can sit beside her, leaning against the double sink vanity. One of the gold handles is trying to dig into my back, but I ignore it.

"Between you and me, I've been thinking about picking up another job." I can spare her the details, as I don't want to tell her how terrified I am of starting over at some new place. That I'm afraid that my body wouldn't like it, and would retaliate if it were to be anything strenuous. I know I'm not in the best of shape, but I figure that in my situation, I don't really have room to be picky. "I can't make any promises, because I don't know what the future holds, but I am *not* going to let money be the reason that I can't fight for you and your brother."

Julie's bottom lip trembles, and I know I've struck a chord in her. Before I know it, she's swinging her arms around my neck and burying herself there. "I love you, Mom."

My eyes clench shut, and I savor her words as if I've never heard them uttered before when it couldn't be further from the truth. "I love you more."

9

Better Than Cookie Dough

Clara

Haven't I cried enough already? Apparently not.

I return home from taking the kids to Joe's new place, and not a minute before eight. I even drove around a few different blocks before dropping them off because I'd be damned if I gave him any more time than what he already had. Emmett droned on and on about how long it was taking, but I could tell from one look at Julie's smirk in the passenger seat, she was aware of what I was doing.

That small little lift of her lips meant the world to me. Like we were two girls against a world that was coming at us. And by world, I mean her dad.

Emmett had been in a bad mood ever since returning home. I know he blames me for his lack of electronics, but it stems from him not keeping his grades up to begin with. I lost track of how many times he pushed his glasses up on his nose. You would think that if he wiped that scowl off his face they might stop sliding, but I guess he hasn't figured that out yet.

Joe was ready and waiting for us on his front porch, stalking toward my van with Chassidy nowhere in sight, thank goodness. I did my best to calmly explain to him that Emmett's grades aren't acceptable at the moment, and all I was met with was a response of, "You'll get them up, right, kiddo?" to our youngest.

He patted Emmett on the back and they went inside without offering me a goodbye. Guess I'm on my son's shit list, too.

The massive two-story home swallowed him up within its tan exterior. The black shutters on each window are no doubt for looks only. It doesn't look like they're even functional. I'm sure he has brand-new appliances in every room and a giant television to boot. The most I've seen of the inside was from the listing online before it was taken down with the sale. I had gawked at the price tag, and almost lost my eyeballs in the reaction.

Julie hugged me tighter this time, harder than on the floor of my bathroom. Neither of us wanted to let go, and I glared at Joe the longer it went on. I still don't know what *I* did to warrant this attitude from him. Why is it okay for him to be angry, but not me?

The entire ride home I was in a daze, beating myself up with feelings of confusion swirling around and meddling in places they shouldn't be. Nothing on the radio could tune it out, so I gave up on that, self-doubt and fear of my unknown future the only things keeping me company.

Now here I sit, alone in my garage after all the lights have gone out. The air in here is growing heavier and hotter the longer I sit. But perhaps it's just because the cold air from the vents isn't hitting me head-on anymore.

Plucking my phone from its position in the cupholder closest to me, I go to my messages. My finger hovers over Seth's text from last night, prompting me to reply since I haven't yet, and it was left in an unread status.

He literally just left this morning after an amazing night of sex. I know he didn't give me a timeframe of any sort. Pretty much the all clear to contact him whenever. But is it too soon?

Just how bad do I not want to be alone tonight? I have to work tomorrow, and I'm tired already. But the thought of seeing him again has me typing out a message before I can argue myself out of it.

Too soon?

I press send. And only then does it register that he might take this as a desperate plea for a booty call. Is that even what I want? More sex? Do I even try to follow up that message to try and backtrack?

I'm halfway through another message when I see little bubbles working on a reply, and I hold my breath. What if I really was nothing more than a quick fuck last night?

The bubbles stop, and my spirits drop at the mere thought of him trying to ghost me. Is there any chance he could be aware that I'm staring at my phone, waiting and wishing for a reply in my favor?

There is something off about Seth, but I just can't put my finger on it. First of all, the obvious. Why the hell is he with me when he could be with someone without a bunch of baggage? Second, who the hell just decides to take over and do your lawn and expect nothing in return? Okay, so we had dinner. But then he paid for it! Then, he follows me home and fucks me?

I'm still reeling from how good it was, but maybe it was only because it had been so long since I had sex.

No. It was fucking amazing and unlike anything I'd ever experienced before. That's the damn truth.

Everything okay?

It's a short reply, but even so, I get my hopes up. Especially since he's at least talking to me. I suppose he could still shut me down, though, and I don't know what might hurt worse. But if it works out, it beats being alone again.

> If you're busy, it's fine.

A few more bubbles go off, and then I have an answer that makes me both anxious and a tad giddy.

> Be there in fifteen.

I swallow hard, not knowing what to expect when he gets here. Judging by the kiss he left me with, I hope he might make me forget my name tonight. Rail me until I pass out so that I don't let my troubled head get in the way of sleep. But even so, I know it probably isn't the best way to cope with my emotions. But when have I ever gone about dealing with my own stress in a healthy way?

Rushing inside, I quickly take my shoes off and run to the bathroom to brush my teeth. Again. I switch into another bra—one without underwires—so if I sleep in one, I'll be more comfortable.

Setting my alarms for the morning, I go ahead and place my phone on the wireless charger at my bedside and close the blinds so it will be darker if we end up in here. I don't want to presume, but I want to be prepared.

I'm switching some clothes over to the dryer when my doorbell goes off, sending my heart into overdrive. My palms are already growing sweaty, nerves gathering quickly as I approach the front door.

My hand hesitates on the handle and I'm grateful for the solid door between us that shields me from view. When I gather enough courage, I unlock the deadbolt and open it. But the sight that awaits me has me choking on air.

"What the hell happened to you?" I shriek as I take in the sight. Seth looks like he has been in a fight. He has a cut on his arm that looks angry, a bruise beginning to form on his face, and his posture is off, making him appear shorter. "Do you need to go to the hospital?"

"What? No, I'm fine." He shakes his head as he welcomes himself in. I step outside to have a look around, but am unable to locate his vehicle. I'm not sure if I should be searching for danger lurking in the night in addition to the missing truck or what.

"Then why do you look like you've been in a street fight or something? How did this happen?" Great, is he involved in something that could possibly threaten my family? The mere thought of it almost has me sending him packing, muscles and all. "I've got enough shit going on in my life. I can't handle any more."

"Relax, Clara." He sighs as if his beaten stature is no big deal. His facial hair does nothing to cover the purpling on his upper cheek.

"I can't!" My voice rises higher than I mean for it to. "I can't jeopardize my kids for whatever this is."

I cross into the living room. The soft glow coming from the kitchen is the only thing casting light in here. I sit on the couch and bury my head in my hands, wondering if I ever should have sent that text and welcomed him back.

The sound of shoes hitting the floor in the entry is soft, but then he begins to close in on me. I resist the urge to look up and into his face. He might have been knocked around or some shit, but he still looks fucking amazing. It isn't fair that he can still look delicious even in this state.

"Clara." His voice caresses over my skin like a thin, soft blanket. He lowers to the floor and when he does, he draws my hands away and into his. His eyes are still shining bright. "An old family member paid me a surprise visit. Needless to say, we had more than words."

I gape at him. "Your own family did this?"

His face falls sullen. "Unfortunately."

"But..." I search his face, longing to reach out and touch it but afraid that the slightest graze might cause him pain. "I thought you weren't in touch with them anymore?"

"I'm not." Setting my hands down in my lap, he rubs his hands back and forth against my outer thighs, almost in a comforting manner, but I'm not sure if it's meant more for him or me. Funny, because I feel like I should be the one comforting him right now given his family history. "I guess when my new landlord ran my credit for my application to rent, one of my cousins hightailed it here."

"I don't understand," I begin, still confused. "They're the ones who wronged you. How in the hell did you get in a fight like this?"

"I'd rather not talk about it." His movements on my legs stop and I can feel my face pinching. "At least, not right now."

I hold my breath, still concerned about Seth and the condition he's in, and this surprise visit of a family member from his past as well.

"Is everything alright with you?" He looks up into my eyes, and while I note the sadness that's pulling at them, it almost feels like I'm seeing my own reflected back at me. "I thought you were getting your kids back today?"

My head begins shaking before I can even mutter a single word. Tears are threatening, burning my eyes, and dammit, I'm tired of crying. I'm exhausted from trying to hold my shit together. It feels like all I ever do is stress, worry, and wait for the next thing in my life to go wrong.

"All I've ever wanted out of my life was to be a mother," I start, and for the life of me, I don't know why I'm bringing this up to a stranger who I only officially met yesterday. The poor sap has no idea just who he took to bed last night. "Some people figure out what they want out of their lives. Their dreams, occupations, whatever. But me? The only thing that has been a constant want and need, was to be a mom."

"There is absolutely *nothing* wrong with wanting that." Seth lifts a hand and his finger swipes away at a rogue tear on my cheek.

"But I'm struggling, Seth." I draw in a sharp breath, agitation beginning to dig at the corners of my mind. "And Joe, he—he just loves to dangle it in my face that it would be nothing to take them from me. If I piss him off, he'll drag me back to court for full custody, and he has the financial means to do that, whereas I don't."

My voice is cracking from letting out the voices inside of my head. From speaking my fears verbally. I begin to confide in Seth about Joe, still in shock over how he pulled the wool over my eyes this weekend. And worse, my daughter thought I'd be mad at her for something her father was responsible for. I would never dream of doing that, no matter how pissed off I am at him. But right now, I'm at his mercy, and I fucking hate it.

"Do you really think he would do it? Take them?"

I blink as I look up, trying to squash my exhausted nerves. "I don't even recognize Joe anymore. I'm afraid he would do it, just because he can. Whether he really wants them or not."

The man I married is gone. As much as it pains me to say, I know it to be true. I don't know what I ever did to make him resent me like this.

"But he's never pulled anything of this magnitude before?"

I shake my head no. My lips feel swollen as I roll them in before speaking again. "I'm sorry to unload all of this on you. I'm sure this isn't what you had in mind when I texted you."

"Seems like we're both dealing with some crap."

I scoff. That might be the nicest way to put things.

"But maybe we can deal with it together. Neither of us have to go through it alone." Seth resumes his soothing tactic of rubbing my legs and my mood lightens ever so slightly at that word.

Together.

I still can't believe that Seth wants anything to do with me in the first place. Something just doesn't add up. And while a part of me likes the attention, and hell, *revels* in our sexual encounter last night, I still have trouble believing he would have any kind of attraction to me in the first place. Maybe he was just horny and needed to get that out of his system. Perhaps we're going to head into a friendlier territory now that he has. Even though his hands on me might lead me to believe that thought is a lie I'm telling myself.

I'm still a bit wary about his altercation, and with a long-lost cousin to boot. Just what kind of family did he leave behind that they're willing to drop him for not being able to have a child and now they show up unannounced and bring about a fight? I don't know what his family member looks like after their incident, but I have a strange bit of faith that Seth was victorious in the outcome.

"Are you sure I can't get you some ice?" My fingers gently skim the side of his face, not realizing I'm reaching out until he turns into my touch, closing his eyes. The relaxing effect it has on me is almost instant. His facial hair is so soft, reminding me of his chest. I'm not sure if he conditions it or what, but it isn't dry or scratchy in the slightest.

"I've been icing most of the day, but thank you." He turns to kiss my palm and my breathing shallows. I didn't realize just how deprived I've been of touch. Of physical touch. It's something I have gone so long without that this one, small act means so much more than Seth railing me last night.

It's too soon. Too quick to be getting hung up on feelings for a man I just met. My heart is already breaking at the mere possibility of losing my kids; I can't put myself in a spot to let it further crack when this man eventually decides to leave me too. I mean, why wouldn't he? I'm well aware that he stated that he would stay, but I have no rhyme or reason to trust this man.

"Do you want me to stay the night again?" His golden eyes find mine, a pleading in them that makes the beating in my chest take a stumble.

"I wasn't aware I had the option to say no last night," I tease him, letting out a bit of a laugh.

Seth cocks a grin, a naughty one that sends replays of last night bouncing around my head. "You didn't."

"I still don't know you that well. I mean, who's to say you're not going to murder me or rob me blind in the middle of the night?"

Admitting that out loud feels like screaming about the elephant in the room, but I don't shy back from it because in truth, and I can't explain why, I don't think he would do either of those things. But the Negative Nancy in me still has a part of her guard up.

"Clara, I promise that I have no intentions of murdering or stealing from you. I will steer clear when your kids are home and give you space when you ask for it. But if you *ever* want me here, all you have to do is say so. No questions asked."

I nod slowly, eyeing the mark on his arm again. "Are you sure you're okay?"

"Yes. I've left my street fighting days behind me and sent my cousin packing." His cocky smile returns, and as much as I want to offer a playful jab at him, I resist. The man has already been through one beating today, and while my touch might pale in comparison, I don't want to risk an ounce more pain than what he might already be in.

"What time do you have to work tomorrow?" He stands, then proceeds to sit beside me on the couch, and close. His thigh nestles up right next to my leg as he draws an arm up around my shoulders.

"I have to be there at eight. I start setting alarms at six fifteen, though."

"Start setting alarms?" Seth questions as he places his free hand on top of mine, lacing his fingers through to hold mine. My heart skips a beat and I struggle for a moment to remember what he just asked.

"Yeah, I...I start my alarms earlier because I like to hit snooze a few times."

"Well, I will make sure that you get up in time to get ready for work," he states, as if making it his own personal mission.

"Are you an early bird?" I let my hand leave his and turn it over, letting our palms touch as we intertwine our fingers again.

Seth shrugs. "I can be. Not always the case."

"What about your job? How soon do you normally start working again after a move?"

He sighs through his nose, rubbing his thumb across my index finger. "Normally I would have my office put together by now. But with my uninvited guest today, things got thrown off-kilter."

We go quiet for a minute, alone in our respective thoughts. I'm still worried for Seth. And while that problem helps drown out my own sorrows, the longer we sit, the more uneasy I grow.

"Are you sure that this isn't going to be a problem? Your family finding you?" I turn my attention toward him, my head casting a shadow on the lower half of his face.

"I think he got the message. I don't want anything to do with the family that wrote me off so callously. I've got my own life now. One that now revolves around you."

My heart skids to a stop like the roadrunner in those old cartoons. My mouth drops as I stare at him. Confusion and flattery are alternating like neither one knows how to be triumphant.

How do I even respond to something like that? Maybe his cousin did a bigger number on him than what I originally thought.

Seth's hand forms around the back of my head and he draws me close, letting his lips brush against mine and stealing any sense of coherent thinking I have left.

10

Wake-Up Call

Seth

Clara is almost passed out on the couch. We've talked for hours, about any little thing we thought to bring up. We traded stories from when we were children, work drama—because who doesn't have that—and the list goes on and on. I'm falling even more in love with her every time she speaks.

It isn't all fun, though. There were times when the conversation veered toward touchy subjects and traveled to alleys of sadness. Were it not a work night, Clara told me she would have brought out the alcohol at the mere remembrance of some of those memories. The scare her family had when they thought her brother was killed while stationed overseas. How Julie had ended up in the hospital as a young tyke with a severe case of pneumonia. How Emmett had broken the same arm two years in a row because he was a bit clumsy, like his mom, and the second time he had knocked himself unconscious with the act. These stories eventually led to how she had found out about Joe cheating on her, and the divorce papers.

One thing has become clearer the more she talks and the more she shrinks her posture beside me. She is self-conscious, and her own hardest critic. While she doesn't come right out and say it, it's evident in the way she speaks of certain situations. Her nerves about being in the way, her worries of not being the perfect mom with the crafty ideas and snacks for school, how she compares herself to others. I am going to make her see just how beautiful and desirable she is. It might make her uncomfortable at first, sure. But she deserves to see herself just as I do—a woman who loves fiercely and puts her family at the forefront in all that she does. It's something my parents never did.

If today had been uneventful, I would have carried her off to bed, but Clara smacks me on the chest when I try to. She keeps reminding me of my injuries, telling me that I need rest, and ice. I eventually let her get an ice pack since she won't stop pestering me about it. She brings me three.

There's no way I can tell her just how bad were the situations and fights I've been through in the past. Because I can't tell her about the animalistic side of me. Growing up, I wasn't always this lean and muscular, and I was picked on quite a bit until I finally went through my first change on a full moon. Things started to align after that. I began to find my stride in life and take better care of myself. Began taking a stand against some who sought to beat me down. Carter and his older brothers, to name a few.

I strip down to my boxers and let her curl up on the bed and get comfortable before I form myself around her. It takes some slight rearranging, but I finally find a spot that doesn't bring about any discomfort and I settle in.

Tonight was different. Perhaps I owed it to her for fucking her last night when I couldn't think about much else. I have to say, it is slightly easier to be around her now. While her scent still has me salivating at times, it's more manageable. And the fact that I didn't completely freak her out after being so forward last night, that she asked me to come back again tonight, makes me feel like I have a win in my corner.

Bending my head, I inhale deeply, savoring her closeness and reminding myself that I have found her. Who would have thought that after all this time being alone, I might finally have another shot at something I wrote off so long ago?

A purpose. A reason. Someone to look forward to being around and with. The kids are the damn icing on the cake.

Clara is passed out cold as the morning creeps around. She's turned a couple of times but other than that has been a pretty sound sleeper. I, on the other hand, have been dozing on and off. I'm still troubled by Carter's surprise visit and bothered by the news of my dad. I didn't even get as far as to ask what's wrong with him, but a strong part of me really doesn't care what is claiming his life.

Maybe I'll wait a year and look up his obituary. Morbid, probably, but I don't see any reason to waste energy on the bastard. He doesn't deserve the title of father.

I can just barely make out the time on Clara's phone behind her, and wish for the minutes to slow down. I'm not ready to lose her to her workday.

Six ten.

Clara kicked off the covers about half an hour ago and hasn't tried to reach for them since. My eyes roam over her body, covered in a large T-shirt, and now that I look down, I find that she went to bed without any underwear.

A bra, but no underwear? That doesn't sound comfortable. Why is she doing that to herself?

Six eleven.

My eyes fixate on her bare ass and my cock begins to straighten. There isn't much to the fabric with these boxers, and it's soon jutting out with all of the naughty thoughts coming to life.

Will she be mad if I wake her? Treat her to an early morning orgasm so she can start her day off on the right foot? The more I think about it, the harder I get. I reach into my waistband and give myself a few strokes, suppressing a groan.

Her phone on its charger changes to six-twelve, and a challenge of my own making is at the forefront of my mind.

I'm going to wake her before her first alarm goes off.

Carefully, I roll her onto her back, still blissfully asleep and un-aware, and I part her legs. Positioning myself down between them, I bury my head between her thighs and part her so my tongue can lick up her length. She is so smooth and soft, and fuck, if she doesn't smell so damn divine.

My lips and tongue go to work, stroking and coaxing her to awaken by nothing more than greedy lashings on her clit.

Six thirteen.

I'm barely able to glimpse the clock from my position. I finally hear a breathy moan leave her throat. "Oh…"

She raises her hands toward her face, as if she can rub the sleep away, and when my lips close in to suck on her again, she lifts her head to find me between her legs.

The devilish triumph I feel satisfies my ego in all the right ways.

"Seth," she mewls, and the heavenly sound of her voice has me sucking on her harder. Her face screws tight as her head slams back into her pillow. "Oh, Seth."

I wrap my arms around her thighs and hold her tight, applying more pressure with my tongue as her hips try to move.

Clara's hands are trying to figure out what to do. They're roaming her body, in her hair, pulling at her face as she tries to accommodate what she's receiving. I want to see her grab her own breasts, squeeze her nipples and add to the experience she's having, but they're hidden away.

I dig in more, my cock painfully aware that it could be inside of her, but this is all about her coming undone by my mouth alone. I would sweetly drown in her if it kept those sounds coming out of her throat.

"Se…" Her hips try to jerk, signaling that she's getting close. Her hands find my head and she's trying to suffocate me but I love the feel of her nails on my scalp. She's grasping as the air leaving her lungs pitches higher until she reaches the peak.

I shake my head, my tongue a hard protrusion that has her back arching as she cries out. I keep sucking on that little nub, her body shuddering as she continues to spasm in pulses. While I don't want to leave this spot that I find so satisfying, she's attempting to pull me off.

With one last pull of my lips, I raise my head. Clara whines, her body shaking as she tries to find her equilibrium again. Her eyelashes are fluttering as she tries to focus on me, and I release her legs, letting them fall to the sides.

Her alarm starts going off, and I smile at what I just accomplished. Granted, I only meant to wake her by this time, but I guess I was a greedy motherfucker.

I lick my lips, grinning ear to ear. "Good morning, Clara."

After being denied a shared shower once again, I make my way out and into the kitchen. I'm pulling my clothes on as I go, eager to get some coffee started for the both of us. I start mine first in the hopes it will cool enough for me to down it before she has to go. I then find the iced setting on her machine and hope that I'm getting it started correctly. I should have been paying more attention yesterday.

Leaning up against the counters, I gaze about the kitchen. It's rather large—or at least, bigger than what I'm used to. Mine now is pea-sized compared to this. The upper cabinets reach up toward the ceiling, and there's an island that I'd like to clear off so I can have Clara for dessert.

My cock is practically screaming at me as I think about hoisting her up onto the surface. Better yet, the dining table in the next room would be a better height to take her if I were standing. My head tilts to the side, and I imagine my Rose opening up for me.

Clara comes out of the hallway in a rush, shrugging on a top over her lacy, cream tank with a moderate neckline and that moon necklace of hers.

She really is fucking perfect.

A blush creeps into her cheeks as she makes eye contact with me, and her steps slow.

"I tried to start some coffee for you, but I'm afraid I don't know how you make it."

Tucking her hair behind her ears, she approaches the fridge and pulls out the milk and a bottle of creamer. "You didn't have to, but thank you."

"For the coffee or the wake-up call?"

Her eyes bulge as the redness in her face becomes more prominent. I bite the inside of my cheek, a bit too amused by her reaction.

"Both...I guess."

She's unable to bring herself to look at me, and while I like her honesty, her uncertainty has me moving in closer. There's a pause in her movements as she mixes up her drink. I try to take notes on what she's doing, but I'm too distracted by the sight of her.

"You guess?" I move her dark hair away from her face, and she stills as I bring my lips to her skin. I inhale as my lips brush against her temple, leisurely skimming it. "Should I wake you tomorrow with my dick instead?"

Brown eyes shoot up again as her lips part on a sharpened breath. Her pulse is quickening, adrenaline pumping through her veins. Judging by the far-off look that overtakes her, I know she's envisioning me doing that.

"Awfully bold of you to assume you'll be back tonight." She tries to steady her voice, but I'm already onto her. She shakes the bottle of creamer and pours a splash of it in, stirring with her straw before grabbing a bottle of syrup stashed nearby.

"I will be," I begin as I take a step back to retrieve my coffee. "Because I want to cook you dinner tonight."

She pauses after adding some milk, shooting me a look that I can't quite decipher. "Dinner."

I nod. "Yes, dinner. I noticed you have a grill stored in the garage. Could I use it?"

She rolls those lips again, and I fight off the thought of what a sight they would be wrapped around my cock. Hell, I would even take her hands right about now.

"Honestly, it probably needs to be cleaned. I don't even know if there's enough gas in the tank, either. It hasn't been used in a while."

"And what time do you get off work?"

"Four. But I need to run a couple of errands after work, so I probably won't be home until after five." She takes a quick sip of her drink and thinks on it for a moment. She must have mixed it right, because she takes the cold items back to the fridge. When she returns, I pull at her waist, drawing her in.

Clara's gaze flashes from my eyes to my lips, then back again. It's like she's trying to ascertain my next move. "D-do you want me to make anything?"

"Absolutely not, it's my treat." I grin right before I take her mouth. My hands are securing her to me, arms holding her close as my tongue darts in to chase after the sweet drink she's made. At first, she's slow to return my fervor, but she soon concedes, arms wrapping around and pulling at me as if I could get any closer. We could meld into one another and that still wouldn't be enough for me.

I walk her back against the island, her ass pressing into the cabinets as my groin tries to find a way to nestle between her legs. I'm about ready to lift her onto the counter and try to indulge in my earlier imaginings, but her hands are trying to push me away.

A hand brushes against a sore spot on my back and I hold back a hiss. I don't want her under the impression that she can't touch me for fear of hurting me. Going without her hands on me isn't an option.

"Seth," she breathes, trying to catch her breath. "I'm...I'm going to be late for work."

I tug at her bottom lip with my thumb, enjoying how plump it is. "Sure you can't call in sick?"

I would gladly do so for today, even though I already requested to use half a day of vacation time. If it means spending my time with Clara and chasing her around this house, I would call off the fucking week. I have enough time built up; I could do it.

She weighs my words for a moment, then shakes her head. "I can't. I'm sorry. I have to get going."

My body fights the thought of taking a step back, but I reluctantly do so. She tucks her brown hair behind her ear again, then grabs her coffee and rounds the island to find her purse on a stool and drape it over her shoulder.

"I'll see you out then." I chug the rest of my coffee and immediately take it to the sink to rinse it. Our cups are still there from yesterday, a small token of my previous visit.

Get used to having coffee with me in the mornings.

I can't help but wonder if she uses the dishwasher for these things or if she washes them all by hand? It would be nothing to wash them really quickly, but I'm sure she doesn't want to leave me here alone, unattended.

I follow her out of the house and into the garage. The breezeway between buildings hits me with a brush of cool air as she unlocks the next door and makes her way in.

"Have a good day at work." I offer her a light peck of a kiss as she opens her car door, and it's enough to bring out her smile.

"You too." Clara climbs into her van and before I know it I'm taking off in a jog. If I stay another moment longer, she will definitely be late for work if she's supposed to make it to Pembrook by eight.

Due to Mr. Nosy Guy yesterday, I parked my truck about a block away and out of his sight. I'm happy to find that no one is watching with cautious eyes and questions about my being here.

Driving to the gas station—again—I nab a few slices of breakfast pizza, a donut, and a small container of milk. Cooking for Clara tonight gives me the perfect excuse to go to a grocery store and buy some damn food.

Practically inhaling my pizza, I'm about halfway through my donut by the time I get back to my place. My good mood takes a nosedive as I find my dear cousin's car still parked outside.

Motherfucker.

Slamming my truck door a bit too harshly, I make my way up to the door. My foul mood and this uninvited guest are threatening to ruin my whole day at this point. Just as I reach the door, the handle turns. I have half a mind to kick it in due to the man who has overstayed his failed mission of a visit, but when I see the state that Carter is in, feelings of guilt and partial regret are quick to seep in. They're emotions I'm not used to experiencing, and I shove them down deep.

His right eye is swollen shut with a busted lip. Shoulders are hunched over, and there are splotches of red bleeding through his shirt. Due to his debilitated state, I'm not sure if he would even be able to drive, let alone see well enough to do that task.

Ignoring his injuries, I choose my words carefully. "What are you still doing here?"

I don't know why I'm giving him the chance to speak. After our fight, I told him to leave me the hell alone and never come back. He can tell the family whatever he wants, but there's nothing and no one that could persuade me away from my decisions. In a nutshell, that is. My true words might have been a bit harsh, but I straight-up told him that I would end him if he's still here when I get back.

I didn't tell him how long I would be gone, but I'm not complaining about the reason I was away all night.

"I know, I know." He practically cowers before me. The man needs a damn shower, he smells awful. "I was going to leave, I promise. But I think I lost my wedding ring during our tussle."

I snort. I hadn't heard the use of that word since my grandpa was alive, and he died a few years before I left. Anytime us kids got involved in fights, he always called it a tussle.

"They'll work it out. Just let them tussle."

His smoke-infused hack of a voice was one to also utter the "boys will be boys" remark, time and time again. I fucking hate that line.

He encouraged fights, saying they would make us stronger in the end. He would simply sit by and watch, even as limbs were being broken and flesh torn. The apple hadn't fallen far from the tree with my father. Another reason why I don't give a rat's ass about his upcoming date with death.

There isn't a doubt in my mind that my grandfather would have written me off just like the rest of my family. Good riddance.

"Janet will have my head if I lose it. She always makes me leave it at home when—"

I hold up a hand to silence him. This is the first I've heard him speak about his partner, and while I want to send him packing, I don't want a pissed off wife coming after me over a fucking wedding ring.

"Where have you looked?"

Carter tilts his head, neck popping and releasing some built-up tension. "I've looked in the backyard where we shifted and made it to the tree line, but I haven't had any luck yet."

Annoyed that my plans for the day are being thwarted once again, I exit the front door and round the house. His steps are uneven as he follows some distance behind.

Our fingers elongate when we change, nails sharpening to claws as they do. The clearing in the backyard where we shifted is the most logical place for the band to have slipped from his finger. Granted, I was lunging at him before he had fully changed, but I wanted to send a message not to fuck around with me.

If some ring stops him from going home to show them the damage I inflicted, then what in the hell did I beat him up for? I could have killed him, but knowing he has some sort of family of his own stopped me from doing so. That, and the fact that I've found my mate has me rethinking some things.

Great, Clara is going to make me a softie. She's doing it already, and I hadn't even realized it. When issues are brought up within a pack, they're often dealt with—more times than I care to admit—with death. It's an outdated and ludicrous practice that I've never fully been able to comprehend, but it's still ingrained in me. My old pack isn't the only one that operates that way, either.

"Is that why you won't come home?"

My eyes begin sweeping the torn up ground. I'm going to have to level things out back here. I need a shovel or something to flatten down our markings and crevices in the earth. An agitated sigh blazes through my nostrils. "What are you going on about?"

Carter keeps a small distance between us. Smart, considering I could have torn him apart yesterday. And while I'm still healing from my sustained injuries as well, if he gives me reason, I would finish the job before he has a chance to shift. He wouldn't even see me coming with his lacking sight at present.

"The woman you've been with."

A bolt of anger rakes through me but I'm quick to recover. I can't let him find out about Clara. Carter doesn't need to take back any other information besides the fact that he lost against me and I spared his life. I can't risk the chance of my family using my mate against me. I have no idea why they want me to come home or why my father's news would make them want that. But I won't give them any ammunition to use to begin with.

"Am I not allowed to get laid?" I keep my voice at a level that won't indicate it's anything else but that. It couldn't be further from the truth, but it's the route I have to go.

Carter tries to laugh, but is then grunting from the pain it must cause him to do so. "Guess the bachelor life is treating you alright, then."

Sure, you can think that.

I spot his ring near the back steps and my eyes narrow. My temper threatens to surface again at how fast and easy it was to find. Had Carter really been looking, he should have been out of my hair long before now.

My nostrils flare again as I stare at it, unsure of how to proceed. Did he plant it here to buy some more time? Or is his swollen eye making him stupid?

Whatever the case, it's time for him to go. And he had better choose the easy way to get the hell out of my life. I don't think I can be so kind to him the second time around.

11

Head in the Clouds, or in the Dump

Clara

I almost caused an accident on my way to work this morning. Then I typed an extra digit for a card payment at the dental office—thankfully, the poor woman didn't have enough money in her account for the transaction to go through. And I scheduled someone for an appointment on a major holiday, and another for two years from now.

To say that my head isn't screwed on straight is stating the obvious.

The image of Seth giving me oral, trapping my thighs in his arms, has my heart palpitating and my womanly parts screaming at me for more.

More of *him.*

What the hell am I doing? I'm a mom coming out from the other side of a divorce. I'm struggling to make ends meet and worried about the possibility that my ex-husband might try to take my kids away. What am I doing allowing a complete stranger into my life and my home?

"Clara, aren't you going to take your lunch?"

I tear my gaze away from the spot on the wall I'd been staring at to find Sylvie, one of our hygienists, studying me with a hand on her hip. Her cartoon scrubs are a vast contrast to the plain ones that everyone else wears around here.

"You alright?" Her chipper, high tone still comes off as caring, but there's an underlying concern.

I note the time on the clock of my monitor. I'm already five minutes late getting out of here. "Sorry, yes. My head is somewhere else today."

I snag my purse from its little slot beneath my desk and I stand. I'm one of the last ones to take lunch, normally opting to take the later hour so it makes the afternoon go by faster. I thank Sylvie and head out the door and to my van.

For a Monday, today has been unusually quiet. It has allowed me to get lost in thought more than once, and I keep drifting back to Seth when I'm not sulking about my life and my future with my kids.

Funny how this man who came into my life a few days ago has had this effect on me. When I'm not freaking out about everything else going wrong in my life, I am obsessing over him. I guess he has a way of making me forget about all of the negatives and focus on something else.

Getting to know him. Enjoying his company. Heart fluttering at the mere mention of him making me dinner tonight. The fact that I text and he's there, even after getting into some sort of fight with a family member who he's written off.

But damn. The way he makes me *feel.*

Giddy. Curious. Hopeful. Heard.

The thought of seeing him again tonight has butterflies flapping their wings in my stomach. I feel like a teenager, getting high hopes and probably unrealistic expectations after two nights together.

But this morning, though.

I blow out a slow breath as I reach for the handle of my van's door. I shut myself inside and crack the windows to get some air flowing through. It's only about eighty degrees today, not bad for taking my lunch in my car.

Throwing my purse into the passenger seat, I lean my head back against the headrest.

Seth is the first man to show any interest in me since Joe and I split. I still have trouble understanding why, but deep down I one-hundred-percent believe that I deserve to be happy. Especially after how angry Joe and Chassidy made me. I need some sort of distraction, and while I can't comprehend Seth's attentiveness and perseverance, it doesn't make me want him in return any less.

Should I wake you tomorrow with my dick instead?

I bite my lip, an involuntary shudder passing through me at the imagery that invades my mind. I'm at odds with how I should be reacting after his actions this morning. Feasting on me. Waking me from my slumber with his wicked mouth and the force of his tongue. Would it really be so bad to wake up to his cock inside me when I was unconscious from the start?

Another thought shoots through me and I release the hold on my bottom lip. I guess he never specified where he wants to stick his dick. Maybe we need to lay some ground rules.

Rolling my windows down further, I grab a notebook stashed behind my seat for Emmett to doodle in and begin to fan myself. The temperature in the car is rising too fast.

Recalling his words from this morning, my thighs press together and I dig my ass into my seat. I can't get Seth out of my head. His voice, his smile, his freaking body. His facial and chest hair that is remarkably soft to the touch. Eyes like the sweetest honey, falling gently from its dipper.

My chubby ass doesn't belong next to his, let alone beneath it. But holy shit am I smitten. So why am I hiding it? And him? We're both adults, for crying out loud.

No, I'm not ready for him to meet my children after two days. I know he said that he plans on sticking around, but I don't know him well enough to decipher if that's true or not. I don't want to get my hopes up, but I know it's already too late for that.

Before I can talk myself out of it, I pull out my phone and bring up his info. Pressing on his name, I note that I haven't even had the chance to gather his last name yet. After all we've talked about so far, neither of us has even asked. I could have been attempting to stalk him on social media by now. I'm not proud to admit that, but maybe it would help ease some of my worries over this handsome stranger who has blown into Alton and my life.

On the second ring, he answers—a bit quicker than I was anticipating and I panic when he picks up. "Hey, beautiful."

My mouth parts, unsure of how to respond after that endearment. The pause between us is growing.

"Clara?"

"Uh...hi." My eyes dart frantically around my console, as if I might find some sort of response there while my mind is blank. And here I thought talking to Seth on the phone might be easier than in person.

He can be stunning at times, intimidating at others. It doesn't make me crave him any less.

"Everything alright?" There's some sort of movement on the other end and I listen closely, but can't decipher what it is.

"Just on my lunch break." *And can't stop thinking about you.* "A-are you sure there's nothing I can do to contribute to tonight?"

"Well, now that you mention it…" There's more maneuvering of some sort and a small grunt from him. "I could use your expertise on where to get groceries from. Who's got the best meat?"

You do.

Oh my God, Clara!

I slap a hand to my forehead, glad that Seth is miles away from me right now and not able to pick up on how immature I'm being. What am I, back in high school right along with the "your momma" jokes?

"Um…I would say the meat counter at Josten's is really good." There's a long pause and everything goes quiet. "I'm sorry if I disturbed you. I'll let you get back to work."

"No, no. You're fine." More sounds are coming through the phone. and I become curious as to what he's doing. "Sorry, I'm a bit behind on getting my office put together. I took the rest of the day off so I could get this and some grocery shopping accomplished."

"You really don't have to worry about tonight, Seth. It's a nice gesture, really…but—"

"Clara—" The sound of him using my name has me shutting my eyes and tuning into him completely. "Are you alright?"

"Yes." The answer leaves a bit too forcefully. I don't even believe the single-word reply coming out of my mouth. "Maybe."

"Clara…" The sound of my name rolling off of his lips again has me rocking my hips into the seat. "Do you need me?"

In more ways than one.

His lowering tone sends me right back into my bed and our first night together. Our bodies pressed into one another, enjoying what the other has to give. I'm throbbing for him just from the sound of his voice over the phone. The remembrance of the way his touch lit a fire is telling me to turn on the damn van with the air on full blast.

"I'm just looking forward to tonight." My breathing shallows, and I'm pretty sure Seth can hear my heartbeat through the connection on the phone with how loud it sounds in my ears.

"Me too, beautiful, more than you know."

The afternoon passes a bit more quickly.

I receive a text from Julie after school, a small message letting me know she and Emmett made it to the activity center alright. They'll stay there until her practice is over and Joe picks them up. At least, it had better be him and not Chassidy.

My spirits have lifted slightly and I smile as I interact with each person who walks through the door at the dental office, be it a child, parent, or the elderly. I'm lucky enough to finish the day better than it started.

I make a beeline for the exit at closing time, flipping the lights off in the waiting room as I return to collect my belongings and power down my computer. I wave a few goodbyes as I head out the door with a spring in my step. I drop off the mail from work and make a few runs to pay some bills, and the next thing I know I'm speeding down the highway to get home.

This thing with Seth—whatever it is—is giving me something to look forward to. There's little doubt that he will stay the night a third night, and I smile to myself.

Last night was nice. Talking, getting to know one another. We didn't need to have sex to enjoy each other's company. And although I want it to happen again, I'm pleased that the conversation never seemed forced. It flowed naturally, like we were two souls who are on the right track.

It still feels a bit early, though, to be thinking so far ahead. But I can't help it. The possibility of never spending another night alone. The chance at finding love again when I thought I never would.

Pfft. Love. It is *definitely* too early for that.

My mouth twists as I recall the scars on his back. While Seth might not have revealed that information, it's clear that he didn't exactly come from a loving and secure home like I did. Sure, his parents are together like mine, but the way his mood plummets at the mere mention of them causes me to withdraw further questioning. He did divulge that he was bullied for most of his school years until about halfway through high school. Only then did things start to turn around slightly. But I still don't know the extent of that.

There's no sign of Seth or his truck when I arrive home, only the sounds of neighbors mowing their lawns filling in the breezeway as I make my way into the house. I kick off my shoes and make a dash to my bathroom to get out of my work clothes and freshen up. I barely get through brushing my lower teeth when my phone goes off. My eyes widen when I see Seth stating that he's here.

With a quick brush of my upper teeth, I spit and rinse my brush, then fly out of the bathroom like a mad woman and come to a skidding halt at the front door. I try to slow my breath, forcing my frenzied air to calm down as I unlock the door.

Seth has two reusable grocery bags in hand, and he's wearing gray shorts and a tank without the sides ripped out. The broad grin on his face as he looks me over causes me to blush already. I open the door the rest of the way to allow him entry, and he makes his way into the kitchen to set things down.

"Get your home office set up okay?" I place myself on the opposite side of the counter and lean down on my forearms as I watch him begin to take out the contents of the bags. Steaks, seasonings, potatoes, and vegetables. There's some sort of brown box that looks like a dessert, but he's quick to swivel and put it in the fridge before I can decipher what it is.

"I did. Hopefully your day was more exciting."

I scoff. "Not in the slightest. I would have rather spent it with you hooking up a computer. Could have been there for moral support."

"Aw...miss me, did you?" The corner of his lips turns up, his facial hair begging for my touch.

I can feel my face heat further at the mere thought of him between my legs this morning, that enticing mouth of his eating me out to high heaven.

"Guess you could say that." I don't want to sound too desperate. If I didn't need the money so badly, I might have taken the day off just for the hell of it. But on the other hand, I have been stockpiling my vacation time in case of emergencies.

Noting how the mark on his arm has improved dramatically in our time apart, I come around the island, my hand reaching out to touch him.

"Damn, what kind of witchy medical shit do you have? Your arm looks so much better." I shake my head in disbelief that the injury to his arm has healed so much within a short amount of time. Seth shrugs, as if it's nothing. "I told you, it wasn't that bad."

I raise my brow, not buying that. I remember how beaten he looked last night. Even this morning, it still looked sore enough to cause him pain, and it did when I touched his back.

Seth, sensing my skepticism, turns toward me and steps forward. His hand tilts my chin up to make me look into those gorgeous golden eyes. They focus on my lips, and he tugs at my bottom one again. How can he make me want to dissolve into a pile of mush with a single touch? With the intensity of the look on his face, my body is responding. I swallow hard, reflecting on this morning again. Seth never even gave me the chance to return the favor.

An unsteady hand moves toward his shorts, and I hesitantly run it across his thigh until I come to a considerable bulge. The material is thin, granting me enough of a feel of his member hardening beneath.

"Think dinner can wait a few?" I grip him harder, and I swear one of his eyes twitches as his lids lower. My hand is full of him, and that excites me and wracks my nerves as well.

"What did you have in mind?" He pulls at my hips but I step back, drawing him into the dining room by his hands and pulling out a chair for him. I'm not sure I would be able to reach him if I were to get down on my knees.

Seth throws me a quizzical look, and I muster up whatever courage I can find to reach for his waistband. Hooking my fingers into it, I drag his shorts down his muscled thighs before pushing on his chest for him to sit.

His behind no sooner hits the chair when my hand runs down his length, back and forth, and he closes his eyes as his head tips up. His Adam's apple protrudes as he swallows.

His cock is so smooth, large, and my mouth is practically watering as I feel a bit of precum leak from his tip.

I lower to the floor, positioning myself between his legs, and my mouth is on him in mere seconds. My tongue glides over the top, tasting him briefly before plunging him into my mouth. When he hits the back of my throat, his body tightens and a low growl forms in his chest.

Damn, it's sexy as hell to hear a man turned on.

Once I find a rhythm, I go at it. I find way too much joy in the groans coming from him, and it urges me on. I'm not sure when or if

I could ever be as sneaky as him with his little wake-up call for me this morning, so this will have to do.

Seth's hands are on the side of my face, and I draw back on him until I find the crease at the base of his head before looking up into his eyes. Unblinking, I descend down his shaft again, taking him as far back as my throat will allow. I swallow, and his eye twitches again. He's so fucking beautiful that it hurts. How is he so damn delectable?

Seth's hand wraps around at the base of my neck and he starts to take control. I surrender to it, letting him work me how he needs to, and taking it.

Until he grows rougher. The pressure he puts on my neck is building, and each time he hits the back of my throat, it's threatening my gag reflex. I barely have time to recover after each encounter, and the combination of him and my saliva is slowly leaking out of the sides of my mouth. I struggle to keep my eyes open. I want to see him, memorize this vision of him before me, but I'm losing the battle.

Seth becomes more vocal, groaning his appreciation, and as much as I want to try and fight to regain control, I can't deny how hot it is to hear him and the satisfaction he's gaining from it.

I try to cough, but he rams his cock back in and before I know it, I'm choking on his eruption. His cum runs down my throat, the thick coating almost suffocating me when combined with the fullness trapping it back there. Tears are leaking from the corners of my eyes, but all I can do is attempt to swallow over and over again even though I can hardly breathe.

When his hand loosens on my neck, my head shoots back so fast my body can't compensate for the sudden action and I land on my ass, panting and swiping at my mouth with the back of my hand.

Seth flies off of the chair and pins me on the ground, barely allowing me enough time to recover before his mouth is on mine.

"Fuck, Clara," he murmurs as his kisses become more measured. I'm still struggling to breathe and trying to catch up on the air my lungs need, but damn. Sucking him off was even more gratifying than I thought it would be. It was totally worth it.

He leans up, legs on either side of my mine, and he begins to undo my capris. I lift my hips to allow him to draw them down, and while I feel crazy exposed in the light of the dining room, I'm so worked up I almost don't care. He stops dragging them down at my knees and lies beside me, his hand diving in before I can even get a word out to stop him.

Thumb circling my clit, his fingers begin to work in tandem, and I'm quickly throwing my forearm over my mouth to stifle the needy moans that keep leaving my throat.

Seth removes my limb and his face hovers over mine. My face pinches as I attempt not to shoot my uneven breaths into his face.

When my eyes reopen, he's studying me with a positively sinful grin.

"Consider this our foreplay, Clara." He adds another finger, filling my entrance. It pales in comparison to the way his length felt inside the other night, but I still crave it. I whimper as he reacts to my whining, hanging on the noises I make as if he can conduct my body like a symphony. "Tonight I won't stop until you're howling my name."

12

Lose One, Gain Two

Clara

I don't think my body has ever been used this much. Not even on my honeymoon with Joe.

Actually, scratch that. My body *definitely* has never been used to this extent. I hate comparing Seth to Joe, but sadly, it's all I have to go off of. Joe was my first everything—first date, first kiss, and my first when it came to sex. His tastes were...I guess you could say, uninspired and dull.

There was no passion. No needy grasps or calling out of names. With Joe, after he found his release, it was time to shower and go to bed.

Seth peppers me with kisses while keeping himself buried inside of me even after we're both satisfied. And while he's still asking for me to remove my bra or accompany him to the shower, he respects me and my wishes and gives me the space I need.

I wish I was comfortable enough to completely let down my guard like that, and maybe someday I will be. But I still fear that he might go running for the hills if he really *sees* me.

Hell, most days I don't even want to look at the reflection staring back at me. All I can seem to see is what's wrong. I hate that I do that to myself, but at this point in my life, I don't know how to stop. My breasts are most definitely lower than he might suspect, and there are stretch marks on those, my stomach, and other places that I'd rather keep under wraps. My C-section scar is a bit more hidden, but for some reason, that doesn't seem as embarrassing as the stretch marks. Sure, some of them are from bearing children, but not all of them.

Lifting my shirt slightly, I run my fingers over my stomach, gaining a sour face when my skin isn't smooth and blemish free. Quickly, I lower it, discouraged from thoughts of really letting Seth see me.

Parting with him this morning was, dare I say it, a bit difficult. Julie and Emmett will ride the bus home today and the little routine Seth and I have established will be put on pause for the time being. He even offered to come and mow the lawn today while the kids are at school and I'm at work. As much as I wanted to let him, the thought of giving him a key to the garage is the only thing that stopped me.

I don't know why it bothers me, considering I've spent every night with him in my bed this past week. Seth has cooked dinner every night and helped with the housework even though with the kids not home, it's been light. It's still nice, though, having help in the simplest of tasks and without asking. He even took it upon himself to fix the dishwasher with a quick trip to the closest home improvement store. Dare I say it, he's already getting around the house as if he lives there.

Well, except for the upstairs. I declared that off-limits because I know the wreck that awaits in Emmett's room. I already did a sweep to make sure he hadn't snuck any food up there and nabbed any dishes that might have tried to escape to the room of no return. That's going to be task number one for him when he comes home. I'm so excited to have him and Julie back, I'm willing to let them pick dinner tonight and go from there.

There was only one game for Julie to cheer at this week, and one parent meeting for Emmett. Seth never pried or asked to tag along, thankfully, not putting me in a weird position to have to turn him down. His consideration and understanding about my failed marriage and the aftermath I'm still working through is remarkable. And a bit suspicious.

I let out a long sigh as I pull into the garage. As happy as I am that they're coming back for their week with me, I hate to feel like I'm losing something else in return.

As I slip out of the van and swing my purse over my shoulder, the garage door opens to reveal Julie. Her straight hair is pulled back, revealing a worried look that brings all thoughts, good and bad, to a screeching halt.

"Julie, what is it?"

She comes barreling toward me, a sob leaving her lips, and I stumble at her impact. For such a skinny thing, she can certainly throw her body weight into something. The force of her could have knocked me over.

"Julie, honey," I plead as I try to pry her back enough to look her in the face. She hiccups, trying to collect herself enough to talk. "You're scaring me, what's wrong?"

I fear that the worst is about to happen. That my own daughter is going to be the one to tell me that Joe is coming after full custody of the kids, and is intent on ripping them away from me. My mind is on high alert as I struggle to try and keep my expression void of anything but concern until she tells me what in the hell is going on.

This can't be it. Not now. Dear God, please don't do this now.

"It's...Noah." She hiccups again, swiping at her tears that won't give up. "And Dad."

The boy she likes, and her father. Jesus, what the hell happened to warrant this kind of reaction from my little girl?

I set my purse down on the hood of my car and turn my attention back toward her. "Tell me everything."

She sniffles again, trying to clear up her emotions enough to get through whatever she's about to disclose. She starts with the fact that her brother always gets to have friends over to her dad's new home, but whenever she wants to invite someone over—in this case, Noah—Joe puts his foot down. Mags lives in the outskirts of Alton, so seeing her is easy as pie when Julie is with me. Noah, on the other hand, lives closer to Pembrook, and their school is between the two towns.

Julie and Noah go back all the way to first grade. When they were little, they would tell everyone they were married and were the best of friends. They played together at recess, went to each other's birthday parties, and when they were lucky, had the same classrooms. Now that they're in middle school and have about seven different teachers spread out across the three-story building, they hardly get to see each other much, from what I've gathered.

When I was little, I thought boys had cooties. But not Julie. It has only ever been Noah. And when she started becoming interested in boys, her sights never swayed from her childhood best friend. It's been a touchy subject at times, as I know how scared she is to put their relationship in jeopardy by admitting any feelings she has toward him, and while she's thirteen going on fourteen soon enough, I remember just how heavy those emotions were at her age.

Noah has never given me any cause for concern. His parents, a teacher and a mechanic, are great people. They pride themselves on their five children and the young man that Noah is becoming.

"He won't let me hang out with him at all. I know the rules. Door stays open. Parents have to be home. But he doesn't care! He just asks why I can never bring any girls around? Girls are mean, Noah's not!"

I know she meant to exclude Mags from that statement, but I choose not to bring that up. Girls—and grown women, even—can be fucking mean.

I could probably name about ten girls Julie's age who are the best of friends with her one minute and ice-cold the next. It's hard to keep track nowadays of who we're on good terms with, but there are always two constants in her life that never give her any grief—Noah and Mags.

"Hey, hey," I try to soothe her as I pull her into another hug, squeezing her as tight as I can and willing her to feel better. "Listen to me."

Holding her out at arms length, I look into her glassy eyes. "What if you invite Noah over this weekend? You know I don't mind it. We can order pizza. Get you guys your big bag of Skittles. I can hide out in my room and you guys can have the living room."

"You don't have to do that, Mom."

"Yes, I do. I know how much he means to you, and yes, you know the rules. Now, I can't speak for your father and how he chooses to run his house..." It pains me to say that as nicely as I do. "But here, I want my kids to be happy. Noah has never been a problem. And as long as it stays that way, *we* shouldn't have a problem."

"What about Emmett?"

I sigh, knowing how he always tries to butt into whatever his big sister is doing, teasing and trying to embarrass her in front of company. That kid will let out a fart in passing just to get a rise out of you, and burp nonstop until it annoys the hell out of you just to draw your attention away from whatever is going on.

"Well, somehow, he managed to get his grades up over the week, so he gets his electronics back. I'll see if he wants to invite someone over, and if he does, well, we'll go from there."

"Really, Mom?" She blinks at me with hope in her young eyes, her tears finally ceasing as she waits for me to confirm.

"Yes. Now go call Noah and work something out. Other than your practice in the morning, the weekend is free."

She springs across the short distance between us and wraps her arms around my neck. I hug her with a grip equal to her own. Her happiness warms my soul, and when she turns to leave, now with a pep in her step, I take a moment to myself.

Julie is growing up. I knew it was inevitable. She's old enough to know right from wrong, and while most of the time I trust her to make wise decisions, I know that might not always be the case. But for now, it's simply two friends getting to spend time with one another.

Lord help me when Emmett starts hanging out with girls, though. That little sneak is going to be a pain. I just know it.

I snatch my purse and head inside. I'm barely shutting the door behind me when I find my son in the fridge with a jar of pickles wide open, shoving one into his mouth.

My jaw drops slightly and I click it shut. Kicking my shoes off, I observe him munching the pickle faster to try and speak, though he doesn't chew enough before opening his mouth. He gives his glasses a shove. "When did we get pickles? These are good."

We didn't, Seth did. Now my son is eating one of his favorite snacks. I should have known that my youngest with a bottomless stomach would find the pickles, even though I had tried to maneuver the container to the back of the fridge. Did he sniff them out or something?

Seth and I have had dinner together every night since our "date" at the Chinese restaurant, so why wouldn't he have some snacks here?

I insisted, actually, since I didn't know what he liked or wanted. I don't foresee myself going to the grocery store with him anytime soon, so I told him to bring a few things over. Lucky for him, I have an overabundance of free toothbrushes and samples of toothpaste from work, so he has that area covered as well.

I sigh as I let my mouth form into a secretive grin. Guess I'll be getting a replacement of those pickles, seeing as Emmett is going after another, dipping his fingers into the jar.

His hair is growing longer and could use a trim. I'm shocked his father hasn't done it himself. He isn't a fan of men with longer hair. Or facial hair for that matter. He used to shave every morning to make sure he was clean and stubble free for the day. I hated all of the little shavings he left over the sink. He barely even lifted a finger in any sad attempt to clean up his messes.

Nope. That was all for me to deal with.

Seth's beard is neat, though. I admire how it shapes around his face. The way it brushes across my skin and tickles me here and there. How it...

There I go again, spiraling down my obsessive trail about Seth.

The rest of the night moves on quickly. Since we all decide to make homemade pizzas tomorrow instead of ordering, I make the quick trip to town to get some chicken strips and fry baskets, and we devour those with a plethora of different sauces and watch a new movie that's streaming.

Come to find out, they're practically dining out every night with their father, and the thought of making our food tomorrow is more exciting than ordering from their favorite pizza joint. I'm more than happy to oblige, offering to go get what we need from the store while Julie is at practice tomorrow.

Emmett disappears to his room at about nine and offers a nonchalant "goodnight" as he ascends the stairs. I was met with an annoyed groan when I told him his friend Baron can't come over until his room is cleaned and vacuumed, even tipping him off that I'll be getting on my hands and knees to check under his bed and the closet so he doesn't try to stash anything there.

Julie follows about a half hour later, giving me a tight squeeze before she, too, heads up for the night. I'm beginning to turn off lights downstairs when my phone goes off and I snatch it from the couch on my way down the hall. Seeing Seth's name light up on the screen has me shuffling into my room and closing the door quietly.

Kids make it home ok?

I type out a quick reply, asking if he's busy, and as soon as the message says it was read, an incoming video call from him lights up. His face comes into view, oddly similar to the selfie he took on my phone earlier in the week for his contact info. I'm not about to admit how often I've stared at it, studying him in our time spent apart like some lovesick puppy. As much as I want to do the same now to the live video before me, I have to pick it up before I run out of time to answer it.

Tucking my hair behind my ear, I swipe at the screen and sit on my bed, scooting up against the pleated headboard. "Hi."

I offer an awkward wave as I'm met with his comforting smile.

"Hey, beautiful."

I roll my eyes, the corner of my lips moving up with the little nickname he always uses when we call each other. "Yes, they made it home alright. Thank you for checking in."

"Everything good on the Joe front? Do I need to cut the power to his house? Slash his tires?"

"No." I grin, appreciative of the figurative lengths he's willing to go. "Luckily, I didn't have to see or speak to him today, but he still managed to upset Julie. I've got it under control for now, though. Can't say the same for when the kids go back."

Julie's words from last Sunday ring in the back of my mind. Her admission that she wants to live here and not with her dad. My recent fooling around with Seth hasn't been helping in my search for a part-time job somewhere. There has been *zero* job hunting.

I try to keep my voice low, knowing that Emmet's room is practically on top of mine. "Tell me about your day, though. And when can I come see your place?"

Seth lets out a small laugh as he looks down and back up again. The camera moves when he does, showing off his bare shoulders, and I remember riding on top of him and how my hands dug into them. They were so firm and tight and—

"I think I should get the rest of my things sorted out this weekend. When you're ready, just say the word and I'll bring you over. Just know, it's nothing compared to your place. I tend to pack really light on my moves and it's kind of bare."

"I don't care." I shrug even though I'm pretty sure he can't see it. "It would be nice to see your place for a change." I pause for a beat, then keep going. "It's kind of strange, though, being apart tonight. The kids have gone upstairs and I don't know what to do with myself right now. Thoughts are racing too fast to read, not enough focus to try and watch something."

There's an energy to expend since sex has practically been a nightly thing for us now. Well, except for the night he showed up injured.

"What are you in the mood for?" His voice dips down, deepening and speaking in that tone that could quickly have me melting into a puddle. I seriously don't understand how he does that.

I consider the chance to be bold, or just simply tease him. I ponder my words for a moment while making sure I can still make out the sounds of a game upstairs. For whatever reason, having this barrier of a phone between us has me growing some confidence. "That depends, are you naked?"

I keep my eyes focused on his image on the screen, his face not giving anything away as his chin dips down. "I can be, but what about you?"

A rising urge to strip and continue our call together has me bolting. "Hold that thought."

I lay the phone on the bed, so the camera just reflects the ceiling on its screen. I poke my head out and into the hallway to make sure the coast is clear, and when I close my door, I lock it. I shimmy out of my clothes so fast, depositing them into a heap on the floor, but I pause on my bra.

I guess I'll get to be in control of this, and what Seth sees. I can hide what I want, show him what little I deem fit to be seen. I slip my bra from my shoulders and retrieve my earbuds from my nightstand, plugging them into my ears before resuming my position on the bed. At the last second, I pull the blue sheet up and around my chest, tucking it in under my arms.

On a giant inhale, I finally muster up enough courage to pick the phone back up.

"Is it weird that I miss you?" I confess, feeling a bit shy about saying it out loud.

"Not at all. I would much rather be sitting next to you." His eyes are searching his phone screen, as if they're trying to decipher what lies on the other side of it.

"Touching you instead of touching myself." His words in my ears stall my breath for a beat, and my hand wavers, showing off my naked shoulder.

"Lean back, Clara." Seth's commanding voice has me doing just that. I slink against the headboard, my back curving as I do.

My heart is beating faster, my blood already pumping and Seth isn't even here. "Now what?"

I await further instruction, studying his face, and I can't decide if I want to focus on his mesmerizing eyes or those delicious lips.

"Part your legs for me."

My feet separate, sliding across the mattress, and even though I'm covered, I shiver. It could be from the central air that's kicked on, but I don't think that's to blame.

"Answer me something, Clara." My name on his tongue shouldn't sound so damn sexy. "When you're by yourself, do you come with your own fingers or with a toy?"

My face lights on fire. I'm sure the shock of his question is more than evident in my expression, but I can't bring myself to look at my image in that little box on my screen. I open my mouth to speak, but nothing comes out, and even though I can't exactly look him in the eyes, my gaze leaves the phone.

"Clara." He growls my name into my earbuds and my eyes close, enjoying the rough sound a bit too much but also nervous that if I don't comply, there won't be anything stopping him from coming over. While I do want him here, I don't want to chance any encounters with him and kids just yet. That, and, if he has his way with me, I don't think there is any way humanly possible to stay quiet. When it comes to anything sexual with this man, I am anything but noiseless.

"A toy," I say, blushing at the admission. Joe thought sex toys were dumb and that I shouldn't have any need for them. Little does he know, I got more action with my vibrator friends than I ever got with him. During this past week with Seth, the "O" machines in my nightstand have never even crossed my mind. Seth knows how to take care of me, that's for sure.

"Get it out and show it to me."

For whatever godforsaken reason, my mouth runs away from me and I look back at his face on my phone. "Which one?"

His jaw tightens and his eyes close. His reaction has me internally grinning to myself. Bet he didn't see that coming.

"Something...clitoral?" He pinches the bridge of his nose and I bite my bottom lip. I have about three of those. One that's super quiet, leading up to the most powerful one that would probably have me reaching an orgasm in about thirty seconds with Seth on the phone.

"Oddly specific for a guy, but yes."

When he reopens his eyes, it's like they're staring into my soul with their severity. "I don't want anything inside you besides my cock."

My mouth dries up like the Sahara Desert and I know more color is creeping up and into my face. I would much rather it be him, too. But that would be playing a dangerous game right now.

I don't know why I push to tease him some more. I don't recognize this side of me coming out to play. "Too bad." I pout. "There's a blue one that has a penetration feature."

"Fuck," Seth mutters, and I have to turn my face away to stifle my amusement. "You either grab something or I'm coming over there and climbing in your bedroom window."

I shoot him an incredulous look. "You wouldn't."

"Don't tempt me," he warns. I try to swallow, but fail.

Setting my phone down again, I fumble in my nightstand to locate one that I think might suffice for Seth's...request. Settling on a light pink vibrator that fits in the palm of my hand quite nicely, I return to my stance on the bed and pick up the phone again.

Readjusting my earbuds, I settle on the screen, but now Seth is nowhere to be found. I search the small surface, trying to decipher what's going on as it shows near darkness.

"Seth?"

A light flips on and I'm met with a stark white-and-black bathroom coming into view. It's so clean, harboring just the bare necessities that one might need as if staying in a hotel. And when Seth comes into view at the mirror above the sink, my stomach is doing flip-flops.

His naked frame is almost on full display for me, and the camera is angled just right to show off his hand on his very prominent erection as he strokes it back and forth. Once. Twice. Slow movements of his hand that have me clenching my thighs together at the mere remembrance of what it feels like for that very thing to enter me.

If he thinks he's getting a camera view of my toy at work, he is sorely mistaken.

"Be a good girl and turn your toy on. I don't want to come without you."

Well, fuck me.

It's on the tip of my tongue to remind him that I'm a woman in my early thirties, but damn, if that isn't one of the hottest things he's ever said to me. I am out of my freaking mind.

This is not how I thought things were going to go on my first night without Seth staying over. My breaths are so miniscule it's making my chest ache as I dip a hand down beneath the sheet, toy at the ready. I hold the button down until the vibrations come alive.

It feels like I'm watching a porno and Seth is the one and only star of the show. His immaculate frame fills the screen, the light from above shining down on his shoulders and making his muscular upper half appear larger.

He pumps his cock again, and a groan fills my ears with the sweet sound of him. I place the toy on my clit, and my breath hitches as it makes contact, my body beginning to hum along to the sound of the little tool that goes to work on me.

I struggle to hold the phone to my face. My motions soon became choppy. While I want to focus on the act of Seth stroking himself, and damn, is that a hot sight to see, the rising need to rock against my vibrator has me moving too much.

Seth remains poised, giving himself a few slow strokes before beating it off hard a few times and then finding a steady rhythm again. It's similar to how I fisted him a few nights ago, keeping him guessing on what would come next.

I want to reach through the phone and touch him. Want to wrap my hand around that cock and curl my fingers around it. I want to stick it in my mouth like I did at the damn dinner table and work him over. But I have to say, watching him do this with his own hand is an erotic sight that's pushing me higher on the hill with my little pink friend.

"Seth," I pant, trying to remember to stay quiet. But the sounds of him are filling my ears and drowning out whatever noises I'm making. Air is entering and leaving my lungs quicker now as I circle the toy around. My mouth drops, unable to stay shut any longer.

"I'm going to fill that mouth again," he bites out between pumps.

It's a promise I know he will make good on, and I look forward to it. "I...want...that."

"Shhhh..." he tries to silence me, but his need is overpowering him as well. His voice is growing louder, grittier as he pushes himself, and I so desperately want to be there for his impending orgasm. "How quiet can you come for me, Clara?"

"I..." My vision wants to betray me as I climb higher. I squint, face pinching as I try to fight off the rising need to become vocal. "Seth...I..."

"I know, beautiful. Come for me, now!" His bark sends me over the edge, pushing me off the cliff that I had quickly risen to. My body spasms as I snap my mouth shut, trying to fight off the moans that want to erupt in the wake of my orgasm.

I whimper as I turn the toy off, hips rocking along with the waves of the aftermath.

"That's it, beautiful, yes," he hisses as he jerks himself off more fervently. When I reopen my eyes, I find him shooting his cum onto the white countertop, the arm that holds the camera faltering as he finds his release and his back bends. The muscles in his abdomen tighten with each breath, the lines and divots from his heaves showing off the beast of a man that he is.

This man is dangerously irresistible. His golden hues somehow manage to sweep my breath away in the camera. A recognizable hunger, more than evident. But it isn't enough to sway me from the crash afterward.

Embarrassment begins to seep through as the realization of what just happened sinks in. I close my legs and curl up onto my side, a bit flustered and confused by what just transpired.

The earbud on my opposite ear falls out as I turn, taking in the sight of Seth's aftermath as his face fills the screen again.

"Clara," he hums. There's a softness to his voice now, the comforting one he normally uses to help me get to sleep afterward. It's soothing and sweet and...caring. "I don't know if I can stay away from you for a week."

I blink at him, trying to comprehend what he's saying. My negative thoughts and worries begin bombarding my mind now that my earlier high is fading away. I don't want him to stay away, not really. But the thought that the distraction that he is might jeopardize my plans and the future I seek with Julie and Emmett...

It hurts. No, it pains me to think that I have to choose between my newfound happiness with Seth and my children. My kids are everything. And this past week, I did absolutely nothing to try and figure out my money situation in case the worst happens and lawyers get involved again.

I can't let Joe try and use Seth against me. I can't let Seth get in the way and risk losing my kids in the most god-awful way imaginable. I have to get out of this before it goes any further.

But I already know, without a shadow of a doubt, that I am already in too deep.

"I...I have to go." Tears are beginning to well in my eyes and I can't look at the concern that's crossing his face any longer. "Goodnight, Seth."

13

Just My Luck

Seth

I don't know if I fucked things up with that video call, but a large part of me believes that isn't the case. I tried to call Clara back, hell, even texted her, but was just met with a message telling me goodnight.

I've been camped outside in the woods in my wolf form all night, with my sights set on the back of Clara's house. I saw the kids wake and practically race to the living room about half an hour before Clara came into the kitchen. There are a few slivers of windows in the dining room that allow me a narrow view of what's happening inside. Knowing my way around her house by now helps me figure out who's going where and when.

I'm not normally the stalking type, but after Clara hung up with me last night, I couldn't wind myself down. She had been in a good mood, playful even, when we started, but somewhere things went off track. I don't know what I could have done to bring an abrupt change of pace, other than my remark about not being able to wait a week without her.

While it is true, I don't think that would be enough to scare her away. I want her to know that she's wanted. I need her to know how I feel about her. But perhaps I'm still coming on too strong even in my attempts to not do that.

Just as I'm about to take my leave, the back door opens and Clara steps out with her iced coffee in hand. Her legs are bare, and I have little doubt that she's wearing an oversized shirt underneath that black robe of hers. She has about three different robes she likes to rotate through. Were I capable of smiling from ear to ear about how well I'm getting to know her, I would. That is, until I make out her face as she finds my gift.

I had only gone one night without her by my side until last night, and I thought it fitting that she wake up to something that might make her smile. I'm devastated to say it has the opposite effect.

Clara cups a hand over her mouth, her face falling as she scans her backyard and skims right over me in the tree line before making a dash back inside her house. How she managed not to spill her coffee on the way is baffling.

She didn't even touch the rose that lies on her seat outside. The first one, I found tucked in a small vase in her bathroom near her makeup stash. I don't think Clara would take to material gifts so early in our relationship, but I thought flowers wouldn't hurt. Until now.

What the fuck did I do wrong?

Sticking to all fours so I can stay low to the ground, I bolt out of there. My mind is racing faster than my body can carry me as I weave in and around the thick of the trees and toward the highway.

I realize I hadn't been thinking clearly. Crossing a highway in broad daylight never even crossed my mind before now.

Either I shift back and go streaking across the four lanes, or I wait for a lapse in cars and make a break for it. I sit back, calculating my options. Guess my choice of home wasn't the best when it comes to checking up on my mate. Especially in this form.

Knowing I'll be faster on four legs, I wait. And wait. There's finally a break in cars and I dart across the highway like there's a pack of wild animals behind me chomping at my ankles.

Once safely across and buried in the trees again, my mind settles on Clara. Well, I guess I wouldn't say *settles*.

I barely get a whiff of something before a bullet goes buzzing past, landing in a tree on my left. I skid to a stop briefly to discern where it's coming from. There's someone in the distance who reeks of cigarettes and cheap beer, brought to my attention by a shift in the wind.

I have no choice but to take off and alter my route back home. My clothes will be of no use to me, as changing back would probably give this hunter a chance to catch up. I can stifle the sounds of my agony, but I can't speed up the process it takes to return to my human form.

My feet beat the ground, digging in and undoubtedly leaving tracks behind that might draw concern. Guess I've found a new task for myself today—covering up the damn paw prints I've left behind.

Another bullet whizzes past me and I change course again. I huff out my agitation as I speed up. Whoever this is, they have a decent aim to have gotten so close to me not once now, but twice. I would have thought that the trees around me would be enough cover, but apparently not for this marksman who now has me on his radar.

A clearing comes into view and in it, a decent-sized pond that barely harbors any algae. Strange for it to be out here in the middle of nowhere. I survey the area quickly before making the rash decision to find a moment of safety therein.

Taking in a deep breath, I leap into the water and my furry frame submerges itself. I let out a guttural roar as I will my body to change back. My body comes alive with a scorching fire that overtakes me. Hair begins to shed, and even though I plummeted into the pond that is much deeper than it looks, I can still hear the sounds of my body snapping and reshaping itself into its smaller frame. I struggle not to gasp for air, knowing that I'll drown myself if I do, twisting and thrashing around as much as the pond's resistance allows.

Above me, the water's surface begins to appear, and I hold my hand in front of me, barely able to witness my claws retracting along with my shrinking extremities.

Head pounding and quickly losing oxygen, I push myself harder and reach the surface just as the sound of a gun goes off. I flinch as birds take flight from their trees and I begin checking my body for any signs of injury that may not be registering yet while I gulp for air.

When I look back to the point from which I jumped into the water, an older man stands at the ledge, shotgun in hand and a cigarette hanging out of his mouth. A fresh one, judging by its length. He wears a tattered red flannel shirt, torn jeans, and boots that are covered in muck from trudging through God knows what. Looking at his unkempt hair that's obviously overgrown and greasy, I think that the man needs a fucking dip in this pond more than I did.

The gun doesn't scare me at this point, even though it's been fired at me a few times now. The last, seeing as how I'm unmarked, must have been fired into the air as a warning shot. What is more unnerving is that I have just stepped foot into another wolf's territory.

"You lost, young man?" The cigarette between his lips bobs as his Southern accent becomes evident. It doesn't fit with how everyone else speaks around here.

I stay put, waiting in the water until I can figure out if this stranger means me any true harm. No wonder he has such good aim. The bastard knows what he's dealing with. For someone who's a smoker and probably inching toward fifty if I had to guess, I'm surprised that he was able to keep up with me long enough to take those shots.

"Yer trespassin'." His face remains emotionless and I honestly have no idea which way this will go.

"I'm sorry, sir. It won't happen again," I try to reassure him, but his face remains unchanged.

"You must be that new boy that moved into Harold's place."

Of course he knows who my landlord is. And the thought of this man aging me down is picking on nerves that I would rather leave alone. I have done a lot of growing up—too much, in fact, to be considered a fucking boy to him.

"I am," I respond clearly. "I'm renting it—"

"I don't want any trouble," he's quick to cut me off. "This *town* doesn't need any trouble."

"That's the last thing on my mind, I can assure you."

He tips the barrel of his gun in my direction, and on reflex, I hold my hands up in defense as something swims past my toes.

"Then why in the hell are you out here in broad daylight? Do you have a death wish?"

Absolutely fucking not. "With you on the other end of that gun, apparently."

There's a moment where everything falls silent and our eyes connect. An unspoken argument forms between the two of us although our voices are nonexistent.

Even through my tussle with my cousin that carried itself into the woods, I never picked up on the scent of another wolf. Now that I think about it, what I smelled was those damn cigarettes he's lighting up. Guess I have a neighbor closer than I thought. One who I will regretfully have to tread lightly around.

It's probably safe to assume neither of us wants any trouble. Especially since unbeknownst to him, I am going to be around for a long, long time. I will never move again unless Clara makes the decision to do so—if she ever does. If she wants to live out the rest of her life in that house, I will be by her side.

When the man is taking too long to decide, I lower my hands back down and offer a bit more of an explanation without giving too much. "I was concerned for a friend of mine and was checking in. I planned on getting back before sunrise but stupidly, as you can see, I didn't."

His eyes narrow, the blue of them hardly visible from my position and the sun taking over the sky. "Anyone else livin' with ya?"

I shake my head in denial right away.

"Then who else was there? I'm not stupid."

For fuck's sake. "An unwelcome somebody paid me a visit. He won't be a problem. He's already gone."

He snorts, a puff of smoke leaving his mouth. "You boys sure tore up some ground. Not sure I believe ya."

"I didn't say it was a pleasant visit." I keep my tone stern but try to hide my frustration with this ongoing conversation.

I need to get home. I have to check my phone to see if Clara has reached out. This delay is quickly eating away at me, and an odd stench that has begun to emit from this pond is urging me to scald my skin in hot and soapy water. The longer I float in it, the worse the smell becomes.

"Look, I apologize for any inconvenience. It was not my intention to cause you any upset, and I will be more careful."

Finding another wolf practically in my backyard was certainly not high on my list of probable worries, but it's quickly escalating there. I've been so focused, blindsided by finding my mate, that I haven't even mapped out the area and figured out routes and such for the next full moon, which is only a few nights away. What I fear now is that the wolf before me might have a pack.

They could either want me to join them, kill me if they deem me some sort of threat, or try to run me off. None of which fit into my agenda. It might be slim, but there is a chance that this man is a lone wolf of his own. If that's the case, perhaps we could choose to coexist and pretend we know nothing of one another.

After all my time moving around the country, what are the chances that in the small town of Alton I find my mate *and* a fucking werewolf?

Perhaps I was better off sticking to bigger cities all this time. But regardless, nothing is going to take me away from my Rose now that she's in the picture. Clara needs me. And dammit, I need her, too.

"If you'd kindly lower your gun, I will gladly get out of your hair and off of your property."

The man's eyes narrow more as ash falls from the end of his cigarette. My patience is wearing thin, waiting for him to decide whatever the fuck he's going to do.

When the gun finally lowers, I begin swimming to the nearest bank on my right.

"Yer naked," the man states. Knowing that he can't see my face, I give the biggest eye roll of my life.

Coming from a big family, I had to get comfortable with the naked body pretty early on. Hell, before my first change I was witnessing family members stripping and transforming, returning from runs in nothing more than their birthday suits. Now, getting used to my own body and exposing it to others, that did take some time.

Once I went through my first change and started working out on the regular, gaining muscle and surpassing others in my physique, I became more confident. I was no longer the overweight kid, and once I knew how to throw a punch, take a hit, and defend myself, I wasn't the laughingstock anymore. I knew what my body could do and how much it could take.

Being naked around this man? Worse has happened, even if he did hold me at gunpoint.

The odor coming off of me is repulsive as I exit the pond. The dirty water is going to sting my nostrils all the way home, that I'm sure of. I swivel and note how the man has been lingering on my form, pushing away my irritation at him doing so as I begin to take my leave.

The grass beneath my bare feet is overgrown as I traipse through it. It doesn't bother me so much when I'm in my wolf form, but now that my sensitive skin is exposed, I don't like the feel of it.

"This is a good town," the man calls after me as I begin my departure, careful to listen to any sounds that indicate he might change his mind about my release and put a bullet in me. "Good people."

To anyone else, this man might come off as a protector of sorts. But there's an edge to his Southern tone that leads me to believe that there's more, and I don't like not knowing the man who threatened me with his own gun. Before coming to this town, I always made it a priority to try and figure out property lines and so forth, though I only knew what was visible on the county assessor's website. I have the impression that this man's claim to the land behind my rental property is more than what I was initially led to believe.

I rushed into the decision to move here. I didn't do my due diligence, the research I normally undergo before settling somewhere. And once I was here, everything became about Clara. I was practically setting myself up for failure.

The man's hands are still on his shotgun as I turn to face him. He's ready to take aim should the situation present itself. "I know you have no reason to believe me, but I mean no harm or ill will toward the people of Alton." Joe lives in Pembrook now, so he is excluded from my remark. "Again, I apologize for my intrusion. It won't happen again."

We study each other for a beat, and thankfully, his eyes remain fixed on my face. I can't say the same for my backside as he nods slowly and I leave the man behind and begin to make my way through the woods.

His scent becomes more faint in the direction I take. My eyes and ears would be better if I wasn't in my human state, but I can't risk coming across anyone else. I would rather someone catch me naked and fumbling through the trees, and lead them to believe it was a drunken accident. I have used that excuse before, and if I have to use it again, so be it. I won't lose any sleep over it.

Before long, I'm at the tree line, and I have to hang back a bit to keep cover from the road that draws closer before it stretches out and away from me again. The rear end of my rental home comes into view, and I let out a sigh of relief that I made it back, even with my interruption.

I scan the area for any sights or sounds of life, and when I detect nothing of importance, I dart out from the trees and to the back door.

A key is stored in a little Ziploc bag behind one of the rose bushes, and I sift through the sun-bleached mulch to find it. A thorn drags across my forearm and I grunt, frustrated by how wrong everything is going right now. My hand shakes as I retrieve the key and head for the door, eager to get to my phone.

I'm a mess from head to toe as I stumble into the kitchen and slam the door closed, the blinds clashing against it. My hair is all ratty, my feet are covered in earth, and I smell horrid, but that doesn't stop me from nabbing my phone from its charger and checking for any calls or messages.

But there's nothing from Clara.

Zero texts, but two missed calls and one voicemail from someone else. The area code from the number glues me to the floor that I stand on.

While I'm distraught that none of them are from my mate, I'm growing more and more perturbed about the family that just won't fucking leave me alone.

Tapping on my voicemail, I put it on speaker phone and listen to a voice that I would recognize anywhere, even if it has aged a bit since I last heard it. I can tell by the message that it was planned out, each phrase meticulously chosen and spoken with emotion meant to stir something in me. It's the end that finally tugs at some strings I thought were long gone.

"It's time to come home, Seth. Please, please come home."

I want to believe that the whole message was planned. That it was all a part of a ruse to get me back when Carter failed. But there's a break in her voice on that last word, a crack that opens something painful inside of me.

Home.

I can't bear to listen to it again. I can't hear my mother calling me to come back to the one place I swore I would never visit again.

My mood falls somber as I place my phone on the counter and head toward the bathroom. It's like I'm having an out-of-body experience, not really present in my frame that stalks into the shower and turns the knob until it's as far to the left as it will go.

The water burns as I step beneath it and I hiss, bringing me back into my body and reality. A scorching blaze is erupting on the back of my neck, beating on me relentlessly as I try to concentrate on the anger and suppressed memories that threatens to rear its ugly head.

I guess letting my cousin live was a mistake, providing him and my mother with a false sense of hope. I hadn't wanted to kill Carter, to leave his wife a widow and his possible children fatherless. I thought I had done him a favor, but now in hindsight, I realize it had probably given them the wrong idea.

Alton is my home now. Clara is my purpose. My world revolves around her and everything she holds dear.

And I'll be damned if I let anything or anyone interfere with that.

14

Radio Silent Isn't an Option

Seth

Clara has left me in the dark. A place I don't want to be, but I'm forced into when I know her kids are present.

My last call to her was on Saturday night. Nothing. The last text I sent, Sunday night, but no reply of any sort once again. The days are now blurring together. It feels like the earth has fallen off its axis and I'm free-falling. I don't know which way to go from here and it makes me sick to my stomach. It's now fucking Sunday again and my Rose has left me without any kind of explanation.

I can't focus on work. I've missed meetings and an important deadline that caused me to get a written warning for the first time ever with my job. Clara hasn't posted anything to any kind of social media channel either, and it feels like she's tortuously ripping me out of her life.

And thanks to the voicemail from my mother, I began doing something I swore I would never do—stalking everyone that I could within our family. It was a shitty attempt to try and keep my mind busy and prevent me from hiding out behind Clara's house, which I've been doing more than I care to admit.

Sure enough, Carter has a wife and four children now. My ex-fiancée has the same amount of kids, and going off of the picture-perfect and pristine family pictures she puts online, it looks like she's trying too hard to convince everyone else that she's happy. I, however, am not buying it.

The family I never really felt like I belonged to has grown so much in my time away. They're practically strangers to me now. And it isn't until I see my father in a wheelchair, with my mother behind him, that Carter's news comes up front and center.

My parents are almost white and gray now, with wrinkles that I don't remember and more frail than I would have expected. They were never known for any displays of affection, and yet in this photo I'm fixating on from Thanksgiving of last year, my mom's hand lies on my dad's shoulder, and his hand is covering hers.

He looks sick. Eyes sunken in and hair thinning with a receding hairline. Scruff on his face and a forced smile while his body is being whittled away to nothing more than bones.

My mother, on the other hand, looks exhausted. You can see it in her eyes, but her posture remains prim and proper. She has stopped dyeing her hair and wears it much shorter than I can recall her doing.

Together, though, they're beginning to show their age. *Good riddance.*

Slamming the lid of my laptop a bit too harshly, I toss it to the side of me on the couch and bury my face in my hands. My mother hasn't tried to contact me again after that voicemail, and it has done more mental damage to me than I thought it would.

My father can't hurt me anymore. My mother can't stand by and watch without saying a word. My so-called *family* turned their backs and pretended not to see the battered and bruised young boy who wanted nothing more than for it all to stop—the terror, the suffering, the longing for someone to put me out of my misery because maybe then I could finally get some rest.

So why am I curious about the family I've written off? Why am I diving down this dark path and seeking out what information I can find on my past life and those in it? I am losing my fucking mind.

I shoot daggers at my phone, glaring at the time as it changes.

Clara's kids should be long gone by now, and I could probably make it to her house in less than ten minutes on my own two feet. I haven't left her any more roses for fear of her last reaction happening again, but that hasn't stopped me from lurking in the trees every night, making sure she's home safe and sound and that nothing is amiss.

I won't text or call to give her the heads-up that I'm coming. It would give her the chance to lock up or worse, to run away.

Damn, I hope it never, ever comes to that.

The temperatures have decided to dip down in the evenings this week and into the fifties. October is here, bringing in changing leaves and dropping humidity. The townspeople are already putting out Halloween decorations and some are even placing uncarved pumpkins on their porches. I'm a bit surprised by how many are getting involved with the upcoming holiday.

Except for the guy sitting in his driveway, who I think still wants to shoot me. Him, and my neighbor who I haven't had the pleasure of coming face-to-face with again since our meeting at the pond. Larson Weils, as I found by his property records, is practically living off the grid as well as he can. He's a mystery of his own that's both intriguing and frustrating as hell. Even with my scouring of the internet, his trail has only led to the house and an obituary for a wife who died some time ago. Even that was lacking in information.

Eager to run, knowing it will bring up my body heat, I take off. I don't know how long I'll camp out in the woods behind her house if

I stay out there again. I dress in some black sweats and a dark hoodie, trying to keep myself hidden as best as I can.

I have found multiple routes that allow me to stay out of sight, and I've found out which houses have outdoor pets to avoid and where to dodge streetlights. I know I look suspicious, so I have to stay out of the eyes of the people of Alton as best I can. If I were really out for exercise, I would have a bright shirt on to alert others of my presence, but I don't want any attention. No one is to know of my comings and goings to Clara's house. Her being on a dead-end road, with a forest behind her, works to my advantage.

As I near the back of her home, I grow more cautious. There's a glow illuminating the back porch, and my steps become more hesitant the closer I get. What I didn't anticipate is Clara sitting in her chair, all wrapped up in a plush gray blanket.

My heart aches for her as I observe. The woman has taken up residence in every fiber of my being. She is rooted into my DNA at this point, and our separation is only hurting me more.

I remain at enough of a distance to stay out of sight, and crouch down. She is still as she stares ahead and to my right. Just her and her thoughts in the night, alone.

At least, that's what she might think.

I want a closer look, and I survey the surrounding darkness. I have to tread carefully so I don't cause any unnecessary noise and spook her.

An audible sniffle can be heard, and when a hand of hers emerges from the blanket, she swipes away at her face. In that one move and sound, all of my struggles over my past life come to a screeching halt and vanish as I focus on her.

Why is she sitting out here all alone? I could be comforting her, taking care of her, *loving* her. She shouldn't even have to ask it of me.

Drawing my already silenced phone out of my pocket, I curve my free arm around it to dampen the brightness so I can type out a text to her. I only hope that she has hers nearby.

> Is it weird that I miss you?

Using the very words she spoke to me not so long ago, I press send. I don't want to focus on my problems, and I want to see if this might open the door for her to talk. And if she doesn't want to do that, I would gladly just hold her until her spirits lift, until she is ready to confide in me. That is, if she would let me.

Time ticks on at an agonizingly slow pace. Trying to make myself comfy in my spot is pointless. Being so close to Clara without being able to talk or touch is almost worse than my message being left unread. I assume she left her phone inside, and that makes me feel even worse—that she wants to be alone and not let anyone reach her. Until the blanket around her loosens and her phone-filled hand comes into view.

I lean forward and onto my knees, trying to catch a closer look as she studies her device. The urge to bolt from the trees and come skidding down in front of her becomes prominent. It's so clear that something is wrong, given her almost catatonic and statue-like state. The casual swiping of tears that I can't see from here is chipping away at my heart.

A quick glimpse of her thumb moving across her screen has me rising to my feet, an anticipation building and the hope that she won't full-out shut me down. If she does, I will be showing up at her front door. She can't do that to me. To us.

There's a short buzz in my front pocket and I draw out my phone again, looking at the message notification.

I can't do this anymore.

My thumb flies over my screen and I hit send a bit too forcefully.

What exactly are you referring to?

Pressing the screen to my chest to smother the soft glow, I can hear a sob leave her throat before she swipes at both eyes again. I brace myself against the nearest tree with my free hand. The stretch of time it takes for her to respond is testing my ability to remain unseen. She wouldn't be able to pull this crap if I was standing before her.

No. She's attempting to take the easy way out.

My phone buzzes again and I pause a beat, trying to prepare for the response awaiting me. I'm not sure what has gotten into Clara. Whether it was my doing or not, I am sure as hell going to find out.

This. Us. Whatever it is. I'm sorry, Seth.

My eyes close, the sound of another sob racking my ears. I'm not angry with her, just confused as hell. She owes me an explanation, and I highly doubt she has one good enough, seeing as how she thinks she can escape me by phone.

There are words clouding my mind in a jumbled mess. Replies that would come off the wrong way if they aren't coming directly from my mouth. Text messages are so dull and lifeless compared to the emotion needed for the conversation that we need to have.

I'm not going to give her the chance to run and hide from me. I will stare into those beautiful brown eyes and coax the truth out of her. If trying to cut things off with me is bringing her this kind of sorrowful reaction, there has to be a reason. She's scared of something. *Running* from something. And I have the sneaking suspicion that it's not solely about me.

Thumb skating across letters, I give her a short window to announce my arrival.

I'm coming over.

Pressing send, I put my phone in my pocket. Even if she texts me back, nothing will persuade me otherwise. I'll wait a couple of minutes before I leave my hiding spot. I will beg and plead through the front door if she doesn't let me in right away. I have all night, and I would gladly wait.

I know the moment she reads my message because her back straightens and the blanket falls from her shoulders. She stands from the chair, the rocking hitting against the back of her legs. Snatching her blanket and rushing inside, she turns off the porch light. It allows me the darkness I need to come out of hiding.

A flash of her brown hair crosses the narrow window as I enter the grassy plane of her backyard. I choose to use the breezeway between the garage and house in the hopes of thwarting any escape attempt, should she try. Now that I'm on the pavement, my steps become quieter. There's a motion sensor that I set off on my way through, but I carry on, careful to listen to any indication that Clara might be coming this way.

The path turns and leads me toward the front of the house. The lights from behind and the front porch are now the only things providing any kind of illumination.

Pulling the hood off of my head, I make my way up the composite steps that lead me to her doorstep. I'm caught off guard when the camera above her doorway is missing, and I fixate on it. Nothing but a cord remains in its place. Like it was ripped from its home, severing it from the base.

Not bothering with sending her a text, I knock on the door and call out her name. I try to hide the urgency in my voice, masking it with concern.

My body responds as she looms near. Clara moves in closer behind the door and I swear the hair on my arms stands on end in anticipation. My heart rate spikes, recognizing her presence and longing for her scent to fill me up.

"Clara, please. Talk to me." I raise my voice enough to make her think that I'm not aware that she's so close.

We wait there, and as much as it pains me, I remain patient. I stuff my hands in the pocket of my sweater and lean up against the wall of the porch, staring up at the darkened sky above. "I'll wait."

I will give her all night if I have to, as much as that isn't what I want to do. I push off of the vinyl siding and lie down on the porch, feet toward the door so I can get a better look at the blackened abyss above, dotted with stars. If I'm intimidating her, perhaps this will put her mind at ease, even if just a little.

Time stands still, but this deck is unforgiving on my back. I crack my neck before drawing my arms up and behind it to give my head a rest from the planks below me. I'd better try to get comfy if I'm going to wait for Clara to come to me. She needs to do so on her own terms, and when she's ready. As much as I loathe waiting, I feel that it's the right thing to do instead of hovering and acting like the big bad wolf.

I grin to myself as I think about that children's story.

That wolf and I might not be so different. I practically blew in weeks ago and claimed Clara. An unforgiving storm of power swept me through her door and devoured her. Had the wolf in that story found his mate, oh how things would have taken a turn.

My body goes rigid as I hear the click of the deadbolt. I keep my face calm and collected as the knob turns. I refrain from shooting up and racing to her side. I remain silent and still. She will come to me, I know it. My Rose is almost ready.

"What are you doing?" Her voice is small, barely reaching my ears but still pleasant to hear. There is a tensity in my muscles that begins to dissolve just from hearing her speak.

"Waiting for you to let me in." Into your home, your mind, and your heart. I've got nothing but time.

"Seth...I..."

The tremor in her voice is almost enough to shake me loose and make me go after her, scoop her up into my arms and reassure her that she is strong and she can conquer whatever is troubling her. And I'll be by her side every step of the way.

"Isn't it cold out here?" Her voice becomes clearer as she steps out of the door and draws closer to my feet.

I shrug, still gazing at the sky above. "I've got a sweater."

My body begins to panic without my permission as she disappears from view beneath me and I hear the door click shut. I fear that she has left me out here on my own, but then her blanket-wrapped body comes back into view and she lies down beside me. Her body, too many inches away.

Let her take the lead, I repeat to myself, over and over like a mantra as I hold off a little longer. And it works.

"I can't do this. I can't keep doing whatever it is that we're doing."

"Getting to know each other?" I press lightly.

The night air is growing colder the longer I stay still. The black cover overhead feels like it's stretching on into eternity, while at the same time threatening to swallow me up if Clara keeps going like this.

"I have to think about my kids, Seth."

"I've never asked you not to. I know you're a mother. I know how much they mean to you. I haven't even met them yet, but the way you talk about them, the stories you tell and the way your face lights up at the mention of either of them…" I blow out a long breath. "I only hope I get the honor of meeting them someday."

Her breath catches, enough to drag my gaze and turn my head to look at her. Tears are streaking down the side of her face, a trail forming for new tears to fall faster. Her nose is a little pink and the skin around her eyes is splotchy. Either she's removed her makeup or she's rubbed it all off by now. In her sadness, she is still captivating, even if it hurts me to see her like this.

"You don't understand," she chokes, her voice straining to hold it together.

I prop myself up onto my forearm to get her to focus on me. "Then help me understand."

"But why?" She sits up, hugging the blanket in close as if it's going to help keep a barrier between us, like an imaginary wall she's trying to construct. "Why do you even want anything to do with me? We only met last month. I don't even belong with someone like you in the first place."

Whoa, curveball.

"According to who? To you?" I'm almost offended. Is this really Clara talking or is somebody else putting this idea in her head?

Her gaze shoots to mine and lands briefly, before it darts away again.

"Clara," I urge her. "Did someone say something? *Do* something?" My attention shifts up to the camera that's been ripped from its place, and she follows. Her shoulders sag before she hugs the blanket tighter, uncomfortable.

"You're going to think I'm an idiot." Her lips thin as she focuses on something in her mind. "I *am* an idiot."

"Tell me." My mood is spiraling downward as I wait for some fucking explanation as to why Clara is trying to end things with me. Why a camera has been torn down from outside her door.

"Joe knows about you."

I take a second to mull that over. I can see how that's cause for concern for Clara. Especially considering she was keeping us on the down-low. While I'm ready to ditch everything and jump into a life with her, due to the bond she knows absolutely nothing about, in her mind we have only known each other for a couple of weeks. It's no wonder she's so skeptical of me. Of us.

But fucking Joe? I know he's an asshole, but I'm not scared of him. Is he using this newfound knowledge of me to try and take the kids? How is it that he could cheat in their marriage but not allow Clara the chance at being with someone new now that they're divorced?

"What do you want me to do?"

"You need to leave me alone." Her voice betrays her as she raises it. She is pissed, and rightfully so. But I'm not the one deserving of her anger. "I can't...I had a plan. I *have* a plan, but I can't do it with you in the picture."

Just tear my fucking heart out of my damn chest. She can't mean it. I refuse to believe it.

"I can't have everything, Seth. Life would never be that kind to me. I'm barely making ends meet. Even though I refinanced the house to a thirty-year mortgage, the monthly payment and taxes eat up a lot of my income. I need to find another job so I can start putting money away in case Joe tries to drag me back to court. He's made it blatantly obvious that I don't have the means to beat him when it comes to money. There is no way I'll let that bastard take my kids away from me simply because he can afford to.

"And, icing on the fucking cake, a front row seat for you as to why I'm a dumbass—it never, *never* once occurred to me that Joe still had access to the damn camera out here. He's been watching you come and go ever since you came into the picture and..."

Clara is shaking. Words, body, and all. Hell, I'm fucking livid for her. I'm trying to bite it down and hide it, but I know my eyes are alive with a vivid fury.

Joe had no right. What a fucking piece of garbage.

"And we...Seth, we never made any sense to begin with. We don't belong together, and I don't know what you see in me, but—"

"Don't even finish that fucking thought," I warn her, and her eyes snap to mine and her mouth shuts quickly. "Joe doesn't get to rule your life, not anymore. He doesn't get a say in what you do or who you see."

"Seth, he—"

"I'm not finished." I move closer and her back presses against the wall behind her as I do. "With Joe aside, name one good reason why we don't belong together."

Her mouth parts as her eyes dart to my lips and back up again before she blinks away. There's an answer stirring in her eyes, but she's unable to spit it out. I take hold of her chin and force her to look at me. She tries to resist, and pulls at my wrist to get away, but it doesn't work.

"I'm just a tired mom." She breaks, fresh tears forming as her lashes flutter rapidly. "A tired and out-of-shape mom with trust issues. I don't even remember what it's like to be happy anymore, because the last time I thought I was, it was all a lie. You belong with someone fit and beautiful and desirable." She swallows hard as I carefully examine each word that leaves her mouth, trying to make sense of it all.

"You deserve someone who can run with you. Someone who doesn't binge on food as a coping mechanism. A woman who can pick up and move with you when you decide it's time for a change in scenery."

I release her chin and turn my face away, stricken with the sting of her statements and gutted by how she could possibly talk like this.

"We don't fit, Seth. It could never work between us."

15
The Weight of Words
Clara

I'm not sure if Seth will be angry or relieved that I'm pushing him away. I don't know if I was just a fun game for him while he's here in Alton, a quick conquest or fuck until he decides to move on. Which eventually, he will. I know he stated that he plans on staying here a while, but I don't know what that means to him. A few weeks? Months? His lease is only a year, if I remember correctly. And knowing some of the cities that he's called home in the past, I don't think there's anything of importance in this small town to keep him here.

As much as it hurts to drive him out of my life, lose the one thing that has brought me happiness instead of the loneliness the walls of my home bring in my children's absence, it has to be done.

Seth deserves someone who can keep up with him in every sense of the word. As much as the mere thought of it suffocates me, I know that isn't me.

Joe's snide and harsh remarks about Seth and myself had blindsided me, rocked me so hard that I felt as if I'd been left out in the middle of the ocean with no land or rescue in sight. I felt powerless, useless against Hurricane Joe and the destruction he creates just for hell of it. Because he can.

It fucking makes me sick.

And now here Seth is, inches away from my face after my dismal speech, and I wish I could hear whatever thoughts are going through his head after my words have come to a halt. He's still and silent. The dark hoodie he wears hides the movement his chest might have for breathing. That is, if he's breathing at all.

This could go one of two ways. He could accept the unflattering truth that left my lips and move on with his life. We could go our separate ways, and I will never forget him—I will undoubtedly cling to the memory of him and our short time together. I mean, the sex, the attentiveness, the communication is all stuff you would hope for in a man. I knew it was too good to be true. There's no way in hell I deserve him.

Or, and I don't think that he will, but he could put up some sort of resistance, claim he wants to see where things could go. As much as anyone would love someone like Seth to fight for them, for the chance of being together, I don't believe that will come into play here. Not for me, anyway. I'm not worthy of what he has to offer or give.

For once, Seth's eyes don't hold the candle of brightness in their golden hue. It's almost like they have dropped five shades darker. They've never appeared that color in the confines of my purposely ill-lit bedroom.

The urge to cry in the silence is growing stronger. I am so fucking tired of bawling my eyes out, stressing over every little thing and having no one to confide in about this fling.

I try to rise, and he moves too. I'm actively pushing away at Seth's chest to give me enough room to stand and flee back into my empty house that will swallow me up like a black hole.

Seth's hand reaches out and snatches my wrist. My rising stance falters as he rises with me. And when his focus returns to my gaze, my eyes shoot open. Any trace of wetness in them evaporates when he sets his sights on me. My mouth goes dry too, all thoughts of trying to fight him fleeing away into the night, never to return.

Seth closes in, backing me toward the front door, and my heart begins beating around in my chest like a damn ping-pong ball stuck in a machine. He zeroes in on me, his mood taking a nosedive into something I can't decipher. Something troublesome? Frustration, maybe? But there's a glint of something sparking, rising to life as his facial expression shifts again.

"You're missing something." His low voice isn't threatening, but it puts me on edge not knowing what he's referring to. I thought I was kind of clear. Things are over. They have to be.

Reaching around me, he opens the door, and I step up and over the threshold, still being held hostage by him on my wrist. It's a firm touch, but not one that hurts.

The door slams behind him with a kick of his foot, and I flinch, but his grip tightens ever so slightly. He tears my blanket away with his free hand and gives it a toss to the side.

"Correct me if I'm wrong, but..." He finally releases his hold and draws that arm up beside my head, planting his palm just above it as his face draws close enough that his breath grazes me. He looks almost lethal in the shadows of the hallway. The faint light from the kitchen subtly brightens half of his face, making him look beautiful on one side and sinfully dangerous on the other. He focuses on my lips before he stares into my soul and continues, "Not once did I hear you say that you don't want to see me anymore."

My breath quickens, my chest hitting his with each inhale, and I swear he's growing closer even if I can't see him doing so. I *feel* him caging me in.

"Not once did I hear you say that you don't want me."

I try to blink away. The unease at the severity of his leering state is too much. But Seth is having none of that as he brings me back to face him, his thumb skirting across my bottom lip as he does.

"The day you can convince me that you don't want me, is the day that I'll leave you alone."

Placing a hand on my hip, Seth drives his groin into me. I'm momentarily stunned by his erection. He's so hard I'm brought to my tiptoes in response.

"But that will never happen," he warns, his voice low and gravelly. "Know why, Clara?"

His touch on my hips, now *that* is bruising. His fingers dig in, keeping me in place until one word escapes my mouth, and it sounds weak and pathetic.

"W-why?" My heart is beating so hard beneath his stare that I think I might collapse. But with him pinning me here, I don't think I would make it very far.

An amused grin sweeps across his face as I wait for his answer. Like he knows something that I don't.

This isn't going at all how I expected.

"Because I'm not going anywhere." His head dips down and his lips brush against mine in a small caress. "I will never make you feel unloved or weak." Another light kiss touches my lips, and my eyes close as I focus on the delicate touch when his other hand is so harsh.

"I will never make you feel anything less than desirable." His hips draw back only to roll into me again, and a whimper leaves my lips as gives me another kiss, but this one more firm.

"I get to decide what I consider beautiful, and Clara—" He coaxes my lips open after my name, and my eyes are fluttering open to see him. He could stop hearts, I swear it. Send both men and women to their deathbeds. "Any man who has led you to believe you are anything other than that, doesn't deserve the air you breathe."

I'm struggling to do precisely that. *Breathe.* As much as I'm hanging on every word that leaves him, I can't take in enough air. The walls are closing in, and I feel like I'm going to break under the pressure.

He doesn't mean that. This isn't some fairy tale.

Seth's hand leaves its spot on my hip and he drags it along my side, drawing my shirt up until he can place his hand on my waist. He lays it flat along the side of my stomach, and I squirm against him but I can't go anywhere.

"Your stretch marks show that you've created and given life. Your body tells a story of how you have lived your life thus far. A canvas of all of the fucking wonderful, amazing things that it has done. That *you* have done."

His fingers wrap around to my back and he's driving me forward and off of the wall. My hips press into his and the lack of air in my lungs is growing more and more painful.

"You're so hard on yourself because you haven't had anyone to share your burdens with in so long."

He's right. It's exhausting keeping things bottled up to myself. Tears are streaming down my face and my eyes are wide open with the realization that's setting in. It's too much. *He's* too much.

"I can be that for you, Clara." His lips catch a tear on my cheek as he skims the surface. "Let me be everything you need."

Seth's request pushes me over the edge and I break down. I'm gasping for air as my upper half makes impact with his chest and my exterior breaks into unflattering sobs. A combination of disbelief, awe, and fatigue are all whirling around, and none of them seem able to come to the forefront to be victorious.

In a swift move that catches me off guard and halts my crying, Seth sweeps me into a hold and I cling to his neck in a panic. "Seth—"

"Don't even start." He presses a kiss to my temple and carries me to my bedroom. He doesn't groan or grunt as he does so, but it doesn't do anything for my nerves that he might hurt himself in the process. I've told him before that I'm too heavy for him to do this, and here he is doing it again anyway.

Setting me down on the bed, he tells me to lie down. I'm not in the mood for sex, and judging by his erection that he made me very well aware of, I have every reason to believe that he is.

Seth disappears for a moment, and I tuck my hair behind my ear as I try to sniffle, but my nose is too stuffy. When he returns, he's carrying the gray blanket I was using, and he kicks off his shoes beside the bed before climbing in and draping the cover over us.

A flood of relief surges through me as he settles and I turn away from him, my back to his chest. He readjusts to form around my frame.

His words are too much to process. His presence, too overbearing for me to think straight. But dammit, why is he so adamant to stay? He could have left and I would be binging on cookie dough bites or ice cream until my stomach hurts, lost in the misery of losing him and on my way toward figuring out a life after him. But now?

He is persistent about inserting himself into my life even after I tried to push him away, forcing himself into my home and my heart even though I thought that what I was trying to do was right.

We don't fit, Seth.

My earlier statement comes back, and while I reflect on it briefly, I can't deny that the feel of him behind me is having the exact opposite effect on me.

And it scares me how perfect he feels.

—)●(—

My body is stiff and the side of my face hurts from being smashed into my pillow. I don't think I moved an inch last night, as I'm in the same position and Seth is still holding firm to my waist. I can't make out if he's awake yet, and my phone isn't on my nightstand to get a glimpse at the time. There isn't much light coming in from behind the curtains, and I'm starting to think we'll be getting some rain today after all. You never really know if you can trust the weather forecast around here.

I guess the time doesn't really matter, though. My work is closed today due to a federal holiday. My bosses don't have to close since we aren't in sync with any federal offices, but I think they just like the excuse of getting three-day weekends in occasionally. I'm certainly not going to complain about that.

It doesn't take long for my stress to creep back in. While my memory did a pretty good job of bringing up Seth's words first thing after I awoke, the hope I had in them is short-lived.

I don't deserve him. I don't know what in the hell I did to even rope him in and tie him down. Even if I want to believe that he has an interest in me, that he likes me at all, it doesn't help with my plans to try and get my kids back. Would he really still want me if they were around here full-time?

Seth doesn't know what he's in for. He can't understand what he's getting himself into. Sure, he might have wanted kids at one point in his life, but trading in his freeing lifestyle for a woman and her two children? It still doesn't make sense.

A low rumble sounds at my back and I still. It isn't a snore, but it is a strange occurrence that I haven't experienced with Seth before. I snap a hand over my mouth to suppress the laughter that threatens to spill as it happens once again.

What the fuck would you even call that? A garbled grumble of a bear that's dying in the woods?

When it occurs a third time, I lose it. The hilarity reaches its peak and I can't hold it back any longer. I lean forward, an awkward croak of morning giggles leaving my throat and already putting me in a better mood.

"What? What is it?" Seth sits up behind me and I soon do the same, but I struggle to look him in the eyes as he rubs the sleep away from his face with his thumb and forefinger. The sound of his hands running through his facial hair afterward makes me want to reach forward and tug on it myself.

"It's nothing." I wave my hand as if I can persuade him to drop it. Of course, that won't be the case with him.

"Clara, what's so funny?"

More giggles erupt as I try to figure out how in the heck I'm supposed to describe the sound that just came through his chest.

"Was I snoring or something?" He's growing concerned with my inability to give him an answer.

Another fit of laughter has my face reddening and my cheeks hurting from the strain. "I would *not* call that snoring."

Seth is waking up more and more by the passing seconds. I hate to have awoken him in the first place, but damn, is there any chance that he's aware of the sounds he's capable of when he's sound asleep? Will I be the one doing the honors of informing him of that?

"Clara," he urges, my light and fun mood starting to grow contagious as he presses for more. "What is it?"

I blow out a breath, still trying to recover from my outburst. "I don't know what that was. It wasn't from your nose like a snore, but it wasn't like a growl from your chest either. It's like it got stuck in the middle, and the rumble shook my back."

God, it even sounds ridiculous trying to describe it. I press my lips together as he studies me. The light in his golden eyes has returned.

"Sounds...bizarre. Sure you weren't dreaming?"

I smack my hands on the knees of my folded legs. "I most definitely was not!"

There was no mistaking that. If he starts it again, I'll have to find my phone and record it. I'm not going to be made fun of for hearing something that came out of *him*.

"Hm..." Seth turns pensive and my merriment comes to a brief halt. Snoring is one thing. Making sounds that are reflective of a dream or nightmare is another. This? This is something else entirely.

"I don't suppose you could replicate it for me."

"Absolutely not. I'll save myself the embarrassment." I beam at him. I'm more than eager to try and catch him making that sound again, and I want to see the look on his face when he finally comes to terms with it. A bit childish of me, that I can admit. But hearing something so strange, from this chiseled and muscular man before me, was entertaining. I'd like to think that he won't take it too seriously.

Seth draws closer, my humorous state fleeing as he leans onto all fours and his face is mere inches from mine. I don't think he cares much about personal space. He seems to need to invade mine most of the time, almost like he can't help himself.

Knowing I didn't have the chance to brush my teeth before I fell asleep last night, I'm closing my mouth faster than my next heartbeat.

"How would you like to come see my place today? Keep in mind, it's bare minimum necessities." It isn't fair that he doesn't have morning breath. "Maybe I could take you out for lunch after?"

His eyes are searching mine, and as much as I want to lean forward and kiss him, I can feel myself trying to pull back. While it is intriguing to finally find out where he spends his time away from my house, he hasn't exactly been very forthcoming with information about it either.

"Only if you want to," I start. "We don't have to."

"I want to, Clara." His knuckles brush my cheek and I turn into it, reveling in the small touch.

"You said a lot of things last night." My head dips down, leaving his hold, and his hand returns to the bed to support him in front of me. "I still don't understand why."

"Do we have to understand it if it makes us happy? You...you make me happy, Clara."

A lump starts to form in my throat. With the sincerity of his words and that look on his face, either he's a damn good actor, or he's feeling this to his core. He's making it impossible not to believe him.

"I've been running for so long. Alone for most of my adulthood, and from the moment I first saw you, something clicked into place."

I give him an incredulous look. "Don't tell me it was love at first sight, I swear."

A sly grin crosses his features as he reflects on something before returning to look at me. "I won't say that, I promise. What I will say is that I stand by everything I said last night."

My heart skips again. It might need to be shocked back into a steady rhythm if he really does stick around. He's said a lot of things. Made me *feel* plenty. I still don't believe that I deserve this man in shining armor before me.

It's a bit sad to admit, but within the short timeframe I have known Seth, he has already managed to go leaps and bounds ahead of what Joe ever accomplished. With Joe, there was no romance or swooning. No sweet words and promises. Perhaps that's why it's so hard to believe in Seth's declarations.

No one has ever spoken to me the way that Seth does. Looked after me and listened like he has been capable of. I want to believe that if I haven't scared him off yet, then maybe there is an ounce of hope that if—better yet, when—my kids come into the picture, that things won't change.

But I am scared of the pieces of me that would be left behind if I let Seth in and this doesn't work out. I don't think I could take another betrayal. Another heartbreak that would take so much.

Seth is right, though. While I definitely don't understand the why of it all, he makes me happy. *I* am happier when he's around. I want to think that should he meet Julie and Emmett, once the initial awkwardness wore off about their mom being with someone new, that they would love him too.

In time, I can very easily see myself doing that. Loving him. He would make it too easy, and I am already falling.

16

Progress

Seth

This van is too big for Clara and her kids. It feels like a boat in comparison to my truck. She assures me that it comes in handy with the stow 'n' go seats and when she's carting kids around to games and sleepovers, even if those days are getting to be fewer and further in between.

Guess I'd better get used to her "mom van." Her words, not mine. My truck definitely isn't equipped for a multitude of kids. I'm sure they wouldn't mind riding in the back of it for fun, but I guess that is more frowned upon nowadays.

Funsuckers.

Joe. I'm obviously referring to him. Julie and Emmett have never ridden with the tailgate down and legs hanging, letting the wind whip through their hair as they go driving around wooded bends and gravel roads. I don't think I rode in the front of a vehicle for most of my teen years. That is, until I was finally able to get behind the wheel of one.

I direct Clara to get to my place, and we're soon pulling down the drive. Thankfully, my truck is the only one present. The little white house has all of the blinds closed and from the outside, you might assume that someone is home but perhaps not awake yet. I let out a sigh of relief at the sight.

My family still knows where I am. That alone is almost enough to keep me awake at night and a constant at my mate's side.

"Huh..." Clara cuts the engine and grabs her purse. I watch her study my little house that pales in comparison to the size of hers. It would be nice if we could stop wasting time and she would invite me to live with her already, but I know that's jumping the gun. In her book, anyway. I am more than ready.

"So you really do have a place of your own."

I raise a brow, trying to decipher what she means by that.

"What?" She shrugs, her breasts dangerously close to hitting the steering wheel. She isn't that short, but with how close her seat is, you would think she's closer to five foot than five foot five. "For all I knew you were homeless and slumming it with me. Camping out in my backyard when you didn't have a free place to stay."

I'm briefly stunned into silence, both concerned by her accusation and yet suspiciously curious as to why she thought that in the first place. If only she knew that every night she sleeps alone, I really have been lurking in the woods behind her house. I don't think that would go over real well.

"Do I smell like the outdoors or something?" Even though it was a week ago, that stench from the pond is still ingrained in my senses.

"No, no." Blush begins to creep up into her cheeks as she opens her door and gets out. In a flash, I jump from my seat and meet her on her side, taking her hand in mine. Although it catches her off guard for a second, hers quickly molds into my hold. I'm fishing my key out of my pocket as I lead her up to the front door.

Opening it, I lead her into my living room and draw up the blinds to let some light in. Even though it's a cloudy day with the chance of rain, it still helps brighten the view of our surroundings. I didn't realize that my living space was so cave-like until now. Guess all it takes is having company for me to figure that out.

"I guess, a tour?" I take her purse from her and set it on the couch as I begin to show her around. She is quiet and reserved for the most part, examining things here and there, a free hand skimming surfaces when she gets close enough.

"Wow," Clara remarks, and I pause before we can leave the kitchen and dining area. I note her lingering stare out of the back door window. "The woods are so close. You have like, no yard."

I shrug. "The front of this place is all yard. Not that I have much use for it." I need the trees, and the quick jaunt out to them has been pretty convenient so far. Clara's house is a bit further away from the tree line, but not far enough that I can't keep a watchful eye on her.

Not ready to let her find the rose bushes planted along the backside of the house, I draw her away from the kitchen and continue on. I lead her down the hallway, so narrow that she has no choice but to follow behind me instead of beside. I flip on the bathroom light to illuminate the oddly chosen black-and-white scene. There is only a small circular window on the opposite end that I don't even bother covering up.

Clara sucks in a sharp breath, and when I take in her face, color is creeping into it once more.

"Feel like you've been here before?" I tease, growing harder as I recall our little video chat. My sweatpants do absolutely nothing to hide my erection, not that I want them to. Not in the slightest. I want her to know how I feel, especially when it comes to her.

Her bottom lip falls, eyes widening as she shifts her stance, and I know what she's visualizing. I had wanted her to see all of me, witness me coming, and for her viewing pleasure only.

Weaseling myself beside her, I angle her body until her back is at my front. With a slight bend at the knees, I gently press my hardened length against her until she is bracing herself on the doorframe. My lips brush against her ear. "We could create some new memories in here."

The air is thickening around us and the thought of taking her from behind at the sink while she claws at the spot where I came is eating away at me. She'd look fucking divine as she tries to prop herself up while I ravage and savor her.

"Is that a part of the tour?" she inquires on an exhale, head falling back and onto my chest. My hands are wrapping around her waist and making their way toward the fastenings of her jeans.

"For you, it is." I nip at her ear and she gasps. That little sound is music to my ears as I rock my hips into her, eliciting another right off. Inhaling her sweet smell, I let it fill me as I burrow into her neck and part her hair to make way for my kiss.

She relaxes into me as my hands undo her button and zipper and then make their way under her long-sleeve tee. Her flesh is soft and warm and I want to rip her garments from her body. But considering she doesn't have any clothes of her own here, she may not be too happy if I were to carry through with that.

I groan as my eyes close, trying to decide which scenario to go with. Adrenaline is pumping through my veins and a hum of need is making itself very well known. If I don't pump my cock into her soon, I might explode from the friction of grinding into her ass. There are so many ways I could take her in this small space, all of them trapping her here and completely at my mercy.

"Maybe I just want a replay from our video."

My brain skids to a halt. She cranes her neck to look at me, that knowing gaze of lust upon her face. But there's something else there, too.

A small smirk lifts the corner of her mouth just before she speaks again. "But I want to see the rest of your place first."

God. Fucking. Dammit.

She squeezes past me, patting my arm as she goes further down the hall, and I forget how to function for a moment. There are only two rooms left to go, and I'm not going to let her think she has won for long.

I stalk down the hall, and just as she turns her head to steal a glance at me, her brown eyes widen with a fleeting moment of fear. I point to my left, then my right, keeping my words clipped. "My office. Our bedroom."

Hand snapping out, I seize her arm and drag her into the room I have barely used since moving in. It's a bit dark, but still bright enough to make out every strand of beautiful hair atop her pretty little head. Reaching down, I pull off my shirt and give it a toss before reaching for the hem of hers. The sudden change in course is still registering on her face as I claim her lips and try to reach for the closures on the back of her bra, but her arms are quick to try and thwart me. She's no match for me and my strength, and she knows it.

"Seth," she pleads as she breaks our kiss.

"Did you not have a bra on for our little video chat?"

Her mouth opens to say something, but the only response I get is a tiny squeak. Clara diverts her eyes. Her fingers tighten on my biceps, as if that might stop and hold me back.

"Don't think I didn't see those bare shoulders. And we can take this back to the bathroom if you like."

She takes a brief moment to think it through before shaking her head slightly. "That...that was different."

"What are you afraid of, Clara? I want you. *All* of you. Is that not enough?" I don't know how else to ask, how else to beg.

"I..." Her eyes are fluttering, her discomfort growing increasingly obvious in the silence between us. "They're not..."

Her broken words and explanations that won't come are twisting something within me. She is shutting down and putting up a wall over a bra.

I'm not going to have that.

Swiveling to my dresser, I pull open the top drawer and retrieve a tie—one out of the two that I own. I rarely wear them except for the occasional work conference, and I can't think of a better use for one than for right now. I am going to break down Clara's barrier, one crack at a time. Not even her insecurities can keep me away.

I tie the red strip around my eyes, firmly securing it at the back of my head, and proceed a couple of steps until I can see Clara's feet coming into view. I reach out my hands and wait for her to take them. When she does, I let my thumbs smooth over the backside of her hands, trying to calm her racing heart.

"Promise I won't look. Not until you're ready." As bad as I want to worship her body, I know that I have to do this for her. One small step into earning her trust for our forever endgame. It's been clear that she's uncomfortable with her body, and I don't want to press my luck and send her running. Especially when I have just gone the past week without her. Perhaps this will give her the chance to do things on her own terms, give her the courage to take a small step of trust.

If she thinks her large breasts are going to send me on my way, she couldn't be more wrong.

"You promise?" she whispers faintly, and I have that urge to go down on my knees again. I meant what I said. I want *all* of her, no matter how I get it. If that means blindfolded? So fucking be it.

"I promise. You'll be the one to decide when I can take this blindfold off."

I step in closer, trying to gauge where her mouth is from my height. Her hands leave mine, and next thing I know, they're pushing my waistband down. I grin, all too eager to be stripped down for her. I only hope that she'll do me the honor of letting me do the same with her clothes.

As her hands glide down my legs, I can feel her eyes on the bob of my cock as it's freed. There's a brief pause on her descent down, and I bite the side of my tongue to hold off a broadening smile. She holds my clothes at the bottom, allowing me to step out of them, and when she disappears, I remove my socks and give each one a toss. I can hear her removing her clothes and the shimmy of her hips as she pushes her jeans down. I catch a small glimpse beneath the blindfold of her feet pushing them to the side and I snap my eyes shut, afraid that if she gets one small inkling that I'm stealing a peak, we'll lose momentum.

Clara's hands are uncertain as she takes mine and hesitantly places them on her waist, just above her hips. My fingers sink in and it's hard holding back when there are so many things I want to do to her. I have to remind myself that we have time.

Her chest brushes against mine and I still, recognizing that there's nothing separating my chest hair from her bare skin. My cock is pressing into her and her hand wraps around it, catching me off guard. There isn't much room between us, but she strokes it anyway from root to tip and my head falls back, lost in her touch.

No matter how many times I have beat myself off on my own, nothing could ever compare to Clara's handling of me. I'll never touch myself again. This is just too damn divine.

Precum is beading up and she takes my shaft and drags the tip of it across her belly in a slow draw. My fingertips dig deeper into her skin as my senses go haywire. Stripping me of my sight and denying me the chance to witness my beautiful Rose working me over at her own leisure is driving me mad with desire.

The very thing that Clara doesn't think that she is. *Desirable.*

Knowing it's a risky move, I allow my hands to climb up, and I can imagine the trails of goosebumps left on her pale complexion as I do. She holds her breath as I reach the sides of her breasts, and I lift them up into my hands and give them a gentle squeeze.

Fuck, they're huge. A groan slips free as my thumbs skate across her nipples, their peaks just begging to be licked, sucked, and pinched. Damn, what a sight it would be to slide my dick between them.

The thought of needing bigger hands comes to mind, but a part of me enjoys that they spill over at my touch. I can handle her, and she will come to revel in the sensations I can provide for her.

Clara's hand has stopped moving, and I take that as my sign to make a move. Whether she's ready or not, I am going to find out. Carefully lowering one breast, I seek the base of her neck and tilt her head up. As if I can stare through the tie and into her eyes that are no doubt growing bigger, I pull at her hair.

"The only place I'm coming today is inside of you." My words are rough, her stance faltering as if she's still arguing with herself over this whole interaction. I don't give her another chance to overthink. "Bend over the bed."

One hand stays on her for guidance as she hesitantly follows my order. When she comes to a stop, I use one of my feet to push hers apart to grant me better access, and I smooth my palms over her plush ass, gripping and pulling. I only wish I could see the redness they're creating in their wake.

Fingers sail past her pubic hair and hurry for her center. I circle a few teasing strokes of her clit before diving in to see how wet she is for me. Her insides squeeze at the intrusion and a hum leaves my lips in appreciation of how ready she is. I twist and turn, bringing moisture out to circle some more around that little nub that has her whimpering for me as she pushes her hips back.

She's hungry for me, and I am more than happy to feed her growing appetite.

Nestling the head of my cock to her entrance, I let the warmth radiating off of her pulsate as my thumb plays with her beneath it. The pressure intensifies and her voice turns raspy. It is damn intoxicating.

Her hips shoot back, my erection diving in so fast I barely have time to comprehend it and I'm bending over her from the sudden impact. I'm clawing at the comforter as a cry leaves her lips when I impale her. I'm rendered useless for a moment, trying to get my bearings at her abruptness. Her insides are squeezing my dick so hard I have to catch my breath, fearful that I'll come too fast.

"Fuck, Clara," I growl, and I'm fleetingly curious whether the sound is anything like what she was poking fun at this morning.

"Take it..." she whines, and I tilt my head up as if I can see through the makeshift mask, even though if I tried, it would be very minimal. "Take it off."

I rip the tie off of my head violently and settle on the sight of her naked before me.

Fucking exquisite.

I can see everywhere my hands have clutched onto her. Light pink marks are evident. There are lines across her back from where her bra was secured, and I swear I'm the one who's going to go weak in the knees now that she's finally laid out for me.

"Fucking beautiful." I let my voice carry over her as my hands smooth over her backside and up toward her shoulders. She's trembling beneath me as I go, still adjusting to my length that she took it upon herself to thrust onto.

How did I get so lucky?

Every inch of every curve, and every whimper that leaves those lips, is mine.

Knowing what it must have taken for her to gather the courage to tell me to take off the blindfold, I decide to give her a choice. My hands are still roaming over her, memorizing every dip and staggered breath as I keep my hips stationary. For now.

I bend to kiss her back and a shudder runs through her. Her brown hair moves as if she wants to turn and look at me but she doesn't.

"Thank you," I murmur across her skin. She might be face down with those breasts smashed against the bed, but it still feels like a win. "How will you take me, Clara? Steady, slow, and calculated? Or fast, hard, and destructive?"

I'll fucking break her back and mine if she takes the last option. And I will cherish every single minute of it. I just have to know that she's ready for it. Being without her for days on end has messed with me.

She takes a moment to decide and damn, don't I wish I could just make the decision for her and go wild, but I eagerly await her response. I need to know what she wants from me right now in this moment.

"Destructive," she mewls as she presses her ass against me, as if we could get any closer. "Make me forget about everything else but you."

I grin, probably a bit mad in doing so, but Clara never stops surprising me. I am in for the fucking ride of my life with her, and I am going to marry her someday. Mark my words.

Taking in a deep breath, I sit up and grab onto her hips. Hopefully she won't care about a few bruises along the way to ecstasy. I want her to look at them and remember this. This moment where I fuck her without mercy. Drive us both to the point that we lose our damn minds in the process.

I draw back and shoot forward, and her body threatens to plummet forward but my hold on her is fierce. One warning is all I give her, and then I'm off.

My thrusts are so fast that she can't keep up with her garbled cries and she can't even support herself on the bed. Her upper half is growing lax as she takes each and every strike I give. Her hands are grasping the bed, but nothing gives her what she's looking for.

Shouts turn into cries and cries turn into shrieks. Even those morph into something I have never heard come out of her mouth before, and it only drives me harder and faster.

My muscles are working overtime, veins in my arms protruding with the increased need to steady her and keep pushing forward. If my Rose wants destructive, I'll give her that, and then some.

She feels fucking magnificent beneath me. Every time I touch her, it's like the first time all over again and I can barely contain myself.

I beat into her, over and over again, unrelenting as I find my release gathering on the horizon. Bucking into her harder, my spine threatening to stiffen, I'm growing too hot but I push on, burying my dick inside of her and never stopping until I know she can come too.

A pained scream tears from her throat and she's pleading for me to stop. At least, I think that's what she's saying as her body begins spasming. She's shaking so violently that my orgasm consumes me and my body comes to a screeching halt as I let out a booming howl of satisfaction. I don't think I've ever come so hard in my entire life, and my body is misfiring, trying to figure out what in the hell we're supposed to do right now. I can't collapse on top of Clara, even though that's exactly what my frame is threatening to do.

I'm fading fast and need to lie down, but I fight it as I scoop up Clara's legs from the floor and onto the bed. She sounds like she's crying, but her head is buried in her hair and denying me the chance to check for sure.

Crawling onto the bed, I draw her close, pushing her hair out of the way so I can see if I've caused any damage. She shakes but doesn't pull away, and when I see her eyes, they're closed but tears are still managing to escape.

A tense fear consumes me, and I'm afraid that I've gone too far and freaked her out. Or worse, hurt her.

"Cla—" I clear my throat, trying to get a clearer tone. "Clara, are you alright?"

I'm brushing her hair that keeps falling into her face, bringing her body in as close as it will go while still being able to look into her eyes when she opens them. When she does, I go numb, waiting to see how bad I fucked things up.

I can't decipher if it's hurt, hate, or a combination of the both. But it strips the air from my lungs. No words will come from my lips again until she speaks. I am terrified.

"What the hell was that?" She swipes at her cheeks before her head leans back down on the bed again. Her voice is ragged. "Who are you?"

She forces a small laugh and only then do I release air, closing my eyes to try and bring myself back down from my near heart attack.

My lips turn up as I kiss the top of her head, heart still beating wildly as I try to settle down. Then I look her dead in the eyes and keep my face as earnest as I can possibly manage. "I'm Seth Woods."

She smacks me with the back of her hand, another laugh coming through, and this one...this one seems more natural.

If only she knew I am going to be the last and only man who is going to love her unconditionally, no matter what life throws our way.

17

A Day Out

Seth

I feel like I just got laid for the first time. It couldn't be further from the truth, but the stupid grin I have plastered on my face as I walk hand in hand with Clara even has her blushing.

"Stop it." She bumps into me, but it does nothing to mess with my proud stride. She's embarrassed, and it's cute.

We had lounged in my bed, talking for about an hour before we finally felt as if we could control our limbs enough to support us. As much as it pained me to give her privacy in the bathroom to get cleaned up, I stayed behind, my body sprawled out and spent without a stitch of clothing on.

I was still drifting up and in the clouds when she came back into my bedroom fully dressed. When her eyes roamed over me, it was almost enough to make me drag her back in for another round, but she winced when I pulled on her a bit too rough. I hadn't really meant to break her back, but after all, she did say she wanted it to be destructive.

My naked ass waltzed out and into the kitchen to retrieve some pills for pain relief and a bottle of water. She struggled to keep her gaze up as she took it from me, and I couldn't help but thrust my hips forward and poke her, watching as the redness surged into her face in her feeble attempt to push me away.

And now here we are, walking across the parking lot of a restaurant in Benson as if we're two lovebirds on their honeymoon or some shit. Even though we're passing the lunch hour rush, there are still plenty of cars and people around the area. I can tell that Clara is growing nervous. She's hoping that we won't run into anyone she knows here, compared to Pembrook where she works and her kids spend half of their time.

"We don't have to do this if you don't want to," I state, the same line I've said about four times since we left my rental. It's by her own admission, not mine, that she wants to stick it to Joe someday. That she can be happy without him.

Didn't take anything else to convince me. I would worship her and show Joe what it's like to be head over heels for my soon-to-be wife.

Doesn't matter if it takes weeks, months, or years. I will make her mine.

Well, years might be pushing it. I want everyone around to know that she is taken now. By me.

We're quickly shown to a booth inside the country-styled restaurant. There are cowboy hats, horseshoes, and lassos adorning the walls. Croons from Southern musicians play just loud enough to help with background noise, and while it isn't my favorite type of music, I know I can get used to it and let it fade away so I can focus on my other half.

Clara slides into the seat and I pause, trying to decide if I want to sit next to her or on the opposite side. The hostess stands by awkwardly as I war with my inner dilemma.

It isn't until Clara cocks an eyebrow at me and my failure to move that I finally give in and sit on the opposite side. We're handed our menus and I stick my left leg out and toward her side of the booth, letting it brush past her leg.

Brown eyes rise to mine and I only offer a slight upturn of the corner of my lips.

"Stop it," she repeats, and it only furthers my amusement.

"Going to have to be a bit more specific about what I need to stop with." I take a swig of my water and turn my nose up. Gross, I hate faucet water. I might be part wolf, but I still have taste and preferences.

Another woman comes by, dressed in some sort of Western attire with a bolo tie. She looks too young to even know what it's called, but she takes our drink order with a smile and is off before a woman's voice cuts through on the speakers in a new song. Her twang almost makes my face pinch.

Maybe I'm not going to be able to do the music here.

"I'm going to have to tell Julie and Emmett," Clara begins, her lips rolling anxiously. "That is, if Joe hasn't told them already. I asked him not to, but—"

"He probably has," I agree, and I can sense my anger rising toward the piece of shit. "I stand by what I said before. I will stay away unless you tell me otherwise. I don't want to make them uncomfortable. I will only come into the picture when you, Julie, and Emmett are ready."

"And what if they're not? What if they don't want their mom seeing anyone?" The worried look she wears wounds me without my permission. I clear my throat, hating the thought of something like that happening. I can't deny that it's a possibility. Her kids have only ever known life with their parents together, and now Joe has left their mother for Chassidy.

"Then I'll wait, because *you* are worth waiting for."

She shakes her head, as if my words aren't enough.

"I'm serious, Clara." I lean forward to grab her attention, and don't continue until those pretty eyes are on mine. "I know it's hard to believe, but I'm all in. I know why you may have your doubts, and you have every right to question it. But in the meantime, I will keep trying to prove it to you until you're ready to accept it."

Beneath the table, her leg jerks upward but then quickly returns to its spot as if she forgot mine was right beside it. It reminds me of how often she bounced her leg at that Chinese restaurant when she was anxious. Perhaps she really is coming around to me after all.

"You're very persistent." She rolls her lips again and all I want to do is take them against my own. I don't even care who's watching. "But you don't exactly strike me as patient."

"I'm not saying it won't be a struggle on my part," I acknowledge. Even though I want the transition into her life and into her home to be a smooth one, I know that might not be the case.

If she were a werewolf and aware of the mate connection between us, there would be no waiting. Clara would fall into step and share the air I breathe as we become one. I would have marked her as mine with my bite at the first chance I had, and the rest would be history.

Since she's a human, that isn't the case. How can I explain to someone that their body, their *soul* calls me home? That a single word from her lips would have me kneeling before her to carry out her every whim? We are meant for each other, *made* for one another. Two pieces to be made whole by our mate connection. I want to believe that she feels it too. Even though it might not be glaringly obvious like the alarm bells ringing in my head, she has to feel something more, doesn't she?

If my truth were to come out now, I'd scare her off faster than a dog spazzing out about fireworks.

Just for the record, I'm not scared by them. They're annoying as hell and stupid creations, but that's about all.

My work phone buzzes in my pocket, and although I want to have full focus on Clara, I apologize so I can check it real quick and stow it away on silent. But the number. That damn area code is determined, and it's picking at my last nerve. I'm going to be hell-bent on finding out how they got my work number in the first place.

"What's wrong?" Clara's voice turns wary, and I shake my head to try and smooth away the face I'm making. She's smart, knowing something is off when I slip up and don't school my emotions.

"It's nothing." I try to glide over the incident nonchalantly, but her face is telling another story.

"Seth," she attempts to persuade me as she raises a brow again. It's clear she's not going to let up, and I try to decipher the best way to tell her that my family won't leave me alone. That after ten plus years, they're coming out of the woodwork and trying to get me to come home. I've made it a point to tell Clara that I'm not going anywhere. Told her time and again that I'm here to stay. This news won't help her, let alone us, in any way. So I skirt around it. At least, I try to.

"I wasn't fully honest about why my cousin paid me a visit." I know that line is a hook and I have her fully engaged now. Yet, I can't look at her until I deliver the reason why. I need to see her reaction when I do.

"He was here to inform me that my dad is...sick. Guess he's got an expiration date." Anger threatens to rise as I talk about someone I wrote off so long ago. I am pissed, perturbed, and so fucking confused about why I'm letting it get to me in the first place. He doesn't deserve an ounce of sympathy.

"How...what?" Clara's stunned reaction is a bit more animated than I anticipated. "Oh my God, Seth. What's wrong with him?"

I shrug, feeling suddenly cold about it all. Clara is taking this news a lot differently than I did, and she doesn't even know a single person in my family.

"You don't *know*?" Her rough exaggeration on that last word is perplexing.

"Why should I care?"

At the worst possible moment, Ms. Bolo Tie returns to take our order and I haven't even had a chance to flip through the overbearing menu. I tell Clara I'll order whatever she's having, and her mouth closes for a moment. I can tell she's getting riled up. She orders some sandwich with a side of potato salad. I say my thanks to the waitress before being met with a dead stare from Clara.

"What?" Why is she taking offense to this news, like I've somehow wronged her?

"What do you mean, *what*?" She kicks me beneath the table like some toddler, and the impact barely even registers in my brain. "Seth, this is serious."

Clara genuinely cares, without knowing any better. It's evident in the way her tone pitches higher while she's still trying to keep her voice down. In the way she leans forward and the worried look she wears. I guess I haven't given her much detail about why I wish my father was already dead.

"So serious that they wait until this news to try and reach out? I'm not buying it."

"What are you not buying? Do you think they're faking this or something? Why would they stoop so low with a story like that?"

I never really considered it could be a lie—after seeing those pictures that I came across on the internet, I know better. Something is wrong with my dad. Something is draining his life away. An uneasy feeling rises in my chest. I hate that this is taking up so much space in my head and apparently, my body as well.

"Maybe they're trying to make amends." Her eyes are darting around the table as she tries to form her thoughts into words, but I don't like how she's springing to the defense of others that she's never even met.

"Well, I'm not interested. They've had plenty of time to do so before now."

"But..." She's growing more frustrated, and not in a good way. I fear this might be pushing her away instead of closer. This isn't how I was expecting this conversation to go. "But being faced with death, that can really put things in perspective. Death is final."

"I know that." I try to keep my response level.

"Then why are you writing them off?"

"Because they wrote me off." My teeth are grinding against each other as heat begins to ooze over my skin. Nasty agitation is growing the longer we stay on the topic, and I don't want to go down this road. "If they're seeking forgiveness, I'm not going to give it just so he can die with a clear conscience."

Clara gapes at me. Worse, it's like I can see her pulling away even though she doesn't move an inch. It's in her eyes, like a wound I inflicted upon her and she's rendered speechless because of it.

I am hurting her, and it isn't even about her. It's about me and my shitty past that I don't want to burden her with. It's my decision not to act on this news, this revelation. Now, my inability to care or do something is having a negative effect on the relationship I'm striving for right in front of me.

In tandem, she closes her mouth and her whole face falls into a sadness that brings my hand up to my chest to rub at it. I can't look at her. It's one thing to see her broken and dealing with her own life and troubles, quite another to be the source of something new. This bothers her, and because of that, it's weighing heavier on me now, too.

"Would you regret it?" She's almost drowned out by the music playing and the voices around us, but her words keep repeating back to me in my head before she opens her mouth again. "Would you regret not saying goodbye one last time?"

I didn't tell anyone goodbye when I left the first time.

I want to snort out my denial of a reply but I'm afraid of the reaction I'll get if I do. Instead, I'm met with various emotions hitting me from different angles and attacking me.

My old life I left behind. The family I cut ties with, who did nothing to put us back together after I left. It's quite clear now that they had the means to find me, and it took my dad on his deathbed to get them to reach out. I sure as hell wasn't going to be the one to do it. That door to my life was closed, and now it's being beaten down, splintering with each strike and chunks flying off in different directions. I am being torn apart by a past and a hurt that I thought I had locked away and thrown away the key.

Guess I was fooling myself.

"Are you speaking from personal experience?" I turn the attention back on her, hating the way I feel right now. The spotlight being on me is too much at the moment, and I need to turn the tables. I can't go back there. I *won't* go back there.

Clara's shoulders sag forward a bit as she looks absently away. Only then do I muster up enough courage to really look at her. I thought my family problems and my lack of involvement was troubling enough for her, but this? Whatever she's thinking about is downright depressing. My heart aches for her, and I don't even understand how when I know nothing about the why.

"I had an uncle," she begins, and I wait for her to continue. "Well, a great uncle, but whatever. He was a bit weird. One of those relatives that you exchange pleasantries with and try to scoot out of the conversation and away as soon as you see a chance at an exit." Her gaze turns downward, and it looks as if she's rubbing the palms of her hands together in her lap. "An alcoholic who drank like it was his job or something. You never knew if you were going to get happy-go-lucky Marvin or raging, lunatic Marvin."

Clara sits back in her booth, crossing her arms beneath her breasts. "The last time I saw him, I was at the grocery store with the kids. I didn't want to run into him, and dreaded the conversation I would have to somehow stir up. So I took my cart full of food and Emmett, hauled Julie by the hand to the checkout lanes, and got out of there before he could see us."

Her throat constricts as her eyes begin to well, and I'm about to ask her to stop but she beats me to the punch.

"A month later I found out he was sick and in the hospital. I was going to go visit the next day, but I got a call in the middle of the night that he had passed. The kids, they probably don't even remember him. Nobody in the family knew that he was in AA or that he had been turning his life around. Even had a few sobriety chips, and when we cleaned out his place, there wasn't an ounce of alcohol to be found. Even found his list of people he wanted to...to make amends with."

I don't even know what to say. I know that our scenarios, and the people involved in them, are different, but that doesn't negate the fact of what she's getting at. My father was directly responsible for not only physical abuse, but mental as well. And the fact that my mother stood idly by told me that nobody would be coming to my rescue. That, I had to do for myself.

"Promise me you'll think this through, Seth." Brown eyes shift to mine and I'm frozen solid, pinned by the unexpected sting of her story and the regret she's reliving. "Just because he's got an expiration date, doesn't mean it won't happen sooner than you think."

For the first time since meeting Clara, I don't want her to be right. But goddamnit, I hate to think that she is. She is beautiful, smart, and insightful. Caring, a little daring, and surprising me when I least expect it.

She is made for me. Even with all of the fucked-up bits that are rising to the surface. I know it will be a struggle, but she will make me a better man because of it. One worthy of her love.

I lay an outstretched arm on the table and open my hand for her. She eyes it warily before bringing her hand up and I take hold of it to assure her, muttering words that are merely that, until I can actually bring myself to follow through with it. "I'll call them back."

Her expression still holds the sadness lingering from her confession, but it doesn't stop her from offering a small upturn in the corner of her mouth.

Now I just have to decide what in the hell I'm going to say to my mother.

It takes a little bit of time, and multiple visits from our waitress, but the mood at our table eventually turns around.

Clara has a knack for finding good food around here, I'll give her that. The potato salad is top-notch, and I practically inhale the sandwich. The bread is crisp with a crunch that I sink my teeth into. The meat is divine and not too salty, either. I may not be a fan of the atmosphere and the attire the employees are wearing, but the food speaks for itself.

When the bill comes, I don't even let our waitress set the check down before handing my card over. I should check it to make sure everything on it is correct, but I don't want the chance of Clara slipping in to pay for it.

Her bottom lip sticks out in a pout at my quick action. "You didn't have to do that."

She crosses her arms below her chest again and I set my elbows on the table so I can lean a smidge closer. I'm not going to bring it up, at least not point-blank, but Clara has been honest with me on more than one occasion about her money troubles, and I'm not about to add to them. She is already taking care of a house on a single income and all the bills that come along with it. When you figure the responsibilities and food needs of three people under one roof, it's no wonder she's so stressed.

"I didn't, but I wanted to." I let my leg graze against hers, reminding her and myself of how close we are beneath the table even if it feels like we're too far apart above it.

I should have sat next to her.

It takes some persuading, but I finally get Clara to agree to spend the day out and about with me here in Benson. There are tons of stores and a large shopping mall all within walking distance, and once I sign for my bill—and check it—I take Clara by the hand and lead us out.

I am more than ready to run away from the country music that will be haunting me and my dreams for the next week. If we ever eat here again, I might have to bring some earplugs or order it to go.

The sky is taking a turn, now stormier than when we first arrived. It doesn't worry me in the slightest. The wind picks up as we head into a department store, and a shiver runs through Clara, her hand jerking.

I try offering her my sweater, but she declines as she grabs a cart and puts her purse in the top tier.

"What's your style?"

My attention slides to her, confused by her question as we turn to the left. When I fail to provide an answer, she rolls her eyes. "For decorating. Your place is too empty, too..."

"Boring?" I offer, and she grins.

"I didn't say that."

I chuckle lightly. "Moving around a lot, I never really saw the need to worry about it. My clothes, office stuff, and sometimes my TV if I get a really good one, are all I take with me."

"Maybe I have too much crap." She contemplates, her lips twisting to one side. I want to put my hand on her waist, but I know Clara is already going beyond her comfort zone being out in the public eye with me.

"You don't," I argue. "You have a house that you've lived in. Memories that have been made. You have a home. I have a rental."

"So you're probably limited as to what you can do." There she goes again, getting lost in that head of hers.

I don't want to decorate a place that I don't plan on staying in. I want to live with her, but I can't come right out and say it because I don't want to start backtracking from the direction we're headed. I honestly have no idea if I can hang or mount anything on the walls of my place. I don't have any family pictures or sentimental objects.

"How about we find a new comforter for your bed?"

Her head snaps at me and I can't help but dive in further. "Don't think I didn't notice that tear in the corner. You could use a new one."

"It's at the bottom of the bed. I've practically forgotten all about it." She shrugs. "Anyhow, bedding is expensive. I've been meaning to try and patch it up, it's just low on my priority list."

I take the cart from her and steer us in the direction of home decor, weaving around a few people until I manage to turn us down the aisle we need. There's a wide array of colors, plenty to choose from, and my eyes bulge when I see the prices on them.

Fuck, they really are expensive. I bought my current set online a few years ago for a fraction of the price.

"Enlighten me." I gesture to both sides as she crosses her arms. She's not loving this idea, and I can't say I blame her. She's really not going to like it when I try to buy her one. "What would you choose?"

She locks eyes with me, not doing me the courtesy of at least glancing about to convince me that she's even considering it. "What if I said the old lady floral on your right?"

I look over to see the most god-awful print that looks like it belongs in another decade. It reminds me of something that my grandma would have had on her bed. Bushels of flowers tied by little pink ribbons. I'm pretty sure I would smell her house if I opened that bag. If there's a freaking dust ruffle in there, so help me.

Calling her bluff, I lift the bag and give it another once over, trying to cover up my disgust. "Guess we'll get two of them."

Both of her brows rise and her bottom lip falls away from the top. "Two?"

"Yeah." I place it in the cart and bend to pick up another. "That way when we wear out the first one, you'll have a backup."

It takes a beat for the realization to register, and then she's dashing toward me and fumbling to take the second package from my grasp. "You ass."

Her hiss is enough to bring forth lighthearted laughter from me as she sets the both of them back in their respective places. She's calling me names now. I like it.

Clara stills as she straightens her back, focused on something behind me, all funny business now aside. There's a scowl in place that has me turning in an instant to witness what has disturbed our little lovers' dispute.

Fucking toothpick.

Tits practically getting ready to leap from her low-cut sweater that probably cost more than these gross bedding sets, it's Chassidy. Coffee in hand while pushing a cart full of clothes in the other. She does absolutely nothing to hide the way her eyes roam my frame, which is infuriating considering she's supposed to be in a relationship with Joe.

"I don't think we've formally met." She turns and leans an elbow on her cart, pushing her hips to the side and plastering a smile on her face. She's putting on a show and I couldn't care less. "I'm Chassidy."

The fake sweetness in her voice has me cocking a brow. "I really don't care."

There's a flash of something malicious in her eyes before she slips her composure back into place.

"Well, that's just rude." She feigns innocence as she glances at Clara then back to me. "I was only trying to—"

"Are the kids here?" Clara is stepping up to join me at my side and while I want to hold her hand to steady her, I decide to stay completely out of it. I don't want to overstep even if I want to protect her. I know how much she hates Chassidy and her part in breaking up her family. The only good thing to come from it was that Clara is now free of that marriage and a space for me has been made.

"Does it look like they're here?" She glances to her right and left, apparently unaware that we are unable to see her surroundings from our viewpoint.

"Then fuck off, Chassidy." Clara's words are heated, venom spewing from her lips, and I can't help but grin my approval.

Chassidy stands there, gaping at the audacity of my mate. I wonder how often her mouth is open for men in the same capacity. She'd better close it before somebody's dick falls in.

"Not sure if you flunked out of high school or something, but that means bye." My statement angers her, and if her tan skin could show any inclination of it, it probably would have. With a flip of her blonde hair, she practically stomps off like a child.

I pivot to face Clara, and there's a gleam in her eyes as her head turns in my direction. I like this side of her; it could be fun.

18

What PDA?

Clara

I want to kiss him.

The urge to throw my head back and laugh at the fact that he just called out Chassidy and her lack of understanding is strong, but instead I'm hurling myself at him and throwing my arms around his neck. I kiss him hard as he leans over to accommodate my shorter height. His beard brushes my chin and I run a hand along his face in appreciation.

Never has Chassidy hightailed it like that before, and while Seth didn't completely step in and take over to get rid of her, that one line that came from him means so much. Finally, it feels like someone is truly on my side, willing to help me stand my ground and not let me be pushed aside.

Seth is too good to be real. I still don't understand it, but I am happy. His words on the matter couldn't be more accurate.

When I try to separate us, he deepens the kiss, tongue sliding in, and I swear my underwear is going to dissolve with the need that's quickly accumulating and making my head spin.

But my body aches. Seth taking me from behind was a mix of both moderate pain *and* intense pleasure. I had never been fucked so hard in my entire life, and I'm pretty sure I'm going to be popping pain medication on rotation for the next several days in the aftermath. My heating pad might have to come into play too. It's like my ass landed on concrete over and over again. Add that to his dick impaling me, and that's a concoction anyone would be sore from.

A hand puts pressure on my hip and I suck in a sharp breath. Only then does Seth release me and take a step back.

He's concerned, looking at me, possibly trying to decipher the reaction to his touch. I cross my arms, a bit shy. "You really know how to put the 'D' in destructive, don't you?"

"In you, yes."

I'm stunned for a moment, trying to fish my head out of the gutter as I squeeze my thighs together, as if that will do anything to stop the arousal that's trying to make itself known. My face is starting to burn and I'm growing uncomfortably hot when just minutes ago I felt a chill.

I'm out in public, for crying out loud. This is ridiculous.

Clearing my throat, I turn away from him to look at the various bags of bedding, but everything is a blur. I can't focus on anything long enough to even figure out if I like it or not.

What I can admit, is that I like whatever Seth has on his bed. It felt luxurious under me as he pounded into me. I grasped and pulled at the fabric as if it could save me from him. Not that I really wanted saving, but nevertheless, I couldn't deny how good it felt on my bare skin. There were no puckers or seams to be torn. No fancy threading or designs, just a solid color of comfort. "What kind do you have?"

Seth draws closer and sticks a hand in my back pocket as he turns me to face the opposite side of where I was looking. His hand is probably a quarter the size of my ass, but that doesn't take away from how good it feels for him to handle it.

My arm comes around his side, although I don't have anything to grab onto but hard muscle. It never ceases to amaze me just how rigid and toned he is. It isn't too much like some bodybuilders, but he's still a walking and talking sculpture.

Outings with Seth have been pretty minimal thus far, so today is only our second time. I don't miss all the double takes and looks that he draws. He acts as if he's completely oblivious to them all, and maybe he is. But it still makes me feel less than.

I know what they're thinking as we walk side by side together. My mind is incapable of shutting off the negative thoughts, and unable to ignore the stares and lust coming from other shoppers. It doesn't seem to matter their age, either. From giggling teenagers to an older woman riding on an electric scooter, he has an effect on everyone he passes.

By the time we find ourselves headed toward the checkouts, we have an odd mix of home furnishings, toiletries, and food-related items. There's one painting that caught my eye. I merely complimented it and when I tried to move on, Seth retrieved it and gently set it down in the cart. It isn't necessarily anything special, no discernable people or objects, just wavelike brushstrokes that start from a deep green and eventually morph into a shade so light you'd barely make out a green tint if it wasn't for the color beside it.

"For my living room," Seth stated as he stuck his hand in my back pocket again. I don't think a minute passed us by while inside the store that he wasn't touching me in some way. His hands always found their way onto me.

"I'm going to run to the restroom real quick before we head out. I'll be right back." Offering him a forced smile, I wait for his acknowledgement and then make my way to the bathrooms I know to be hidden on the other side of the coffee shop. It's usually far less busy here than the ones on the other end of the store. That, and I don't want to double back to get there.

Swinging the door open, I'm grateful to find that there are so few occupants. Noticing that there are some empty stalls at the opposite end from where I entered, I go to the last one and quickly shut the door behind me so I can have a moment of peace without everyone looking and judging. I hate that I care and that it bothers me so much.

Why? Why can't I shut off this damn mind of mine and turn a blind eye to them all?

Fanning myself, I try to get a hold of the tight ball of nerves in my stomach and take a few deep breaths. By the time I hear a second toilet flush and I'm pretty sure that she has left, I unlock the door and head for the sinks. I scan down the line to see that there is still someone present and I carry on with the washing of my hands so I can make my way out to find Seth and get out of here. I think I've had enough social interaction with the world for one day.

Turning away from the hand dryer, I come to an abrupt stop. There's no covering the look on my face as I come to be a few feet away from Chassidy. It's like she's been waiting for me, arms crossed and blocking my exit. I swear to God if she starts tapping her foot on the ground, I'm going to slap the bitch.

Why in the hell can't I get away from her?

"What's wrong, Clara? Afraid of flaunting this fling around in Pembrook?"

Yes. No. It's none of your damn business.

I try to step around her, but she moves to block me. Pretty immature and annoying as hell, so I take a step back. I'm pretty sure I can pin her down with half a butt cheek if she doesn't move. It'll still leave room for Seth's hand.

"What do you want, Chassidy?" I adjust the strap of my purse before it can fall from my shoulder.

"Just trying to figure out what that man...sees." Her sneer as she looks me up and down is threatening to make me see red.

My hands are fisting. She notices, and a satisfied smirk takes over. There's little doubt in my mind that together with Joe, she's seen the video footage of Seth coming to the house night after night. The invasion of privacy, the betrayal of it all, is infuriating.

"Well, try not to have an aneurysm figuring it out," I remark, but my voice wavers. Not from nerves, but from being so ticked off that I can't cause any bodily harm without getting myself arrested. Why this woman keeps testing me, I don't know if I'll ever find out.

Chassidy hums to herself, and I can tell she's gearing up for something. She's practically giddy about it. While I may want nothing to do with Joe anymore, it seriously baffles me what in the hell he sees in her. Besides her petite body, perky boobs, and gray-free hair, how is it that this woman played a part in the end of my marriage?

"I can't imagine he'd actually want to stick his dick in you. It'd probably get lost."

I swear I'm fuming like my head is about to blow its top. I don't even think, and my mouth starts moving. "At least he wouldn't stub his dick like other men when they try to enter *you*."

A boisterous cackle sounds from behind, and I jump as a toilet flushes. I'm overcome with a serious case of embarrassment, not knowing who in the hell has remained so insanely quiet until now.

The woman who exits the stall has beautiful braids with a deep red fastened into them. A nose stud is prominent on her face with her big lips wearing a bold shade. Her outfit and name tag are a dead giveaway that she works here, and I hold my breath as she continues to chuckle, making her way toward the sink.

"You'd best get lost, li'l blondie." She steals a glance at Chassidy before she breaks out into another amused laugh. "Dick stubbin', ha!"

Her laugh is infectious, and I can't fight off the effect it has on me as I turn to see a horrified Chassidy. She can't even bring herself to look at me before she bolts from the bathroom, her sweater dropping off of her shoulder and revealing her pink bra strap as she goes.

"*Girl.*" She draws out the word and it takes a second to register that she's referring to me as she tears off a brown paper towel from its dispenser.

"Sorry about that. I didn't realize we weren't alone."

"You don't need to apologize." She waves her ring-clad fingers at me as she tosses her paper into the trash can. "You just made my day. She sounds like a real piece of work."

My eyes bulge, weighing the idea of how much I want to divulge to a complete stranger. But you know what? Fuck it.

"My ex-husband cheated on me with her. Now I have someone new in my life and...well, feels like she's trying to go after him, too."

"What, that li'l thing?" She shakes her head, moving toward the door and I'm following after her, more than ready to get out of here. "Sheesh!"

Chassidy is nowhere in sight when we leave, but Seth is quick to flag me down and the worker just steps ahead of me, coming to a standstill as I catch up to her side.

"Now I know he ain't wavin' at me."

"That would be my someone new." I smile at her and she does a double take of the tall, bearded, and muscled man that's heading our way. I notice as he draws closer that the items in the cart are already bagged, and I can feel a mini argument coming up the moment we're out of the store.

She blows out a breath, and it's only then that I get a glimpse of her name tag without it being too obvious. Tanisha.

"Honey, I don't know anything about your ex, but I think you're better off." The way she leans over slightly to speak to me as she sizes up my man has me feeling all warm inside.

My man.

Can I be warm and get chills at the same time? I must be getting a fever or something.

"Do you have a brother?" Tanisha asks Seth when he gets close enough, and the heat overtakes me.

Seth, as polite and charming as ever, smiles at her question as he tips his head down when he catches something with his eyes. "Aren't you married?"

"I don't *have* to be," she teases back before unleashing another maniacal laugh. All I can do is bury my head in my hand. With all of the rings on her, I can't even begin to tell if she's really married or not. Maybe she just likes to accessorize.

"You two lovebirds enjoy yourselves." She leaves without another word and I offer her an awkward wave as I join Seth at his side. He's quick to put a hand over my love handles, just above where there might be bruises surfacing. I guess I'll find out later if that's the case.

"What did I miss?" He gives me a light squeeze and I almost jump. I don't think he meant to tickle me, but the twinkle in his eyes tells me he knows how to tickle me now.

"Can we hash it out on the way home? I'd kind of like to get out of here."

"And which home are you referring to?" There's a spark in his facial features, baiting me. All thought is lost as I try to recover.

Ours. His. Mine. No, his. "Just, out of Benson. Please." I leave his touch behind and know he's fast to follow after me, the cart quickly coming into view in my periphery.

"Lead the way, beautiful."

We're at Seth's long enough for him to put some groceries away, and we pick a spot for him to hang his art piece. The living room seems like a great idea until we realize he doesn't even have any nails to put in the wall. His toolbox is pretty minimal, and when I say that, I mean it's smaller than a shoebox. Knowing that I have some nails at my house, we're soon heading in that direction.

The day seems to have gone by too fast considering what little we've done. Mess around, eat, and shop. Even then, we only went to the one store and I felt spent by the time that was over with. What little energy I had depleted quickly when I started arguing with Seth about paying for everything that was in our cart. I hadn't meant for him to go off and do that while I was in the bathroom recovering.

Although, he now wants to dub Chassidy "dick stubber" and honestly, I'm not complaining. The bitch needs to let up. I loathe the fact that she's a constant around my kids, and so help me if she ever acts like that around them? I'll probably end up spending a night in jail.

I'm shuffling around the house when we return, grabbing items that Seth needs for his place. A hammer, nails, and some leveler thing that I've never used. Returning from my room, Seth strolls up to me and places his hands on the sides of my face, getting too close, too fast.

"What?" I search his eyes wildly, trying to decide if he's going to break me with a round two of today's earlier attack. I know I asked for it, but I don't think my body could stand it, no matter how much I want to fool myself into thinking that I could take it.

"New comforter is in the wash, and I've started a bath for you."

I'm well aware of how puzzled I look. It doesn't stop him from kissing me on the forehead and leading me away and toward my room.

"I saw you popping some more pills," he starts as he winds me through the house like he lives here now. Which in a way, he kind of does. When we enter the bathroom, I notice that there are a couple of other items I hadn't given much thought to when he was grabbing them. Sneaky guy was picking up things for his time spent over here. It's a bit bold of him, but I can't deny the practicality of it.

"I promise I'll leave you alone for a bit." The water is already running in the tub, steam coming off and flowing up and into the air. "Take your time. I'll wait for you out in the living room."

Placing a kiss on my cheek, he starts to leave. As kind as his gesture is, I spout off, a bit more panicked than I mean for it to sound, "What are you going to do?"

He pauses for a moment. While I am grateful for a break and the chance to do a little self-pampering, I hate leaving him to fend for himself around here. But then again, I guess his comfort level around here has grown exponentially if he's buying his own set of things to stay at my house.

There's a pause before he lets out a long exhale through his nose. "I'm going to make good on my word and make a call."

His face falls into one I don't see too often. Seth got pretty worked up at lunch, and I know his past is still hurting him. No doubt the news of his father is bringing things to the surface and I can't imagine dealing with it if I were in his shoes. Being estranged from your family for so long and then coming back into the fold with grim news would mess with anyone, I imagine.

I'm well aware I don't know his family like he does, but I don't want him to miss this opportunity to patch things up. If that's even in the cards. But I also don't want him to come to regret this decision to find out what's happening and what they want.

Curiosity almost gets the best of me. It's on the tip of my tongue to ask him if the scars on his back have anything to do with his dad, but I shove it aside. I'm too afraid to ask. Too frightened of the truth and what bringing up something like that might do to Seth.

Being a mother myself, I want to say that I'm sure his mom would want to hear from him. The thought of going over ten years without speaking to either of *my* children? Just tear my heart out of my chest now.

There's still so much that I don't know about Seth. But I choose to believe that if he's giving them the time of day with a phone call, there has to be a glimmer of hope, right? It seems like for him to even consider calling them in the first place, there has to be something there still.

I only hope that no one from his family will cause him any more pain than what already occurred in the past. What he chooses to keep hidden. Seth doesn't need that. I want him to heal if possible, before it's too late.

19

Stay Gone

Seth

I can't decide who to call.

Do I want to rip my cousin apart for providing some sort of false hope that I might possibly return? I could have fucking killed him, but I held back. Damaged him? Sure did. But I let him return home to the family that I now know he has. A part of me wants to yell, shout, and threaten his life until he ends the call.

That could be a bit therapeutic.

However, I can't do that right now. Not here with Clara so close by. I can't take a chance of her overhearing things that might be said. Someday, when I am absolutely certain that I won't scare her off, I'll tell her everything. There won't be a single secret between us. But for right now, everything is so new and she's too skittish. I can't risk it. I don't fault her for it—she has good reasons.

I'm rummaging carefully through the home office that's on the other side of her bedroom. Ever since Clara confided in me about her money troubles, I've been trying to decide how and if I can help her.

She isn't going to take on another job. Absolutely not. While I admire her willingness to do so, it would take time away from her kids and me. Her heart is in the right place, but she's already stressed enough. Adding another job on top of it all? It might be more counterproductive.

Finding what I'm looking for, I whip my phone out and take a couple photos of the paperwork before stashing it back in the filing cabinet. The desk beside it is a bit big and bulky, not very practical for a place where I could work. But maybe once I come into the picture full-time and need to set up shop, I can rearrange and turn things into a home office that would work for me.

I look about the room, taking in the wooden built-in bookshelves with plenty of empty space. A few photos of the kids are scattered about, making a mini time capsule of Julie and Emmett's growth through the years. It doesn't seem like much time is spent in here, and it's tidier than most of the others. The white curtains are always drawn closed, and the area rug feels like it's hardly ever trampled on.

I'm already imagining making room for my things. A possible chaise for Clara to lounge on while I'm in here working. On breaks, I could fuck her on it and then we'll resume our normal activities after. I wonder if she reads anymore. The lack of books makes me wonder if she's moved on to something else or if she just doesn't have the time to take part in it.

My hours vary every week. While I might get forty plus in a normal one, I make my own schedule. As long as I get my shit done, nobody really cares about it up the food chain.

I cringe, thinking about how messed up I was without Clara this last week. My once impeccable work record was tarnished by a verbal warning. I guess there's a first time for everything.

Sure, there are a few meetings and kickoffs for programs that are nonnegotiable, but I try to work around them. Sometimes I pull all-nighters, loving the quiet atmosphere and lesser interruptions so my workflow can go smoothly. But seeing as how I now have someone to share a bed with, I might have to work out a more logical schedule. We'll figure it out; I have full faith in that.

I grunt, knowing I'm doing everything I can to put off this damn phone call. I'm dragging a hand through my beard, scratching my chin as I lean toward the possibility of calling my mother. I'm torn about the idea.

Recalling her voicemail, I know she's more than likely going to get emotional again, and I don't really want to experience that in the moment. The mere thought of it makes me more uncomfortable than I care to admit. Where was that emotion when I was begging for my dad to stop?

Perhaps if I can convince her that I'm staying gone, that I'm not coming home and not even a dying father can bring me back, then maybe she'll call off Carter. I fear that the longer I wait, the higher the chance of him or someone else coming to Alton. I can't have that. No more surprise visits or phone calls; it needs to stop.

The running water from the bathroom ceased a little while ago, and I hope Clara is enjoying her alone time. I'm not going to be far from her once this phone call and that bath end.

I will have to be more careful with her tonight. While she hasn't outright complained or shown any regret about our earlier engagement, she has been trying to hide the aftermath of it. She deserves this time to rest and relax, but damn, do I look forward to doing that again.

My cock is hardening and I have to push those thoughts away. I need to make good on my intent to call, and I don't want this looming over my time spent with Clara until I get it over with. I won't let this be the cause of any more problems with her. It needs to be taken care of, and swiftly.

I step out the back door and take in the scene of the woods that I have come to know pretty well by now. The sun hasn't shone at all today, and the cloud cover, along with the incoming night, has already darkened the trees and dampened my view. I can pinpoint exactly where I was last night, and I hold focus there as I take a seat in the chair opposite Clara's.

I can't help but wonder if Joe ever sat out here when Clara was his. Correction, she was never his. He was merely holding my place until I came into the picture. Giving her children when I couldn't.

I crack my knuckles at the mere thought of his dick going anywhere near her. He didn't deserve her and in the end, hurt her. My fists would like to meet his face, first off. The rest, well, I'll decide as it comes to me. If there was a way to get rid of him without further damage, without hurting Julie and Emmett, I would gladly stoop that low. Just from seeing images of him online, he looks like a douchebag—there's a smugness and pride to him that makes him look arrogant.

I don't know the first thing about being a father figure to a nine- and thirteen-year-old, but I will make sure to be everything they need without being too overbearing. Damn, I can't wait to meet them.

I'm stalling, again. I realize that as a gust of wind sweeps past me. It's enough to send leaves from their trees and carry them off. I focus on one of them intently, watching it until it disappears into darkness before I bring my phone out and scroll to find the number I wanted to forget and click on it. Who in the hell even has a house phone anymore?

I hold my breath, stiff as a statue as it takes a beat for it to start ringing.

One. Two. Three rings.

Just when I think a victory is in sight and I'm headed for an answering machine, the line shifts and that familiar voice picks up. I swear the temperature has just dropped ten degrees.

"Hello?"

Words fail to come, and I'm still staring off after my lost maple leaf, as if when it returns, it might bring my mind back with it.

"Seth? Is that you?" She sounds older, but there's still that familiarity that tugs at my chest without my consent.

I can't move, at least my body can't. It's like I've been strapped down to this rocker by thick chains and rolls of duct tape. But not my lips.

"Hi, Mom." It sounds wrong to even call her that anymore.

"Oh!" Her voice breaks on that one sound. Alice Ries is acting just as I suspected she might, but it doesn't make it any easier to hear. And I thought getting through that voicemail was difficult. "Seth, oh my. Seth!"

Her words become more hushed as she tries to clear the thickness gathering in her throat so she can string together more coherent sentences. Steadying breaths are gripping me in a way that I don't like, and I grow more and more uncomfortable.

We've hardly even begun.

"I can't talk long," I start out, trying to set the mood with a clipped tone. The line goes quiet for a moment and I start to think that the call might have dropped. One glance at the screen and I know that's not the case.

It's on the tip of my tongue to ask what's wrong with Dad, but I stop myself. I want to keep this as plain as possible, try not to show too much interest in the case that might give her false hope.

"It's been fourteen years, Seth."

Has it? I stopped counting after ten. If I tell her to keep counting will that get me off of the phone faster?

"I'm not coming back," I state, trying to keep my voice even yet stern so there's no misunderstanding.

"But..." Her voice breaks again, and can't help but wonder if this is an act or if she truly feels broken up about it. How can I tell when I don't really know my mother anymore? How much has she changed, if any, since I last saw her? A lot could happen in fourteen years. Hell, so much has changed in me just since I met Clara.

"But your father, he—"

"He's dying. I heard." I'm remaining cold and distant, the only way I can afford to be. The way I remember *her* to be.

"Seth." Her voice turns more serious, like it's bordering on the point of scolding.

That's it, let me piss you off. I can tell Clara that I tried. Hopefully, that will be enough. "Still not coming back."

The line falls silent again, and while I don't want to find myself alone in a room with her, I can't help but wonder what she's doing at this exact moment. Is she alone or are there others present? I can't even tell if I'm on speaker phone or not, though there are no obvious signs of it. Is my father in close proximity and listening to the conversation? If he is, he's doing a good job at staying silent.

"You have a duty to this family, Seth. It's time to stop running around and come home. You're needed here."

Funny, how you don't say that *you* want me home. It only deepens my need to get out of this talk as quickly as possible.

What could I possibly gain by going back to Colorado? She didn't do anything to try and calm my dad down in his wild and violent outbursts. Disappeared when my grandfather joined in and the two of them took turns making my life a living hell. Thank fuck one of them is already dead.

And when the news traveled about my inability to have children, you would have sworn that I was damned and had cursed our family. Aunts, uncles, cousins, and even extended family members acted like I had the plague or something.

Perhaps if I'd had a different upbringing, if my mother even *tried* to put her foot down even once, maybe this story would be different. Does she even miss me at all? Is it that far-fetched to want my mom to *want* me to come home out of more than just duty? I don't care if I am their only child. They washed their hands of me before I even left.

"Look—" I lean forward in the chair, feeling rigid as I do. "Let me be perfectly clear. I am *not* going back there, and if anyone else even attempts to come and try to convince me otherwise, they will never return. I did Carter a favor, I won't make the same mistake twice."

I almost hang up, but for whatever reason, I wait. I don't know if she'll raise her voice at me or backpedal to try and diffuse the situation. My nostrils flare, and there's a shake in the arm I'm using to hold up the phone.

There are too many memories. Too much irreparable damage. I've spent so long running from the past that won't just stay buried.

"What happened to you, Seth?"

Isn't that a loaded question? I grew up and moved on. Paved my own path in life without Mom and Dad in the picture.

"What...why won't you come home?" Her voice is on the verge of getting emotional again. "Out of all of the places you could go, what is keeping you in Iowa?" Her voice rises on the name of the state I'm living in, and by the sounds of it, somehow it offends her.

"I don't know how else to put this. I'm not coming back. There's nothing, and I mean absolutely nothing, that you can say or do to convince me otherwise." And that's the fucking truth. I don't care if my old man is in a casket next week. I'll be absent from the visitation, funeral, and graveside service.

"I just don't understand. What on earth could be keeping you there? Haven't you been away from your family long enough?"

I've entertained this phone call longer than I anticipated. I could go with something along the lines of "You're all dead to me" to wrap things up, but that doesn't seem like enough.

"Did you meet someone?"

My attempts to part with my mother come to a screeching halt. "What? No."

"You did, didn't you?" Her tone turns almost chipper and I'm standing from the chair and looking out into the woods as if something out there will help me ward her off of this trail.

"I didn't say that." My response is short as my mood dips down into something foul.

"Oh, Seth, you didn't have to! Why else would you refuse to come home?"

Had Clara never come into the picture, I *still* wouldn't be willing to go back there. Not even if hell were to freeze over or there was a zombie apocalypse and the only safe haven was on my family's estate.

Absolutely fucking not.

She's rattling on and on about meeting her and the pack she's from. Already trying to butter me up with excitement when there is zero chance that I am going to admit that I have indeed found my mate. She's quick to assume that she's a werewolf. If my mother were to find out that Clara is very real and human? I don't want to imagine her response to that. It's a fifty-fifty shot, which way it could go. I've already disappointed her once without even trying, why put icing on that cake?

"Even if I had, it doesn't change things. I want nothing to do with any of you, Colorado, *nothing.*"

"You would really throw away your family? Your own flesh and blood? You *will* come home, Seth!" Her temper is rising, as is mine. I can feel my bones beginning to vibrate. I can't do this. Not now.

"Let me remind you that you threw me away first!" I'm shaking, overcome with the need to change with my roiling anger. "It'd be in your best interest to forget about me. You stopped being my parents long ago, don't try to make up for lost time now."

I hang up and smash the phone onto the iron railing. Pieces fall to the ground and I'm left with the carcass of what's left behind.

I'm seething, so lost in thought and flashbacks from my past that I don't even realize that Clara is present until I catch her sweet scent. It's mouthwatering, it truly is, but it doesn't do enough to calm me the fuck down.

I'm trying to suppress it, the change that's attempting to take over, but not even when I look at her do I feel like I can hold it off.

"Seth." She holds her breath, a worried expression on that face that any other time I would take in my hands and kiss away. She's in a robe, her legs bare to the October air, and she's holding them together as if she can keep them warm without a stitch on them.

"I need to go," I grit out, unable to say much more. My spine is expanding, as if a live wire has just zapped it and it's trying to signal for the change even though I'm fighting to hold off.

Not right now, not in front of Clara. It's not the right time. Our situation right now, our relationship, is too delicate to be thwarted with the news of who I am.

Of *what* I really am.

"Please. Don't." Her voice is falling quieter as she pleads for me to stay.

My gums are starting to burn, and I can feel my teeth protruding from behind closed lips. One look at her and she'll know something is off. If I wait any longer, I'll jeopardize everything.

"I...I need to run." I speak through my tightly clenched jaw, knowing that my voice sounds forced and jagged. Definitely anything but normal.

In a swift move, I hurl my body over the railing and onto the ground below. My back almost doesn't bend enough to let me, and the balls of my feet sink into the ground. I take off in a sprint for the tree line. Hair along my arms is growing rapidly and my body is trying to change on its own timeline, but I push through, pumping my arms harder as I will my legs to carry me faster and out of view. I do my best to keep the agonizing sounds of my change to a minimum, for fear that Clara might hear. I can't have her coming after me or alerting any authorities to strange sounds in the night.

I only hope that she'll give me this time to work this out of my system, this built-up tension and hurt that I need to burn off in the only way I know how.

Only then will I come back to her, ready to move on and forward, even though I thought I already had.

20

Stupid Chick That Gets Killed First

Clara

There's a sharp snap and a shuffle, a sound like Seth might have fallen to the ground. Like someone just skidded to a stop into a mountainous pile of leaves but far beyond what my eyes can see.

I stare out into the darkened woods, still trying to comprehend that Seth took off like a bat out of hell and disappeared in them. He isn't even wearing any shoes!

My heart is beating rapidly, rising up my chest and into the base of my throat as I whisper-shout his name, but I can't make out any other sounds besides that of my staggered breathing and blood pumping through my veins.

I only caught the tail end of his discussion, and while I could only hear his end of it, I know that it must not have gone well. My stomach feels like it's holding solid rocks inside of it, weighing me down with an uneasy feeling.

I put Seth up to this. I was adamant that he contact his family so there wouldn't be any chance of living with the regrets. I should never have tried to compare what little I know of Seth's past to my uncle's passing. My heart was in the right place, but who am I to say what he should and shouldn't be doing? I have no control over his life or the past he has tried to move on from. We're still getting to know each other.

What if they *are* the reason for those scars on his back, and I was pushing him right back to his abusers? What have I done?

Thoughts plague me without slowing, each one more troubling than the next. Should I be concerned that he didn't want to talk about it and instead wanted to run into the woods? That doesn't exactly sound healthy, or safe for that matter. He has no shoes to shield his feet. No phone and therefore no source of light.

A roll of thunder in the distance makes the rocks in my stomach heavier, and I'm balling my fists. The failure to figure out what I need to do is eating me up.

Clearly, Seth's head isn't in the right place, and I fear for him in the woods by himself. They stretch on for quite some ways, and not even I have ventured that far into them. He could get lost in there if he's not careful.

This is stupid. *I* am stupid for running after a man and into the woods to try and find him. But I don't think I'll be able to sit and wait and do nothing when he is obviously hurting.

There's a crack in the sky, illuminating dark and ominous clouds on my right, and I bolt into the house. I'm tearing off my robe and hauling on clothes to help shield me from the dropping temperature. I stuff my phone into my sports bra for good measure.

I throw on my mowing shoes, aka the crappiest pair of shoes I own, and come skidding to a stop at the kitchen sink in search of a flashlight that turns out to be dead. Things are falling out of drawers and clattering to the floor as I scour through them. I don't have any time or care in the world to tidy the mess I make as I keep digging to find the ridiculously large batteries I seek in an unopened package. I make quick work stuffing them inside the flashlight, and once it flips on, I almost face-plant on the kitchen tiles but catch myself.

I'm no runner by any means. I am fully aware that I'm in no shape to try and chase after Seth with a storm rolling in, but it doesn't stop me from trying. The harsh intake of air is already attacking my lungs as I make it to the tree line and flip on the flashlight, quickly finding out just how dark the path ahead of me is.

"Seth?" I call out as I begin to make my way in. There's another grumble from the sky, and whatever storm is moving in is doing so fast. The breeze picks up, sending a shiver through my body.

In hindsight, I should have at least snatched his shoes from the house and brought them with me, but I was in such a hurry I guess I was lucky to have even thought to bring a flashlight. I know my phone battery is getting low, so I didn't want it to be my only source of light. If I manage to get lost, I need something in case of an emergency.

I call out his name again as I come to a brief stop to catch my breath. Evening my stance, I glance back to find that my house and any lights that are on inside have already disappeared from view. Even with the coming fall and the trees ridding themselves of their leaves, the wooded area is still dense. I'm being swallowed up by darkness. The lack of life around me and the absence of the small town of Alton is raising the hair on my arms.

This feels like the beginning of some horror flick, and I am going to be the first one picked off because of their stupidity. Fat chance in hell I could outrun some serial killer.

Fuck. What am I thinking?

My flashlight is weak in my surroundings, and the increase in rumbles above me is doing absolutely nothing for my nerves. Another crack sounds, and when the lightning flashes, I can barely make out the treetops above.

"Seth!" My voice is shaky, and while I might have stopped my lame attempt at running, my heart is still racing. Joe and I never let the kids venture far, knowing just how deep the woods run. We drew red marks on some of the trees at one point, letting the kids know the furthest point they were allowed to go, but those have long vanished over the years.

There's a snap of a branch on my left and I jump, dropping the flashlight from my hand and momentarily blinding me in my feeble attempt to retrieve it. I'm all thumbs as I try to steady it and look ahead to see if a deer or something might be the cause, but I can't make anything out. The night is swallowing up the beam of light, and the urge to talk myself into retreating already is growing stronger.

Seth shouldn't be out here alone, but then again neither should I. But at the same time, I feel responsible for his pain. I should have stayed out of it. His family and past, it's none of my business. Yes, I wanted him to reconnect when there was a chance of him losing his father, but at what price? That phone call seems to have done more harm than good. The exact opposite of my intent.

The light pitter-patter of rain begins to fill my ears as it falls. I inhale, shaky and weak. My body is growing colder the longer I'm out here, and as much as I want to try to go after Seth, I force myself to entertain the fact that he could be out of the trees and running the streets of Alton right now. Maybe even on his way back home. I force myself to believe that. Perhaps he really did just need to be alone so I didn't see him upset.

My dumb ass trying to track him down seems more like asking for disaster.

Plops of rain begin to hit my head and I glance up, as if I can tell the water to fuck off. So much for the bath I had.

Just as I'm mustering up enough courage to trudge my way back through to head back home, there's a rustling of leaves from behind. My breath hitches, and I listen intently to see if I can decipher just how far, or close, it might be.

It's normal to see deer and rabbits regularly around my home. It shouldn't be any big deal that one might be caught out here in the storm just like I am, but I can't shake the feeling that I am being watched. Maybe it's my overactive imagination playing tricks on me, and the countless scary movies Joe forced me to watch, but I can't seem to shut my brain off from that possibility.

The rain begins to fall heavier, dampening my hair and rolling down my face. I swipe away at it as I try to find the strength to swivel and begin to charge my way back home, but there's another sound that has my free hand snapping over my mouth.

Something snarls from up ahead.

I open my mouth to call for Seth again, but nothing comes. Not even a squeak. Fear is seeping into every blood cell in my body, and terror begins to set in. In all of my life living between Pembrook and Alton, I have never encountered more than deer, squirrels, birds, possums, and other animals that I wouldn't consider frightening. But this? Every siren that could possibly sound off in my head is doing so, and at full volume.

I have never had any reason to fear the woods, until now.

My eyes are soon burning, tears forming and descending as they mix with the falling rain that's obscuring my already poor vision. My sweater is growing heavier, and while I want to get the hell out of here, my feet act like they were cemented to the ground below.

My posture jerks as the sky above me lights up and thunder travels in and roars in my ears. How can something so bright up above barely give me any grace down here?

When my eyes lower, they fall on something up ahead that freezes me to my core. Something, and I don't know what in the hell it is, is looking at me. Its eyes and pointed features are slanted in my direction. It's on all fours and hairy.

With another roll of light, I barely discern sharp and high ears. While my mind is trying to convince me that it's some wolf, it isn't like anything I have ever seen before.

It snarls, its mouth flashing a menacing set of teeth that tells me it is all predator, through and through.

And I am now the prey.

While my eyes might have steadily grown more accustomed to the dark, it has done nothing to aid my logical thinking. I am a freaking lamb to the slaughter. I have nothing to defend myself and I just stand there, frozen in terror.

Until it moves.

The creature acts as if it's sitting back, but that couldn't be more wrong. It begins to stand on its hind legs, showing off a great stature that would no doubt tower over me. I know that running will probably give it reason to chase me, but I don't think waiting for this beast is any better at this point.

A shrill scream rips from my throat as I pivot. The light from my hand is bouncing about madly as I dart around trees and try to hop over tree roots and fallen branches. I expect to hear footsteps behind me or the gnashing of teeth, but there's just the sound of me, attempting to run in a panicked state in the hopes of finding my way back home.

I'm not sure if I will die by the tall monster I encountered or if a heart attack might take me first.

Just when I think my body is failing and going to give out on me, I hear something coming up on my side. I dodge behind the nearest tree as lightning and thunder collide above and I struggle to take in a breath. The air in my lungs hurts, and I'm pretty sure I haven't had this much adrenaline coursing through my veins since a high school physical education exam.

Something snarls again, and I'm on the verge of giving up. The bark behind me is wet and rough, and a piece breaks off and falls as something else growls from the opposite direction of the last.

Two of them? Fucking two?

I'm dead. There's no way I'm outrunning two wildly unnatural-looking beasts. While I might have my phone on me, I don't want the last message my children get from their mother to be of her damn death while being ripped to shreds. I'll be a fucking buffet for whatever in the hell they are. Will I even have any remains left to be found by morning? How long will it take for a search party to be sent out?

I'm on the verge of sobbing, sending up silent prayers to whoever might be listening to save me and help me find a way back to my house and to my children. I beg that they aren't left to fucking Joe and Chassidy. I can't die leaving Julie and Emmett in their care. I won't.

I take off again, but trip over something and I scramble to get up. Dirt packs in under my nails and wet leaves are sticking to me as I lift my head and come face-to-face with light golden eyes. My brain is confused for a moment, trying to connect them to the one and only person I know to have such a beautiful gaze, but it's all wrong.

Brown fur forms a face like that of a wolf, but its snout is much longer. While everything in my body is telling me to run, I recognize something else.

This isn't the one that was snarling at me earlier. Its mouth is closed. Its hair is lighter, and it doesn't have that menacing look that sends chills through my entire body. Its head is at eye level, and while we're maybe a few feet away, in some remarkable and yet baffling way, I know it doesn't warrant the fear that I felt moments ago.

But the threatening sound from behind me does.

I glance back, finding the darker creature on all fours again, and drawing closer. Its steps are muddled with the storm that's taking over my auditory senses.

The one before me growls and somehow manages to leap and take flight over me. It attacks the other one, and while I'm momentarily taken aback by the fight taking place, I use that distraction to my advantage and get to my feet so I can take off. Teeth chomp and bodies collide as they strike each other and roll about. It draws my attention for a split second, and my shoulder hits an outstretched and low branch. I hiss in response to the impact, finding torn fabric and the sting of a fresh wound.

The creatures fighting behind me only drives me harder and faster than my legs are willing to take me. The earth beneath my feet is growing slick and muddier as I go, making it harder to get my bearings. It's like the forest is trying to keep me here.

One of them lets out a strange and garbled shriek of pain, and it sends a chill straight through me. I have no idea at what point I lost my flashlight, and while I want to reach into my bra for my phone, I don't think I'll be able to get a good enough grip on it to hold on to that, either. And with the rain? Good. Fucking. Luck.

A speck of light comes into view, and while I want to let out a victorious cry, that comes to a halt as I trip over something again and fall hard. I groan as I roll to my side, cupping my elbow as I try to recover from the abrupt stop in my getaway. My chest heaves, but I attempt to prepare myself to push through the pain in my throbbing knee and arm.

I'm almost there.

I've almost lost all sense of why I came into the woods in the first place, until I hear a strained yet familiar voice.

I scramble up, my feet digging into the mud and coating my shoes with its thickness. I'm soon panicking for not only my life, but his as well.

"Seth!" I screech as I hear him let out a howl of agony. Fresh, hot tears are quick to form.

Odd and indescribable animalistic sounds come from the darkness and I'm searching it wildly, afraid of what might decide to pop out. Something is moving up ahead as I take a weary step back, and then another.

I'm too scared to call for him again, afraid of leading either of those things directly to me. Especially now when I'm so close to home. But the fact that Seth is still out there frightens me the most. He could be dead before any cops make it out here, and even then, who would believe a mad woman talking about creatures that stand taller than her that have no business being anything more than fucked-up figments of my imagination?

"C-Clara!"

Chest thudding wildly, I take a step forward, scanning where I think his voice came from, and call out his name again. I'm moving in that direction when a figure comes into view.

I stall for a moment, willing my eyes to focus so I can be certain. Seth's face rounds a tree and before I think, I take off toward him. The rain, thunder, and lightning show are still filling the air, but I push on until I get close enough to really make him out.

I'm stunned to find a stark naked Seth trudging through the muck and nearing me. My footsteps come to an end as I look him over in a panic. "What...? Where are your...? What happened to you?"

Seth looks like a wild man, mud and earth caked on him to make it look like he has been living out here in the woods for ages. Not even the rain is hard enough to wash away the clumps on him, but as he swipes some of it away, I catch a glimpse of a wound on his chest.

Scratch that. Wounds? They look like claw marks. Four distinguished marks on his chiseled chest like Freddy Krueger slashed him.

And then it hits me as I look into his eyes. Alive, wild, bright, and golden, even though we're shrouded in the night. The same eyes I saw on one of those things before I began running for my life.

Water is running down my face as the rain picks up again. Its force is almost deafening as the sound fills my ears. It seeps into my parted mouth as we both stand there, staring at each other. My sweater is sopping wet and holding me down like a weighted blanket, making it even harder to catch my breath.

Just as Seth goes to take a step, I take an unsteady one back and hold my hands up in the air to stop him. He's not running for his life. Not a single fear showing for whatever in the hell was in the woods.

"Clara, I can explain." He holds out his arms as if he's trying to cautiously approach an unpredictable and scared animal. I know I don't stand a chance, not a single fucking one, but I turn anyway and run.

21

Every Rose Has Thorns

Seth

I should be used to running around naked by now, but not when I'm trying to chase after someone who's actively fleeing from me because she's terrified. I can smell the fear radiating off of Clara as I close in on her in her backyard. I'm still sore from my shift, rendering me slower than normal.

We're in the clearing halfway between her house and the woods by the time I catch up and cut her off. Her eyes are alive with fright, the browns of them almost swallowed up by how large her pupils are. She's trembling as she stops, her body shaking, and I know it's not just from the outdoor cold and her soiled clothes.

Clara is scared, and painfully, rightfully so.

Fuck. Fuck. Fuck!

This isn't how it was supposed to go. Clara wasn't supposed to come after me, and dammit, if that stupid, nosy neighbor of mine could just get it through his thick skull that I'm not a threat in the first place, none of this would have happened. Larson must have thought I was going after Clara when it was the exact opposite. I was trying to protect her from him. How was I to know this dipshit has been stalking me?

As soon as I shifted into my wolf form, I caught onto his scent. And when Clara entered the woods, that put her on both of our radars. The real kicker was that Larson thought he could take me.

He might have had a good swipe at me, but he didn't stand a chance. I threw him against a tree and bent his hind leg until I heard it snap. He scurried off, limp and defeated, while I changed back to my human form and chased after my Rose.

The very one who is now looking at me like I murdered someone in front of her.

It's too soon. Clara finding out about me and all that I am—she's not ready for it. Our relationship will be over before it really had a chance to gain momentum.

"Clara, please. Just let—"

"No!" She shakes her head as she tries to step to the side. I can only imagine the shitstorm that must be swirling around in her head, trying to make sense of things. Of what she just witnessed.

"You don't...no!" She's shaking her head, full of disbelief and fright. I'm sure she wore the same look when Larson stood on his hind legs to try and intimidate me. And worse, exposing himself further to Clara.

He made the situation more chaotic than it needed to be.

She's trying to skirt around me, trying to figure out how she can make it to her house and away from *me*. She knows my secret. Even if she doesn't know how to fully admit it to herself and put a name to it yet. A name to what I am and what she just witnessed. I'm not exactly a fluffy and fun-looking furball of fun, the exact opposite of a domesticated animal.

Clara's nose is red and her face is blotchy with color while she's being washed out at the same time. I want to hold her and tell her that everything is alright. Explain every little detail of my upbringing and life to help her come to terms with what I am, but I know that she isn't in the right headspace.

But I don't think I can just walk away, either. I can't leave her alone to come to terms with all of this on her own.

Her eyes dart around briefly, signaling that she's going to try and make a break for it again, and when she does, I cut her off. I catch onto her around her middle, spinning her around to face away from the house, and when she tries to scream, my palm comes up to silence her. She's frantic, fighting against me and bucking violently, and I lose my balance, sending us both toppling to the ground, but I'm quick to recover. I pin her down and steady myself on top of her as I do. She's crying profusely, but I can't let us separate. Not now, and not like this.

"Clara, please. Please just listen to me," I urge and beg.

"No, no, no, no." Her head is shaking back and forth as she pleads for me to let her go. My heart is breaking at how wrong all of this is. How horribly south this has gone, and holding her down is only making it worse. "My kids. Please don't take me from my kids."

Just when I thought things couldn't get any worse and I couldn't feel any lower, there it is. It's gutting to think that Clara believes I would be capable of such a thing. It hurts worse than the blow Larson landed to my chest. She really has no idea just how much she means to me, how I would literally put my life on the line for her and her children. Harming her is one thing I swore I would never do, so why does it feel like I'm doing exactly that right now?

She can't even stand to look at me, and that alone speaks volumes. As much as I want her to take a second and listen to me, I fear that it would fall on deaf ears. It stings, to even consider leaving her, especially right now. So, I give her a choice.

"Listen to me carefully, Clara." I still the fight in her long enough to gain her attention. Her face is pointed away and eyes are firmly shut, but she's listening. The rise and fall of her chest beneath me, mildly slowing. "I know you have no reason to believe otherwise but I would never, *never* harm you or do anything to endanger you or your children."

She tries to take advantage of my loosened grip, but I'm quick to recover and her face pinches in disappointment. Clara's hair is plastered to the sides of her face, the two of us sinking into the ground the longer we remain here.

"I'm going to give you a choice, and no matter what you decide, I will honor it."

I don't fear her going to the cops or reporting a wild animal sighting. I know she's smarter than that. When she tries to describe what she saw, no one will believe her. Worse yet, if her ex-husband should find out anything regarding the matter or claims, it would only further fuel him to take action on the one thing Clara seems to fear the most—Joe taking Julie and Emmett.

Clara is too selfless to risk that. They mean too much to her, as they would to any good mother. The kind of mother I wish I had.

"I'm sorry for what has happened. This is *not* how I wanted you to find out." My body is blocking the downpour from most of her body, but streams are running off my sides and from my hair, dripping onto her in steady measures. "I can leave if you wish. Leave, so you can try to think more clearly and we can pick this all up later. Or, I can stay and I can tell you everything. And I do mean everything, Clara."

She still can't look at me, choosing to keep her face turned away, and it's like my insides are being twisted. I'm losing her, I can feel it.

"Either way, you will learn my truth. I'm just letting you decide on the when."

We're incredibly lucky that she lives on a dead-end road and the houses in her part of the neighborhood are so far apart. Hers is set back far enough from the road and the next door neighbor that nobody would be able to see us in our current position. And with the storm that's rolling through, no one may have even heard a peep from what has happened tonight.

I release her arms and carefully stand, watching her the entire time. She keeps still for a few beats before opening her eyes and blinking.

Slowly, she draws her knees up and goes to stand. Her clothing sags and her face makes my chest ache. My injury and the discomfort from it are long forgotten already. She's been through the ringer tonight, and it's all my damn fault.

Well, and dipshit Larson. I'll deal with him soon enough.

"Clara." I instinctively reach out to touch her and she recoils.

"Don't fucking touch me!" Her heated expression is sending me through pits of despair and agony. Her voice is growing hoarse as she begins to put some distance between us. "Don't come near me. Don't talk to me. Just...don't."

I'm breaking. My body is reeling from the loss of her and the wall she's putting up between us. My heart is cracking open, and I'm losing the precious connection that gives me life. My other half is on the verge of rejecting me, and while I know she doesn't know the seriousness of that, it doesn't make her words hurt any less. A part of me will die if I lose her. I hate to be dramatic, but I honestly don't know how to move on if she isn't in my life.

I don't know how to come back from this. I fully believed that by shielding her from the truth for a little while, I was doing the right thing. But maybe, just maybe, I was merely thinking of myself in that, too afraid of losing her and scaring her off, which is exactly what's happening before my very eyes.

A lump is forming in my throat as the sky lights up and the rain threatens to drown us. As much as I want to try and convince her that everything is going to be alright, I'm having trouble believing that right now.

"I'm sorry," is all I can manage before I turn away, giving her the time and space to flee from me. From us.

She doesn't hesitate to do it, either. I shudder as I hear the back door slam and I'm left alone. Just me and the storm, reeling in the wake of an evening of disaster.

Time moves differently without Clara in the picture.

In the days that follow the incident and her discovery in the woods, time crawls. I am quick to go out and get a new phone, and even send her a message to let her know that I have a new number, but she leaves it unread. She won't even offer me the decency of a "fuck off" reply. Hell, I would even take that right about now. Being left all alone and in silence and without her—now, that's downright miserable.

Days crawl by and they bleed into weeks. The grass around my rental dies as we move into November. Most of the trees have lost their leaves now and the air has a bite to it when you step outside. That doesn't stop me from visiting Clara's house every night just to check in on things.

I never catch her outside, and as much as I want to leave her back porch full of every fucking flower known to mankind—or the most I could possibly purchase from a flower shop—I know that it isn't in my best interest to do it. Especially after how upset she was after receiving one the last time. The bushes behind my house have finally met their end, just as lifeless as I feel now.

This time, I really am in the doghouse. Both literally and figuratively. Clara has shut me out and it hurts worse, so much worse, than when I voluntarily up and left my family.

As time passes, they haven't even tried to reach me again. I find it suspicious, but overall, I'm just grateful to be left alone by my mom, cousin, and anyone else who might think it's their job to get me to come back. Even if they don't have this new phone number, they still have my work cell. They have the means to find me if they wanted to.

"Seth?"

My name snaps me out of my thoughts and back into my work meeting. I'm in my home office with three different computer monitors before me and a meeting pulled up with about half a dozen coworkers.

I'm not even sure how long I zoned out for, but it was enough to render me absolutely clueless about whatever the hell we're talking about now.

So many of these meetings are pointless. Check-in's and updates that could easily have been an email in the first place to spare everyone the waste of time that they usually are.

I don't care about the conference coming up or whatever tea Shirley is drinking today. I don't give a rat's ass about the company's new and improved logo and the meaning of the colors that were chosen for it.

Great, fine, let's fucking move on.

"Sorry." I bite down my attitude and try to put a smile on my face but it feels too forced. I probably look like a crazed man right now, but I really couldn't care less. "I've been having some connectivity issues today and the hot spot is being temperamental."

My chat goes off on my right screen and I see a new message from Dante, who finds these meetings just as insignificant as I do. He's the closest to me in age out of our group and we both started around the same time.

> *They want to know if you're going to the conference.*

I type out a quick thanks as a reply leaves my lips. "Still undecided. When was it you had to know by?"

"Next. Wednesday." Juanita, my boss who is usually charmed by me, is obviously annoyed. She's been married three times and when she's taken, she laughs at all of the jokes and pokes fun at herself and others in lightheartedness. But when she's in between husbands? Look out. She's got the attitude. As she does with me right now, biting out her words in short reply. Her bright red lips are always a distraction that pulls at your eyes when you're on these video calls.

That, and Tracey's orange cat who always finds its way into the camera's view. That stinker is always causing mischief, whether it's in front of us to see or in the background.

"Then you will have my answer by Tuesday." I try to flash a deeper smile but it gets me nowhere. I think it's safe to say that there's no man in sight for her right now; she's too grumpy and clipped.

Somebody send her a man, please.

The rest of the call is mainly small talk and the rest of the team discussing the conference in San Diego. Normally, I would try to go to this one. It's a good chance to check in and hang out with everyone. And when I say everyone, I mean Dante. We're usually thick as thieves, bonding and bitching about work and life under the sun and moon.

That is, until he brought his new wife last year.

Dante left his bachelor life behind for her, and while I'm happy for him, it does cause me to rethink going to the conference this year. I don't like feeling like a third wheel.

Now with Clara bouncing in and out of the picture, it makes the decision to go that much harder to make. Therefore, I haven't provided an answer about the trip yet. Fleeing to the West Coast with Clara had been a thought at one point. Taking the kids to the beach if they knew about me by that time. But my life has gone up in flames and the fires haven't shown any signs of being extinguished yet.

By the time the meeting is over, my phone is ringing with Dante's name displayed across it. I wait a few seconds before answering, knowing that he's going to come at me with questions about the conference and my lack of involvement in the meeting. I know we're coworkers, but I like to think that we're closer than that. A friend that I have, no matter where I move to.

"Hi." I breathe out slowly as I pinch the bridge of my nose, standing so I can stretch myself out.

"Are you really considering not going to the conference? You love San Diego! What gives?"

Dante's voice is more concerned than anything, and while he may not know of my secret that Clara regrettably discovered too soon, he probably knows me better than anyone else.

I don't want to bother him with the third wheeling topic, so I weigh the thought of some truth. I let it slip a while ago that I had met someone, so he already knows that there was somebody in the picture, but I wasn't exactly very forthcoming with any information after the fact.

"Normally I would jump at it, sure." I make my way out of my office and toward the kitchen so I can start to scrounge up some food. I don't think I've eaten anything since lunch yesterday and we're clear into the next afternoon. "Things are just a little up in the air right now. I'm not sure if going on the trip is the right thing to do."

"Meaning?" He's quick to press as I start grabbing some items from the fridge to make a sandwich.

I slam the door a bit too harshly, the contents in the door rattling in their places and it sounds like something falls over. "Meaning, I've fucked things over with someone and I'm trying to figure out how to fix it."

And so far, failing miserably.

Apparently all it took was my inability to control my anger for everything to spiral out of control. If I could have just swallowed my frustrations and fought off the change, talked things through with Clara instead of trying to run, maybe she wouldn't have shut me out. Maybe she'd still be speaking to me. What I wouldn't give to hear her voice right about now.

Don't get me started on fucking Larson. He was quick to get after me for shifting on a night without a full moon, and now he's doing the same and stalking me? *Me?* I haven't heard a peep from him since that night. I hope he's learned his lesson not to meddle with my life.

"This the same woman you met when you moved?"

"Yes," I sigh, my heart feeling heavy. "Her name's Clara."

"That's right, Clara." I only briefly discussed her on our last one-on-one call, but apparently it was enough for him to remember her. I never brought up random women I hooked up with. Never flaunted them as prizes, either. I had needs that needed taken care of sometimes, but didn't bother with the whole dating thing. I was always upfront with them too, letting them know that I never planned on a hookup being anything but that.

Until Clara came into my life.

"Well, what did you do?"

"Quick to assume it's me?" I feign innocence, even if some might say it's the furthest thing from the truth.

"She's a divorced woman with kids and you've been living the dream life of a single bachelor for as long as we've known each other. The math isn't mathing."

I'm partially offended, but we both know he's right. And while I can't tell him exactly what transpired to lead to this disruption, I also can't deny the minor weight it lifts to be able to talk about my sad excuse of a love life. Well, now that I actually want one.

"So you do remember her." A fraction of a smile breaks across my face, one that doesn't feel fake.

"How could I not? I know you must be serious about her if you even brought her up in the first place. It's not like you."

My ham sandwich looks like a toddler made it. Meat is spilling from it and mustard is squeezing out through a cut in the wheat bread. I might have been a little heavy-handed.

"What are you going to do? How are you going to fix it?" he pries, not letting up.

"I was waiting for her to come to me. Giving her some space."

Dante groans, and I can picture him at his desk burying his face in his hand. He is tanned, as if whatever religion he believes in blessed him with that dark skin that women lust after. Back in our single days together, they were quick to throw themselves at him first. "And how long has that been going on?"

I toss my sandwich onto a paper plate and leave the table to go look out my back door. A squirrel takes off and darts up a tree, leaving the scene empty and void of life.

Lifeless. That's kind of how I've been feeling lately.

"More than a few weeks."

"Fuck, man." He's beginning to sound annoyed, and that edge in his tone is putting me in the same mood as well.

"She isn't answering any of my texts and I'm not going to hound her, either." I stand my ground, hoping he'll see that it's not like I haven't been trying. How else is Clara supposed to react when she comes across two werewolves in the woods on an evening of severe thunderstorms?

"Have you given her a reason to?"

"I've told her I'm sorry. I've apologized."

"She needs more than words, Seth." A woman's voice, though distant, interrupts our conversation.

I didn't know that there was a third person listening in. Dante must be having some quiet words with her, as both of their voices become mumbled and it sounds like they're arguing through whispers. It isn't until I hear his wife demand the phone that I hold my breath.

"Hi, it's Susan." I could recognize her high pitch anywhere.

"Hi, Susan." I'm hesitant to talk to her and feel too exposed with her jumping in. She also works from home, but for some makeup company. It kills me how much people can make through cosmetics. Meanwhile I'm busting my ass with programming, fixing, and creating programs, without any kind of recognition for it most of the time.

"Sorry to butt in..." *No, you're not.* "But remember that actions speak louder than words. If you really like this...Clara?" She mumbles something, then comes back. "Clara. Then you need to show her that you are fully committed."

I am committed. What the fuck does she know?

"Oh! What if you bring her to San Diego? We could go on a double date!"

I exhale sharply. There isn't a fat chance in hell I'm going to get Clara to go halfway across the states to a conference when I can't even get her to talk to me.

Dante must be trying to wrestle the phone back from Susan. Their little argument grows, and I'm half tempted to hang up.

"Weeks? He's waited too long already," she snaps as Dante picks up the phone, a little short of breath for a moment.

"Sorry, Seth. Talk to you later?"

"Yeah, talk later." I end the call and stow my phone in the pocket of my sweats.

Committed.

I let out an odd snort, irritated that Susan has the audacity to give input when she has only met me once and knows nothing about my relationship with Clara.

I'm giving time for her to come to terms with what she saw in the woods. Trying to be patient when I know that her world and the man she thought she was getting to know have been turned upside down. I'm not going to badger her until she finally comes around. No matter how hard it is.

And action? What the hell action could I possibly take that wouldn't drive Clara further away from me? It's a miracle she isn't trying to pack up and leave after what she witnessed outside her back door. Not that I'd let her, but still.

It leaves me to wonder how I can get her attention in the first place. I can't show up when the kids are present, and they're there until Friday evening. I don't even care if she starts screaming and throwing things at me, I just want to see her again. And not through windows like some pervert.

It's evident that my texts aren't doing the trick. She hasn't done me the favor of responding to a single one. So obviously, I need a new plan.

Committed.

A thought I've had a few times resurfaces. It's the reason I was snooping around in the office in Clara's home in the first place.

She will most likely be livid if I carry it out, but it will draw her out and directly to me. It will definitely rile her up, and I'll gladly take whatever reactions come my way in the wake of it. My Rose won't be able to ignore it.

Pulling out my phone again, I bring up the pictures I took to make sure I have all of the information I need before taking an action that could completely backfire, but I already have my sights set on seeing it through.

Now, I'll just have to wait until Clara finds out.

22

He's Got Balls

Clara

The child screaming in room four is getting on my last nerve. Normally, I would be composed and understanding of a kiddo who is scared of the dentist, but today is not that day. The young boy has been here before and has never had a cavity, but it doesn't stop the little guy from screaming bloody murder when he's leaned back for Dr. Neiman to look at his teeth.

I get it, I'm a mother. I should give a little grace and just ignore it like I normally do, ready the stickers and treat basket for when the child is freed and ready to go, but I can't seem to turn my sour and unforgiving mood around.

I've been like this for weeks. Going through motions with fake smiles and niceties that I don't mean.

With the holidays drawing nearer, I applied at a retail store for seasonal help, and I even have an interview tonight. Not sure how I'm going to convince them to hire me when I don't have a reason except for needing the money. I don't like the idea of selling myself as someone who would be a good fit amongst all of the younger and freshly turned adults who are no doubt applying as well. But I know

I have to make right on my promise to Julie, and I can't let this shit show with Seth ruin that.

Just the mere thought of his name in my mind has me standing as the child wails again. It's like nails on a chalkboard, and my mind instantly takes me back to the woods, bearing witness to the creatures who stood taller than me with claws that could gut me.

The other receptionist, Melissa, eyes me warily. Her pink blouse is too bright for my bad mood. Curls too perfect, and makeup pristine, without a line or dry patch in sight. Screw her and her flawless complexion.

"You okay, Clara?"

Fuck, no.

As if she can sense what I didn't speak aloud, she straightens her back and her eyes widen as if I'm about to attack.

I don't even ask her if it's alright, I just state what I'm going to do, knowing she's not going to question me. "I don't feel good. I'm going to take a break."

Grabbing my purse, I head for the door, completely forgetting my coat as I go out the back and into the parking lot. I was late getting here this morning and my van is at the back of the employee parking row. I mutter a few curses as I hug myself, trying to fight off the chill that cuts through to my skin.

Fuck November and the coming winter months. I hate this upcoming season and the weather that comes along with it. I start my car and turn on my seat warmer and heated steering wheel.

I'm all out of sorts and have been for a while now. My head is not right, and I know it. I blame Seth for all of it, even if I can't comprehend it.

Sometimes, I wake from a dead sleep, reliving that night over and over again, but I'm being torn to shreds by monsters. Only, the ones in my head are even worse than what I actually encountered in the woods. It plays on my memories and distorts them, making me question what *actually* happened in the first place.

Every day since, I hang on to the fact that it was all too good to be true. That *Seth* was too good to be true. Of course this gorgeous man is fucking nightmare fuel, and to boot, he wasn't even alone. Someone else was in the woods...*something* else.

Seth texted me once a day for a while once he got a new phone. I would swipe the message notification away as soon as it came through. I don't know and I don't care why he still saw the need to contact me after everything that transpired. Yet I can't bring myself to come right out and block him either, and I don't know why that is.

As much as it pains me and as much as I enjoyed my time spent with him, I can't deal with whatever the hell he is, and I can't risk putting my children in harm's way either.

So why does losing him feel like that other creature tore my heart out that night? I lost what little happiness I had found. I think of Seth's golden eyes on that beast that was barely a few feet away. Why did I let myself get caught up in the romance and feelings he spurred alive within me when we were together? It isn't fair. None of this is fair!

My phone buzzes and I take it out to see that a calendar reminder has popped up. The mortgage is due today and while I am pretty sure I have enough money in savings to cover it, I pull up my online banking so I can make sure.

I fail my fingerprint recognition three times, prompting me to enter in my password instead. My warring thoughts are messing with my head and the remembrance of my password. Upon the third try, I get locked out.

"Fuck you!" I scream at my phone, my face growing hot. Even though I'm stewing, I call my bank to get unlocked, and while I'm at it, I ask for my savings account balance.

The chipper voice of the teller on the other end of the line speaks with a clarity that's hard to miss. "Eleven thousand, twenty-four dollars and thirty-one cents."

I blink a few times, having trouble comprehending the words that just came out of her mouth. I know I heard her correctly; her articulation was annoyingly good. "I'm sorry, what?"

She repeats the same number again, and I shake my head.

"Are you sure you have the right account pulled up? I don't have that kind of money."

I know she's already asked the normal security questions, but there's no way I have that much in my account and don't know about it.

"I just need to make my mortgage payment and I should have enough in savings to cover it for this month. But that...that is not my savings."

The line goes quiet except for the occasional clicks of what I assume is her keyboard. "I'm not showing that you have a mortgage."

Is this chick new or something? My agitation only grows bigger from there.

"Oh, okay. I see what happened."

If I could shoot daggers with my eyes through the phone at this girl, I would be.

"It looks like you got a wire back on the second and it paid off your mortgage. The overpayment just went into your savings account."

I'm shaking my head again. I don't have time for this nonsense. "I still owe over one hundred and forty thousand. I haven't even—"

"Clara, I'm looking right at your account. Can you go ahead and try logging into your online banking so you can see what I'm looking at? Your temporary password is Tuesday135@."

I'm half tempted to hang up on her, but I resist, wanting to prove her wrong. She has probably reset somebody else's online banking as well and I don't expect to get into my account either.

I put her on speakerphone and begin typing in the credentials, and a fleeting moment of confusion sets in as it prompts me to enter in a new password. I'm about ready to blow my top when I try entering in the password I thought it was before and it tells me I can't reuse an old password.

Stupid technology.

I alter the password a bit and once I'm in, my whole body goes rigid.

> Savings Balance: $11,024.31
>
> Checking Balance: $412.13

"Um..." My brain short-circuits and my thumb is dragging at the screen to try and view my loan which is usually after my checking account, but there's nothing there. "You said it was a wire?"

My heart is speeding up, trying to figure out why in the hell my mortgage is gone and there's enough money in my savings account to take care of house payments for almost a year.

"Yeppers," she states again, too cheerfully. "Came in on the second."

"Does it say where it came from?" I'm clicking on the savings account to check its history, and I can't see anything besides the amount and the memo line reading "Incoming Wire."

"I should be able to. Give me just a minute, I need to put you on hold."

The most horrid wait music comes on and my head is all over the place. Eleven thousand dollars? Ten of which came from this unknown wire? There has to be some sort of mistake on the bank's end. While this would be an answer to my prayers and help with my financial struggle, I know that it isn't right. I can only imagine the panic the person this was meant for might be feeling if this money went to the wrong person, wrong loan, and wrong account.

"Sorry for the hold, we just wanted to make sure that all of the wire's info matched up, and it did. It really was meant for your account, and it came from Seth Woods. Does that ring a bell?"

Holy. Fucking. Shit.

What in the hell is he doing? Is my silence not enough to tell him that I want nothing to do with him and whatever freaky shit he has going on?

"Ma'am?"

I'm buckling my seat belt and putting my van in reverse as I offer a clipped goodbye and dial my work. I tell Melissa that I'm sorry but I'm going home for the day. I don't even offer any details, just that I'm not getting any better and that I'll see her tomorrow. I'll deal with the consequences of my decision then, because I can't mentally deal with it right now.

Once I hit the highway, I'm blazing down the road going fifteen over the speed limit. I almost have a heart attack as I swear I pass a police car, only to see in my rearview mirror that it's one of the old and retired vehicles that has its emblem removed.

The sky above is a dark gray, much like it was on my last day out and about with Seth. The last time we talked and ate together and…

My jaw clenches tighter as I try not to focus on the good parts of what we once had. I can't travel down that rabbit hole, not now. I need to stay focused and concentrate on what Seth has done.

What is his angle in all of this? Why in the hell would he fork over that kind of money? I have been shutting him out of my life, ignoring his apologies and pleas to talk, and now he goes and does this?

I don't want him or his stupid money!

The moment I think that, my anger falters. While I firmly believe that I don't need him to swoop in and save me from money problems, it's the first part that pains me more.

Would losing him hurt this much if I didn't want him? Why does his absence wreak havoc on me in the first place, when I was fearing for my very life in those woods? If Seth was one of two of those things, I know there has to be a lot more where they came from.

It's the reason I look out of my house and into the trees from darkened rooms. The reason I shuffle from my house to my garage as quickly as possible as if something might make an effort to make a meal out of me. The panic that I feel each time I have to even entertain the idea of going outdoors in the first place is all-consuming. I used to love having nature at my back door and now, I'm scared of it and what could be hidden in there.

I take the only exit there is to Alton and turn to go over the bridge. My heart is racing as I channel my anger to stay focused on the task at hand. I'm not going to give Seth any indication that I'm coming. Not a chance to run and hide, not that I think he would.

No. I'm hoping to catch him off guard when I unload on him. He isn't going to get the courtesy of knowing about my arrival ahead of time.

But the moment I see his truck, I'm having second thoughts. Knowing that this is the first time I'll see him face-to-face since his naked frame pinned me down outside of my house in the pouring rain is having an odd effect on me.

My palms are growing sweaty even though I turned off the heat in the steering wheel. My breaths have grown shallow to the point that my head is growing fuzzy with lack of air. This stomach of mine is forming knot over knot in an attempt to keep me strapped down to my seat.

The mere thought of seeing the breathtakingly handsome man again is putting more pressure on me than this damn underwire bra is to my ribs. Lord help me if his shirt is off—I can't deal with the distraction of him and his body. I have to stay mad, but I already know that my mood is slipping as I slam my vehicle into park and get out.

Not even bothering with the doorbell, I bang my fist on the screen door.

"Seth!" I shout, but I'm slipping already. What if it isn't the human man that meets me at the door? What if that wolf-like thing greets me instead? Would it even fit inside this house with his low ceilings?

I am going in blind and unannounced, quite possibly the stupidest thing I have done since letting him inside my home in the first place.

Brainless me, I beat on the door and call out his name again anyway.

The door swings open, revealing a thankfully clothed and devastatingly attractive man that my memory will never let me forget. His bulky arms are on full display from a royal blue tank. Very reminiscent of the first time I laid eyes on him and the day he mowed my lawn. His wolf tattoo suddenly carries a lot more meaning as I try to bring myself back into the present, reminding myself of why I ditched work and drove out here to meet him face-to-face.

"I don't know how you did it, but I'm sending it back," I fume, voice shaking. "All of it!"

Seth remains expressionless even though I am the exact opposite, and it drives my temper further. He opens the screen door and I take a step back, not taking that as the invitation he probably meant for it to be.

"Come in, Clara," he instructs cooly, but I shake my head vehemently.

"I will not," I declare.

"We're not doing this outside. You either come in voluntarily, or I will haul you over my shoulder and do it myself."

"I'll scream." I take another step, knowing that he has picked me up time and time again. He could make good on his word.

Seth steps out, crossing his arms and holding the door open with his back. He looks to his left, right, then directly at me, and I still. "Go ahead."

Mouth growing thin, I choose not to argue with him. He steps further to the side and nods for me to enter. I skirt around him as much as space allows, and walk inside but quickly turn to face him again as I back in.

Like an idiot, I left my phone in my car. I showed up without any kind of plan or exit strategy in place. I'm intent on yelling at him for somehow finding out enough information on me and my financials to pay off my mortgage and then some.

Seth closes the door, sealing me inside, but he doesn't lock it. It still feels like I'm being trapped, and I'm growing warier by the second. His place hasn't changed at all since I was last here. The painting he bought at the store is still sitting by the wall it was meant to hang on, and the house is just as clean and spotless.

"You had no right," I begin, trying to fill the silence that falls between us. "I don't need your money. I don't *want* your money."

I remain on the other end of the living room that houses the bare minimum of a wide flatscreen and couch. The only items on the end table are the remote and a coaster. Must be easy keeping a place clean when you only have yourself to look after.

Seth crosses his arms again, face unchanging, and it only angers me more.

"Who the hell does that, Seth?"

"Is that really the only reason you came to see me?" His lips barely move as he speaks to me, but the weight of his gaze is heavy.

"Y-yes," I stammer, unable to look at him any longer. "I don't need your charity. I can take care of myself."

Seth takes a step forward and when he does, I back into the wall behind me. His presence alone is filling the room and putting me on edge. I feel like I'm being held captive by a wild animal in its own cage. One I let get too close, time and time again.

"I think you're lying to yourself. And me."

My eyes dart to his golden ones, but I divert them again.

"I'm not..." I search for words, but I'm having difficulty stringing them together with him so near. "That's a lot of money, Seth. I've never asked for your help and I don't need it. I don't need you."

That last part hurts as it leaves my lips, and I swear I stop breathing. While I didn't mean to try and wound him, it feels like I'm doing just that to myself in the process. I hate how much I want him and how good he makes me feel. But there is so much more to him that I don't want to know. And dare I say it, sometimes I wish I had never met him, even if it is gut-wrenching to think of.

"You've been ignoring me ever since that night, Clara. Denied me the chance at an explanation." His volume stays steady as his arms fall to his sides. Only then does the realization sink in.

"You did it on purpose." My jaw drops, realizing I have just fallen for the trap he set for me. "The money. You knew I wouldn't ignore it."

I hadn't thought twice about confronting him once I found out, and while I had my doubts the closer I got to his place, I still pushed on. I was totally blind to the possibility that this was his plan all along.

The predator from the woods created this game, and now I am confined to his home and utterly at his mercy.

Seth has me right where he wants me.

23

Clean Slate

Clara

The living room feels like it's shrinking and I can't center my thoughts. I came here on a mission to tell Seth off and to leave me alone, and now here I am, backtracking and curling up into a metaphorical ball in the corner. I might as well be rocking back and forth until somebody comes along to take me to a psychiatric hospital.

I don't want to talk about that night. I don't want to rehash the details and the fear that crept into my entirety, and the belief that I could be quickly snatched away from my children. I don't want to come to terms with any of it.

"Clara." Seth's voice oozes over my skin, and the calming effect has me inching away as if I can become one with the wall to try and put more distance between us.

"Don't," I warn, but I feel weak speaking. "I can't do this. I don't want to talk."

"Then just listen to me, please. That night—"

"I don't want to talk about it, any of it!" I shoot back as my eyes began to burn. I sink down to the floor, knowing that I have no way out of here without him capturing me. I don't stand a chance in any kind of escape, even with doors unlocked.

"Just leave me alone," I wheeze, slipping my hands along my scalp, grasping at the hair on my head between my fingers.

"I can't do that, not anymore." His soft voice is growing nearer and I peek up to see him sit on the floor close by, crossing his legs. "I've tried not to come off as too overbearing, but now that you know...now that you've seen what I really am, I think it's time to have a serious discussion. One I hadn't planned on having for quite some time because I have been scared shitless that it would push you away. *Drive* you away from me. I'll be damned if I'm going to lose you because of what I am."

Hot tears are falling from my eyes, trailing down my cheeks as I hang on to that last line. "What if you already did?"

Seth swallows hard, the bob in his throat capturing my attention. For a moment, I can feel myself opening up, wondering what on earth he could possibly say to try and sway me into thinking he isn't some creature of the night that's going to be the death of me.

"You asked me what I meant when we spent our first night together. When I said that you were made for me."

I had brushed it off as something merely said the heat of the moment. It seemed like an odd thing to say at the time, and while he never had mentioned it again, I still clung to that memory—Seth suspended above me as his hips drove his hardened member into my core. How amazing he felt and the way he seemed to mold to me.

"With my kind, someone like you only comes around once in a lifetime."

My kind.

I don't even bother swiping away the remnants of tears on my face. My mascara could be running, and I don't give a flying fuck right now. Seth has already seen me cry, a blubbering mess on more than one occasion, and he didn't bat an eye to indicate he was uncomfortable with it.

"You, Clara, are my once in a lifetime."

My heart skips without my permission, betraying me without my say-so. Seth has no right to talk to me like this, not after what I've been through. Not after he hid something so...so...

Disturbing. Unsettling. Fucking frightening.

"You have no right," I begin, more tears quickly on their way. "No right to say things like that to me. I don't even know who you are. I don't even know *what* you are."

Memories flash, both of the woods and from vivid nightmares. Sharpened teeth and claws, hairy limbs, and large bodies that are easily triple my size. Ripping flesh from bone and tearing screams from my mouth until I wake up. What might have been a few minutes, in my feeble attempt to run for my life, felt like an eternity. Images bore into my head, creating a crater that I can't pull myself up and out of.

"You look absolutely nothing like your fucking tattoo." Tears keep streaming down the tracks of the previous ones, landing on my chest. Small wet spots are beginning to form on the material.

I didn't mean for my observation and comment to come off as funny, but I can detect a small smirk on Seth's features before he masks it. "No, I really don't."

We sit in silence for a bit, neither of us moving except the occasional blink or heavy sigh that I try to stifle. While I might not feel in danger around him at the moment, I still don't know where we can go from here.

We.

Referring to us as such is still mind-boggling. How can I possibly think of us like that when I'm bouncing back to a previous conversation that Seth and I had. We don't fit. Whatever he is, it isn't natural.

It isn't plausible. It defies reason and the world I grew up knowing. So why am I not trying to leave anymore? I planted myself on the floor, already giving up with my half-ass speech and not taking my leave after saying what I thought I needed to.

Using deflection instead of figuring that out seems like the best option for me right now. I draw my knees up and rest my head on my arms.

"Who did you end up calling?" I may not want to talk about that night out in the woods, but that doesn't mean I wouldn't like to discuss what transpired before. What led him to get that upset, destroy his phone, and leap off of my back porch and into the night?

"What?" His confusion is evident, my change in subject doing exactly what I wanted it to.

"Who caused you to smash your phone to smithereens?" I haven't even been outside to pick up the broken pieces since it happened, too fearful of what might be lurking beyond my sight. I don't think my fat ass would get lucky enough to escape a second time.

"My mom." His answer is so quiet. A suffering becomes evident that registers and tugs at me uncomfortably. "Is it so wrong to think that she might have missed me since I've been gone so long?"

My brow rises, my full attention on him now. "What did she say?"

"It's more what she didn't say that bothered me. Hell, even if she tried to put on a show to pretend she wanted me, it would have been better than her 'you have a responsibility' spiel."

"Your dad?" I push, even though I hate that he's having to go through this again because of my eagerness *not* to discuss the hairy side of things.

"He's a part of it, but that's not all of it." Seth stretches his legs out and to the side, still giving me ample room to do as I please should I decide to do the same. "My family tracked me down, not only because he's dying, but because they want me to come home. Even though I might not be capable of procreating, they want me to take over their estate. Take my place in a pack that goes back for decades."

I can't believe that I'm going there. That I'm going to actively discuss things that I know absolutely nothing about and dive into this background and history with him. "Are you not a part of that pack now?" I swallow hard. "Or any others?"

Seth shakes his head. "Nope. Haven't been a part of one since I left. I've come across a few others in passing over the years. Some want nothing to do with me, others have approached me. I never had interest in joining any of their ranks."

Guess he really is a lone wolf.

I swear the temperature drops in here as I contemplate asking about the other...*thing* that I met that night. The intimidating one that stood on its rear legs and had my life flashing before my eyes in that one action. It's this precise moment that I realize my nightmares have been charged by him. Seth was never the one haunting and plaguing my headspace.

"But..." My voice is growing wary as I try to bite back the nerves that are surfacing. "There was another one with you when..."

I'm struggling to say what I want to. Maybe if I can trick my mind into thinking that I'm in some sort of role-playing game, I can try to speak more freely without sounding like a lunatic.

"That would be a problematic neighbor of mine. Afraid we've crossed paths a couple of times now and neither visit has been exactly pleasant. He crossed a major fucking line that night."

"Neighbor?"

He nods his head. "You might know him, I guess. Larson Weils?"

I swear my eyes can't get any wider before they try to pop out of their sockets. "Larson? He's a...he was in the...? That was *him*?"

I don't know much about him, to be honest. He always keeps to himself but is friendly should you find yourself near him. I only really see him at festivities the town puts on and that's about it. I don't believe him to be married or have any kids, but he has lived in Alton for a lot longer than I have.

"He was under the impression that I was here to cause trouble. His words, not mine. I guess when he thought his gun didn't scare me off, he would try to deter me from you, and this town, another way. Had he not been stalking me that night, things would have turned out differently."

"As in, you'd still be hiding this...secret." I motion between us. "From me."

Seth sighs as he rubs the side of his face. "I had every intention of telling you someday, Clara. I want you to know me. All of me. My past, my hopes for the future, everything."

"When?" I blurt, trying to figure out when in the hell he would try to drop a bomb on me like that. And how would he have told me? Would he have given me a leash with instructions to call on him or would he expect me to just believe his word?

Okay, maybe that's a bit harsh. But in reality, how on earth would I ever believe that something such as this, this other side of him, was even possible?

I would have had to see it to believe it. And while the circumstances might have been different, I would have still found myself right here in this exact spot. Struggling to come to terms and understand it when my mind is telling me not to. Even though I saw it and lived through it, I still want to write it off as if it never occurred.

"I was going to tell you when our relationship was in a stable place. We've been so hot and cold, I was terrified it would scare you off before we even had a chance to get started, and now look at us. That's exactly what happened."

Looking up through my lashes, I study his golden eyes. The very ones that I have grown enamored with. The tenderness and wickedness he can wield with them makes my heart skip at times and beat faster at others. They are the eyes that I knew wouldn't harm me in those woods.

"And where do you see this 'us' headed?" I want to know these so-called hopes for the future he speaks of, and where he sees us going. If he's going to be honest right now, this would be a good start.

"You want the truth?"

I nod. "Nothing but."

My forearm is starting to ache from the weight of my head but I keep it there anyway, trying to steady myself and keep as still as possible even though the rest of my body is begging to move into a different position. I may only be in my thirties, but sometimes the aches and pains want to inform me otherwise.

Seth's gaze further pins me to my spot, holding so much power that all my body's ailments are soon forgotten.

"I'm going to marry you someday, Clara. I'm going to show you unconditional love like you've never experienced before, and I'll be the only man in your life for the rest of your existence. I want to help you be the best version of yourself, while joining you in raising your children. Show them the world while teaching them street smarts and everyday skills needed so they can achieve whatever they want out of their own lives. I want to be everything you need, and then some."

I'm trying to wrap my head around his words. The way he delivers them, never pausing, like he rehearsed this over and over. "What romance novel did you crawl out of?"

His brow rises, and it only deepens the humor ricocheting in my head. My head finally pops up and I let my knees fall to the side, relieving some of the pressure on my tailbone too.

"I..." While I'm flattered by his willingness to help raise my kids, he hasn't even met them yet. That is a lot of words and a tall order to fill. "Are you some kind of hopeless romantic or something?"

"When it comes to you, yes."

"But why? Ever since you've come into the picture, since you've moved to Alton, you've been attached to me."

Seth's head turns toward the kitchen, and while his facial hair covers a good portion of his face, it looks as if his jaw tenses, but I can't be certain. I notice his reluctance to answer, and it gives me a moment to let my eyes roam free over him without his heated stare.

The way his muscles curve and cave. The rise and fall of his chiseled chest beneath his tank. But it's the wolf tattoo that I get hung up on. Its mouth is hanging open, rage evident. The detail of the black piece is piercing, especially considering its meaning now. Seth's openness about severing the ties of his past might not have been the whole truth, but now, I can see what he kept hidden. His pain.

"If you were like me, you would have felt it. Sensed it as soon as we were close enough."

I return my gaze to his face, and he sits up straighter, crossing his legs in front but hanging his head low.

"Felt what?" The only thing I can recall is how this incredibly hot man wanted to help *me* mow my damn lawn. The piece of eye candy who had no business being as attractive as he was, taking pity on me and my inability to work the riding lawn mower.

"The mate bond."

I squint my eyes, not understanding. What kind of freaky paranormal shit is this? "What bond?"

"Think of it as two halves becoming one. Two souls recognizing one another on a level that sometimes, we can't even comprehend, so we feel it. You, Clara, are what I need. What my mind, body, and soul craves every minute of every day. Once you came into the picture, once I found you, there was no *me* anymore. Just us."

Weird. Romantic, sure. But weird.

"So, this is some weird love at first sight type of thing?"

His chest falls on a heavy exhale. Even if I can't hear it, I can see it. "If that's how you need to look at it from my perspective, then sure. But it's so much more."

Seth has always been so quick to accommodate. Understanding my requests for him to stay away when my kids were home and never pushing when I felt uncomfortable in my own skin. To be honest, I'm rarely comfortable in it, especially when things get intimate. I can't even see most men hanging around while I cry and complain so early in a relationship. But he was always there when I needed him. He stayed.

"Clara..." He leans forward and I grow tense. "I'm sorry that I wasn't able to control my anger that night. I'm sorry that I ran away after that phone call, and I'm sorry for every single fucking thing that transpired after that. Not to sound desperate, but I don't know how to live, let alone act, without you in the picture."

"That doesn't give you the right to use money to draw me out," I add, still perturbed that I fell for it in the first place. But I guess I let my madness get in the way in the heat of the moment of discovery. I guess I'm not so different from Seth when he ended that phone call with his mother and his emotions got the best of him.

"That, I'm only partially sorry for."

I flinch, taken aback. "Partially?"

He nods. "You've been open and honest with me from the start. One of your biggest burdens, aside from not having Julie and Emmett all the time, is money. If I can grant you and your troubles a little bit of relief, then it's worth it. *You* are worth it."

"Seth, it's a lot of money."

"Take it. It's done. The money wasn't doing me any good anyway. Just building and gaining interest in accounts that I have no plan on using. But this? I can help. I *want* to help you and the kids."

"Because you think that you're in love with me." I'm still having trouble believing this whole bond thing.

"Don't you see it? I *do* love you, Clara."

Well, those are words I don't expect to hear from anyone else but my kids nowadays.

There's a softness and warmth in his eyes that makes the gold in them pop even more. I want to brush off his claim, but it has a firm grasp on my chest and deeper than that even—my heart. I thought that I wasn't worthy of being loved again, that that ship had sailed away.

And yet Seth keeps coming back. Driving us together again no matter how many times I try to convince him to do the opposite.

While I still can't come to terms with what he is, I can't deny that I do feel something for him. It scares me, but I do. It has been so long since I've had these types of feelings, and while the woods might have heavily swayed me from confronting them, I am finding myself tackling them now here before him.

"Love is a very strong word." I consider my words carefully as I speak aloud.

"And yet it still isn't strong enough to convey what I feel for you."

I look at him, finding him studying me just the same as I am him. The urge to swallow down my nerves is a strong one, but I fight it off and try to change the subject.

"I should probably get going. Julie has practice after school."

Seth's face falls for a moment, as if saddened by my news. I have no idea how long I've been here, but I can't let it interfere with the schedule that doesn't cease just because I'm having man problems.

He stands and steps in closer, offering his hand, and though I hesitate, I take it. I'm pulled up to standing and he steps in again, almost pinning me against the wall. Air leaves my lungs as his breath fans across my face. My lips part as I look into his eyes, searching them for his intent.

"I suppose it's probably too much to ask for a fresh start." His chest is dangerously close to mine, and I'm afraid that if I take a deep breath, my breasts will hit him.

"Might be kind of hard to do that…a lot has happened."

His eyes land on my lips, and I can't help but do the same to him in return. I know well enough that if he makes the first move, it'll be game over. We might be inches apart, but something is telling me to throw my arms around him and surrender. I may not be willing to acknowledge and discuss what all he is and what that means for the *us* he claims there to be, but imagining a life without him is dark and grim. These past weeks without him have been bleak.

"Please don't shut me out again. I'll get on my knees and beg if I have to," he pleads, his brows moving toward one another.

The image of him on his knees before me is an unexpected one, but I wouldn't put it past him to do it. Just the same as I know he'll pick me up and carry me off, ignoring protest after protest. I haven't known him to back down on his word.

"Let's just take this one day at a time." I use the wall to slide out of my place in front of him and make my way toward the front door. The air that expands my lungs almost hurts. I hadn't realized how little air I was taking in.

I don't hear him rushing after or following me, but as I open the door, I offer a few words to try and put him at ease. It's all I can offer right now. "I'll text you tonight."

24

Beer and Wine

Seth

I've been putting this off for a while, but my visit with Clara has apparently given me the boost I need to go and confront my neighbor.

There hasn't been a peep from him, no whiffs of his awful choice of beer or cigarettes to pollute the air, and it's been nice. But since there's no end in sight, no idea when I might stop renting this house and move into Clara's, I need to try and make nice. Truthfully, I don't want to, but if Dipshit and I are going to coexist, we need to figure out a way to do so without a repeat of what happened with Clara, or any other humans who might find themselves in our way.

Changing into jeans, solid boots, and throwing a sweater on, I head out the back door.

I enter the tree line just enough to hide me from the main road that curves back and forth. Within a few minutes, the cold around me is nipping at my nose and I stuff my hands into my pockets. I have always been stubborn with cooler weather. I hate the bulkiness of coats and often go without. The restraining fabrics didn't allow me to move how I want, and at times, it feels like a straitjacket. At least, that's what I assume it to feel like. But there could be five feet of snow and my dumb ass would still be out shoveling in nothing more than this.

If I ever move in with Clara, and I have full hope that someday I will, I'll have to change that mindset. I have to be a good role model for Julie and Emmett, and if Clara tells them to wear a coat—and I have a feeling that she does—then I will as well.

I smile to myself, wondering what I might have in common with the two of them. Surely there will be things we can connect on. While I washed my hopes of being a father down the drain a long time ago, I am excited about the chance to be a part of their lives in whatever way, shape, or form they'll have me.

As for their mother, they will never doubt that I love her. That I do anything other than worship the ground she walks on. I will show them what it means for two adults to be in a loving and stable relationship. It's something that I hope one day they will strive for themselves, and not settle for anything less. I know the life Clara and I will have together won't be perfect, as nothing in life is. It takes work, communication, dedication, and love for one another to survive.

It's relationships like what I'm describing that I witnessed in the place I used to call home in Colorado. My parents were fucking terrible at their job of raising me, but their mate bond is strong. Family members that were lucky enough to find their soulmates were the same way with their companions. Sure, they all had their troubles and arguments at one point or another, but in the end they conquered whatever battles they faced and it made them stronger in the long run.

There's a change in the wind, and the smell it brings with it stalls my footsteps on the dry earth below. I catch the remnants of a stale cigarette and the sound of a click in distance, and I duck just in time for a bullet to go whizzing by.

I've already entered Larson's property, and I've skirted around the pond by now. I can barely make out a log cabin just ahead through the trees. I dart behind a sizeable one, trying to figure out how best to handle this situation.

I don't do guns. Even though my family was rather fond of them, I thought of them as a cheat's way to win. Once I began gaining muscle of my own, I enjoyed physical combat all the more. It feels powerful, being able to take someone down with your bare hands and nothing more. But I hate to admit that I feel stupid coming armed with nothing more than a pocketknife.

"Larson, I just want to talk!" I peer out from behind the wood at my back to see if I can make out anything else up ahead, but I can't.

"Fuck you!" his strained accent shouts back.

This is going well.

Just as I'm asking myself why I bothered to come out here again, my mouth is opening once more. "I come unarmed. I'm merely hoping to talk and square things away."

That's partially true, but he won't be able to see the knife I have hidden on me anyway. I hope that I don't have to use it at all.

"You broke my leg, ya bastard!"

Yep, he's definitely pissed. Perhaps if he wasn't such a heavy smoker, it wouldn't diminish his healing capabilities. Going off of the smoke in the air, he has chosen to keep up with that bad habit instead of getting better faster.

Still don't regret breaking his leg, though. Fucker shouldn't have shifted and been out hunting me in the woods that night. Clara never should have seen either of us.

"Stop smoking and you could have recovered by now!" I shoot back, but quickly realize that my mouth isn't helping my case any. "Sorry, sorry. That was uncalled for."

I roll my eyes, grateful for the cover the tree has given me and the distance still between us. I wait silently, listening for any indication of movement. All I can picture is him poised to take another shot if I give him the opportunity.

"We both made some mistakes that night. I'm just trying to figure out a way to not let something like that happen again."

"The only way that'll happen is if you leave. Pack up and go!" he barked his words out. From the sounds of it, I was willing to bet he had a cigarette between his lips.

"I can't do that!" I answer, growing more and more agitated at our yelling back and forth. "Look, I didn't want to say anything before. I don't know you, and I don't know this town like you do..." I struggle with what I'm about to say next, but pummel through it. "But I've found my mate."

I take a deep breath before stepping out and into view. "I'm here to stay."

I'm too exposed. I'm risking my life with an older man who has a crazy good aim and yet here I stand with my arms up in the air in surrender. He could easily end me if he wants to, and I'm hanging on to a sliver of hope that he won't. That he'll understand what it means to find your mate and the ties that come along with it. I know nothing about him or if he has ever had one of his own, so I know I'm playing a very dangerous game.

"Git yer ass up here," he mumbles before raising his voice again. "But no funny business or you get a bullet in the skull."

"Understood." I lower my hands as I slowly begin to walk forward. His cabin becomes clearer, a small little place with a roof that needs work. The front porch, where he's sitting in a rocker, is drooping in the middle and looks like it needs to be torn up and replaced. He's got a thick flannel button-up jacket on, and while I don't see any wrappings on his leg, he's got it propped up funny. He follows my movements with his rifle as I draw closer.

There's a spot just off the deck where he throws all of his cigarette butts. I can't even begin to decipher how long they've been accumulating. I guess he's just lucky that his home hasn't gone up in flames by now. No wonder he carries that stench with him wherever he goes.

"Clara's your mate?"

I nod, careful not to break eye contact with him. "She is."

"That woman's been through a lot," he huffs out, momentarily dropping his scrutinizing gaze.

"She has," I agree. "And I'm afraid that our altercation the other night has only added to it."

His unshaven face shows signs of remorse as he lowers his gun. My tense muscles sag a bit in relief at the sight.

"Why are you always comin' and goin' in your form? Isn't the change on the full moon enough? Yer crazy, boy."

"Maybe I am crazy to put myself through it so much, yes. But I'm protective. Until I find myself living under the same roof as her, I will watch after her by any means necessary."

The change can happen quickly. Shifting into another form grants me easier access to all of my senses and the capability to move swiftly. While it is certainly painful, it's worth it in the end to me, to be able to keep tabs on her when I'm not predominantly in the picture yet.

"Life hasn't been kind to me in regards to a mate."

"It hasn't necessarily been kind to me until recently. Until Clara, that is." I try to keep details to a minimum. I'm here to seek peace, not a best friend.

"Is she alright? After our quarrel?"

I want to scoff in amusement at his use of the word "quarrel." Dip-shit here was no match for me from the start. Just a fucking distraction that put unneeded stress on Clara and me.

"She's not even a wolf."

My lips tighten, knowing that he's well aware of how rare a case such as mine is. I still suspect that he doesn't have a pack of his own or the need to tell others of me and my situation, but I don't want to divulge everything to this man.

"We're trying to figure things out," I state, reflecting on our conversation from earlier. We will do exactly that, in time. As much as I want Clara to push all of the negative things aside and accept me, there's still so much we haven't discussed yet. She's hiding. Holding back the questions she should and could be asking, resisting the chance to ask them. The longer she does that, the harder it will be for her to come to terms with it all and finally learn to trust me.

"Does yer pack know?"

I shoot him a look, unsettled by his new line of questioning. "I don't have a pack. Not anymore."

"Do they know that? Why does that fella keep comin' back?" The suspicious look he gives me is bone-chilling, and I work hard to stow the unease trying to rise to the surface.

"Scraggly beard. Stocky frame. Beer belly?" I try to describe Carter without giving his name. He's the only one to have visited me here. The only one to my knowledge.

"I caught his scent outside yer place just after you got here. About a month ago, someone with a Colorado plate used my driveway to turn around and spit his gum out. A few days ago, fella used the drive again, but he saw me out here this go-around. I waved my gun at him. Can't soon forget his stench. My yard's not a trash can."

I should have known when he stayed, using the excuse of a lost ring to buy him some time before departing. He had an agenda and my warning was not enough. Even with the beating he took, too much mercy was granted. What in the hell have I gotten myself into?

"Take it ya didn't know." The man pops open a worn and red cooler at his side, retrieves a can of beer, and tosses it at me. I look at it for a moment, deciding if I really want to let my guard down and drink it. Is this his version of an olive branch?

"I told him that if he ever came back, I'd end him." The thought of killing my cousin is a sore one, especially after seeing the family he has back home. But the fact that he's made the trip up here two more times, after our first encounters, has my brain going haywire.

Not even the phone call with my mom was enough if he was here days ago.

Fuck.

"You must be pretty important if he's risking his life then."

"Or he's just fucking stupid."

"Watch yer mouth, boy. Or I'll have to wash it out with soap."

I smirk at him, knowing we have a heavier and darker conversation on our hands. "I'd like to see you try, old man."

With that, I crack open the beer.

I hate to admit it, but Dipshit—I mean, Larson—isn't all that bad.

We talked for hours and past sundown before I began to make my way back to my house. Dare I say it, I even apologized for breaking his leg after he apologized for stalking me that night.

My visit might have been a rough one to start, but by the end, we had come to an agreement. An understanding of each other and expectations set up for our plans to share the tiny town of Alton. He's been living here since before I was even born, in the same house that he had once shared with a wife, but he lost her to disease before they could even try to start a family. He's stayed ever since, not willing to part with the one place they ever called home together.

The more beer he drank, the looser his lips became. He was spilling more and more information about his life without me even trying to pry it from him.

One thing is a clear rule between us—should my cousin Carter show his face again, he won't be reporting back to anyone else anymore.

Larson admitted to taking a few lives over the years from those he wouldn't bend to. Packs he wouldn't join, sides he wouldn't take. He never did say what he did to dispose of the bodies though, and I knew well enough not to ask. But he made it a point to say that none of them have been found to this day.

We have more in common than I initially thought, and I would do better to remain on his good side. I know how well he can make use of firearms, something I don't take lightly.

I no sooner make it back to my place when my phone buzzes. It's the first notification since I've been away, and a natural smile crosses my face when the name and picture I have waited so long to see appear on the screen.

A fucking wolf though?

My body is practically numb from the cold even though my belly is warm from the cheap beer I've consumed. My thumb is skating across the keypad, but another message comes through before I can finish mine.

Is that even what I should call you?

My shit-eating grin only broadens further, and I pivot, rounding the house so I can make my way over to her place. Her kids might be home, but if this is any indicator that she might be willing to open the door and talk things through, I'm all for it. Let's clear the air.

I erase my previous message and type out one that I hope gets her riled up a bit more than she already is.

> You can call me whatever you want, beautiful.

I take off in a light jog, but I quickly find out that it's a bad idea. I haven't eaten anything since this morning, and it's like the alcohol in my belly is sloshing around to make that fact well known. I slow down the pace to a quick walk with long strides. Even through the darkness I can see my breath on each exhale. I make little puffs as I toy with the shapes I make.

The light on my phone doesn't even get a chance to dim before there's another response.

> Great, I ducked a werewolf.

> Fukked a wolf.

> Dammit!

> *Fucked a wolf!!!

I come to a stop on the other side of the bridge that crosses the highway, laughter forcing itself out of my throat, and I'm unashamed by it. I don't know what's gotten into Clara, but it's hilarious. I have little doubt that she is cursing out the autocorrect on her phone.

Picking up the pace, I take my usual route to remain unseen. I'm not wearing as dark of colors as I normally do, but I stick to the shadows and move as quickly as I can without angering my stomach for its lack of carbs to soak up the drink I've had.

I bite my tongue, trying to think of a reply as I turn onto the alley before I come to her street. This is a bold move, showing up like this. It could be the beer kicking in and clouding my judgment, but Clara's opening up a door that I want to bolt through right now. She didn't want to discuss it earlier, and I'm hoping that now, we finally can.

I scan her street to make sure no one is out and about, and when I see that the coast is clear, I whip out my phone again.

> Are you going to make your wolf huff and puff before you let him in?

There's a bit of cringe to it, but I bite it back and send it anyway. I focus on the light coming from her bedroom window. She must have seen the message, because there's a flash of a shadow crossing as I make my way up the steps to her front porch. There's still a cord hanging from when she ripped the camera from its perch up there. Little does she know I have already bought another one, a better one to replace it. And three other cameras for good measure. I just haven't gotten around to setting them up yet.

I can sense her behind the door before the deadbolt unlocks. She whips it open so fast, eyes wide as she takes in the sight of me on her darkened doorstep. I flash a broad smile, making sure my teeth are showing. Her robe is cutting dangerously low on her chest and I'm already imagining my hand running along that exposed skin.

Her attention on me falters as she looks around nervously before dragging me in by a fistful of my sweater. I'm light on my feet as she closes the door and pulls me down the hall and into her bedroom.

That vanilla scent of hers is mixed with something. There's a hint of fruit that I can't quite place, and it isn't until I see a bottle on her nightstand that I make the connection as she shuts her door and locks it.

Guess we've both been drinking. No wonder she was a bit off-kilter and amusing in her texts. In the low lighting, I can't decipher how much of the drink is left, but her face is flush with color, letting me know that she's already had enough to make her round face redden from it.

"What are you doing here?" She grips the top of her robe closed and I withhold the urge to let out a sigh of disappointment.

"Sounded like you wanted to discuss some things."

"But the kids are home," she shoots back, nervously pointing at the ceiling.

"Guess we'll have to be quiet then." I offer a smile that comes off more mischievous than I mean for it to.

"Maybe you misread my messages." Her eyes are struggling to keep focus with mine and I don't know if it's just because she's embarrassed or if there's more alcohol at play here. "Maybe you're reading too much into them."

It isn't that far-fetched to think that neither of us have our heads on straight right now. This could be another recipe for disaster, and yet my feet are moving in the direction of her side of the bed, and I snatch the bottle. There's more liquid in it than I thought there would be. I bring it to my nose, confirming that it's what she's been drinking, before I take a swig of it.

The top drawer on her nightstand is open a crack, and as much as I want to open it the rest of the way to see what kind of goodies await there, I refrain.

I've never been much of a wine drinker. It always tastes like rotten grapes, but it smells better on her than this red one tastes. I notice an undertone of blackberry, and it's my new favorite smell mixed with her sweetness.

Clara's eyes broaden and her lips part. Her hair is pulled back, exposing her neck, and all I can think about is gluing myself to it and making her bend to my will.

"I think you want to do more than talk." She rolls her lips, and I can feel my cock hardening in my jeans. As much as I want to take her—and I always want to—I know that we've both been drinking and I don't want either of us walking away from tonight with any inclination of regret.

"Have we not discussed that I want to do everything with you?" I take another swig without thinking, then set it back down on the stand before I make it a habit.

Something is brewing between us. An unspoken need with lustful stares, and I wonder if her body is screaming for the connection we create as much as mine is right now. There's never a time that I don't want her, even though my judgment might be slightly impaired right now.

"But..." I round the bed and sit on the edge, nearing her. The new bedding looks good in here; it's a shame I haven't had a chance to test it out yet. "I will resist touching you because once I start, I won't be able to stop. We don't need either of us regretting anything that could happen between us tonight. We can just...talk."

Clara's eyes slant, and I struggle to keep my focus on them. All my brain seems capable of seeing is my hands roaming over her body, ridding her of that robe and anything that might be hiding beneath it. Especially that damned bra I know she has on. Fuck, if I could just tear that off of her, it would be a glorious night.

But I won't touch her—I can't. Regret can be a powerful thing, and I don't want it to taint our time together.

At the same time, I can't deny how devastatingly sexy my Rose looks. I wish I had brought her a bouquet of flowers so large she would struggle to hold it.

Fuck it, I'll buy them tomorrow.

Get ahold of yourself, Seth.

Clara moves closer, focusing on my lips as her legs drive my knees apart. My constricting jeans make me want to moan in protest as the fabric brushes against my erection. When she sets her hands on my shoulders, she tips her head to the side and I'm powerless to resist my arms that rise and settle on her full hips.

"You're touching me." Her voice grows sultry and I close my eyes, replaying those words in my head as my fingers press down and into her flesh. "That means you can't stop now."

25

Ducking Wine

Clara

I'm nervous. Perhaps more now than before I found out he is some sort of creature of the night. We're just going to go on ahead and say wolf for now, even though the ones I grew up learning about are much smaller and less scary than what I encountered that night weeks ago.

While I know that we still have things to talk about, and glaringly obvious things at that, I can't deny one thing.

I have missed Seth.

Seeing him today, even after my road rage and flying down the highway to confront him, did something to me. His words stirred emotions and feelings that I wanted to embrace, even though I didn't think that I was worth it. And now, with the help of liquid courage, I finally have him all to myself.

I'm a bit apprehensive about putting my hands on him, but once I do, my body relaxes. My hands skate up his neck and toward the sides of his face, and I hold him there, my thumbs brushing across his facial hair. The way his eyes close, as if he revels in my touch, is enjoyable to watch.

I lean forward, and my mouth drifts across his to test the waters. His grip on my hips tightens further and when it does, I pull his body closer to diminish what little gap is left. What started out as slow and languid turns into something feverish and devouring. His tongue is quick to find its way in, licking and tasting everything in its path like he is trying to retrieve whatever remnants of wine he might find in me.

And I savor it in return, moaning into his mouth as one of his hands moves up my back and presses me into him.

"Clara," he groans into me, and I'm quick to shush him. A small burst of a laugh sounds from him and my hands go in search of the bottom of his sweater. Seth is quick to accommodate, helping me rid him of it and whatever shirt he has beneath it. I run my hands through his chest hair, delighting in the feel of the hardened muscle beneath. His skin has a chill to it from the fall weather temperatures that are starting to plummet in the evenings.

"Will you still want me in the morning?"

I pause a moment, trying to process the meaning behind his question. Does he really think that the wine I consumed is at play with my actions here? Sure, I am buzzed, and it has given me a slight boost in confidence. But I'm having trouble seeing a reason to *not* want him. I think that's part of my plight. Wanting him is as easy as breathing. Even painfully so at times.

Wolf problem aside, and pushed *way* to the side, Seth still makes me happy. Even if I am so freaking confused and baffled by this new revelation. This other side of him. There is always a part of me that longs for Seth, craves him and his presence even when things are crumbling around me. Even after that night, and Seth being front and center of the drama, my first thought was to call him night after night and I had to talk myself out of it. Is there any piece of me that is strong enough to stay away?

I highly doubt it.

"Only if you still want me."

The affection his face holds tells me what I already knew. What he confessed to me earlier today and had me reeling in that information since. I capture his mouth again as I begin to try and fumble with the button of his jeans, eager to take him inside and quell the need that's blossoming at my center.

Seth helps, lifting his hips to move his remaining clothing down. No sooner has he done that and kicked off his shoes, I'm pushing him back down and onto the bed.

His cock hits me at my backside as I follow him down. The absence of my underwear makes me painfully aware of how easy it would be for him to enter. Little does Seth know, I was prepared to take care of myself tonight. With my wine and a guilty pleasure movie pulled up, I'd planned on watching it with my drink of choice before pulling out a toy to help get me off.

I was too wired for sleep, my mind repeating the afternoon with Seth and his confessions nonstop in the time since.

Groping my ass, he soon finds that I am bare down below as my robe moves up toward my hips. He moans in appreciation and I giggle as I try to quiet him as he rumbles. I feel like I'm in high school, trying to hide the fact that I have a boy over. Afraid that one wrong sound will alert someone that something is going on. Should I be more bothered by the fact that it's my children who are upstairs?

Fingers find their way inside my heat and I break away from his lips. I rock back onto them, realizing how much I have missed them. I've missed *him* and what Seth is capable of making me feel.

The energy pulsing through me each time we're together is unmatched, along with the excitement and promise that comes with it.

Seth begins drawing out the moisture of my arousal and circling my clit. My breaths quicken as I grind against his fingers. Even though I have broken away, his head tilts to kiss along my jawline and he buries his face in my neck. With how hard he's sucking and pecking me, I have a feeling there might be marks from him by morning.

The head of his cock comes in contact with me and Seth drives himself in.

My mouth parts into an "o" as he enters, dragging it out so I feel each inch of him until he's buried deep. Fingertips digging into him, I'm vocalizing my pleasure loud enough that it's his turn to shush me. He laughs lightly while doing so, the movement shaking me, and I tighten around him. Everything tightens.

His fullness is captivating, grabbing my attention as I settle and adjust. How many weeks has it been since he has been inside of me? It's been far too long.

I'm not ready, but he begins to withdraw and he thrusts his hips into me again. My eyes shoot open to find his golden hues looking at me in wonder as he tucks stray hairs behind my right ear. We have never fucked in here with the light on, and while I'm grateful that I'm still wearing my robe and bra, I am even more enraptured by the beauty of the man beneath me.

He bucks into me again, and I snap my mouth shut but not before a strained whimper leaves my mouth. The pleasure is radiating through me, my blood raging with fire and desire.

"Hush, Clara," he soothes as he cradles my face in his palm. "No one else needs to know that I'm loving you. Not tonight."

He drives in again and air shoots through my nostrils on an exhale. I don't know how in the hell I'm going to be quiet. He's going to have to gag me or something to keep me from letting the house, the neighborhood, hell even the town of Alton know that we're fucking.

Loving me?

I try to brace myself for the next strike but I'm still rocked by his words. I'm ill-prepared and slap a hand over my mouth, and rather painfully, as more sounds try to escape. I'm beginning to perspire beneath my robe, the smooth fabric clinging to me in places I'd rather have nothing touching. Nothing but him.

My mind is scrambling, trying to figure out how I can continue to take him and come silently. I've never once doubted his ability to do so without a sound. Even if he should happen to finish first, he will make sure that I'm taken care of before leaving me.

"Pil...pillow." I reach out an arm but I can't grab mine. Seth is quick to retrieve the opposite one and I take it, wedging it between us.

He moves faster and without restraint, thrusting into me, and my head plunges into the soft fluff. I know my face is screwed into an unflattering one as I take each thrust. The pillow acts like a barrier to stifle my building cries of pure bliss.

I don't understand how he gets enough momentum beneath me. Each strike is like a hammer driving a nail into the wall, and the torturous yet delicious climb is consuming me.

My mind goes blank, focusing on nothing more than smothering my growing shrieks and continuing to take Seth and everything he's giving me. He's fast, the slickness between us growing and providing more lubrication and granting him all he needs to push both of us to climax.

I'm pretty sure I'm going to suffocate myself as I find my release, gripping onto the pillow as I scream. The orgasm is almost too much, ravaging my body almost as much as his destructive manner when he took me from behind on his bed. He stiffens beneath me, a growl vibrating his chest, and my memory threatens to take me to a place I don't want to go—I'm met with a spotty vision of beasts lurking in the shadows.

I come up, desperate for air, and it comes rushing in and expands my lungs. I blink rapidly, eyes trying to adjust to the light from my bedside table that I had forgotten all about. When I look down at Seth, his face has morphed from one of satisfaction to something else entirely.

Worry.

It's in his brows as he looks at me. In his mouth as his lips part, on the verge of saying something. His hands are swiping away at hot tears I didn't realize had fallen.

I'm pretty sure my head is buzzing as I fail to take a deep enough breath. It's like I'm swimming in murky waters and I can't find my way to the surface.

"What is it?" he whispers as he sits up, raising me with him. I'm wobbling, struggling to keep myself upright, and his cock jerks inside of me. I'm still tensing around him in steady pulses, the remainders of my orgasm still trying to work itself out of my system.

"I'm scared," I exhale, and my throat feels raspy. I need water. Something to help my parched throat as I admit something out loud for the first time ever.

I'm scared of losing my children. Of the lengths Joe will go in order to get them. And even though Seth has taken it upon himself to relieve me of the big financial responsibility of my house, what if it still isn't enough? Now, I am scared of the unspoken elephant in the room. Or should I say wolf?

"Scared of what, Clara?"

Through wet eyelashes, I look at him. I'm pained by the words that are trying to leave me and I don't want to see the effect they have on him, but I know they have to be said.

"Of you." A shaky breath rocks me as more tears follow. I'm a damned mess who doesn't know how to stop crying. "Of what you are. What that means for...for us. For my family."

There's more of what he is out there, that I am undoubtedly aware of. I can't focus on anything else but this other side of him. It directly affects me, complicates things beyond all measure.

Maybe I have the wine to blame for this after all—for the truth coming out. For being bold enough to message him in the first place regarding the one thing that I haven't been able to bring to the surface and talk freely about. I hate hiding from it, but I'm afraid it will do more damage if I keep it tucked away like I have been.

"The only time it will get in the way of us is on nights of the full moon. Those nights, I don't have a choice. I will change into what you saw, but I will remain out of sight. I don't go off stalking or hunting anything. It's more of an inconvenience than anything else. Just think of me camping out in the woods until I can come back to you."

"But what about that night? It wasn't a full moon. And there were two of you." I hiccup and snap a hand over my mouth, embarrassed by how loud it was. It might have been one hell of a storm that blew through, but in the days thereafter, I had looked up the moon cycle to find out what that night was.

"I let my temper get the best of me. I left to try and work things out in the only way I knew how. I wanted to run. I wanted to feel the agony that the change puts me through." Seth rubs a hand through his facial hair, pausing. "What I hadn't intended was for Larson and his suspicions of my intent to get in the way. You got caught in the middle of our rift, and I don't think I'll ever be able to forgive myself for you finding out like that."

Seth kisses my forehead, a warm press that does little to help my warring thoughts and recurring memories that are choosing to remind me of what I witnessed.

"I never did ask, but...why *did* you follow after me?" He's willing me to look at him with his grasp on the tip of my chin.

I work to swallow, but the dryness that has taken over my throat isn't going away anytime soon. "I heard the tail end of your conversation. You smashed your phone and then ran off. You ran off into the fucking woods, Seth. With a storm coming." Then I add with a whisper-shout, "And no shoes!"

Seth shushes me and my rising voice, lifting a finger up to my lips. His gaze turns up toward the ceiling and while I can hear nothing, it doesn't stop my heart's decision to speed up.

A creak in the flooring of the hallway above alerts us both that someone is up, and I can't decipher which kid awoke. Seth helps me off of him and I wince as he slips out and takes off toward the bathroom area. I can only assume that he's hiding. I'm kicking his discarded clothes under the bed when my door handle starts to jiggle.

Thank goodness I locked the door.

"Mom?" Emmett's voice carries through, thick with sleep. I rush over, making sure my robe is tightly closed. I swing it open to reveal him in his sleep shorts, rubbing at his eyes with the brightness of my room shining on him.

"Everything okay?" I'm out of breath like I just made a mad dash through the house. "What's wrong?"

His hair is flat but sticking in weird directions. I keep telling him to let his hair dry before he goes to bed, but he never listens.

"Can you keep your show down? It's too noisy."

I'm glad he looks too tired to recognize that the blood has probably drained from my face at the likelihood that he overheard Seth and me. Even more horrifying, me in particular.

Emmett's not even alert enough to scan my room and find that the TV was turned off a while ago due to no activity. I blink, trying to rearrange my panicked thoughts as I usher him out and into the hallway so he can make his way back to his room.

"I'm sorry, honey. Go back to bed." The further I walk into the house, remnants of mine and Seth's exchange become more and more evident as it begins to leak out of me with each step. I stop at the bottom of the stairs and offer him my apology again, crossing one foot in front of the other to squeeze my legs together.

Once he's up and out of sight, I hurry back to my room, lock the door, and when I round the corner to the bathroom I run into Seth's solid frame. He's fast to embrace me, drawing me in, and I'm soon softening into his giant hold. Well, as much as I can while trying to hold my legs together.

I try to clear my throat before speaking. "I…need to get cleaned up."

There's a heat in his eyes, threatening to make my knees buckle.

"I have work tomorrow," I clarify, trying to communicate that it's getting late and I need to try and put whatever this is on pause until we have more time. That, and I am already feeling emotionally drained.

"Does that mean that I need to go?" His thumbs move back and forth against the sleeves of my robe, a tenderness to his touch. Even though he has already spent himself inside of me, his erection is still hard, trying to nuzzle its way between my legs. I take a step back.

"I want you to stay." I breathe out, breaking eye contact as I move past him. "Let me shower real quick." Not giving him a chance to ask about doing so with me, I enter the bathroom and shut the door. There's barely any light in here, coming from the one and only window that has horizontal blinds tucked into it. I pee real quick before ridding myself of my robe and bra and turning on the shower, letting the hot water come to life before I adjust it to the temperature I need.

Technically, I don't need to wash my hair tonight, but I feel like I need the therapeutic rush of water over my body to help me focus my thoughts and center myself. The water scalds me when I first step in and I hiss as I back away and grab hold of the knob to slowly work it in the opposite direction, putting my foot in and out of the stream repeatedly until I decide how hot I can take it.

Taking a deep breath, I step into it and let it fall on me. It cascades down my head and body, water running off of me in steady droves. I hold the air in my chest as long as my lungs will let me and tip my head down as I exhale a slow and controlled release.

It's barely detectable, but the shower door opens and I freeze. My eyes open in alarm as it shuts again, but without my doing. I want to go into a panic. It might be dark in here, but you can still see enough. Every curve, roll, hip dip, and my drooping breasts are going to be on full display.

I hate it.

Seth is so perfectly defined and unbelievably attractive. My body has never experienced anything remotely like that in my entire life. I have never been proud of the figure I have, even before I had my kids.

Head turning over my shoulder, I see his frame in my periphery. "What are you doing?"

I didn't think that my darting off and closing the door behind me would be any indication of an invitation for him to join me in a shower. He has tried to before, but always listened when I steered him away.

"You don't need to hide from me anymore, Clara." His hands skim my hips until he takes hold and his chest presses against my back. "I'm not."

"It's not the same," I choke out. I'm about ready to drown myself under the water to fix this damn throat of mine.

"Maybe not." His chin settles in the crook of my neck. "But I don't think I can convince you of how perfect you are for me any other way."

I suck in a breath as his hands move from their spots, over my stomach and too swiftly, to my breasts. I don't think they've seen a perky day in their lives and I've always been ashamed of that. Like there's something wrong with me.

Large hands take hold of them in unison, scooping them up until water begins to make its way to the skin they've been covering. My eyes flutter down to look at how they overfill his hands and yet he still gives them a gentle squeeze before finding my nipples and rolling them between his fingers.

The sight of him doing so and the pressure are almost too much. No one has ever touched me like this, ever. Hell, I've never even played with them myself because I'm so unhappy with this chest of mine.

Seth is bringing shaky feelings to the surface and newfound sensations that I have never experienced up and into the light. So I do the only thing my brain lets me do. I lean back into him, letting his erection press against my backside. I close my eyes so I don't have to dwell on the scene before me, wallowing in my self-doubt that's trying to tell me to run away.

That is, until he opens his mouth again.

"I'm going to claim and love every inch of you, Clara Rose. Mark my words."

26

Shifting Tides

Seth

Damn, I missed being by her side. I've had little sleep since being back in her home and bed, but it's all worth it. I just can't shut my mind off.

Correction, *our* bed.

It was well past one in the morning when Clara finally passed out. She kept trying to keep up the conversation, asking me about little things here and there. The topics varied, from shift-related things to everyday life, then back to family and the shit show that I could now start speaking about freely. We weaved in and out, around so many things, that it was hard to keep track of all we discussed. But I wouldn't have it any other way.

I knew it was coming. The moment she would ask about the scars on my back. In all honesty, I was surprised it took her so long to inquire about them. I held nothing back, letting her know it was a combination of my father and grandfather's doing. I was a late bloomer of sorts, and they thought beating me would bring about the change when I wasn't working along the timeline they wanted. Sadly, I think they just wanted to use my delayed shifting as an excuse to keep beating me.

One wrong look was all it took to get backhanded so hard that one time, I put a hole in the wall when I couldn't gather my balance. If I forgot to set the dinner table promptly by six, my grandfather would break the nearest limb of mine within his reach. If I failed to pull a weed out in the garden when passing by, my dad shoved me face-first into the ground to make sure I could really see it, a foot between my shoulder blades, waiting for me to dig out the nuisance.

If I was ever caught outside on a full moon, they would taunt and terrorize me. Chasing me down like I was the prey. Slashing through clothes and sometimes down to the bone in their attempts to get me angry enough to bring on the change they so desperately sought after in me.

When Clara started crying, I fought to regain my composure. She kept apologizing profusely for trying to get me to reconnect with my family. Blaming herself for putting me in a position to bring back my disturbing past. She was angry, sure. But it seemed as if she was mourning for the young boy being mistreated and beaten, completely taken aback that my own family would commit such atrocious acts.

Even when she calmed after I dropped that bomb of knowledge and I thought she might be ready to drift off, she switched gears and changed the subject entirely.

It was amusing when she tried asking what I expected in return for the money I'd used to pay off her house. I joked about a blowjob for every ten grand and was met with a slug to my arm. The strength in her strike told me that she had intended for it to hurt, so I feigned that it did before backtracking. Clara got flustered so easily, especially regarding anything sex-related, but there was always a glint in her eyes to show how curious she was. I knew she was imagining the things I put into her head, and it only delighted me more.

One thing, however, that I would have to get clarification on because I knew she was dipping in and out of consciousness, was her comment about me meeting Julie and Emmett. I tried not to seem too overzealous at the mention of it, and she navigated the topic elsewhere before we could go much further.

It was like I had a first-class seat to her thoughts swimming through her head as they came and went. That was the only way I could describe it, as we jumped from one thing to another.

Even after the passing time, our room smells like sex, heavy with lust and the scent of our bodies combined in the one act I know I will never tire of. We showered, but it hangs in the air as a constant reminder that we are together again. As if her snuggling next to me isn't enough for me to know that this is real.

At some point I drift off, until a thud sounds upstairs, indicating that someone is awake. Footsteps shuffle about and a groan indicates that it's Julie. A door soon slams and it jostles Clara for a moment before she buries her head back into my side.

With a side glance, I make sure that the bedroom door is locked, but I can't make out if it is or not. It has the push button lock, and from my angle, I'm not sure. I let my eyes close as I focus on Clara's breathing and the occasional bump or sign of life up above, and it isn't until I hear someone racing down the stairs that I slip from the bed and dart around the corner to hide out in the bathroom like I did last night when Emmett awoke. I step into the shower and back against the wall as Julie tries the door, but there's nothing but a jiggle of the handle. The cold tiling sends a chill through my heated skin.

"Mom!" She begins knocking on the door and there is a rustling of bedding and a curse before I hear Clara get up. "Mom, do you have any lunch money?"

"Sorry, sorry. I think I missed setting my alarms."

Shit, my bad.

I had checked Clara's phone throughout the night, keeping up with the time, but it never crossed my mind that none of her alarms had gone off. And I should have known—she has a lot of them.

I sit down in the shower, drawing my knees up to rest my arms on them to make myself comfortable. My breath catches as my ass makes contact with the floor. As much as I would like to wrap up in something, there's something exciting and naughty about hiding out in here. A bit immature, but I choose to find the humor in my situation.

For three people living under one roof, there sure is a lot of commotion just to start the day. Emmett won't stop trying to get out of going to school, complaining that his stomach hurts one moment and then inhaling a package of pop tarts the next. The bickering between brother and sister begins as soon as they're both awake. They fight over the bathroom upstairs, call each other names—for which Clara scolds them—and you would swear they were getting ready to engage in a fistfight until their mother steps in.

I never had any siblings of my own, but plenty of cousins that acted like that when they were younger. When we were little, we were all a bit close. But there were never any sleepovers or birthday parties. Just occasional holidays when everyone got together. Not having anyone in my school grade meant not seeing them as much there either.

Enter puberty and the wolf changes, and it fucked everything up. Literally. Best friends became enemies. The girls became envious and mean-spirited. Hell, even Carter and I were somewhat tight until he went through his first change. It was a bit sad, really, how far we all drifted apart. You might think that becoming werewolves would bring us closer, but it wasn't like that. Not for our pack. We put up with each other because we had to. We protected our secrets because we needed to.

Maybe if I had a brother or sister, things could have been different for me. Especially now. If there was a sibling who could take over for me, it would make my life a hell of a lot easier. But then, if I would have had to share the burden and mistreatment bestowed upon me, perhaps it is better off this way.

My parents tried for years before and after me to have another child, but for whatever reason, my mom had miscarriage after miscarriage. She never could seem to carry another baby to term. Multiple doctor visits, natural remedies, and visits to different states in the hopes of something taking and working, but it never did. I'm not even sure when they decided to stop trying, but at some point, discussions of it had ceased entirely.

I'm so lost in thought that I lose track of what's going on until I hear Clara saying goodbye to the kids. I stay put, waiting for her to come and find me because I know it's killing her to not know where I've been this whole time.

I wait silently, more than ready for her to find me tucked into the farthest side of the shower. Naked and for her eyes only.

She pads into the bedroom and stalls briefly before continuing. My beautiful mate walks right past me, a quickness to her steps as she searches, and I grin as she heads toward the closet. In hindsight, it might have been less harsh on my ass had I gone in there, but this was the first thing I thought of.

Clara comes back out of the closet and pauses, and it's like I can hear her thinking out loud, wondering if I'm still here and if I am, where I'm hiding. She hesitates to take a step forward, her silhouette on the frosty glass showing off every curve I roamed with my hands last night, and in this very space.

We may not have fucked in here, because judging by her lack of a silent orgasm prior, we would've had to hold off until there was no one else in the house. There isn't a pillow in here for her to hide in.

A wicked smirk forms as I remember how she tried to switch pillows, since she had been hollering and moaning into the one I normally used when sleeping over. I told her I wanted the reminder of her shoving it in her face between us, of her pleasured cries as she screamed into it.

My dick is growing harder the more I reflect on those precious sounds that came out of her. Stifled or not, they were burning hot.

Clara moves and passes by the sliding door that's slightly ajar before coming to an abrupt halt. At a slow pace, she retreats, taking two steps backward as her brown eyes peer into the shower to make sure that she saw correctly.

I beam at her, flashing a smile that has her crossing her arms and providing a smirk of her own. Her hair is full and voluminous, untamed due to her sleeping on it and not having styled it yet. I wonder if I can convince her to stay home today. I know I could definitely use another go on the bed now that we don't have to worry about young ears nearby.

"Morning, beautiful." I stand and her gaze drops straight down to my erection. She diverts them, and I only broaden my grin.

"Morning," she replies, voice warmed up already having to get after her kids time and time again. "I had to shove your clothes under the bed last night. I'm sorry."

"Absolutely nothing to be sorry about." She steps back to let me exit the shower but I draw her in, letting her back curve as I take her mouth. The way she molds to me, wraps her arms around my neck and kisses back, has my mind on a one-way track. I press the head of my cock into the apex of her thighs and she moans, only to cut it off and push me away.

"I have to get ready for work." She swallows, and the avoidance of eye contact tells me that she's struggling to come to terms with that statement herself.

"Do you?" I tease as she steps away again and I try to close in on her.

"I do." There's a light in her eyes, and those two words do something to me. I hope the next time I hear her say something like that, I'm slipping a ring onto her finger and she's taking my last name.

As much as it pains me to leave her, to separate after these last twenty-four hours, I make it my mission to make sure I can come back to her tonight. Sure, we might have had a little interruption last night, but it won't wound me in the long run to sneak around until Clara is ready to make our relationship public, starting with Julie and Emmett.

"Then I will let you get ready." I put my hands behind my back, assuring her that I won't lay my paws on her again, and plant a kiss on her cheek. She's paler without any makeup on, the smoothness of her cheek just begging to be held in my hand. Her eyebrows are lighter too, a few shades brighter than her hair color.

I set out to find my clothes, kneeling on the floor to retrieve them and dress. I go without my sweater for a while but bring it out to the kitchen. The kids have left cups and wrappers out on the counter and I shake my head as I clear the stuff off. Once that's done, I start the coffee maker, deciding that this will be the first morning I can try tackling her iced coffee. It has been a while since I watched her make it, but I gather all of the known items she needs and wait for the ice-filled tumbler to fill.

Glancing at the clock, I know Clara will be in a rush to get out of here. I only hope that I don't mess this coffee up so bad for her that she'll have to start all over from scratch.

There are no measurements when she does it. She adds a few things, stirs, and tastes, then adjusts if needed. I only sampled her drink once, and I try to remember the sweetness that attacked my taste buds as I take a sip now. I wince slightly, but add a dash more creamer before topping it off with her white chocolate sauce that she always does a quick squeeze of a heart with.

I finish just in time for her to rush out and into the kitchen, tugging at the bottom of her burnt-orange sweater. The fall colors outside have nothing on the hue she's wearing. Mother nature should weep for her beauty.

I hold the tumbler out for her as she tucks her now straightened hair behind her ears. She studies it for a moment, confusion evident before accepting it.

"You made me coffee?"

I nod as I hold my breath. The tint looks right, but I still have no idea just how close it is, or if I completely bombed it.

Her lips move over the straw and she takes a swig, and then her eyes snap up to mine as her shoulders sag.

"Not too bad." She sets the cup down to retrieve a light jacket she has on one of the dining room chairs. The emblem of her workplace is embroidered on the right side and the hazy purple of it clashes with her sweater, but it's only a minor inconvenience compared to the solid black of the rest of the jacket.

"I'm sorry, I have to go. Can you see yourself out?"

"Only if I can kiss you goodbye." I don't skip a beat. I wasn't going to let her leave without one anyway. At least this way, she'll come to me.

"Just a kiss," she warns.

Guess I'd better make it a good one.

Her lips are free of any gloss or lipstick and I take her mouth, coax her open so I get a taste of her to remember her for the rest of the day. She holds on to my arms to steady herself, her head trying to back away but I only follow her. My dick is straining against my jeans as she begins to pry away and fix her top that had been inching up.

"I'll see you tonight?" I ask, praying that we're getting back on track. Everything leading up to now tells me that we are, but her confirmation is what I seek.

"I'll text you." She turns her attention away as she grabs her purse and coffee, but I can see a playful smile spread across her face as she turns away and heads for the door.

Yes, you will.

I'm an hour into testing a new program and I'm about ready to blow a gasket. These problems I'm encountering should have been sorted out during testing, and the fact that we're fixing them now, a week before going live, is a huge problem that has me cursing at my computer monitors every other minute.

I need a fucking swear jar, but then my ass would be broke. I'm pretty sure I'm making up some new words at this point. I'm *that* fed up.

The heat kicks on and I push up from my desk, shaking its contents as I make my way over to the vent in the floor to shut it. I'm too damn aggravated and hot because of work. I tear off my shirt as I turn on the ceiling fan. It comes to life, but its blades are too slow and I pull the chain until it gets to its highest speed.

I stand beneath it, savoring the rush of cool air that hits me. I wait a few moments, collecting my thoughts before I decide on a course of action that will lift my spirits and...maybe Clara's too. Admittedly, last night I was a bit under the influence, but not enough to strike my memory from me.

Retrieving my personal phone, I begin to search for florists. There are a few in Pembrook to choose from, and after searching through reviews and photos, I select one and make the call. While I would like to do the order myself and in person so I could have the personal touch of signing the little card, this will have to do for now.

But I also know that we aren't public yet, and I am her little secret for the time being. Would an admirer do much harm to her day-to-day life?

I choose to think not.

Grinning like a fool after I've placed my order with a delivery for this afternoon, I sit back down in my office chair. All of my work problems are forgotten as I try to imagine an unsuspecting Clara at work in an area I've only seen pictures of online. How stunned she will be when she finds out that the delivery is for her. From the sounds of it, she works with mostly women besides one tech and one of the lead dentists. I hope she won't be too embarrassed with the attention they draw. If she is, maybe she'll get after me for it later.

My work phone rings and I groan, barely giving it a glance as I swipe to answer.

"Hello," I gruff out, trying to clear my voice and I reach for my water.

"Seth—" There's a familiarity to his tone, one that turns my spine stiff as a board. "You're as stubborn as they come, you know that?"

Has hell frozen over? Are pigs flying? Is the apocalypse near?

I swear all of the hairs on my body stand on end.

Dad.

He's obviously aged, voice grown tired and weak as if he's been a smoker all of his life when I know for a fact he never touched anything of the sort. Even though his state is diminishing, he still carries that authoritative tone, just like his father before him.

"You really upset your mother."

"You guys really need to stop calling my work phone. It's a company phone and they can trace all of my calls, emails, and texts."

"Then maybe you shouldn't be so hard to get a hold of."

"Just because you're dying, doesn't mean I forgive you. Any of you." There is hatred lacing my words as I stare at the bottom of my center monitor. The silver strip of it is just enough to hold my focus.

"Forgiveness?" he barks out, and coughs through a laugh. "You're a grown man, Seth. Fuck forgiveness, you've got a duty to this family, this land, and this pack."

"Spare me the lecture." He hasn't changed. He's still the same old man I grew up with. Spitting image of his father with the piss-poor attitude that I remember. The only ones he truly showed affection to were my mom and his mother. "I've already warned Mom that—"

"Oh, I am well aware." He hacks some more, enough to make my nose turn up in disgust at the wet sounds muddling through the phone. "But you're a numbskull if you think you're going to continue on with this...this lifestyle that you've chosen. It's time to come home."

"My *home* is anywhere that you are not."

"Then you should have no problem coming back after I'm gone. To take your place."

My fists are balling and the urge to send one of them through my desk is rising. My body is starting to vibrate and I struggle to take a deep breath to fight it off. I swore to Clara that I would only shift on nights of the full moon—when I have no choice in the matter. If I can just get this family from my past out of the way, I can do that. They bring out the worst in me, and that isn't a lie. Especially as of late.

Numbskull. Pathetic. Failure. Worthless. Miserable excuse for a son. And those are just a few of the things he used to call me over and over again *after* becoming aware of my infertility, to show his disappointment that his one and only son couldn't carry on the family line. Knowing that a father could have so much disdain over something, a matter that was completely out of my hands, was what pushed me out and away. Made me leave and never turn back. The final fucking straw before I started to put my life first for a change.

My mom, always present but in the background, didn't help matters either. She did nothing. *They* did nothing but tear me down lower than I already was after losing my ex-fiancée and the future I was hopeful to create.

I'm fucking fuming. "I don't want to be the cause of death and destruction in our own family or the pack, but if I'm not left the hell alone, there won't even be bodies left to bury. Nothing for the families to mourn. Is that what you want?"

It's hard to believe he doesn't understand that already. I still can't comprehend why his useless son would be of any importance in a pack that I haven't been a part of in well over a decade.

He laughs, a sick sound that has my blood racing. "You're not capable of such—"

"You don't know what I'm capable of!" I scold. I don't see the need to admit out loud that I have a body count; he probably wouldn't believe me anyway. And I'll be damned if I say so on a company-issued phone. "I am not the same man that left all those years ago."

I don't care to reiterate yet again that there is nothing they can say or do to persuade me otherwise. They keep opening wounds I fought so hard to close. Memories I wanted to forget. I can't even hear their voices without being transported back in time to harsh words and blows coming from the people who were closest to me.

"We're more alike than you think, Seth."

I'm stewing. My nostrils are flaring so large they actually hurt. I feel like a damn bull, ready to charge at something.

"*We* are nothing alike. If I ever had children of my own, I would never treat them the way you did me."

There's a low chuckle of laughter. A deep one that settles down into his chest, and while I expect him to start hacking again from it, he doesn't. "What of children that are not your own flesh and blood?"

I let the line fall deadly silent. Fear seeps into my veins at his question.

"How will you raise kids that are not your own? A teenager even, that's almost an entirely different breed."

He knows.

While I have never admitted out loud to anyone other than Larson that I have found my mate, and I denied it when my mother brought it up, the tone in his voice tells me that he has knowledge of more than he initially let on. Carter has been around at least twice since our initial visit, and a part of me wonders if he ever left. I don't know which is worse—that he's here at all, or the fact that he may not be alone in stalking my mate, her children, and me.

How was I so blinded to those possibilities?

Dread gnaws at me, pulling my mind in a million different directions. I can't be in multiple places at once. I know no one would be stupid enough to pull something at the kids' schools, but there are still two homes they bounce between. And half of the time, Clara is home alone.

Not anymore, she's not.

I grit my teeth. I've endured this phone call longer than I should have, but at the very least, it has made me painfully aware that there are eyes out there watching me, Clara, Julie, and Emmett. I hate not knowing how they are going to use this information to get to me.

"That's something that you will never get to see."

27

Cloud Nine

Clara

I'm in a good mood. No, scratch that. I'm in a *great* fucking mood.

I can't even begin to describe the change that has come over me in such a short amount of time. From being driven mad by the sudden and unexpected payoff of my mortgage and the excess in my account, to welcoming the cause of it all back into my home. I feel like I'm spiraling, but in a good way.

Even my coworkers are picking up on my change of attitude. Yesterday, and for weeks leading up to it, I'll admit that I was in my bitchy era. When my kids weren't around? I'm sure I was even worse to be around. But now I feel happier, a heaviness lifted from my soul. Like the sunshine, poking through the clouds with its streams of light, is telling me that things are going to be okay.

My mind leaves, reflecting on Seth sitting butt naked in my shower as he hid himself from my kids while the hustle and bustle of a school morning unraveled in my house. Maybe I shouldn't take such joy in the fact that he mustn't have had any time to grab something to cover himself. In reality, it was my fault. I was the one to shove his clothes out of sight in the first place.

As much as I like having Seth as my little secret, I want more. I don't know if it's his endless confessions and claims of love that have my head spinning. While I am still weirded out by this other side of him that I have yet to explore much deeper, for now, I am more than content.

I have someone to listen to me no matter the mood I'm in. Someone to cuddle with when I want closeness. Someone to be with so I'm not faced with an empty bed or house. Seth has been my number one supporter since day one, and I hadn't even realized it. Hell, he almost nailed my coffee this morning which was a feat in itself. Rarely do I even get it right on the first try, and it was impressive that he was so close, considering he likes his black. I might have let the ice melt a bit, taking away that slight tang of bitterness, but he doesn't need to know that.

Seth might not be perfect, but I can't hold back the joy that he has reintroduced into my life. And while it scares me, I want to talk it out with Julie and Emmett. I am already trying to figure out what I might say and how I will ease them into the idea that I have somebody new in my life. I don't want to flaunt him in their faces, like Chassidy when she came barreling into the picture. Well, once the affair came to light and the divorce was filed for.

"Do I dare ask what's gotten into you?" Trisha, the one who has taken the brunt of my attitude as of late, wheels her chair into view. She has been filling in at the front desk when needed since Melissa has been home with the flu.

Dick.

Shit, I can feel heat rushing into my cheeks at the mere thought of that. "I'm sorry about yesterday," I divert. "Obviously I wasn't feeling like myself."

"No kidding," she snorts, rolling a pen between her fingers. It has a fuzzy pink ball at the top that matches her scrubs. "Woah. Is it someone's anniversary or something?"

Her attention has left me and gone out and into the waiting room where a man comes in with an enormous bouquet of flowers. He's dressed in all black and making his way toward us as he removes the plastic covering, revealing an abundance of yellow and orange roses. The hues pop against the baby's breath and greenery that are also stuffed into the translucent orange vase.

It looks like somebody is apologizing for something with that massive load.

I barely notice a woman entering the waiting room as the gentleman sets them on the counter before me. He's probably in his sixties, with a receding hairline and white facial hair, but his smile is warm and friendly as he speaks.

"Delivery for a Ms. Clara Rose."

I blink at him, trying to figure out if I just heard him correctly. It's not until I'm jabbed in the arm that I finally break free from the trance the man has put me in.

The bouquet is already gathering attention, both from the people in the room ahead of me and those who aren't working very hard behind. Trisha included.

I stand, almost too stunned to remember my manners. "Um...thank you."

"Of course." He flashes that kind smile again and takes his leave.

"No wonder you're in a good mood!" Trisha has stood to join me, clasping her hands together as she zeroes in on the little white envelope that's nestled between the roses.

Clara Rose, I think. Seth called me that last night, and I have no recollection of even telling him the middle name that I never use. But

I guess with his background and the snooping he must have done to find all of my banking information, I'm sure he came across it at some point.

"Hi, can I help you?" Trisha greets the woman who has joined us at the counter, and I take the flowers and turn away to set them down on a lower surface. I think it's the biggest bouquet I have ever seen delivered here. There has to be three to four dozen roses in it, and it's quite heavy.

Two other techs are trying to crowd me, and I give them a look to back off, but it does nothing to deter their curiosity. I stuff the card into my back pocket, not wanting anyone else to lay eyes on it but me. I know who they're from. The pounding of my heart is making its way up to my ears, but that doesn't deafen the sound of the girls and their disapproval about not getting a chance to find out for themselves.

Their floral scent tickles my nose as I breathe them in.

"Beautiful flowers." I hear an unknown voice cut through the noise of the techs behind me. I turn to find the woman that Trisha is helping schedule an appointment, and I offer a polite smile. "Special occasion?"

Her hair is too dark for her face, making me think that she's coloring it to keep the gray away. If I had to guess, she's around my mother's age, maybe even a tad older. She's new, judging by the patient forms that Trisha is doling out to her and the fact that I couldn't place her to begin with. But there's something familiar about her that makes me think we might have crossed paths before, even if I can't figure out where or when.

I've run into and met so many people at the kids' schools, I'm beginning to wonder if that's the link.

"Thank you," I offer, still beaming with delight. "And no, not really."

One of the techs scoffs and I shoot her an annoyed glare. She scurries off and to the waiting room to call someone to take to the back for their appointment.

"Either that's a big apology or someone is treating you right," she muses. And while I'm a bit perturbed by her ongoing commentary, it still can't sway me from whatever feelings are forming in my chest. Too bad my lunch is over, otherwise I would be taking that time to call Seth to thank him.

Trying not to be rude and ignore her, I offer a few parting words before I excuse myself so I can scurry away to find a quiet spot where I can open the card without any unnecessary attention. "Someone is finally treating me right."

Leaving the little check-in area, I make a few turns until I end up at the end of the hall that leads out to the parking lot. Only then do I take out the envelope and slide the card out. It's a sparkling gold, thick paper with a message typed out that has my heart soaring.

Get used to me loving you, because you'll never go a day without knowing it.

I read it over and over, again and again before holding it to my heart. I rest against the wall behind me, looking up at the panels on the drop ceiling as I try to peel myself off of them and come back down to earth. It's then and there that I decide I am going to talk to Julie and Emmett, and the sooner the better. As long as they have good attitudes after practices and such tonight, I might even do it once we get home.

I'm worried about what they'll think, but I want to believe that they just want me to be happy. But, their opinions and their comfort zones matter. I know I'll have to feel them out, carefully dissect their reactions so I don't misread anything. I never in a million years thought I would finding myself in this position, bringing someone new into the picture.

I'm not sure how long I've been away from the front desk, but my cheeks are starting to hurt from smiling so much. I stuff the card back in its envelope and stow it in my pocket before returning.

There are whispers and murmurs as I round the last corner and see four people looking over my delivery, one of which is even counting the roses.

"Who is it?"

"I don't know anything."

"She hasn't said a word!"

They are buzzing with intrigue and speculation. I choose to hang back, leaning against a bare spot on the wall as I watch them try to figure things out when I know for a fact they won't. Seth has never visited me here and has kept a low profile when he comes to visit me at my house. As far as I know, he frequents Benson more than Pembrook for groceries and such. I know there's a really good chance that none of my coworkers have ever crossed paths with him.

It's kind of funny, observing them and their curiosity.

The new woman returns to the desk, so silently that none of the gawkers and gossipers realize that she has. Her eyes slide to mine before she grins, but there's an odd way that it doesn't reach her eyes. It looks...eerie.

My happy ass strolls up to the counter to take her forms so she can go away. "Thank you. Did Trisha already get a copy of your insurance card?"

My presence hushes the voices on my left and they quickly scatter, leaving me in the dust. Every. Single. One of them.

"I'm afraid I left it at home. Guess old age is getting the better of me." There's an unease creeping over me as she looks me up and down. I don't know what she's searching for, but her dark eyes are beady little things that are trying to decide on something. I don't like it.

"That's alright, who's your insurance provider? I can make sure that we accept it."

"Oh, I already checked. She's good." Trisha bounces back into the picture, producing a little appointment card as she holds out her hand to the woman. "We'll see you next Tuesday, Ms. Ries."

"Mrs.," she corrects as she takes the card, and Trisha offers her apologies before reiterating the title.

Mrs. Ries offers a polite nod of her head. "See you ladies next Tuesday."

She turns away and my next exhale is a bit jagged, and I can hear the air running through my nose. I glance down to take a look at her forms, trying to figure out where I know her from. No place of employment, an address in Pembrook, and nothing is giving me any indication that we have ever met before. Her insurance, however, is one that I don't recognize.

"Do we really take this insurance?" I ask Trisha, who has taken it upon herself to go and smell my roses. I'm wondering how in the hell I'm supposed to get those home without crushing them. The whole arrangement is so big that my car's probably going to think that someone is sitting in the passenger seat and my van is going to ding at me until I buckle them in. The vase is way too big to fit in any kind of cup holder.

"Yeah. She at least knew her carrier name so I could look it up." She spins around, crossing her arms as she approaches me with a grin that has me wanting to retreat. She wants information that I'm not willing to give, which means she's not going to let up until I give her something.

Closing time can't come soon enough.

The rest of the workday is spent warding off multiple coworkers and deflecting questions that I won't answer. They're acting like paparazzi with endless questions, but without the cameras. Actually, Trisha does take a picture to mark the occasion, and I shake my head. I guess a divorced woman with a secret admirer is big news, but the bouquet might be bigger.

I should be exhausted by now. My late night with Seth could have messed with my day, but it hasn't. I think I'm still living on the buzz created by our departure this morning, the flowers he had delivered, and the commotion he caused at work.

Deciding to leave the flowers in the office until the weekend, I make my way out to my van and sigh in relief in the quiet that awaits me. It doesn't last long, though, as I dial Seth and wait.

It goes to voicemail. I can't think of a time when he has let it do that.

"Hey, Seth." I search the windshield, waving as a coworker passes me and only then do I remember I'm trying to leave a message. "I uh...I got the flowers you sent. You really didn't have to do that, but thank you. They're beautiful. I'm getting ready to head to the school so, I'll talk to you later."

There is a strange urge to leave him with parting words, one of which is a four-letter word that I haven't thought about saying until now, and it stalls me. I hang up the phone, looking at it and the way his name disappears after hanging up.

Am I so wrapped up in the romance of it all that I'm considering saying something like that out loud? We haven't even known each other that long, not really.

I shake my head, denying the feelings that are trying to knock down walls to make themselves known.

First and foremost, I have to tell Julie and Emmett. See how they react and if things go well, perhaps we can figure out when everyone can meet.

A ball of dread unfurls in my stomach, afraid that one or both of the kids won't like him. It's not like I'm asking him to move in. Even though he has stayed more times than I can count, it isn't time for that. No matter how much I like Seth being present and how naturally we fall into step sometimes.

Even if he is a werewolf. Once every full moon. And sometimes on more occasions than that. Am I crazy for chasing after this? After the us we could be?

My phone lights up with a text from him and I skim it real quick.

> Sorry, shit show at work. What time will you be home?

Maybe he hasn't had a chance to listen to my message yet.

> Around seven if all goes well. I'll text you later.

His reply is quick and final, signaling that he might really be dealing with some stuff, and I don't want to take up too much of his time.

> I'm looking forward to it, beautiful.

A bundle of nerves.

No, worse than that. I think the little bag of chips I consumed earlier is trying to stab me in the stomach.

Julie and Emmett are already chowing down on their food on the way home. They'd wanted to grab something to eat at the snack shack that was opening for the senior basketball game and luckily, I had enough cash on me for them to pick out what they wanted to eat. I can't think about consuming anything else right now.

I don't know how to start the conversation. Don't know how best to tell my kids that I have begun seeing someone new. I'm not planning on sitting them down and talking to them like I'm going to deliver a blow of bad news, but at the same time, how else can we have the talk? I want to see their faces and gauge their reactions, even if it is terrifying to do so.

During the ten-minute drive home, I push myself further and further down the rabbit hole of self-doubt. The itch to hold off on this news and discussion is nearing the point that I am thinking about sealing my lips until another day. But even I know that I would be just as much of a mess then as I am now. Waiting isn't going to help anyone, especially me.

"Could I steal you guys for a minute?" I blurt as soon as we enter the house. "I need to talk to you guys about something."

Emmett sighs heavily as he drops his backpack to the ground and kicks off his shoes. He's been in a mood ever since I got after him in the gym for throwing Starburst wrappers, embarrassing him in front of his friends. He hasn't been very forthcoming with any information as to why. He's not exactly the talkative type most days, unless he's super excited about something.

Julie, on the other hand, looks worn. Her hair has multiple flyaways and her ponytail keeps sliding down. She's wearing a school mascot sweater that's about two sizes too big if I had to guess, and she's balled her fists inside of it as if she's cold, hugging herself as she slides onto one of the stools at the counter.

"Everything okay?" Julie perks up in her voice only, but I can tell that as soon as she hits the shower and her head lands on a pillow, it will be lights out.

"There's something that I need to discuss with the two of you and…" I use the kitchen island to place some distance between the two of them and me. "And I'm not sure how you're going to take it, but I need you to know."

Julie and Emmett exchange wary glances, fully engaged now, and I dig my fingers into the underside of the countertop.

"How would you guys feel if I had started seeing someone?"

Emmett is the first to make a move, scratching his head as he shoots an awkward glance at Julie, whose face falters. Neither of them say a word, and that speaks volumes in itself.

Oh. My. God.

"You already know," I state. I have half a mind to shit on Joe and Chassidy's names and bring them into the conversation, but I bite my tongue. It was none of their damn business. I don't want to start playing the blame game and pointing fingers, but I really do feel innocent in all of this. Is that so wrong?

Joe snooped who knows how often on the old camera. Running into Chassidy in Benson probably didn't help my case, either. While I thought Seth and I had been victorious in that encounter, it probably just added more fuel to the fire that is Joe and his attitude and harsh words about the possibility of Seth and me together.

Joe laughed. He fucking laughed at me as if it were a ludicrous idea that Seth would want anything to do with me.

While I think I've been careful on my side of things, I still have no idea what went on and what all was discussed around my kids in their time away. Or how long it's been since they've been told but never said a peep about it to me.

"How did you two find out?" I press lightly, but their body language remains unchanging. They look like they're in trouble, when really, they are just caught in the middle of things. A place I never wanted them to be.

"Will someone *please* say something?"

The silence is eating me up. Each second that ticks by without explanation is chipping away at any desire I have to talk about this at all. Here I've been worried about how they would react and now I have no idea just how long they've known that someone else is in my life.

"We...might have overheard Dad and Chassidy." Julie is reluctant to speak up, her voice barely reaching my ears. Neither of them can look at me, and I fear for the worst. That they're not ready and that they don't approve.

"Look, I didn't want to say anything sooner. I wanted to see where things went." We'll just skip the little break Seth and I had due to...unforeseen circumstances. "I just want to know how you two feel about...this."

The kids never had any say about Chassidy and the role she's taken on, whatever the hell she is. But I'm not going to let my relationship with Seth be anything like that. While Joe might have his own interests above all else and everyone else in regards to his younger plaything, I won't let that be the case here.

But at the same time, Seth is too important. What I feel for him is growing and evolving rapidly. I have to know that my kids are okay with this. There has been so much change with the separation and divorce, the split custody, everything.

"Are you wanting us to meet him or something?" Emmett finally speaks, and there is a slight disapproval to his tone as he readjusts his glasses.

I take a second, and a deep breath before I answer him. "Someday, I would like that. But I want to make sure that I'm taking your feelings into account. I won't ask that of you if you're not comfortable with it."

Lord knows Joe didn't give any of us an inkling of consideration before his dick slipped into someone else and fucked up our marriage and household.

"Do we know him?" Julie asks, hugging herself tighter. Her voice is so airy, but inquisitive.

I shake my head. "I don't think so, no. He's still kind of new around here."

Julie lifts her head slightly, as if playing with something in her mind. "Thanksgiving is coming. Maybe we could meet him then?" She then looks to her brother, who is starting to frown. "Unless he has his own family thing to go to."

I'm rendered speechless for a moment. Stunned at the mere possibility of Seth getting to meet them, and the branch that Julie is extending to give it a try. Better yet, give *him* a try, and on a holiday. Now if I can just figure out a way to get Emmett on board.

"I appreciate the thought, Julie. Seeing as how he doesn't have any family here, it would be a nice gesture. But only if the both of you are okay with it."

I'm not about to flaunt Seth in their faces like Chassidy had been. Apparently, I'm not beneath sneaking him into the house without them knowing, but one thing at a time.

"You guys don't have to decide right now, but it would really mean a lot to me if you both could think on it."

Emmett is quick to leave, trotting up the steps to his bedroom. I'm a tad surprised that he doesn't slam the door shut. His attitude toward the matter led me to believe he would.

Julie, on the other hand, sits still at the counter, thinking. I round the corner of the island, hesitant to push or pry any further, even though deep down I really want to know how they knew already. What has been said about Seth and me so far?

"Julie, honey?" I pull her from her thoughts and her eyes meet mine. "If you're not ready for this, I'll understand."

She stands and proceeds toward me before her arms fly out from her sides. The sudden impact catches me off guard, and it takes a second before I return her embrace.

It still baffles me to this day, how big she's gotten. No longer is she a little toddler, clinging to me and following my every footstep. Barging in on me when I'm in the bathroom and sneaking into my bed at night after having a nightmare. The girl before me, my firstborn, is becoming a young woman before my very eyes.

"I love you, Mom," she whispers, and a lump is forming in my throat.

I don't think I really knew unconditional love until I became a mother and had children of my own. I kiss her temple, then deepen my hold on her. "I love you too, Julie."

28

Trouble Is Brewing

Clara

Seth doesn't make it over until almost ten, and switches things up with a backpack in tow. While Emmett never emerged from his room after retreating, Julie stayed up a while with me and we watched a couple episodes of a show before she finally made her way upstairs. There wasn't any more talk about Seth, and that's alright with me. I already did the hard part of confessing, even if it was minimal. That's at least out of the way.

"Can I see your phone?" Seth asks, and I eye him questioningly. Using my fingerprint to unlock it, I hand it over. He hasn't said much since he breezed in through the front door and straight to my room. I still have no idea if he ever even listened to my voicemail thanking him for the flowers, and I want to talk to him about my brief conversation with the kids. But something is off with him, and I can't put my finger on what. He is laser focused, tight-lipped, and...what is he downloading on my phone?

"Care to tell me what you're looking for?" I stand beside the bed, already in my pajamas. I made sure my nighttime routine was done before I gave him the green light to come over. Showered and shaved, teeth brushed and hair pulled back. A comfortable bra on for sleeping, but one that could be removed easily, should that situation arise.

"New app." He tosses my phone on the bed and takes a step forward. His hand is quick to find the small of my back and he drags me in until I'm flush against him.

Maybe the shower was a bit hasty.

His lips find mine as he presses a firm kiss, hard enough to threaten my knees, and I use his arms to steady myself. The muscles beneath my fingertips remind me of just how in shape he is. Not that my eyes will ever let me forget it.

"Just how bad was this shit show at work?" I exhale downward as I let my hands run up and down his sweater, trying to take the chill off of him.

"It's been a very, very trying day. In more ways than one."

For the most part, my day was a good one. Julie and Emmett didn't fully shut me down after the announcement that I have been seeing someone, so it was much better than it could have been.

"Sounds like I should have bought some flowers for you instead."

A shy grin crosses his face as he looks away, then back again. That smile of his...*damn.* "You liked them?"

I nod, sitting down on the side of the bed and pulling him with me. He takes my hand in his, thumb skating across the back of it over and over. "They're beautiful, but you didn't have to do that."

"My only regret was not being the one to deliver them to you myself. Someday, I will."

"I have no doubt." I like the image that springs to mind of him doing that. "And if the flowers don't give everyone at work something to talk about, if you stroll through the door, I think there will be some jaws on the floor."

Seth rolls his eyes as he shakes his head. Does he really have no idea how insanely attractive he is? Maybe he's just used to it by now. On our outings for food and shopping, everyone has eyes for him. I've never known the feeling.

"Just for the record, should you buy me flowers again..." This grabs his attention and his thumb stops its motion. "While I loved the arrangement you sent today—it was gorgeous, don't get me wrong—my absolute favorite flowers are white roses."

His head cocks to the side briefly, considering it. "White?"

I nod. "Yes, white."

"Any reason?"

I never needed a reason to love them, not until Joe. He never understood my love of them, thinking they were boring and dull.

As most brides do, I had worn a white dress for our wedding, and while I wanted my favorite flower to be the star of my bouquet, he and his parents said white roses would look awful in our photos. Colorless blobs that would make my dress look dirty in comparison.

Their solution? Purple calla lilies with white carnations. Make that make sense.

"While roses may come in so many different colors, the white ones don't have to be bold to stand out. Their simplicity is what makes them beautiful."

Seth mulls that over, then his finger resumes again. "Then I shall send you—"

"Don't even." I hold a hand up to silence him. Even though I'm teasing a bit, I don't need even more attention brought on me.

"What if I want to make you smile?" There's a gleam in his eyes as his face shifts into one that could break hearts with a single look.

"There are plenty of other ways to get me to smile. You coming over even though I'm hiding you away, for starters."

Seth beams, and while I'm nervous to tell him that his days of being my little secret are numbered, I can't help but gush about the conversation with the kids. How Julie mentioned Thanksgiving and how Emmett might be the harder one to win over. I know if they give him a chance, they'll find some common ground. And even though he has been staying over some nights, it's not like I'm asking him to move in. I would want that to be a unanimous decision when the time comes. I want Julie and Emmett to be comfortable enough around him to *want* him around.

"I'm not going to lie, I haven't been a part of any kind of holiday celebration such as Thanksgiving since I left home. It would be nice." Seth looks off as if thinking about something that saddens him, before returning his attention to me. It makes my heart ache, now knowing how hard of a past he has lived through. Endured. "That is, if the kids are ready at that point."

My mood sinks to murky levels. Thinking about how many holidays Seth might have spent alone up until this point does something to me. By no means am I a Martha Stewart in the kitchen, but I do take a little joy in preparing meals for gatherings such as this, even if they look a little different now.

"I hope they are," I admit out loud, willing it to become a reality. "Anyway..." I grab my phone and unlock it. "What are you—"

There's some sort of app that has finished downloading with a blue icon that I don't recognize. I haven't come across the name before, but I quickly put two and two together.

"Seth, I don't want another camera. I'm not tech savvy enough to deal with these things." A rush of air leaves me at the remembrance of my stupidity. Obviously, since Joe still had access to the old one and I had been none the wiser.

He takes my phone from my hand and asks for my email to begin setting up my profile as though I never stated my dislike in the matter. And geesh, the glare he gives me when I try to use a password with a mix of my children's names in it.

"Never use your kids' names or birth dates. It's one of the first few things hackers will try."

I counter, "Who in the hell would want to hack into my account?"

"Joe," he states, very matter-of-fact, and I grimace.

"Fine. You're the computer genius, you figure one out. I'll never remember it though."

"That's why you get a password manager."

"Sounds like more hassle than it's worth," I quip, still not convinced. I would probably get locked out of whatever that was and then lose all of my passwords. What good would that be then?

"I don't know why you're doing this anyway. I'm pretty sure I destroyed the camera I took down. And if I didn't, I'll go beat it with a landscaping rock for good measure."

Seth's eyes slide up to mine as he waits a few seconds before turning my phone around for me to see it. Clear, nightly visions of my front and back porch, the breezeway and the garage doors come into view. Their images are too clear, even though it's dark out. I gawk as I take my phone into my hands, looking at the stills as if they're pictures and not a live stream of what's not going on outside of my home.

"How..." I stand, mixed with emotions that are fighting to take the lead. I want to be angry that he did something like this without my approval. Like it's some sort of violation that he had no right to do. But then, I wonder why he's doing it in the first place. Is he merely doing it for peace of mind? To protect me?

"When did you do this?" I'm careful to keep my voice low even though I am wanting to yell at him.

"Today." He sits perfectly still, his head the only body part moving. "Why? I never asked you to."

Seth rolls his shoulders back before resuming his stiffened posture again. "I actually bought the cameras when we took the trip to Benson. After you were made aware of Joe's...you know."

"And I've been perfectly fine without any cameras up until this point." The quality of these things means they couldn't have been cheap. The timing of all of this is strange, too. "Why now, Seth?"

His lips tighten, and I wait for him to respond.

"Promise me you won't freak out?"

Well, that doesn't sound good. I repeat his name, urging him to continue while not giving him any kind of promises when I have no idea what news is awaiting me. "Seth?"

His gaze breaks away from mine and he swallows, the bob of his throat seemingly more pronounced than usual. "Work wasn't the only thing that was shitty today."

I wait for him to continue. While he might have been working, he also somehow found time to install four security cameras around my house when I'd only had one to start with. Flowers delivered to my work. What else has transpired to warrant this many views of my house in the tiny and quiet town of Alton?

"I got a call from my dad."

I blink at him, trying to reel myself back from other topics that it could have been. To my knowledge, it has been weeks since he talked to his mom and that hadn't gone well. And now his dying dad is reaching out? Not only do I fear for his mental health after hearing from him, but I'm scared of what might occur after. Especially after witnessing firsthand what followed after the call with his mom.

"What did he say?" I ask gently, drawing a leg up and onto the bed so I can face him better. I feel like I need to tread lightly, but I still want to know.

"I think he knows about you. About us."

I pause, waiting for him to continue, but he's not very forthcoming. "And that's a problem because…"

"Because no one seems to understand that no means no. I am not coming back. I don't care about their estate or the responsibilities they want me to come home to. I don't want anything to do with any of them, but they won't listen."

He turns his upper half toward me and picks my hands up in his as he plants a kiss on them. "My path has led me here and to you. *You* are my life now."

His touch is firm, as if he can show me by his hands alone how much weight his words hold. While I appreciate his honesty, he's still skirting around the one thing I want him to answer most.

"But why the cameras, Seth? Why install four after talking to your dad? Are you in some kind of trouble? Am *I* in trouble? My kids?"

"It's just a precaution."

What the fuck. He might as well have just said yes.

I stand, removing my hands from his hold. "Precaution for what? What are you expecting to happen? Why do I need four fucking cameras on my house?"

If Seth thinks he has any claim to my home after paying off the mortgage, he is extremely mistaken. I will be the bank's worst headache until they reverse the payment and send all of the money back from wherever the hell it came from if he thinks so.

"Clara, please—"

"Answer me!" I shoot back, heated at the whole situation. My whisper-shout is nearing the edge of what I am capable of in remaining hushed.

He stands and proceeds to near me, his frame towering over. It's so quick that I have nowhere to go, and he backs me up against the wall, arms on both sides, blocking me in. My chest heaves at the sudden change in atmosphere, breasts hitting his chest on each inhale.

"No one is going to lay a finger on you or your children." There's a gruff edge to his tone, one that has me wanting to melt and become one with the wall at my backside. I don't understand how he keeps doing that. "I can't pretend to know the plans that my family might have, but I'll be damned if they use any of you in any way, shape, or form."

"You make it sound like I'm in danger," I express, and rather bitterly. "That my family is in danger. I don't know anything about yours or what they're capable of."

"Beautiful, you don't know what *I'm* capable of."

Seth's words send a chill through me. I know I'm unaware of what all he is capable of—I would be the first in line to admit it. Sure, he can make my heart skip and fuck me until my legs turn to jelly. Provide me with endless smiles and endorphins that keep me going, but what else? Seth is still new. Our relationship, still fresh. I don't know what kind of darkness lurks behind his striking exterior and moving declarations.

"Nothing and no one is going to tear us apart." His hips rock into me and I clench my eyes as I look away. His gaze is too intense, his presence too severe. Yet the way he speaks to me, passion drips from his words. I fight to push him away but he's not budging.

"Don't distract me with sex, Seth. This is serious." I push harder, but he doesn't budge. "I don't even know what we're dealing with here. Are they all like you?"

"Say it, Clara." His body is pressing into mine and I can't even take in a deep breath. My head is spinning, but he's quick to grab my jaw and force me to look at him. "Don't let your fear of what I am hold you back. You're stronger than that."

Shaking my head in denial doesn't work. My body is too weak to push him off and I can't stop the badgering thoughts of what happened in the woods from surfacing, and at full force. The beasts that belong in movies, not in real life. The creatures that have woken me from sleep more times than I can count. The terror I felt, running for my life on that cold, wet, and thunderously dark night.

Even though this thing that he is scares the shit out of me, the man before me doesn't. Sure, I am trapped and under his hold and unable to move, but it doesn't negate the fact that I have immense feelings for this present side of him. The one that is loving, kind, and wants a life with me. The one that keeps coming after me, time and time again, even when I try to push him away. But I don't want to face what he is, what he becomes on nights of a full moon. Will I ever be okay with that part of him?

"I'm waiting, Clara Rose." His lips skate dangerously close to mine, his breath warm on my face.

When my eyes reopen, I'm staring dead at him. "Werewolf."

The word sounds foreign on my tongue as it leaves, but Seth can't seem to focus between my lips and my gaze. He darts back and forth, wheels turning in his head though I'm not privy to the thoughts going through it. I want to be angry with him, but my body is betraying me.

"You're a fucking werewolf," I declare, finding power in the words this time around even though I'm still struggling to keep my voice low enough not to rouse anyone upstairs. Seth's chest vibrates with a sound that I can only make out as a growl.

Now I know why he made that weird sound that morning that had me in a fit of laughter. Only I'm not the slightest bit ready to giggle as I bring my gaze back up to his fierce, bright eyes and he speaks with such damning earnestness.

"I'm fucking yours, is what I am."

It's past midnight and I'm still not tired. Even as Seth fucked me against the wall, I couldn't shut my brain off, but that didn't stop me from orgasming and burying my head into his sweater to stifle my sounds. His pants were around his ankles as he pinned me right where he wanted me. I still have no idea how he kept me in place, but I never slid down the damn wall the entire time. Not until we were both satisfied, that is, and he carried me to bed.

Seth had gone into detail about how far back his wolf genes go, and that it doesn't matter if you're male or female, there's practically a ninety percent chance it carries through. I hate that it makes more sense now. The disdain that his parents harbor for his so-called failure at carrying on their line. The responsibility to carry on their name all fell onto his shoulders and they blamed him for something that he has no control over.

It's infuriating.

I myself never understood the need to carry on a family name. That you have to have a boy to do so, like they are the prized children and superior to the rest. I can't imagine living that kind of life, praising one child just because they are a son. The way they can hold so much significance just because of their DNA seems absurd.

"I should probably tell you something." Seth's voice drags my attention from the ceiling fan that remains still up above us. "I changed my last name when I left. I tried to cut ties with the past and with them in one way that I knew would drive my parents—especially my father—absolutely mad if they ever found out."

He takes in a deep breath, my head on his chest rising as he does, and I think about that briefly. "What was your last name? Before?"

I already know he came from Colorado, and that if I see any Colorado license plate I need to contact him immediately. He gave me a description of his cousin Carter who has been around a few times, and Larson also has him on his radar. It is still alarming, knowing that someone is actively keeping tabs on Seth, and worse, possibly *me*.

I'm still not okay with all of the cameras, but I can see now why he did it.

"Ries," he sighs, and my eyebrows shoot up before my head snaps in his direction. Even in the dark of the room, I can make out his confused expression at my reaction.

"Ries?" I repeat, thoroughly perplexed. There's no way. I mean, what are the chances? "As in, R-I-E-S?"

Seth sits up, taking me with him, and I cross my legs. "How do you know that?"

I swear the hairs on my arms are sticking straight up and my heart begins to pound as I recall the woman who came in today. She had felt familiar, but nothing about her screamed that she had any relation to Seth. She didn't have his golden eyes, hair coloring, nothing.

"There was a woman who came into my work today. Well, yesterday." I search the bedside to my left, trying to figure out why she would have inserted herself into my life and my workplace. A sense of dread is morphing into something worse. "She was a walk-in. Asking about an appointment, but she was very invested in the flowers you'd sent. She kind of made me uncomfortable. At least, more than the rest of the people at work who were excited about the flowers."

Seth scoots off the bed, his naked frame catching the light filtering through the cracked blinds. He likes to sleep with the light of the moon coming in, and as long as we don't have a thunderstorm in the works, I'm beginning to find that I don't mind it.

Retrieving his phone from his pile of clothes, he returns. The brightness of the screen has me curious as well as stressed. When he turns it toward me, he's zoomed in on what looks to be some sort of family picture. Low and behold, the woman from earlier is standing behind a man who is sitting down, her hands on his shoulders. Only in this photo, her hair isn't dyed.

"That's her," I utter slowly, succumbing to my shock.

"*That* is my mother. And my father." The man looks ragged, and even though I don't know him, if I had to guess, he does indeed look sick. There's a hollowness to his eyes and the way his shoulders sag forward, indicating that things aren't well.

"Why is she here? Why is she coming to a dentist's office, of all places? Shouldn't she be here for you? To see you?"

Panic is rising, taking hold of my entirety, and my limbs start shaking. Seth is quick to toss his phone and place his hands on my knees as if he could stop them, but it only dampens the movement. I can still feel it in my bones.

"Do you have an address by chance?"

Screw fucking confidentiality clauses. I don't care who she is. This sneaky woman has an agenda and I am becoming a part of it. So help me if she comes near Julie and Emmett, she will be on the chopping block right alongside Joe and Chassidy.

My face becomes tight, but I manage to shake my head. "I just remember it being an address in Pembrook. I can find out tomorrow."

"Good, tell me as soon as you get it. I'll check things out."

Eyes wide, I gape at him, afraid of what I'm about to ask. "What are you going to do?"

"Confront her," he cuts in, his mind already made up. "And if I had to guess, Carter might be lingering around, too."

My mouth drops lower, trying to figure out how things are going to work themselves out. Carter and Seth's parents have been trying nonstop to get him to come home. To leave Alton and go back to a place that he has tried so hard to leave in the past, but they won't take no for an answer.

Now, I have cameras and his mom is coming to my work? What lengths are they willing to go to? What in the hell kind of family did he come from?

"Seth, what if they don't stop?" My throat is drying and it's having a constrictive effect on my words, straining them. "What if they're using me to get to you?"

Scooping my hands up, he takes them in one before brushing hair behind my ear. Normally something that brings comfort, it now has the opposite effect.

"They are." He exhales as his fingers brush my jawline. "That's why I have to put a stop to it. To them. They don't get to dictate my life and make my decisions for me. They lost any voice in the matter a long time ago."

"She's supposed to come back for her appointment next Tuesday. What am I supposed to do?" With the way days have been flying by, it will be here in the blink of an eye. I know I won't be able to hide the revelation if I come in contact with her again. I'm not an actress by any means.

"She won't be making that appointment, so consider her a no-show." Seth's expression turns wild, his words cutting through the darkness as if it has somehow harmed him. "I'll be taking care of this tomorrow."

29

Hello and Goodbye

Seth

The sky is drizzling, the gray blanket above only deepening my lethal mood.

Clara texted me the address she found once she got to work and I could tell by the errors in her message that she was shaken to find out that the house my mother claims as her own is only blocks away from where Joe chose to settle down after their divorce. It's eating away at Clara, not knowing how long her kids have been close to my mom or my cousin.

I knew my texts would do little to ease her concerns, but I had to try. I let her know that I will reach out as soon as I deal with them.

She was restless last night, and I know lack of sleep isn't doing her any favors. As much as I love our time together, even the secret parts, we will have to get on some sort of schedule that allows her the sleep that she needs. It will catch up to her, without a doubt. That is, if it hasn't already.

I miss the days when I thought Joe would be the worst of our problems. The looming threat of him taking Clara back to court to get custody of the kids. Unbeknownst to Clara, I kept digging and digging into him and his background. Ever since the divorce, he has been spending his money left and right. The house he bought is three times the price of the one he purchased with Clara. His truck, top-of-the-line with all the bells and whistles. He is actively flaunting his money, showing his assets off in more ways than one and burying himself into a financial hole.

I am almost willing to bet that if we call his bluff, he'll fold. But on the off chance he succeeds with custody, he would lose what alone time he has with his plaything, Chassidy. I've driven by and stalked his house a few times when I knew Clara and the kids were home safe and sound. Upon one visit, I even caught sight of a naked Chassidy running through the house, floppy dick Joe not far behind.

I wanted to vomit right then and there. Perhaps I should have done it in his truck which he'd left unlocked that night. I assumed he couldn't park in the garage due to its low clearance. If Joe is home, the truck is out and in the driveway.

Clara and I will figure out a way to exist with Julie and Emmett around full time, that I know. I don't care if we need to find a way to soundproof the walls of our room or what, but the kids will never have to overhear us and our lovemaking.

Hell, what did I just say?

My eyes narrow as I let the word "lovemaking" roll off of my tongue silently. It's something that always made me cringe before Clara, but now the term makes sense. Loving and fucking her go hand in hand. I can be gentle one time, only to ravage her the next. Each and every time is exhilarating, and promises to captivate and thrill me no matter what mood, position, or act we're engaged in. She is my fucking everything.

That's why I need to end the threat of my past, now.

Pulling up to the house number Clara gave me, I roll to a stop and park. The beige-sided house is bigger than my rental, but more worn down. It needs a good power wash to rid it of its grime. The bushes around it need tending to, and the grass is splotchy, making me think that some dog, or dogs, keep peeing in the same spot to kill it off in those areas.

There's a slight movement in one of the front windows and I zero in on it. The shabby curtains are too thick to show me who's behind, but I know they've already been made aware of my presence. I leave my keys in the cupholder, jump out, and shut the door.

I'm popping my knuckles as I look about, noting that there are no cars parked in the crooked pavement of a driveway and yet, somebody is here. The sidewalk that leads to the front door is wobbled and uneven. The whole thing needs to be torn up and replaced. It's a damn accident waiting to happen.

The neighborhood is quiet. Too quiet for the start of a work and school day. I make note that no matter how bad things get in here, I'll have to remain discreet. Last thing I need is someone calling the police for a domestic disturbance or some shit.

It's strange how run-down these houses are; it's the total opposite of where Joe resides. This area has been neglected, whereas the other is a part of an HOA.

The screen door is warped as I approach, but I bring my hand up to it anyway and bang on it. I don't bother with the doorbell. Whoever is here already knows of my arrival, and I'm not going to fake any pleasantries. Not when Clara is involved and they won't stop meddling with our lives.

My breath stalls as the door opens, revealing the woman who raised me. Her colored hair should be graying, a sign of her age that I observed in that family picture online, but it's not. Her frame is still fit and lean, stating she's anything but weak.

"Seth, dear. Come in." She widens the door and I try to keep my face void of any passing emotions that try to surface. It's apparent that she's been expecting me, and she looks to be all business. There are no tears or displays of affection at seeing her son for the first time in what feels like forever. Then again, it also feels like I just left yesterday.

The door slams behind me as I enter, but I don't move a muscle in its assault on my ears. The house smells of herbs and spices, a potent concoction that's meant to mess with my sense of smell, and I fight to breathe through it. It's already a red flag, masking something.

The walls are paneled in the living room. The dated furniture probably belongs in a dump, and the thick red carpet below is worn down in the main paths of travel.

"Have a seat," she instructs, as if we're merely going to have a chat. She couldn't be more wrong.

"I'd rather stand." I cross my arms, making myself still as a statue as I plant my feet firmly apart. "You've got a lot of nerve, showing your face at her workplace."

"I'm surprised you didn't show up sooner." She sits on the brown couch, and I turn my nose up. This house, the decor, nothing about it has my mother's touch. She liked nice, tidy, and clean. Stark whites and pristine dishes displayed only to use on special occasions. Spotless linens, floors, and not a speck of dust. This place is nothing of the sort.

"Clara..." she begins. "Beautiful woman."

She's baiting me, but it doesn't stop my temper from rising. "You had no right."

"*I* had no right?" She scoffs as she looks at the nails on her hand. "You've written us all off. Gone years without any kind of contact. Now you want to keep your mate from me? Seth..." There's a disappointment evident in her tone that has my fists balling. "She must not be that important if you haven't marked her yet."

My calves twitch as I try to stave off the itch to change. "That is none of your business."

Clara is still coming to terms with who I am. *What* I am. I'm not going to scare her off with something such as marking her yet. And if she ever wants me to, I won't go jumping at the opportunity to do so. Even if it pains me. My bite would show other wolves that she is taken and spoken for. A permanent mark on her that they would be able to smell. She has to be sure, without a shadow of a doubt.

"You're weak without a pack. It's a miracle you haven't gotten yourself killed yet."

"Who said I don't have one?" I shoot back, raising a brow.

My mom stifles a laugh as she lowers her hands into her lap. Her sweater is fitted; the fabric looks like it's never even been washed with its vibrancy. "You don't mean that decrepit old man who lives nearby, do you? I bet he's hardly capable of peeing straight."

Larson has a good aim with a gun, that much I do know.

"It's time to come home, Seth. We've entertained this little dramatic leave of yours for far too long. And if you're not going to bring your mate, then we can proceed with the plans that we've already made for you."

My eyes narrow into slits.

Plans? What plans?

"We've already made arrangements with Penelope. Her husband has, let's just say, gotten into some trouble, and she has graciously agreed to take your name as he leaves the picture. You will marry her and raise her children. She will take our family name and we'll all just move on from your...predicament."

I feel like someone has just hit me over the head with a two-by-four. I'm struck dumb and thoughtless for a moment as I try to comprehend the ridiculous story she has just brought to light. The mere mention of my ex-fiancée, the very one I stalked online some time ago, adds to my disbelief.

And only then do I fucking laugh. I laugh at the absurdity of it all. My mother has gone mad with delusion if she thinks I would entertain a single thing that comes out of her at this point. Hell no.

"You've lost your damn mind!"

She stands, smoothing her top down as if it has creases, but it doesn't. Her face gives nothing away, no anger or frustration. Just cool, calm, and collected. That's how she remained when her husband tore into me. When my father chewed me up one side and down the other, berating me one moment and beating me the next. She merely stood by and watched. How could a mother be so apathetic?

My voice drips with contempt. "I've told Carter, I've told you, and I've told my fucking father, that I am not coming back."

"Yes, we're well aware. But it's all empty threats. Being all on your own and packless has made you weak. Coming home will take care of that."

I'm fucking beside myself. Of all the things I've considered, matricide definitely isn't one of them. I also don't know how else to get my point across.

Weak isn't going to be a word in my vocabulary either. If she utters that word one more fucking time, I swear I'll sever her head from her body.

I'm speaking before I can determine the consequences of my threat. "How do you think Dad would feel if you were ripped from this earth before his time was up? And by your own flesh and blood?"

Finally, there's a chip in her exterior. It's small and barely noticeable, but it has me steering myself toward her, deepening her fright. I let my face morph into one that I hope is demonic, and it must work, because she takes a staggered step back.

"Do you think he'd feel it? Your life draining from you as you die from hundreds of miles away?"

"You...you wouldn't." Her eyes widen, her irises practically disappearing with her pupils growing larger.

Hand flying forward, I grasp her neck and squeeze. She's quick to claw at me as she fights to loosen my grip. I'm lifting her from the floor as she struggles, her nails drawing blood on my arm.

"You mean nothing to me!" I shake her as I yell in her face. She flinches, attempting to gasp for air. "You have no right to come for me, my mate, or her children. I owe you nothing!"

I draw my arm back before I shove forward, sending her soaring and into the wall. Her body leaves a considerable mark in it as she crumples up into a pile on the floor. It sounds painful, the way she tries to suck in air to fill her lungs, but I'm too far gone. I see red at every corner and my vision becomes blurry.

I don't want to send this kind of message, but I feel that I have to. Clara, Julie, and Emmett will never be safe until this is dealt with. Until my past is left in the past, for good.

I'm approaching her once more when I sense someone at my backside and I swivel just in time to catch a fist flying my way. Had the odor in the house not taken over my sense of smell, I might have been able to determine that he was here to begin with. I knew there was a chance she might not be alone, but I didn't fret about the possibility of it being my cousin who can't take a hint.

We exchange hits, one after another, but he's too weak. His punches barely graze me. I land a solid one to his jaw, and I swear I hear something crack when he takes a blow to his arm.

"I fucking warned you, Carter," I seethe before my temper gets the best of me. "Don't make me take you away from your family!"

"Stop being a fucking pussy and just come home already!" he shoots back as he spits blood onto the floor, possibly even a fragment of a tooth.

I take the opportunity when I see it. His body is hunched over, giving me ample opportunity to take my arm around his neck, and I squeeze with all my might. The fight in him swiftly diminishes as he loses what strength he had. I'm clenching my teeth as we both drop to the ground and my knees hit the carpet. Although it looks thick, there can't be any padding beneath. It's like my kneecaps hit solid concrete.

"Motherfucker!"

I release my hold on Carter as I feel his pulse cease, recognizing the voice from behind as I take in a full breath of air. Seems like my dead cousin here was only the precursor to the main event. One that I know will prove more difficult.

I don't even try to close Carter's eyes, and I cast a glance at my mom who's still holding her throat. I think she's in shock, of me and what I've done, but I really don't care.

A miniscule part of me holds out hope that I can spare her life. If I have to take two lives in the meantime to get her to understand me, so be it.

Death is how things were dealt with back home. As old and barbaric as it is, it's how conflicts come to an end. How disagreements find a winner. Had I not fled in the night all those years ago, I'm sure they would have attempted to kill me for leaving. So why give them the chance?

Quickly, I stand and swivel to find Carter's eldest brother standing in the doorway of the kitchen. His wrath is evident, seeping from his pores as he takes in the scene that he was too slow to stop. Perhaps, he really doesn't care. Not sure where he was hiding during the previous quarrel, but if he had shown up a few seconds sooner, he might have been able to buy his younger brother a bit more time.

There are splotches of gray in his dark beard, but he shares a lot of physical attributes with his now dead sibling. The eyes and facial features are very similar. But where Carter let himself go with that beer belly of his, Adam is still beefy and layered with muscle.

I had noted his appearance when looking at the family photo online, both members that I know and those who had come along since my departure. If he is guilty of anything, it's most likely the pride that he has in himself and his body.

Adam was also the harshest on me when I was younger. The cruelest cousin out of them all about me being a late bloomer for my first change.

I try mentally preparing for a fight that is more evenly matched, knowing that he won't go down as easily as his brother.

"Still want me to come home?" I gesture toward his brother at my feet, baiting him. I then look over my shoulder to my mom. "Would you rather take one body to go, or two?"

Adam comes rushing at me and knocks me to the ground. Luckily, I braced myself enough for impact that I recover semi-quickly, rolling out from beneath him before he can pin me down. He's quick to his feet, baring his teeth.

My bones are vibrating with power, and while I may want to change, I can't. While I want the strength of my wolf form, he could have his arms around me, snapping me like a twig before I could fully turn.

Like the linebacker he was back in his high school days, he takes off toward me. I throw everything I have into a punch, but he takes me down. I fire off a few shots to his face in quick succession like a punching bag. Spit flies from his mouth and he snarls his frustration.

I barely have a nanosecond before he blinds me with a punch to my face. I swear I see fucking stars and just barely move my head enough to miss another one.

Gaining momentum, I drive my leg into his side. It's enough to put a small distance between us until I can stand again, but what I don't expect is my mother who launches herself onto my backside. I'm prying her arms off of me when she tries to cover my eyes, and when all else fails, I throw my back against the wall and the impact causes her to release me.

I don't, however, have enough time to prepare for the gut punch that Adam hurls. My body caves against my wishes, struggling to take in air as he strikes me from above and sends me to the ground. The way Adam throws his body weight into each attack is damaging. If Clara thought I was beat up after my first encounter with Carter, she's going to hate to see me after this.

My Rose.

There's another blow to my shoulder, one that I'm sure fractures something in there, and I fight back the urge to bellow. The pressure of it is too much, stealing my breath when I'm not even getting enough to begin with.

"Told you he was going to choose the hard way," Adam puffs, his agitation so near it's like I can feel his breaths on my neck. I wait for the next attack, but nothing happens.

I'm fighting the pain, listening intently for any sign of another hit, but I swear my blood runs cold as I hear my mother's voice cut through the pants of my discomfort and exertion.

"He'll never come willingly as long as she's in the picture," she states, and it feels as if she's signing off on Clara's death as Adam speaks.

"Then let's take her out of it."

There's a surge in my blood, one that turns ice to fire, and my body vibrates with it. As if I have suffered no injuries at all, my arms shoot out and take hold of Adam's leg and I attempt to take him down with a strike to the back of the knee.

But I fail as something hits me from behind, blackening my view. I don't even have the time to register the pain, or the fear that they will harm Clara.

30
Ticking Time
Clara

Be it instincts, the never ceasing worry in my mind, or what, I can't stop panicking about him. The flowers beside me are a constant reminder that Seth is trying to get his family to stop pestering him, threatening us and the life we want to try and live.

Negative thoughts are clouding me. They're overbearing, actually. One second I'm scared that he'll give in and go home, just so they leave me alone. While that might grant some sort of relief in that they wouldn't be a concern anymore, the thought of Seth sacrificing himself for something like that is unnerving.

The next minute, I'm trying to figure out how we can even move past this if his visit proves successful. Seth told me he would take care of things, but I have no idea how. His words that he'll never return seem to hold no value to them. Why won't they just leave him alone?

There's finally someone in my life that makes me happy. Granted, he's a fucking werewolf with some baggage that won't get lost, but still. Seth coming into my life has given me something to hope for. Something worth fighting and striving for. I am beginning to believe that I could really have a chance at something, something that I thought was long lost and I would never have. A future with him has been unfolding in my mind for some time, and it's one I want to see through even if I don't know what that might truly look like.

So why haven't I heard from yet? How long should I wait before I grow even more concerned?

"Everything okay? You seem on edge." Melissa looks at me with hesitation, eyes dropping to my bouncing knee, and I place a hand on it to hold it down. I guess Seth wasn't the only one to pick up on that nervous act of mine.

"Just...worried about a friend." Even though it's vague, it's all I can think to admit out loud. It's been three hours since his last text, and each passing minute has me wanting to flee and get the hell out of here. For a Friday, it's unusually quiet, and the same songs playing on the radio are eating away at me faster than the time.

"Flower friend?" She nudges my arm playfully and leans in, her curls falling forward, but I can't bring myself to smile. I'm not sure I can get my face to do that until I know he's okay. I wish I could have gone with him. Be by his side so he doesn't have to face his mother alone. That, and I am kind of pissed at the bitch for coming into *my* place of employment to scope me out.

That's fucking weird, right?

"Yeah, um...flower friend."

"Ohhh..." She shakes her shoulders back and forth as she clasps her hands together. "When do we get to call this flower friend your boyfriend?"

Once I know he's safe and sound.

You know what? Seth could waltz through the door right now with those white roses I told him about and I would gladly throw my arms around him no matter who was watching. I just need to hear something from him. Anything.

"Maybe I'll go check on him on my lunch."

It's like I can hear Melissa screaming at me for details. It's in her body posture as she fully turns in my direction. Her bright and cheery blues make it impossible not to notice.

"Is that all that's got you down?" Her voice lowers as she leans on her hands, hoping I drop something juicy.

When I look up at her again, I sigh. I know she's coming from a good place in asking, even if she is probably going to blab about it later when I'm not around. "He's just got some family drama he's trying to deal with. Guess you could say we're evenly matched there."

Melissa blows out some air, considering my small bit of information. "Don't we all, though? Families are prone to problems. Nobody's perfect. And if they're trying to convince you otherwise, they're lying."

I consider her words, knowing how true they are. From the start, Seth told me about his shitty background with his family. Werewolf and abuse business aside, he never once tried to lie or cover it up. He might have skirted around things, but I hadn't necessarily been prying either.

And I was forthcoming with information as well. To a complete stranger, even. Telling him about my every problem and the need I had for my kids. My hate for Chassidy and disdain for Joe who threw me away like trash. He might still be Julie and Emmett's father, but I fucking hate him for what he did to me and our children. I will never be able to forgive him, and I will take that grudge to the grave when I go.

"I know." I sigh as my eyes roam to the bouquet once more. "I just wish I knew how it was going. I feel like I should have heard from him by now."

"Have you texted him?"

My head shakes in denial, and she gapes at me.

"What harm is a text? Even if he doesn't answer right away, I'm sure he will as soon as he can if he knows you're worried."

She doesn't have to tell me twice. I grab my phone and unlock it, not giving her any kind of pushback whatsoever. "I will do that."

> Please let me know that you're ok. When you can.

My thumb doesn't even hesitate to press send, and I stare at the screen for a few seconds, hoping that I'll see the little notification that he's seen it. The longer I wait, the more anxious I become.

The door opens, and a mother and her three kids come barging in. I cast an annoyed glance at Melissa, knowing that the next half hour, at least, is going to be filled with ruckus and mayhem. The mother doesn't even try to get her kids to settle down, and it usually lands on us at the desk to try and find activities for them to do.

Things pick up from there, and before I know it, I'm bolting for my lunch. I still have no response from Seth, and my heart is thudding about as I jump into my van and start it. I try to call him, and it rings four times before it goes to voicemail. I don't even bother leaving a message for him, I just hang up and throw my phone into my open purse on the passenger seat.

I zigzag through the streets of Pembrook, trying to make my way over to the address I gave Seth this morning without another thought. I have no plan in place. No idea what I'm going to do, but dammit, I have to know that he's alright. My mind and body won't let me relax until I find out.

Once I turn onto the street, I turn off the heat as if the quietness of my vehicle might help me concentrate better as I start checking house numbers. The odd numbers are to my left and climbing, and as I reach the house that I need, I slow to a stop.

It's worn down, and shows no signs of anyone around. There are no cars in the drive or parked out on the street. Seth's truck is nowhere in sight. My spirits fall as I try to piece together where he could have gone and why he wouldn't have told me.

But deep down in my gut, I know something is wrong. My hands are shaking as I retrieve my phone, completely lost and confused. I don't know what to do at this point. I don't know where to go from here. I can't just aimlessly drive around in the hopes that I find him and his truck.

The phone lights up in my hands with that little icon from the app that Seth installed, and my eyebrows lower. I click on it. An image from the back porch comes into view and with it, an unknown man stalking toward the house.

I freeze as I watch him approach. He's tall and bulky, and one thing is for sure, I definitely don't recognize him.

As he nears the porch, his eyes shift toward the camera. As if a lightbulb goes off in his head, he turns and heads off toward the garage. My heart is beating wildly, threatening to send me into cardiac arrest.

Another notification goes off and I click on it, taking me to the garage view. This time, he must have noticed the camera quicker, because he quickly darts away and toward the street.

Seth is unresponsive. There is an unknown man prowling around my house, and while I want to alert the authorities, I have no fucking idea what to tell them. The man could be long gone by the time they or I make it to Alton, and Seth hasn't been missing long enough to be reported as such.

Before I know it, I'm speeding off and out of the neighborhood and hightailing it to Alton. My phone doesn't go off again the entire ride back, and the only thing I can think about is how thankful I am that the kids are still in school so they aren't around for this.

A plan begins to unfurl. Not a very good one, but it's a start. As long as I stay in my van with the doors locked, I should be fine with a quick getaway if this man enters the picture. I remind myself to not make any rash decisions, even if I were to catch sight of Seth. All I know about his family is that they are wolves as well, and that they are very clear about their demand for him to come back home. I don't know if this stranger is related to Seth somehow, but it's too much of a coincidence for him not to be.

I reach the city limits of Alton on high alert. It's usually deadly quiet during the weekdays. There aren't many places of employment here because of its size, so most people commute for their jobs unless they're retired. I scan each road, house, and backyard as I go, and I park a ways away once my house comes into view.

I study it, bringing out my phone for good measure. I want to be relieved that no other cameras have gone off, but at the same time, I have no idea where the man went. I play with the app, finding that I can see a live view on each camera and can't catch anything out of the ordinary on any of them. There are no suspicious cars or bodies that I can place, nothing.

I drive around, careful not to stop, but when I detect no signs of movement, I carry on. My next stop is Seth's place, and I try not to speed and gather unnecessary attention from anyone who might be home in the process. Crossing the bridge, I begin to hold my breath until his driveway comes into view. I involuntarily jerk the wheel when I see Seth's truck, crossing the center line and then correcting myself back into my lane. While I want to be relieved, I still can't shake the uneasy feeling that has made itself at home in my belly.

Seth left Pembrook without a word, and then came home? After a possible confrontation with his mother who he hadn't seen in over a decade? It doesn't seem likely.

I scan over the truck and his little house, but can't discern anything out of the ordinary. I know better than to stop, reminding myself not to be rash in my decision-making. No matter how much I want to storm into his home and find him, I can't.

I keep driving, winding down a road that I have rarely ventured down. Only then does an idea come to me. I don't necessarily like it, but maybe I don't have to.

I turn a bit too harshly, almost missing the overgrown entrance that I assume belongs to Larson. The trees and bushes might have lost most of their leaves, but they still provide enough cover to hide the driveway for the most part. There's barely any gravel visible, and his mailbox is on the opposite side of the road. The numbers are hardly even readable after years of weathering.

Larson is sitting on his porch as I near, and I snatch my phone, tucking it into my back pocket as I get out. He wobbles to stand, cautiousness about my arrival evident as he looks at me. I almost backtrack when I see a rifle next to his rickety chair, but force myself to keep going.

I don't think I have any other options right now, and he is the only one who knows about Seth and me. Better yet, the only one who knows what Seth is, since he is apparently a fucking werewolf himself.

What has my life become?

"Can I help ya?" he grunts out, trying to clear his voice. His porch is decaying, wood rotting, and there are countless cigarette butts littering the ground. I try to hold back my aversion. I'm nothing more than a visitor who doesn't have a leg to stand on in asking for any kind of help from a man I barely know.

"Have you seen Seth at all?" I come to a stop, swallowing hard as I look about the heavily wooded area. Larson lives amongst so many trees you would think he was out in the middle of nowhere. Maybe that's how he likes it.

"Recently? Today? 'Fraid you might have to be more specific, miss."

A shaky breath rakes through me as I look up at the sky. I'm barely holding myself together. If the sky cries, I might too.

"Look—" I swallow, yet it doesn't help the ache in my throat. "I know that you are...that you and Seth are...alike. I wouldn't be coming to you if I had any other options, but I'm worried about him."

By the time I'm able to bring my gaze to him, his eyes have narrowed and his lips have thinned. "What's the matter?"

I go into detail, telling him about Seth's family's persistence and the arrival of Seth's mother. How he was supposed to meet with her this morning and has been silent ever since and yet his truck is home and there has been a strange man lurking around my house. My hands become animated as I talk and spew as much detail as I can, careful not to leave anything out. When I finish, I look up to him with pleading eyes. I know he owes me nothing, owes Seth nothing, and yet I've come for his help because I feel as if I have no one else.

"Can I see this man yer talkin' about?"

I nod like a damn bobblehead and dart up to his porch. The wood gives with each step I take and I hold my breath as I try to bring up the videos of the man from earlier. I play each one for him and he studies it. I knew Larson was a smoker, it was one of the few things I did know about him. But the smell has me fighting for clean air in my lungs.

"He kinda looks like that other fella that keeps comin' 'round here."

"I'm assuming you're talking about Carter, Seth's cousin. Maybe this is a brother or something?"

"Perhaps." His gaze leaves my phone and I stow it back in my pocket once again. "You were smart not going home."

But was I smart in coming here? That's what I really want to ask.

"Why don't you come inside, Clara. I think I need to make a phone call."

Larson starts to move, but I can't bring my feet to follow. The outside of his house smells like an ashtray, and while I'm grateful that he's not turning me away in my time of need, I don't think I can stomach going inside if it's anything like this.

"I need air," I blurt as I walk on wobbly legs to exit the deteriorating porch. "I need...I'm sorry. I'll be out here."

"It's cold." The look he gives me shows his concern, but I wave it off. Wasn't he just leisurely sitting out here all on his own in his flannel jacket?

"I'm okay, really. Thank you, though. I just need a minute." I cross my arms beneath my chest and he scans the woods behind me before taking a step forward and toward the edge of the deck. It groans beneath him and I try not to let the unease it gives me read on my face.

"Well, if ya hear anything unusual. *See* anything that don't look right, you bolt on in here. Got it?" He's taken on an authoritative tone that has me nodding in agreement. He hesitates for a moment, before taking his rifle with him inside.

I shake my hands out as I turn, looking out as far as my eyes can see. I can imagine how quick someone like Seth or this unknown man could traipse through this terrain, and in a short amount of time, too. In my van, it didn't seem like there was much distance between Seth's rental and Larson's home, but by foot if I had to guess, maybe half a mile?

Retrieving my phone again, I note the time and mutter a few curse words. I can't find it in myself to call in to work, so I take the easy way out and text Melissa. She's not my boss, but she's the one I need to contact since there's not a chance in hell I'm coming back today. I only hope that she'll cover for me.

I apologize profusely in my message to her, telling her that things didn't go well and I'll give her all the details once this gets worked out. It feels cheesy referring to my relationship with Seth as some sort of exclusive, but I try to spin it as positive as I can in the hopes that she'll take pity on me.

I send the message along with a silent prayer, trying to dodge this bullet so I can move on with the day and find Seth.

Why did this morning feel so terribly drawn out, and now that it's my lunch hour, time is passing too quickly? The time crunch is very real, given that I only have a few hours until my kids come home, and the presence of that man at my house is frightening. From what I could tell, he came from the woods behind my house, so he could have left that way as well. Or worse, he's waiting there. For what, I don't want to imagine.

My phone goes off in my hand, one message right after another. While I catch a brief view of Melissa's thumbs up of a message, it's the other that has me on edge.

> Everything is fine, beautiful. Can you stop by my place before you go home?

Something still doesn't feel right. Even though the use of his endearing term for me has come into play, I know him well enough to know that he wouldn't just skate over the whole situation with his mother like this. If everything was really okay and he was home, he would know that I'm on my lunch hour. Still, we wouldn't get together until after the kids go upstairs and to bed for the night. He wouldn't ask to take my time away from them.

I take off toward my van and as soon as I shut the door, I start a video call. More times than I can count, when things are going well between us, we've done this. Sometimes it's for my whole break, other times just a quick visit. Regardless, if things are really alright, I know he will pick up.

My face is a bit pink from the cold and I try to reel in my nerves as I look at my image on the screen and wait.

And wait.

Until the call ends.

A message comes through shortly after, furthering my alarm and heightening my fear that someone else might be in charge of Seth's phone right now.

> Sorry, work stuff. Really need to see you. The sooner the better.

Tears are trying to emerge, the burn in my eyes too much to ignore as I get out of the van and begin to make my way back to my spot in front of Larson's house. There's a rustling of leaves that draws my attention and my head snaps in its direction.

I look at barren trees that almost look as if they're turning gray, or maybe it's the sky's color that's making it seem that way. Dry and dying leaves tumble across the ground as a light breeze carries them, and just as I'm about to tear my gaze away, something whizzes past me from behind. I turn quickly but find nothing.

Another sounds off, but this time, there's a thump in the woods. Without a second thought, I'm making a mad dash to the porch. I don't care to know what's out there, but I'm sure as hell not taking any chances and I'm willing to risk secondhand smoke if it means being protected inside his home.

Larson emerges, rifle in hand as he opens the screen door. His scraggly face is set in an intense expression. I'm beyond frazzled as I close the distance between us. While I'm trying to get in, he's blocking the way, eyes fixed on something that I can't seem to find on my own.

There's a distant growl of something that puts me on edge. Something that I shouldn't know of, that I wish I had never experienced, raising goosebumps along every inch of my skin. After another growl, it shifts into something else. Sputtering coughs of a man in pain make it to my ears and I shoot a look at Larson, completely baffled.

A wicked grin lights up his aging face, causing crevices of wrinkles. "Let's go see what I've won."

31

Choose Your Grave

Seth

I don't remember how I got here. I'm sitting in the corner of my living room on the floor, wrists bound behind my back as well as my ankles before me. The position has made me stiff and my tailbone aches, but it all pales in comparison to whatever damage has been done to my shoulder. It throbs, radiating constantly as if it needs to remind me that something is wrong.

I'm well fucking aware.

In this state of being bound, I can't even shift. I'll dislocate my shoulders in the process. These damn zip ties are already cutting off my circulation, and attempting to break them seems risky at this point. Whoever tied me up, they made damn sure that I wouldn't be able to shift. I've counted at least seven of the ties, from what my fingers can reach. The length of my pants is hindering my ability to find out how many are down below. There are too many, some of which are cutting into my skin like a knife and I can smell traces of blood. Even so, goddammit, my fucking shoulder!

The toilet flushes and my eyes dart to the hall and I wait. I have no idea how much time has passed, the cloudy cover ruining my chances of guessing from the direction of the sun's rays.

Footsteps begin, and shortly, I'm graced with another presence.

What is this, some kind of brothers' retreat?

Bradley, the second born amongst the brothers that have continued to show up around here, strolls out, flinging drips of water from his hands to dry them. You couldn't mistake who his family is, though Bradley isn't as round as Carter nor is he as buff as Adam. Their heights are freakishly alike, though.

My mind is scrambling, trying to figure out if he's the reason I blacked out in the first place. How am I so important nowadays that they've called in the fucking cavalry to bring me back?

Bradley wears a cocky grin as he comes to a stop at my feet, kicking the bottom of mine. The move is jarring and my shoulder smacks the wall. I hiss through my teeth, unable to hide the pain.

"About time you wake up. Long time no see." He's got the same hair coloring as his brothers. His sister, however, took after their mother with her golden locks and looks nothing like these shitbags that took pride in ganging up on me.

"Where's Mom?" I ask, looking about. I should be able to pick up on her scent here. The air is clear, and there are no smells covering things up.

"We sent her home with Carter's body." He shrugs, as if the loss of his youngest brother means nothing.

"Too bad. Surely we could have squeezed you in her trunk as well."

His face darkens and he kicks at my foot again, sending signals right back to my injury.

"Fuck!" I grit out, and I'm seeing stars again. That can't be good. But it doesn't stop me and my damn mouth from running off again. "My bad, could have been Adam."

Speaking of, where in the hell is he? I can't hear or smell anyone else present. I don't even have anything telling me that my mother was ever here at my place to begin with. There isn't a trace of her around.

"Where is he?" I look around, but there's nothing indicating anyone but us two.

"We saw your little plaything drive by." He crouches down, lowering to my level. He looks at me as if he's satisfied by something. Amused by whatever thoughts are running wild within him.

I try not to let his words get to me. Clara isn't here, so that gives me some hope. But the fact that she was near to begin with is troubling. Hopefully she knows something is awry, but even so, why isn't she at work? Has the whole day gone by while I was unconscious?

"Adam picked up her scent at her house so she would be easier to track." My chest begins to ache, fear creeping in. "With the direction she was headed, she might be paying your little neighbor a visit. I don't think Adam should be too long, though. That old man's practically a cripple."

"Leave her the fuck alone," I grit out. I know Clara would be no match for Adam. If Larson is home, they might stand a chance. But I have no idea of the schedule he keeps or how he spends his days besides being a porch-sitting, chain-smoking drinker.

"Afraid it's too late for that."

"If you guys so much as lay a finger on her—"

"You'll what?" His fist shoots forward as he sinks it into my side. Sweat is accumulating along my hairline and at the back of my neck. "What are you going to do, Seth?"

"Whatever you want!" I bark at him. Fury is bubbling up within me and I have no other outlet to get rid of it. "I'll do whatever the fuck you want, just leave Clara alone!"

Bradley laughs, flashing his perfectly shaped teeth, and I want to do nothing more than sink my fist into them and knock them all out. He was a lucky one who was blessed with perfect teeth, never having the need for braces, and he loved shoving that in everyone's faces.

"Don't you get it?" He stands and begins to retreat. It feels like he's gearing up for some villain's monologue in a movie. He continues, further proving my point. "We've passed that point, Seth. We know that you won't come willingly. Especially if this woman is in the picture. Even if you were to voluntarily come with us, you'll always try to escape and come back to her. We're not stupid." He snorts, and the sound has me flaring my nostrils. "According to your mom, you haven't even marked her yet. Which, I've got to say, is surprising. What are you holding out on?"

None of your goddamn business.

Bradley leans down again, making sure my eyes are on him as cocks his head to the side. "You want to know what dear Aunt Alice said before she left? Hm?"

I know he's going to tell me regardless. He's on too much of a power trip to leave me hanging when he's finding so much sinister glee in this.

"A life for a life." His smile deepens, driving me to the point of insanity. "You took Carter, now we take Clara."

"Fuck you!" I spit in his face, having let my saliva build during his little rant. It's enough to anger him, and when his fist comes at me again, I dive to the side and he loses his footing. It's enough to give me an advantage and I raise my bound legs up and bring them down, striking him with my heels on his back.

I roll away, muttering profanities as I go. I'm trying so damn hard to break my ties but all I can feel is my skin tearing, and I'm causing more damage to my already weakened state. One snaps, completely catching me off guard. It fucking hurts, but I take in a deep breath and let out a roar of a shout as I fight with all of my might to free myself from the rest.

Bradley has recovered, and while I notice a hole in the wall that I'm going to have to fix, he begins to charge at me. My back stiffens as I bring my legs up and hurl his body across the room, and he lands with a resounding crash as he hits something. The pressure on my shoulder from the act only enrages me more.

I'm blinded by my pain and my will to fight for Clara. All I can think about is Adam going after her, the terror she must be in as my fucking cousin guns straight for her. My only hope is that I can get to her before he does, and if I don't? I had better be ready to take him on when he gets back. If he so much as breathes on her, I will fucking tear his lungs right out of his chest.

Adrenaline is pumping furiously through me as I break free of my bindings. My bones start to crack, and I can't contain the torment my body is going through. I scream, letting it out as the change takes over.

"Fuck! Really?" Bradley groans as he bears witness to my shift. His feet slip on the floor as he tries to stand and makes a break for the back door. I can hear him fumbling with the locks as my clothes begin to tear as my appearance morphs into another.

That's right, run.

My shoulder injury prevents me from walking on all fours, so I take off on my hind legs. Bradley is ripping his shirt off as he flees, taking off and into the tree line.

I don't care about the fucking aftermath if anyone sees me. Clara in danger is enough for me to throw away all of my concerns over secrecy. And as much as I want to charge off in her direction now, I can't. Not when Bradley can come up from behind and attack. I have to deal with him first before they can gang up on me again.

No more surprises.

He's mid-change when I take a swipe at his back. He howls as his face elongates, the gashes on his back splitting open to reveal crimson. I use my good side to land another blow, thrusting him forward and further away from view of the road. I don't even give him a chance to get up as my clawed hand grasps his neck and I drag him deeper into the woods.

Bradley screeches like some sort of bird as he fights between figures. It's like he can't decide which one he wants to take on, and it's to his detriment. I toss him to the ground and let out a guttural growl that scatters away any wildlife nearby.

Splotches of hair erupt from his body, some falling from him just as soon as it emerges. He's scared shitless, that I know. I can see it in his eyes as I raise an arm, anger vibrating through me like electricity.

Looks like a good place for a grave. Once my shoulder heals, of course.

With all my might, I swing, bringing my sharpened nails down to slash his throat. His body convulses as he tries to bring his hands up to stop the bleeding, but it's useless. I cut deep enough that there's no hope for him now, and I watch as his life drains from his eyes.

I hold no remorse. Not for him, or anyone who might love him. To me, he's just another werewolf that got in the way of me being my own man, my own person. Cousin was just a name he wore. Today, he proved yet again why I no longer consider him family.

"Seth." That familiar voice calls to me on staggered breath, and my head turns to find it. Several yards away, my Rose is standing. I don't know how much she's been witness to, and as much as I want to run to her, I can't physically move.

I can see her shock; it's evident from her wide and dark eyes. What I can barely make out is the glistening of tears as they stream down her face. She's like a beacon in her purple sweater, the epitome of beauty even though I know she fears me for what I am.

My thoughts stray to my promise that I wouldn't shift unless it were a full moon. I went back on my word without batting an eye, and I'm petrified that she will pull away because of it.

There's a rustling to the right of Clara, and I lower, trying to make myself appear smaller. I'm stunned to find a naked and bloodied Adam, swaying as he walks along while held at gunpoint by Larson. Ironically, he has a bullet wound around the same spot where he caused damage to me earlier. I have to admire the aim to wound and bring him down. I will be indebted to Larson for this.

Someone is answering some fucking prayers today. I'll be damned.

"You take care of yerself. We'll be at yer house."

I nod once as Larson escorts the only brother still living and breathing in the direction from which I came. What I wasn't expecting is the look on Clara's face when I return my attention to her. My heart breaks as I stand before her, the overcast light of day around us, showing off what I am. There is no hiding in the shadows this time. I am on full display as the werewolf she's too terrified to speak of.

Her bottom lip trembles, and I know it isn't from the weather even though her face is rosy from it. No, it's deeper than that.

I don't know how long we stand there, staring at one another. Her eyes skim across me as she studies everything before her. I give her as much time as I can stand and when I can't bear the quiet we're met with any longer, I turn away.

Taking a few steps, I let my knees lower to the ground as I call on my body to shift back, trying to mentally prepare myself for the strain it will put me through. My face contorts and my arms and legs jerk this way and that. I bite back the added stress of my affliction that only worsens as things snap and change. Hair falls from me, exposing my bare skin to the fall breeze that passes by.

I'm practically panting by the time it's over, tears falling from holding back the pain of it all. I can barely detect Clara's footsteps as she draws nearer, her vanilla scent filling my nose.

I stand and turn to face her. She's cupping her hands at her chest, paused mid-step as she waits. For what, I'm not sure. I don't know if I should apologize for the murder I just took part in, the horror in her eyes, or the overall panic she must be in. Probably all of it, to be honest, but I'm rendered speechless.

Clara launches herself, surging forward and raising her arms as if to take hold of my neck. I stumble back slightly, disoriented by the unexpected reaction from her and the weight of her arm that makes my injury roar to life.

"Ah!" My body heaves forward and she jumps back, clasping her hands over her mouth.

"I'm sorry. I'm so sorry!"

I shake my head, my body at a slant as if it will help ease the pain when I know it won't. Something this deep, I fear I need to go to the fucking emergency room. It's something that I don't have time for. But I know my body well enough to realize that this is more than bruising deep.

"It's fine, I'm fine." I know I'm lying, but I can't help but say it anyway as I draw her in with my good arm. She loops her arms around my waist and I expect her to provide some warmth, but she's too cold. Clara should have a coat or something, and she's in nothing but jeans and a long-sleeve sweater. It does absolutely nothing to contain her body heat. "You're okay? You're okay."

I kiss her head as she nods, and I revel in her sweet smell as I close my eyes. We stand long enough for a shiver to rack through her and only then do I release her and take her hand. She looks at me with those beautiful browns and I don't sense a bit of fear anymore. Something softer resembling maybe…relief?

"I knew something was wrong. I shouldn't have waited so long. I should have—"

"Shhh…" I bring the back of her hand up to my lips and only then do I become aware of the bloody scene that my hand is. Bradley's blood has dried already, but the marks from breaking free of the restraints on my wrists have caused streams of red to coat my skin. I'm sure my shift didn't help with the clotting, either.

"Listen to me, Clara." Her eyes flutter until she hones in on me, and only then do I continue. "None of this is your fault. Do you hear me? None of it. I am so sorry that you've been dragged into this. I never should have let my guard down. Never should have put you in this position." I take a breath before continuing. "You're fucking smart, though, Clara. So fucking smart for not rushing here like you did when you found out about me paying your mortgage. You went to Larson, and I thank my lucky stars that you did."

"I went to him for help. I didn't know where else to turn." Her voice shakes with a frantic tone that begins to rise. "He…he fired off into the woods and I had no idea what in the hell for, but…he shot him. He fucking shot him down, and when we found him, he was trying to change back into…"

We are going to have to work through her inability to speak about the wolf side of things and all of its particulars. But that isn't a problem for today. Right now, Larson is probably cornering a wounded Adam, and I don't like the thought of the two of them inside my house. It's bad enough I have to do damage control to the wall that Bradley put his fist through and whatever else he wrecked. I don't want to worry about any bloodstains or bullet holes that might come from its current guests.

One thing is certain, though. As soon as I'm healed, I'm tearing down Larson's porch and building him a new one to show him my thanks for aiding and protecting Clara. We might have started out on the wrong foot, but now, I am indebted to him. I owe him so much.

"What happened to you? To your mom?"

I lead her by the hand, leaving the scene of my most recent crime, and she follows at my side. Twigs and sticks stab at my bare feet, scraping across my ankles periodically, but I barely notice over the throb on my shoulder.

"She was waiting for me at the address you sent. I think she was giving one last-ditch effort to get me to come willingly, and when I wouldn't, my cousin Carter stepped in. I took care of him just in time before Adam—that's the one Larson shot—came into the picture. He and my mom got the best of me, and I think Bradley back there might have come into play at the end because I was knocked out by something. But I can't be sure. Next thing I knew, I was waking up in my living room. Bound and tied in the corner. I guess Mom took Carter's body back home with her."

"So Carter's...dead?" I can hear her stifling a gulp as she speaks.

"Yep, two for three."

Clara shoots me a look of disbelief. "That's not funny, Seth."

"I'm not laughing. The last thing I wanted to do was kill them, but they left me with no other choice. They would keep coming after me, after you."

We walk a few more steps, my house slowly creeping into view before Clara speaks up again. "That man Larson shot? The cameras picked him up at my house earlier."

I stop dead in my tracks, looking at her straight on. "You were at work, right?"

"Actually, I was on my lunch hour and checking the address I gave you, but there was no one in sight and your truck was nowhere to be found. My phone alerted me and I watched him on the backyard camera as he neared, but once he saw the camera, he went back toward the garage. When he saw that one too, he left." She clears her throat, placing her free hand at the base. "I don't think I ever got a chance to thank you for installing all of those, but I've got to admit, you had impeccable timing in doing so."

I hate that I was right. That my family would try to pull something such as this, warranting the use of them at all.

The thought occurs to me that not only did my mother not come alone, but she brought three of my cousins to try and get me to come back home. In reality, the three versus one ratio is almost laughable now. Why bring so many when they were trying to bring a single person back?

By the time we reach the house, I've broken into a cold sweat. My head is fuzzy, and just when I think I'm becoming accustomed to the pain on my shoulder, it worsens. My steps come to a halt and I know Clara is looking at me in confusion, her mouth poised to say something, but I don't give her the chance to.

"Can you grab me some water and some pills? This shoulder has really fucked me up." I ask as gently as I can, but even I can tell it's not as polite as I intended for it to be.

"And some pants?" she pokes lightly, and I try to smile, but it feels like someone has shoved cotton into my mouth.

"If you insist." I let go of her hand and as soon as she enters the house, my head turns just in time for vomit to rise in my throat. It comes out too fast, dizzying me and worsening the trauma my body has been through. The top half of my body feels too heavy to keep upright, and I start to sway.

So help me if I land on my bad side? I'm a goner.

"Young man, you need a doctor."

I can barely focus as a figure enters into my periphery. He's blurry, and I'm not sure if he's real or not. He sounds like he's here, but my vision feels like it's playing tricks on me.

He's got a ball cap on and a beard that rivals my own in length. At least, I think he does. His body blends in with the background, deepening my uncertainty. He looks like the forest as he gets closer.

"Son, can you hear me?"

Son? I'm nobody's son. Not anymore.

Funny how the man's head floats about without a body. He looks weird. Is he a ghost or something? I have yet to come across anything of the sort since moving here. Great, maybe the woods are haunted and Bradley's going to stick around and give me shit for killing him.

"Seth?"

I turn my head too quickly in search of Clara, but my body gives out, sending me to the ground.

32

Is This the End?

Clara

I'm bolting after Seth as his body hits the ground. The water and pill bottle leave my hands at some point as I skid on my knees next to him.

"Let me see him, miss."

I'm taken aback by another man who wasn't out here just a minute ago. I have no idea if he's a friend or foe, either. I put myself between Seth and him, holding up a hand as if I could hold him off. If he's a fucking werewolf too, I'm screwed. "Leave him alone!"

"Clara," Larson calls out from the back door I left ajar. I'm reluctant to give him my attention, not wanting to let this man get closer to my unconscious...whatever he is, who I'm trying to shield. "I called 'im. He's with me."

Larson turns and backs into the house as he mutters something inaudible, possibly at the other naked man, the one with a bullet wound.

Returning my attention to the man before me, I notice that he's dressed in camo as if he's been out hunting or something. "Who are you?"

"Name's Edgar." He holds out a hand, but when I don't take it, he pulls it back in and stuffs it into his pockets. "Heard you guys were having some troubles. I'm here to help."

"With what, exactly?" I'm beginning to think that he knows more than I'm willing to say out loud. That there are more werewolves than I care to admit in Iowa, of all the damned places. They are literally coming out of the woodwork today and it is beyond infuriating, eating away at whatever sanity I might have left.

"Well right now, how about we start with getting this man inside?"

I want to trust him, but letting my guard down right now seems too dangerous. On the other hand, Seth has just passed out without a stitch of clothing on, and whatever's ailing him has me willing to accept a little help when offered. That, and I'm freaking freezing even though I'm dressed.

Edgar approaches and leans down, grabbing onto Seth's knees and raising them to a bent position. I start to protest as he steps on Seth's bare feet as he goes to grab his hands, but before I can get the words out, he's hauling a man twice his size up and onto his shoulders. A squeak of a sound leaves my throat, momentarily stunned before I take off after him, retrieving the items I dropped as I make my way in after them, closing the door behind us.

The new arrival is quick to take Seth down the hall, as if he knows where he's going. I follow, taking in a scene of Larson on the couch with his feet propped up, hands on his rifle which is pointed at the man in the corner. That one's grunting rather furiously, and I swear he's trying to murder me with his stare as I pass.

Edgar and I get to work cleaning up Seth. I cover his lower half with a towel, trying to give him some modesty even though he's completely out. He has paled, breathing shallow as his chest rises and falls. I keep checking my phone, nervous about how fast time seems to be speeding up. Of all the days this could have happened, it had to be on a workday with my kids coming home after school.

Seth stirs, groaning as his eyes begin to open, and I leap onto the bed at his side. My hand is on the side of his face as I will him to focus on me.

"Seth." I'm relieved to see his golden hues as they flit toward me. "Here, take these." I pop the cap of the pill bottle and grab the water from his nightstand. He doesn't even bother sitting up, just takes the two pills and tosses them into his mouth, chasing them down with the water. I think I would choke if I did that while lying down.

Seth's eyes settle on something, and his gaze narrows. I look over my shoulder to see Edgar standing just inside the doorway, still as a statue and watching us. "That's Edgar. Larson called him."

The camo-wearing man tilts his head as if to nod his greeting. "How would you like us to handle this fellow out here?"

My eyes roam back to Seth, witnessing his jaw tense as he stares at the ceiling. After a few seconds of silence, he finally speaks. "I'd like a word with him. After that, he's all yours. He swallows hard. "Then I think I need to go to the hospital."

Seth looks like he's been in some sort of wrestling match or vehicle accident. He's battered, and bruises are beginning to surface, tainting his skin. There are cuts around his wrists and ankles, and even though the lighting isn't great in the bedroom, the blinds are letting enough in to make me think someone landed a decent punch to his face. He's lucky for that beard of his.

"We'll be out in a minute or two." I try to politely dismiss Edgar and I'm thankful when he turns on his heel and exits.

I return my attention to Seth, afraid to touch him even though I want to hug, kiss, and wrap my arms around him, but I don't want to cause him any more pain. If he's wanting to go to the hospital, it must be bad. Hell, he vomited and passed out cold just minutes ago; of course he's in bad shape.

"What can I do? What do you need?"

He groans again, the sound twisting my heart. I don't think the over-the-counter painkillers are going to give him the help he needs. I want to believe that I have a stronger stomach after having two kids and all of the trials they have put me through over the years, but seeing Seth like this? Seeing a man of his physique broken down in this way? It affects me more than I would like to admit.

"I need pants." His nostrils flare as he exhales. "And one of my tanks if I can get it on."

"Got it." I leave his side and begin rummaging through dresser drawers. Whichever hospital he goes to, he could be there a while. I grab some underwear and socks while I'm at it and then I rush to the closet, opening the double doors. I'm taken aback for a second at how organized it is. His ripped tanks are on the left, T-shirts in the middle, and long-sleeved tops on the right.

Damn. Can he reorganize my wardrobe next time he's over?

I help him off the bed and he hisses, breathing speeding up as he leans to one side for a moment before he stands. I help him into his clothes but stop when we get to the final piece, his tank with its ripped-out sides.

"Where does it hurt?"

He sighs. "Better question might be, where does it *not* hurt?"

"Seth," I warn, not appreciating that at all.

"Shoulder." He rolls his neck, clenching his eyes as he does. "I took a pretty bad hit to my right shoulder."

"Well, thank God you're left-handed then." My tone is a bit more sarcastic than I mean for it to be.

He can barely lift his arm, and I try to ease the fabric into the small space he's created and draw it up and over until I reach his head. It gets to the point where I'm on my tiptoes and he takes over, wincing as he drags the material down.

"Clara." His eyes settle on mine as he teeters. My hands rise by reflex, afraid that he might go down again. His hand cups the side of my face as his forehead meets mine. I grip his forearm, careful to give enough space so I don't hit his markings. We remain still until raised voices fill our ears. They're arguing out in the living room, and it's only growing louder.

Seth takes my hand and leads me out of his bedroom and down the hall. The naked man on the floor lets out a cry of agony, and all I can make out is Edgar leaning over him. I'm not sure if he's torturing him or what, but I look away and into the kitchen. I'm growing more and more uncomfortable as the last remaining naked body strains his voice.

Larson hollers at Edgar to stop and he backs away, and only then do I turn my attention back. The bullet hole is still oozing blood and it's running down his muscled abdomen. Larson hasn't lowered his gun at all, poised and at the ready to shoot. I'm not sure if he has some sort of sniper skill set or what, but I hope I'm never on his bad side. His aim back at his house was nothing short of impeccable. Now if he makes a shot, I'm sure it will be sending someone right to death's door.

"You're fucking weak!" the man bellows, spit flying. His face is flushed red. His ragged breaths make my stomach twist.

"Is that why you and your two brothers accompanied my mom? Because *I'm* the weak one?" Seth shakes his head. "Sounds like quite the opposite, if you ask me."

"Does seem a bit excessive." Larson leans forward, focusing on the man who should be begging for his life instead of getting mouthy.

"Is that everyone who came along or should we be expecting more company?" Edgar kicks at the man's leg, and only then do I see that his hands are bound by rope and in his lap. It's tied over and over again and goes halfway up his lower arms. My eyes trip over the sight of his manhood and I divert my gaze. Do I need to throw him a towel or something? Just because these other men are comfortable around this, doesn't mean that I am.

When there's no answer, Edgar draws an arm back and my body recoils from the scene as a scream tears from the man's throat. The sound fills the whole damn house and wreaks havoc on my ears.

"That's enough!" Seth orders, cutting into the assault.

Heaving, garbled sounds follow in the wake of the shouts, and suddenly I'm glad I didn't have any lunch today. I'm not cut out for this.

"Even if you were to mark her..." His words are laced with vexation, but there's a sinister amusement that follows him as he continues. "They're still fucking coming after you. After her."

I shoot a glance at Seth. Whatever he's talking about with this "mark" thing is the least of my worries. It's the last line that has me shaking—the mere thought that this isn't over. And here I stupidly believed that the problems from today were almost solved. It hits me like a gut punch to think that there will be more of this. More fighting, more unknown faces, and more fucking werewolves.

Seth doesn't look back at me as he leaves my side. He takes the gun from Larson's hands and closes in on his cousin, but he doesn't aim it at him.

"Let them fucking try," Seth sneers. A chill rolls over me like someone has left the back door wide open and the fall breeze is trying to sweep me away. Seth raises the gun and I turn away again, but I can still hear the sound of something being hit. I cup a hand over my view and make a beeline for the front door, not stopping until I'm about ten feet away from the house. I can't bring myself to look at another dead body, if that's what Seth did. I was already at war with myself after the revelation that the other man in the woods had been killed. Even if it was self-defense, it doesn't change the fact that Seth has already taken two lives today. Two relatives by blood, even if he doesn't claim them anymore.

"I don't care what you do with him." Seth's voice is barely audible as he approaches me from behind.

It's not until I hear him come to a stop that I find my voice. "Did you kill him, too?"

It's quiet, and I fear that he did just that. I don't know what to do with this information and with this side of Seth. I am still struggling to come to terms with this werewolf news of his, and now murderer is being thrown into the mix?

"I knocked him out, Clara. He's not dead. Just taking a little nap."

I spin around, a bit cynical. "Was I foolish to believe that this would be over? That we've won? Why won't your family stop coming after you? I can't do this, Seth. I can't risk my family or put them in danger. Fuck, we're all in danger!"

"Clara—"

"No!" I yell at him, eyes burning once again. "How many are they going to send next time? How many family members do you have to kill before they take a hint? This is insane!"

Seth leans to the side, thwarting my rising temper when I swear he goes cross-eyed.

"Don't you dare pass out again," I warn as I take a step forward. "We need to get you to the hospital." It's hard to stay mad at him when he looks like he's been hit by a bus.

"No, you need to get home," he tries to declare, even if it's weak by his standards.

My jaw drops. "You are *not* driving yourself. Are you crazy?"

"I'll take 'im, Clara." Larson is exiting the front door, no longer carrying any kind of weapon. "Edgar will take care of business here. I'll help however I can when I get back."

I don't want to pretend to know the meaning behind his words, and I feel like at this point I know better than to ask.

"Go home, Clara." There's an edge in Seth's voice and it sounds angry, but there's a part of me that believes he's just fighting back the pain that he's in. "Be with your kids. I'll try to keep you updated."

"Do you even have your phone? I know it wasn't you who was texting me earlier." I throw my hands up in the air in exasperation.

He raises a concerned brow. "Guess I'll take my work phone to the hospital, then. I'll try to track my personal one from it."

I study him for a moment, pushing back the sympathy that ebbs and flows with Seth and his predicament. While I appreciate the opportunity to head home, I still feel uneasy parting like this, not knowing where in the hell we go from here.

No matter the push and pull we seem to make a habit of, that's just it. We keep finding our way back to each other. Granted, I know I've been the one who's done most of the pushing away, but this time feels different. While I am confused, scared, and even angry, I don't detect the want to drive him off. I want Seth to heal and be safe. I want him to confide in me about his day and the plans we need to make moving forward.

What exactly does that say about me that I am looking forward to him staying in the picture, even when the unknown threats of the future hang in the balance?

Stepping forward, I resist the urge to drive my finger into Seth's chest, but I meet him with a hardened stare. "I'm mad at you. And we're not done talking about this."

A small, delirious smile crosses his face as he plants a kiss on my forehead. "We can talk until I'm blue in the face, beautiful. As long as you don't shut me out."

The feel of his lips on my skin is calming me down faster than I anticipated, and I'm struggling to hold on to my frustrations. Even as the words leave my mouth, they sound like they're lacking the ferocity I mean for them to have. "In the doghouse is where you belong."

The relief that floods through me when my kids make it home safe and sound is unmatched. I'm standing on the front porch, witnessing their confusion at the fact I'm even home to begin with as they get off of their bus. I made the quick run home and threw my clothes in the wash, soaking my sweater with stain-remover gel in the hopes that it might get rid of the spots I acquired while hugging and caring for Seth.

I've changed into some comfortable leggings and a baggy comfort sweater, hugging myself tight within its clean warmth as Julie and Emmett come up to the front porch to meet me. If I'd had time for a shower, I would have done it, but there wasn't a moment to spare.

"What are you doing home? Is everything okay?" Julie is the first to hit the stairs, backpack slung over one shoulder.

Shit, I'm going to have to lie to my kids. I'm scrambling to think of something that won't alarm them but at the same time, not fully omit the truth. "A friend of mine was in an accident. He's on his way to the hospital."

I realize how stiff my body has become and I have to remind myself to relax.

"You mean boyfriend?" Emmett grunts as he brushes past us. My eyes bulge as he continues on and into the house. When I turn my attention back to Julie, she's waiting for an answer to her brother's question, and I don't know how to respond.

Do I call him boyfriend? I just witnessed him murder someone in the woods maybe an hour or so ago.

"I hate to say that it's complicated, but…"

"It's complicated," Julie states, and I can't tell by her tone if she's annoyed or just trying to process that information. "Is he going to be okay?"

Her thoughtfulness in even asking that gives me a sliver of hope. "I think he will be. We just don't know the extent of the damage yet."

Julie nods slowly. Her deep maroon sweater beneath her coat brings out the color in her cheeks, making them brighter. "Well, I hope he's okay."

I'm not sure if she's saying it out of kindness or the sense that she needs to be okay with it because I'm standing right here, but regardless, I choose to believe it's a step in the right direction.

We decide on a breakfast night for dinner, a skillet scramble of sorts with whatever I can find to throw in it with bacon on the side. I can't help but pick at some of the slices as they cool, and I continue to cook the rest of the package in sets. I'm really hungry and can't stop myself from diving in.

The house smells wonderful. The sounds of bacon sizzling make my stomach growl for more, and when Emmett makes his way downstairs after being cooped up in his room, I offer some to him as well.

"How was your day?" I ask, only to be met with a shrug as he shovels a strip into his mouth and takes another to go. You would think I'd be used to the silent treatment he sometimes gives me, but I'm not. "Anything you want to do this weekend?"

He shrugs again, picking at my nerves, and I have to remind myself to breathe and keep levelheaded. I didn't think Emmett would start shutting me out until his teen years, but it's proving to be quite the opposite.

"Did I do something wrong, Emmett?" I can't contain the question any longer.

Little eyes that remind me of his father's slide to mine, but he's quick to turn them away as he leans over the island counter, chewing. I don't think he's going to offer me an answer, but then he surprises me.

"Julie thinks that we need to meet this guy."

"Shut up!" Julie hollers as she enters the kitchen, shooting a wary glance my way. He sticks his tongue out at her and she's about to slug him in the arm but I clear my throat, pinning them down with my stare.

"I *said* we should give him a chance," she backtracks, shrinking her frame as she puts distance between her and her sibling.

Today has been trying in more ways than one, and this conversation has me wanting to abandon ship already. I've almost hit my limit on stress, but I'm still standing and trying to find a way through it to a lifeboat.

"I stand by what I said the other day. Yes, I want you to meet him, but only when the both of you are ready. He understands that as well. Nobody is in a rush here."

"Well, what if I don't want to meet him? He's not Dad." There's a twist in my gut at Emmett's words.

"Dad's not coming back," Julie mutters under her breath. "You know that."

It's like I've been stabbed and someone is twisting the knife. It fucking hurts. Even if Joe wanted me back, I wouldn't take him. Not in a million years. He chewed up and spit out our marriage vows, threw away countless years together, all for Chassidy. I don't want anything to do with him.

Seth would never do what he did.

That thought emerges out of nowhere, and I try to refocus on the conversation at hand. "I can't begin to imagine how difficult this is for you two. If my being with someone is too much for now, I'll keep him out of the picture. But I'd be lying if I didn't tell you how important he is to me. How important he's becoming."

Even though he's a werewolf capable of murder.

These damn thoughts of mine are running away with the wind.

Julie and Emmett exchange glances between lowered heads. It's almost like they're trying to say something telepathically that I'm not privy to, but can only witness through their actions.

"We'll think about it some more," Julie speaks up, struggling to meet my gaze as she pushes herself off of the counter and leaves just as fast as she arrived. Emmett is quick to follow, and before I can utter another word, my phone goes off.

I whip it out so fast I almost lose my grip and drop it, but recover. There's a message waiting from Seth, and my heart leaps as I pull up the message so I can see it in its entirety.

> Fractured shoulder blade but no surgery. I'm bound to a sling for 6 weeks and getting prescriptions for pain. Hoping to be discharged within the hour.

My exhale is shaky, but I can't deny how good it feels to hear the news about what was causing him so much pain. I type out my reply, resisting the thought of calling him as I turn back toward the stove to check on the food.

> Glad to hear. I've got some yelling to do.

And hugging, and kissing, but mostly yelling. I wish I could be with him right now, but I can't help but admire his nudge for me to go home to my kids. This is where I need to be, no matter how much it hurts to be apart from him at a time like this.

I choose to ignore the heaviness that today has been. Being faced with the other side of Seth that has haunted me since our first encounter is threatening to make me hyperventilate. I saw him shed that form and morph into the one I met not so long ago. The one I have grown to care and long for even in his absence.

I can't deal with that right now and be the mother that I need to be. For now, I choose to be present and in the moment, not taking a single minute with my kids for granted. I know Seth isn't going anywhere, and he will be waiting for me when I am ready for whatever next step we might take.

33

The Start of Something New

Seth

I'm fucking sick of this sling. It's only been fifteen days, and it's driving me absolutely insane. It weighs on my neck and I can feel my arm growing weaker without the use of it. I'm down to only taking medications once a day, since I don't like the way they make me feel in the head even if they do help with the pain management.

My truck is parked outside of Clara's house, in the driveway for the first time ever, and I'm careful as I get out. The first time I jumped from it, it jolted my shoulder enough to render me useless for a moment while I cussed myself out. One wrong move and I was a mess. I'm already dreading the next full moon. I hope I don't reinjure it when I have no choice but to go through the change again.

Shooting Clara a quick text that I'm here, I round the front end of my vehicle and go to the passenger door so I can gather the dish I've brought over for Thanksgiving. Clara insisted on taking care of the food, but I didn't want to show up empty-handed. I don't want to come off as some sort of bum who looks like he's only showing up for the meal. No, I want to be a part of it and provide something. Set a good example for the kids that I'm finally getting the privilege to meet.

I suppose I should be nervous, but to my own astonishment, I'm not. In a way, I feel like I already know them. I've lost count of the nights I've stayed over, the arguments those two kids have on a day-to-day basis, and Clara's attempts to get them to stop. I am more than eager to meet them and begin our lives together.

I know I'm not going to replace their dad, and by no means do I intend to. But I am going to be the best damn stepdad to them.

Clara comes bursting out of the small door at the garage, but I'm not met with her warm and welcoming smile. While I might be excited for today, her nerves have been taking over ever since the kids agreed to meet.

"Let me get that." She grabs the casserole dish from the seat and looks up at me, timid.

"Relax, Clara. Everything's going to be fine." I try to quiet her racing thoughts that I know are taking control. "I'll be on my best behavior, promise."

"It's not you I'm worried about." She sighs as she shuts the door with a push of her hip. My eyes take in the sight of her as she does it, and I hate the fact that I can't wrap my arms around those thick curves that make my mouth water. She might be fully dressed, but I'm imagining her naked body against my truck as I take her, watching her reflection as I ease myself into her, burying my cock until I'm balls deep.

Fuck, get ahold of yourself.

Not having any sex since my injuries has proven to be quite difficult. I'd be lucky if we could manage some oral and hand favors, but Clara has been adamant that I heal. I have to guard my reactions to any complaints around her. Nothing puts up a wall between us like my afflictions, and I try my best to stifle and not show any pain, but I know she knows better. It's tough to fool her.

I put on a small act as I enter the house through the kitchen, taking everything in as if it's new when I've been traipsing around the place enough to know every nook and cranny. The aroma of the food hits me immediately and my salivary glands go into overdrive. The ham smells delicious, and I catch sight of it in a crockpot on the counter. The pineapple rings glisten, and I'm ready to dig in the moment I get the green light. I haven't eaten a single thing this morning in preparation for this, and I'm starved.

Clara sets my dish on the counter and gets out some large spoons for the array of sides she's prepared. There's too much food for the four of us, and while I admire how much work she's put into this, I'm a bit soured by the fact that she wouldn't take me up on my offer to provide more.

"Anything I can help with?" I keep a small enough distance that I'm out of the way as I await an answer from her. Her brown eyes keep darting to the entrances and exits to the kitchen. I know she's waiting to see who will make their way in here first.

"Just stand there and look pretty." She lifts the corner of a foil-covered dish and sticks a spoon in. "Or sit, your call."

I beam at her, admiring her even though she's frazzled. She's been so worked up over this day and fretting about it. I have every intention of doing everything in my power to make a good first impression.

The soft padding of footsteps can be heard, and I can already determine that it's Julie making her way down the stairs. Clara casts a worried look my way as she wipes her palms on her hips and comes to join me at my side as another set of feet begin to follow suit.

I see a young Clara come into view, only her hair is considerably different. When Julie sets her sights on me, she freezes. The abrupt stop has me offering a kind smile, but just as quickly as she came into the picture, she turns and flees back up the stairs. Emmett gives a quizzical expression as she darts around him and goes back to her room. He's quick to give his glasses a shove as they slide down his nose.

"Um…" Clara is just as confused as I am and skirts around me. "Seth, this is my son Emmett. Emmett, this is Seth. I'll be right back."

Her son looks like he has bedhead, a mess of hair that shares the lighter coloring of his sister's. I knew as much from the family pictures that hang around the house, but his hair is longer now than in most of them.

Clara runs up the stairs after her daughter, and I scratch my head, growing suddenly awkward in the silence that lies between us.

"You're dating my mom?" Emmett asks as he enters the kitchen and crosses his arms. He's sizing me up, looking up and down as if he's trying to find something.

Loving, fucking, and cherishing is more like it. Dating feels so simple and formal. But for his young mind, dating it is.

"I have been seeing your mom, yes."

His lips thin, then he rolls them just like Clara does, a small act that has me internally grinning. Emmett gives a small nod as his gaze falls on my sling.

"She said you were in an accident. What happened?"

Ah yes, cover story.

"Wish I could say I was fending for my life battling wolves, but it was nothing more than a stupid accident with a four-wheeler." I almost forget to mention the most important part that Clara wanted me to add. "Seat belts are important."

I'm grateful that the bruising and swelling has had time to fade away before today. I'm not so sure that Clara would have gone through with this meal if I still looked as if I'd stepped out of a wrestling ring.

"I hear you're into games," I switch course in an attempt to change the subject. Little does he know that I've seen his room and the various consoles he has. It's a fucking gold mine in there that I would have killed for as a kid. He doesn't know how lucky he has it.

He nods, his hardened exterior softening just a tad. "Yeah, but Mom thinks I play too much."

I shrug, but the movement came so naturally that I forgot about my injury and I wince slightly. "Just make sure you balance it out. It's okay to enjoy it. Hell—I mean, heck—I like playing too, but don't let yourself get sucked into it."

"What do you play?" His interest is piqued, and I'm thrilled that we've gotten this far in our first conversation.

"A little bit of everything. What's your latest obsession?"

Emmett beats around the bush briefly before he starts unloading on me. He becomes animated as he talks about his latest craze, Guardians 2.0, and once I prove my knowledge of the game, the gleam in his eyes is unmistakable.

"I can bring it up in the living room if you want to see it. I'm on level twenty-nine."

I nod my head, a bit too enthusiastically but encouraging him. "Fu...heck yeah. Let's do it."

I'm going to have to watch this mouth of mine now that I'm going to be in the presence of minors. I know some kids can swear like sailors, but I don't think Clara would take kindly to it. And she's the boss.

Emmett shrugs. "You can cuss, Mom doesn't care."

"That's a bold-faced lie, Emmett Cline," Clara's voice cuts in from the top of the stairs. His eyes widen, knowing he's been caught.

Oh damn, we're using middle names now.

I whisper for Emmett to go get the game started and shoo him away as Clara reaches the kitchen. He's quick to comply, taking off at a quick jog to get away from his scolding mother.

I can't help but grin.

"Everything alright?" I ask as she draws nearer, her scent taking over my senses. It mingles with the various foods as she steps in close.

"You're not going to believe this." Her voice drops as she casts a look over her shoulder before coming back to me. "You're tattoo guy."

My brows lower. "Am I supposed to know what that means?"

Clara bites something back, amused as she rolls those precious lips. "Don't say anything to her."

I draw a little "x" over my heart, earning an annoyed look from her before she replaces it with a smirk. "There's a certain tattoo guy who takes a lot of runs around town. Julie and her friends have been fawning and giggling over him ever since he moved here."

I bite back the hilarity that tries to rise to the surface. Of all the things I could have possibly done to offend Julie, warrant this kind of response upon our first meeting, *that* definitely wasn't anywhere on my radar. School buses are so packed and rowdy to begin with, I've never paid any attention to the squeals and laughter emitting from them in their passing. Even though I know what bus the kids ride, I don't pay it any special attention when out and about.

"Not tattoo guy," I jest, pulling her nearer by her waist until her hips meet mine. Her lips part as she gazes up at me through heavy lids, eyes fluttering as she attempts to swallow. "Wolf got your tongue, beautiful?"

I can feel her heart beating as if it's outside of her body, beating for me, and only me.

Her hand floats up to my face, skimming across my facial hair as that sexy smirk returns, lighting up her eyes. "Something like that."

Also by Krystal Kae

Tethered To You Series

Watching Me

Altering Me

The Rose Duet

Chasing Petals

If you enjoyed this book, a quick rating or review on Goodreads, Amazon, or wherever you got your copy would mean the world to me. Your support helps others discover the book— thank you!

Acknowledgements

Wow, creating this book took me by storm. My first draft took me about a month which is unheard of for me. Mornings, afternoons and nights, I was plucking away at a keyboard trying to tell this story that was supposed to be my first attempt at a standalone. By the time I reached 100k on my word count, I realized that I had failed with that mission.

I think a part of the reason for this was because in everything that I write, there's parts of me within the characters. Sometimes, Easter Eggs or clues that only those closest to me will recognize and some, probably only my husband will notice. Clara was not only closer to me age-wise, but she is also a mother. Maybe that's why this story came to life so fast, because even though she's a fictional character, I could relate to her on some of these levels and could see myself in her shoes at times.

I wasn't sure if taking a break from the Tethered to You series would bother readers, but I needed a break from their world and the darkness behind it. But in doing so, I've also realized that I don't know how to write a story without killing someone off so...do with that information what you will.

There are days when I'm writing and scribbling so fast, I can barely keep up with my thoughts and others when I'm stuck in a deep rut thinking that everything I write and do...sucks. There's been extreme highs and severe lows with this writing journey so far, but there's something so rewarding when you finally get that finished book in your hands that keeps driving me forward.

I want to give a shout out to both the HEA Book Boutique and Book Vault for taking a chance on this author who is still trying to figure herself out. My love for indie bookstores has blossomed so much in these past few years, recognizing all that they do for their communities and the support that they give their authors. Thank you for the opportunity to be on your bookshelves.

To my family, friends, and coworkers that continue to support me on this author dream of mine, thank you. If you're still sticking around after this third book, you must not entirely hate what I'm putting out there. Whether you're buying a book for yourself or copies to give as gift, it seriously means the world to me.

To my friends in the social media community, thank you for cheering me on. Sometimes when I make a post, it feels like I'm shouting into the void so when someone takes notice, it means a lot. There's a lot of you that I hope I get to meet someday.

Rebecca, I was so nervous to ask you to edit this new book but I'm so glad that I did! I feel so incredibly lucky to have had you in my corner once again. Your attention to detail, notes, and thoughts are always appreciated. I seriously couldn't get to where I am without your part in it. Thank you so much!

Last but definitely not least, the husband that puts up with me everyday. Should we still call you by another name for now? Jonah? John? Jack? I'm sure you're shaking your head at my ridiculousness. You're welcome. Thank you for the cover, formatting, and countless hours you put into tweaking everything into our version of perfect in order to get these books out and into the hands of readers. Thank you for your part in ALL of this. I love you!

And for the readers (promise I didn't forget about you). Thank you for giving Clara, Seth, and the first part of their story a chance. If you're new to my work, then welcome! If you've been with me since Watching Me, I hope I didn't disappoint with this new book. I can't tell you how much I appreciate the time you took in reading anything of mine in the first place. I hope you're all here to stay!

About the Author

Krystal Kae lives in the corn-filled Midwest with her husband, children, and pets. Her love of reading and writing started back in high school, but it was over a decade later when she decided to put her overactive imagination to work again and began filling blank pages.

Fascinated by all things paranormal, fantasy, and romantic-you can find these topics the center of her writing universe. When she's not working her full-time office job or buried in a story, she loves to create memories with loved ones, travel, and take long walks in cemeteries.

Get the latest updates at **KrystalKae.com** and follow @krystalkaewrites